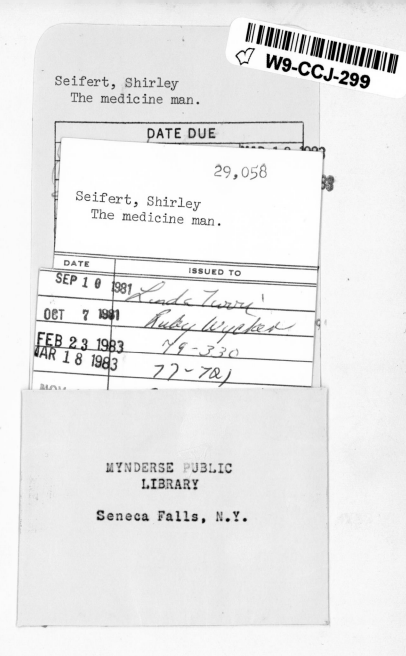

THE
MEDICINE
❧ MAN

Books by Shirley Seifert

Shirley Seifert

THE
MEDICINE
～ MAN

J. B. Lippincott Company
Philadelphia & New York

To Tindy

Author's Note

Now that the time has come to recount those who gave me the most help in presenting my story of the wizard doctor of early St. Louis, I want to mention first those who least expect acknowledgment. They are my patient, tolerant family of one—my sister—a keen copyreader; next, a dear friend and neighbor down the street, who gave aid when most needed, and her nimble, willing children, who acted as messengers; and finally the skilled typist, who, when my typewriter and I developed blind staggers, took over the copying of the final draft. To all these, my sincere gratitude.

In the field of research I am indebted, as always, to the library staff of the Missouri Historical Society in St. Louis—a storehouse of information about any person of consequence who ever lived here or stopped off here on his way elsewhere.

Hours of sitting in a padded chair before a long table piled with books, pictures, correspondence, and other memorabilia repeatedly sent me off with my senses reeling, until I could sift the evidence and keep only what I needed for a true picture. With few exceptions, all the people of the story were real once upon a time. Even Gabriel was taken from a sketch of a farmer driving a charette.

Of Dr. Saugrain one portrait survives. It shows a smallish man in a long, full-skirted coat, his hair flying, going somewhere in a fearful hurry. A caricature surely, but probably typical. How else could he have covered so much ground? I have seen his library—the more than four hundred books which survived the French Revolution, a perilous crossing of the Atlantic, and a succession of owners after that, and now are property of the Society. When I saw them they were on temporary shelves in a secluded corner of the library stacks, awaiting a safer display case in a library addition now being built. They are hardly in a state to be handled much. Consultation will always be restricted, but for me, just to see them, to touch one or two lightly, to obtain a listing of the titles, was evidence enough of a scholar's learning.

To begin, there are tall, formidable volumes on the sciences. Fortunately for me—and the story—science around the year 1800 was not the complex wonder of today. Saugrain's career was drawing to a close before the first steamboat made its way upstream to St. Louis. Electricity had advanced very little beyond Franklin's adventure with a kite string and a key. By refusing to read any text going beyond 1820, I reduced my bibliography considerably and kept within safe depths. Cautiously I did proceed that far.

But it was the man, the patriot, the humanitarian in whom I was most interested. Alongside the formidable science volumes are books on history and travel, and, lighter still, novels, poetry, drama—many paperbacks. So, slowly, with more study of the sources, everything came clear. A drawing of the fine stone house survives, with the stone steps, protected by the iron railing, leading down into a garden plot. Also visible is a bit of fence in ruins—not a fence of stone as some legends say. These are wooden rails in a state of collapse. So I chose to describe French pickets, pointed and very high, because when Henry Shaw settled in St. Louis, with the Missouri Botanical Gardens just an idea in his head, he bought a horse so that he could ride around in the evenings and look over such fences into the town's famous French gardens, Madame Saugrain's among them.

I went outside the resources of the Historical Society on two points only. Needing to know about herbs, I consulted my good friend, Mrs. D. Goodrich Gamble, former President of the St. Louis Herb Society. From books lent by her and her associates, I compiled an interesting list of herbs and their culinary and medicinal properties. My thanks to all.

Finally we come to Tindy, to whom the book is dedicated—

Elizabeth Tindall, formerly Reference Librarian at the Missouri Historical Society, now Principal Reference Librarian at the main St. Louis Public Library. Without her help I could not have finished my story.

Dr. Saugrain's greatest claim to fame was his extending the use of smallpox vaccine to the St. Louis area and beyond. Before him, lack of refrigeration and slow travel made it impossible to deliver the perishable serum to any place remote from the source of supply. Saugrain must have solved the problem, for in 1809 in two separate notices he offered fresh vaccine to all applicants; but no amount of searching on my part revealed his process. Finally, at my wits' end, I remembered how, when I was writing *By the King's Command* and needed to fire an eighteenth-century cannon, Elizabeth Tindall, then still with the Missouri Historical Society, unearthed an ancient encyclopedia containing a detailed diagram of such a gun, with full explanation of the firing process.

So I wrote her this time about my distress. Days later duplicates of pages from old encyclopedias and old medical journals were on my desk. In one, taken from the first American edition of a British encyclopedia (Rees), Dr. Edward Jenner, the discoverer of vaccination, whose dates—1749 to 1823—cover those of Saugrain, discussed at length the handling of vaccine, ending with the words I most wanted to read: "When they [vaccinators] are to be sent some distance, they may be enclosed. . . ." but that is my story.

I do not say that everything in my book happened as I have told it, but any part of it is at least probable. After all, *The Medicine Man* is a novel, a work of fiction, which aspires only to present what Christopher Morley once described as "the mother of pearl of truth within the oyster shell of fact."

PART I

A Long and Difficult Journey

One ✍

On a fine June afternoon in the year 1800, a pair of barges carrying people and freight could have been observed, by anyone watching on either shore, making slow progress up the Mississippi toward the village of St. Louis, capital of Upper Louisiana. No observer, however, showed. The eastern shore—flat, sun-baked clay to where a distant line of trees created a shadowy background, seemed without habitation. The western shore—a wall of gray-white bluffs, with a sandy beach and scrub willows at the base, and now and then an overhang of trees at the summit—seemed equally deserted. A blackbird rising from the willows, a hawk wheeling out against the empty sky, only added to the desolation. A scene of more complete abandonment could not have been imagined.

Except for the boats. They moved slowly, steadily, with a certain obstinacy of purpose, upstream—no slight accomplishment against the current of Father Mississippi, even with the river falling. Both, heavily burdened, rode low in the water. It seemed impossible that square sails, rigged to masts amidships, although filled with a southerly wind, could move them unaided. And yet they did move, one setting the course, the other pursuing—losing, however, a little headway continually, until by midafternoon a quarter mile of water rolled between the two.

For this there was a reason. The lead boat was one of less

than a dozen extraordinary keelboats, generally called galleys, which plied the inland waters of western America and were known to belong to men of wealth or rank. Keeping necessarily the shallow hull of a barge, it was both narrower—about ten feet in the beam—and longer—sixty feet over all. Prow and stern also had been shaped to elongated points, enabling the craft to cut the water smoothly and cleanly against a minimum of resistance. Other differences were mere elegancies—namely, a covered cargo hold, an after cabin with portholes, and an extension of the upper deck forward, meant to provide shelter for captain and crew during a storm. Since it could not have shielded more than a tenth of the thirty-man crew, its shade on a warm day was more valued than any other protection.

By midafternoon the entire crew was posted somewhere—twenty on the sheltered rowing benches forward, eight with pushing poles handy lolling on the plank runways that extended the length of the boat, and two in charge of the steering oar. Every man was ready to swing into action at a word of command; but, until it came, every one rested. Even the steersman hung like a sack over his oar. Only the captain, the bossman, kept unremitting vigil. Ever since noon he had stood close to the point of the prow, his broad back to the boat, moving only to shift his weight a little to steady his balance as the boat met a sudden onrush of water, his eyes on the ceaseless current, the flow of drift in midstream, the sky, the shores, as if any or all might have something to communicate. What that might be nobody but Jacques Cardinal knew. Meanwhile. . . .

Meanwhile an interruption roused the others. Two passengers had emerged from the after cabin and were climbing the ladder to the upper deck. They were a youth of perhaps eighteen years and a gentleman ten or more years older. Other differences seemed more important. The youth, in gingham shirt and coarse cotton breeches rolled above his knees, hurried to the edge of the forward deck and dropped down, dangling long bare legs and large bare feet in space, and appointed himself to watch the captain. The other, as short as the boy was tall, and as neat and precise in his black, full-skirted frock coat and knee breeches and shoes with buckles as the young one was careless, took his stand near the mast, where he could watch everything.

That was the first thing one noticed about this neat, small person—he saw everything, and he studied all that he saw. Now, hired boatmen were not supposed to concern themselves about passengers; but, name of Heaven, *engagés* were men with eyes and ears and other senses. Having no facts in hand, knowing nothing except that here was a gentleman—a man of some importance, or the *Teniente Gobernador* would not have sent his galley to meet him and his family at the mouth of the Ohio— they could speculate; and they had speculated ever since that meeting.

Ah, that had been a thing to see, not to be believed by any-one not present. Here came the barge from Kentucky, racing down the Ohio. Stopping for nothing, it plunged into the Mississippi, which picked it up as if it had been a stick and tossed it aside with such force that the bow buried itself in the mud of the opposite shore. And there the barge hung.

It had taken the rest of that day to remove the passengers in small boats and lighten the load so that the barge could float again. Fortunately there were no leaks. A second day then was spent in dividing the cargo, and two days went for reloading. His family? There were two, bound for St. Louis, carrying with them, it seemed, all their possessions. On one boat they would never have reached the end of their journey. With two it was barely possible.

Finally, early on the fifth day, all preparations were complete. As soon as the last passenger had been counted, the men with the poles would push, first the galley, then the Kentucky boat, away from the landing, and they would be off. However, at this point one of the women, of whom there were four, counting one half-grown girl, took fright at the thought of separation and began to cry. That set the others off, and there was no telling how or when the storm would have ended had not the little gentleman in black clapped his hands with force and commanded all to be still.

He had lacked nothing in inches then. His dark eyes flashed. His hair, worn loose, without ribbon or braid to bind it, stood out from his head. Everyone listened. "We are not parting for-ever," he said, his mouth twitching a little as if he wanted to smile. "We are continuing the journey on two boats because that

(15)

is safer. The captains have promised that one boat shall never lose sight of the other. We will meet each night at the same landing, and finally we will arrive at Saint Louis on the same day, never to be parted again. You understand? *Allons*, let us embark. *Bon-père*, you have all your family on the barge except Jean. We keep him with us on the galley only because of his weight. Jean? Where is that one now?"

That one was already aboard. The young man stood stiff and straight against the mast, his arms stretched out like sticks, ready to take a sail if there should be a good wind, of which on that day, alas, there was none.

Such was the re-embarkation at the mouth of the Ohio. The peppery little man in black assisted his wife, a beautiful young woman with eyes like brown velvet, aboard the galley, then offered his help to a nurse in apron and cap, who followed with two small children—a baby in arms and a little girl perhaps three. Meanwhile, the father-in-law, a strong, quiet man who was never seen to smile, was placing the other young ladies, also charming, aboard the barge, all the while keeping firm hold on a boy of perhaps eight years, with black eyes as bright as those of a squirrel and equally full of mischief.

After that, the days of the long pull up the river were much the same. Each morning everyone had to be counted, then hurried aboard the proper boat, the women always holding back, afraid to trust barge or river. Each evening they would disembark, chattering like magpies. Then all the women and children, led by the older man, would march off to sleep in lodgings ashore, if the landing was near a settlement, only Jean and the professor, or whoever he was, remaining on the galley.

After supper Jean would amuse himself hunting crayfish or frogs, then wash and seek his bed; but hours later the other could be seen on the upper deck, studying the stars, the night sounds, the river, asking himself, perhaps, what was he doing here, with two families on his hands, in this wild and empty land? All the while, to the end of the journey, no man of the crew knew either his name or his station. If Jacques Cardinal, the captain, knew, he did not say. Until the very last night, when a strange thing happened.

(16)

They had moored the boats at the mouth of a creek a league and a half above Ste. Genevieve, and Cardinal had gone ashore to visit an aunt who lived on a farm near the creek. Making his way through the dark, too proud to carry a light, he fell over a low stone wall which he did not expect to find where it was and all but knocked his brains out. His groans and roars brought to his rescue six men with a lantern, who found him bleeding like a wine cask with a hole in it—all over his face and shirt; but, when they would have helped him, he pushed them away.

"Doctor!" he kept saying between groans. "Name of God—Doctor!"

What doctor, the men asked? There was none nearer than Ste. Genevieve.

"On the boat, you fools," he said then. "The little French doctor on the boat!"

Two

On this June afternoon in 1800, the little doctor from Paris, France, looking down from the upper deck of the galley, discovered that by bracing himself with feet far apart, in imitation of the young bossman in the bow, he too could achieve a balance in rhythm with the rolling water. This pleased him greatly.

The mighty Mississippi! How well he remembered his first acquaintance with that river! He had been a student still, a boy similar to young Jean of the bare feet and rolled-up breeches—a boy surrounded, guarded, counseled by uncles, aunts, sisters, and brothers-in-law, to say nothing of two anxious parents, but shaping a career for himself which had little to do with such counsel. Commissioners from England, France, Spain, and thirteen colonies, already calling themselves the United States of America, were meeting in Paris that year—1783—shaping a treaty of peace following the American Revolution. They had argued long over many points of difference; but what threatened finally to close the negotiations with no treaty accomplished was the obstinacy of the head of the American delegation—Dr. Benjamin Franklin of Philadelphia, who would not yield ground in a dispute over a boundary line.

The line was to mark the western limits of the new nation. England, France, Spain, in turn proposed that it should follow the western slope of the Appalachian Mountains. This, they said, would provide all the territory that a weak, inexperienced new government could control. Dr. Franklin stood alone, but sturdily, against that reasoning.

"Gentlemen," he said, "we are dividing a continent. The land beyond the mountains belongs to my compatriots by right of exploration, conquest and settlement. I will hear to no boundary one foot east of the Mississippi River."

Mississippi—young Antoine Saugrain said the name over and over to himself. There was a river he must see!

Ah, how quickly a boy's dreaming became a man's desire! Seventeen eighty-three was the year of his twentieth birthday. That same year a brother-in-law, corresponding with a Monsieur Maxent, a wealthy merchant of New Orleans, had obtained for Antoine an opening there, since America was now fixed in his mind as the land he preferred. To be sure, New Orleans was not his idea of where he would like to establish himself. New Orleans, capital of Spanish Louisiana, was near the end of the mighty Mississippi, and he would have chosen some place nearer its beginning. Nevertheless, since, in view of the New Orleans opening, his kinfolk had also offered to pay for his passage to America, he accepted the offer.

Early in 1784 he set sail from France, never dreaming that it would be November before he could present himself in Monsieur Maxent's New Orleans countinghouse, a specter of his former self, in rags of clothing not his own, his skeleton showing through his skin, his eyes, his cheeks hollow, his hair a brush—destitute except for an oilskin envelope containing his passport and a diploma stating that he had completed in Paris a course in medicine and the natural sciences. Monsieur Maxent examined the contents of the envelope.

"But," he said doubtfully, "these papers were written a year ago. Where have you been meantime?"

Where? In Jamaica, in prison. A British frigate had overtaken the French ship on the Atlantic. He had spent nine months in prison. Finally he had been set free, and given these rags and a paid passage to Europe. He had traded the passage at once for space in a fishing boat bound for the Gulf of Mexico. . . .

"Sit down," Monsieur Maxent said. "Please! I want to think."

The result of the thought was that the merchant, on the credit of Antoine's family in France, had advanced money for new clothing, a barber and lodgings. When this treatment had given the specter the appearance of someone alive, Monsieur Maxent took him to the Cabildo to repeat his story to Señor Galvez, the Governor General of Louisiana.

"But you are a young gentleman," His Excellency said. "Anyone can see that. And you have studied all these subjects—surgery, medicine, botany, physics, chemistry? Señor Maxent, we must indeed find a place for this young man. Now I will think."

While he thought, a ship arrived from Madrid with new orders for Governor Galvez. He had been promoted. He was now Viceroy of Mexico and all the interior provinces. He must leave for Mexico City at once.

"And I will take you with me, Señor Médico," he said. "Why not? New Orleans has many doctors of medicine, none so educated as you, perhaps—but they were here before you. And what about your experiments with minerals? Louisiana has no mines. Mexico is all mines—gold, silver, opals, emeralds. You will make a fortune for both of us."

So, for the remainder of that year and part of the next, he had lived in the Viceroy's palace in Mexico City. He learned to speak Spanish, good and bad. He grew strong and well. But he made no fortune. To begin with, one fifth of all treasure dug from the earth went outright to the King of Spain; and the rest passed through so many hands in the process of refining, accounting and transporting that finally little remained for the original claimant.

But it was waste, more than corruption, that troubled the young scientist. The machinery at the mines was primitive. All implements in this magnificent empire were crude. Once he carried away a sack of dirt and stones thrown out at a smelter and, in his own rock crusher, separated enough pure silver to make His Excellency's eyes bulge.

"Sacred name of the Virgin!" the Viceroy said. "Speak of this to no one. People will be crawling over those heaps like ants."

With medicine the story was even sadder. He had treated a number of patients, from the Viceroy to native Indians, with some success, for dysentery, skin eruptions, worms and lung fever. Then the drugs he had brought from New Orleans were exhausted. Unfamiliar with the flora of Mexico, he had to proceed cautiously with fever draughts. The bark of the cinchona tree, with its priceless, bitter brew, had to be brought from Peru over mountain passes and through jungles—a journey equal to an ocean voyage in time consumed.

"Write a report for Madrid," the Viceroy advised. "The royal council will deliberate . . . *Dios!* You could go after what you want and return in less time than . . . that is how we will do it. I will send you back to France—on a safe ship, I hope—with authority to purchase. . . ."

Fourteen years later, Dr. Saugrain, afloat on the Mississippi at last, could still glow—and shiver—remembering that summer in Paris, when, armed with the Viceroy's letter of credit, he had indulged in a debauch of scientific spending. He had ready finally a chest of all the latest drugs and compounds. He had books on the plants of Central America, poisonous and curative. He had tool patterns and instructions for refining precious metals. He had even a collapsible cabinet, which, when set up, would hold basins, crucibles, tongs, blowtorches, a small furnace, vials of acids, measuring glasses, balanced scales—too many items to be listed—all ready to be put on board a ship as soon as the Paris banker who had honored his letter from the Viceroy about the credit should have word from Madrid, with, perhaps, a partial payment in gold, the remainder to follow.

Word came. The Viceroy in Mexico, Antoine's Viceroy, was dead. He had died within a month of Antoine's departure. All contracts and orders not previously settled were void.

It had required an uncle and two brothers-in-law to pull young Dr. Saugrain out of debt. As long as he lived, to anyone asking what did a young man need most for a good start in life, he must answer: a sufficiency of uncles and brothers-in-law.

Now, again on a Spanish boat, on a river still in dispute, sweating a little over the memory of near ruin, he laughed, frowned, then resolutely turned to scrutinize once more those interesting bluffs on the near shore. Alas, he turned too suddenly. Searing pain, real and present, transfixed him. He had forgotten again that he must never pivot his weight on his right foot.

Three ∽

"Pain is a part of living. It is the furnace that separates pure metal from dross."

Sage Dr. Franklin sat in a great, cushioned chair in his residence on Arch Street, Philadelphia, and spoke the truth as he saw it. The year was 1788. He was an old man, and very ill; but he had risen from his bed to offer food and counsel to a caller who had recently been nearer death than he was at this moment.

Young Antoine Saugrain again blushed for his appearance—his threadbare, weather-stained clothing. This time he had been sent by relatives, made anxious by the threat of revolution, to explore North America for a possible place of refuge. He had landed at Philadelphia the preceding autumn, but, not feeling in need of help then, he had set out at once for the West, only to be made a prisoner by winter at Pittsburgh. However, by spring he had found three good companions, and the four had departed in an open boat, meaning to float down the Ohio. All had gone well until one evening when, as they were preparing to land on the Kentucky side, they were surrounded by Indians. In an exchange of shots, two of Saugrain's party had been killed, and he and the other had escaped only by swimming the width of the river under a hail of bullets to the Ohio shore, running then for their lives through the forest. It was good, Saugrain informed Dr. Franklin, that they had been compelled to run. All that night and the next day they had managed to keep moving through pelting rain and sleet. It was during the second night, when, completely exhausted, they had slept under a fallen tree, that his feet had frozen.

"You may thank God," Franklin said, "that you knew enough to rub life back into them, and that you did not bleed to death from that bullet wound in your neck. What was that stuff you applied to the wound?"

"Agaric," Saugrain said absently. The bullet wound had healed promptly, but the pain in his right leg, his damaged foot, seemed without end.

Agaric—fungus from a tree. He had chewed it to a pulp and applied it as a poultice. It . . . well, finally the bleeding had stopped.

"And you were alive," Franklin prompted, "with courage to swim the river again. And so you reached Kentucky and safety."

No. Of their own power, neither he nor his companion would have reached safety. Some men on a raft saw them and picked them up. He had been stiff as a board when they pulled him out of the icy water. At this point in the story, he had to laugh. All the medicine the rescuers had, besides their rough hands, was a jug of whiskey. They had rubbed both men with that— Saugrain, so nearly dead, with extra vigor. On that last night in the woods he had wanted more than anything a way to start a fire. On the raft, if anyone had struck a spark, his whiskey-soaked body must have burst into a blaze. Dr. Franklin also laughed.

"But you lived," he repeated.

Yes. He had come alive just in time to keep someone from cutting off the index finger of his left hand, saying it would never be any good to him. How could he practice surgery without that finger? It was still stiff. It might always be a little stiff, but it would help to hold things while he worked with his right hand. He had not been so fortunate with his foot. This evening in Philadelphia, his whole right leg was afire. He had not asked to keep the blackened great toe on that side, nor the end of the toe next to it. In addition to frostbite, while fleeing through the Ohio forest that awful night, he had run a sharp stick through the same foot.

"But you are young," Dr. Franklin said, grimacing at his own useless foot on a pillow. "You will heal."

Yes. Dressing his wounds in preparation for that evening's visit, Saugrain, hoping to release some of the demon pain, had made a small incision at the still oozing hole left by the stick. To his surprise, the cut had bled freely—good, healthy red blood. The foot might heal in time. How much time?

(22)

"I still have not seen your Mississippi River," he reminded Dr. Franklin. "Only a small piece of it, near the end."

"My Mississippi," Franklin said, much pleased. "I suppose you might call it that. I remember saying to John Jay, before we had got down to the business of writing the treaty, 'Poor as we are, and yet rich as I know we shall be, I had rather buy at a great price the whole of Spain's right to the Mississippi than sell a drop of its water. A neighbor might as well ask me to sell my street door.'" Then he added slyly, "Spain still keeps control, you know, owning the mouth of the river. How long do you think that will last?"

Sitting there in the warm room before a stove radiating heat, Saugrain borrowed a little of his host's courage and answered impulsively, "It will not last long, I am sure. All of the Mississippi will belong to America finally."

At Fort Louisville, Kentucky, where he had been forced to remain while an army surgeon treated his gangrene, he had heard much talk about seizing the river—treasonous talk mostly, since the plot involved settling up a new nation west of the mountains. It would not come to that, the older man thought.

"How old are you, Doctor?" he asked. "Twenty-five? Surely you do not intend to end your American adventure at that age. You must return to France. . . ."

How could he return, Saugrain asked? Everything he owned—clothing, instruments, medicines, a wallet filled with money—was now at the bottom of the Ohio. How could he explain to friend or kinsman his loss and theirs, his latest failure? Besides, he had no money to pay for a passage home. It was only through the kindness of strangers that he had come back this far.

"You will find a way," Franklin insisted. "Misfortune is not failure. You must return to France, recover your health, then try again."

That evening, warmed by kindred enthusiasms as much as by the Franklin stove set into the fireplace, they had talked for hours —two sick men, one old and one young. In the end Dr. Franklin had offered the money for the return to France and with it a portrait of himself for which he had posed in a Paris studio when he was already past seventy. "A fat old man," he said of the portrait, and, in truth, a round skullcap with a button in the center

(23)

emphasized a certain pudginess; but the artist had written a better description on the plaque: "B. Franklin, Americain."

Through the years that followed, pain had never failed to bring that evening alive again. So now, aboard the Spanish governor's galley, visited briefly by melancholy, Dr. Saugrain cautiously completed his turn toward the bluffs, then found himself unwilling to face them. Could this wall of rock be meant for a warning? An instant later he shook himself and opened his eyes boldly, to discover that, while he mused, the picture had changed. The bluffs seemed lower. More green showed on top. The willows also at the water's edge seemed stouter, healthier, as if they had deeper earth about their roots.

Next, feeling a difference in the motion of the boat, he looked to the bow for the reason. Apparently the bossman had obtained the sign for which he had waited. He stood now, facing the stern of the boat, ordering with a movement of his arms a change in direction. Both steersmen applied their weight to the great steering oar and, as they did so, the galley—slowly, unwillingly, then with sudden consent, swung about and headed toward the flotsam in midstream. Simultaneously, at a spoken command, the oarsmen dipped their blades, driving the boat forward with such a surge of speed that it seemed to race now in comparison with its previous leisurely progress. Saugrain swayed perilously, then steadied himself; and young Jean, watching, laughed aloud. The bossman forward took another look at the current, to be satisfied with the change of direction, then turned once more, to favor anyone who faced him with a satisfied grin, sadly marred by his battered countenance. Red stripes of cuts still raw mingled with the purple of bruises. Unmindful of the effect, still smiling, he addressed the doctor.

"It will not be long now, m'sieu. We must move out a way, to give those big rocks room while we round a bend. After that, we are almost there."

"Good!" Saugrain moved forward to stand beside Jean at the edge of the deck. "In that case, can you spare a minute to let me examine your face? It is the first good look I have had by daylight."

The husky captain winced. He could fight the Mississippi or any other challenging monster with joy and without fear; but he dreaded a pinprick of pain. Undeterred, Saugrain stooped to bring

(24)

himself level with the young man's head and with both hands began probing.

"Do I hurt?" he asked.

"No," Cardinal said. "I can't touch the face without hurting but I do not feel your hands. I know they are there. That is all."

Saugrain spread one, to show the flat fingertips. "I take no credit for these," he said. "I was born with them. Jacques Cardinal, you are in good health. The cuts already begin to heal, and there is no bone injury. You will look frightful until the color fades. There is no help for that. Keep the face clean. Wash with water but do not shave." At Cardinal's grimace he smiled. "If the beard grows, cut it with scissors. Have you a wife? Excellent! She will help you. For the rest, stay sober, and do not walk abroad at night without a lantern."

"It happened on land," Cardinal grumbled. "Nothing occurs when I am on the boat."

"I suspected something of the sort," Saugrain said softly, "but you are not a fish, remember. You must walk on land part of the time. I would like to see you tomorrow, but where? I have no fixed residence at present."

To his pleased surprise Cardinal mentioned a hospital. A hospital had in fact been promised; but Saugrain was old enough now to know that a promise, until fulfilled, was only a promise. By all means, the hospital, he agreed quickly.

"I will have money then to pay you," Cardinal offered.

"You will pay nothing," Saugrain told him. "I am in debt to you for bringing us safely and fast up this great river. We are arriving a day ahead of your expectations—and, I am afraid, the Governor's. That could be inconvenient."

The Governor would have had warning, Cardinal informed him. Watch was kept always on top of the bluffs for boats ascending or descending the river.

It was quite possible, even natural, that an unseen lookout should be stationed on the bluffs. Saugrain had himself thought of such a sentinel. Now, unreasonably, the fact that there was such a lookout disturbed him. However, before he could cover his discomfiture, or pursue it with question, he found something else to think about.

Cardinal, the bossman, still facing the stern of the boat, was

(25)

now looking past the doctor at some object that fascinated him. His eyes were dilated, his mouth was open—in another diabolical grin. Looking in the same direction, Saugrain saw what the object was. For the last five minutes he had been aware of a lively chattering in the after cabin. Now his charming wife, Madame Saugrain, had separated herself from the nurse and the children and was in the act of mounting the ladder to the upper deck. Mounting? She was already at the top of it. Pausing there, she—very correctly—put a question: "Is it permitted?" But then, without waiting for a yes or a no, she stepped lightly from the ladder to the deck.

Four ✍

Antoine Saugrain and Genevieve Rosalie Michau had first met on board a ship. That year was 1790. They were two out of two hundred passengers crossing the Atlantic to new homes in a settlement ready and waiting for them on the Ohio River. At least, the smooth-spoken gentlemen composing the Scioto Company, in selling the homes, had said that such a settlement existed. Every man on the ship, including Dr. Saugrain, carried on his person title to a house and land. The town had even been given a name: Gallipolis. It had seemed a heaven-sent refuge— so safe, so far removed from the terror of the Revolution which threatened to despoil their beloved France.

It was only when the last cape of their homeland was lost in mist that fear crept into the hearts of the fugitives. What did they know of America, really? When in France they had spoken of distance, they had not thought of thousands of miles. It was only when they were far out at sea that they realized the width of the turbulent Atlantic.

They were good people, these exiles. They were not ignorant rabble. They were tradesmen, shopkeepers, lace makers, watchmakers, jewelers. One had been bootmaker to the king. They were loyalists. They had prospered under kings. They had fled to save their lives, never dreaming that they might be exchanging one terror for another.

Conspicuous among them was a family by the name of Michau, the father—Jean Alexandre Michau—a stalwart, handsome man approaching middle age, a worker in leather, a master saddler, the mother a lady of such grace and beauty that one guessed immediately that she had stepped down a little in marrying for reasons of the heart. Happily, however, one could be sure. Jean Alexandre was now on his way to America, meaning to make a fortune there befitting his wife, himself, and their four children —son Jean, a lively boy approaching eight years of age, and three lovely daughters, Genevieve Rosalie, fourteen, Marie Elinor, a year younger, and Sophie Marie, five or six years old. All were charming, but the one who attracted the most attention was Genevieve Rosalie. She was beautiful, with her mother's exquisite manners, and a smile for everybody. On that gloomy ship she was sunshine, falling now here, now there, as she settled an older person in a chair with pillows, or kept her younger sisters and her brother amused, surrounded by most of the other children aboard.

One day, to Saugrain's surprise, she addressed herself directly to him. "Monsieur Docteur, is it permitted? Have you time, please? It is Alphonse here. He has a bad cut. It bleeds."

It did, indeed, ruining her pretty frock.

"The dress is nothing, monsieur. An old one, for shipboard only. I have others. When we arrive in America, where there is good water, I may wash it. Monsieur le docteur, we thank you, Alphonse and I."

That was how it began—his love for Genevieve Rosalie Michau, although at first he tried not to think of it so. She was fourteen and he twenty-seven, with a fortune still to be made. A lovely girl in every way, who would some day be even lovelier as a woman. To gladden some man's heart and home, but not his. Not possibly his.

Then—Gallipolis, Ohio.

There was no such town. No houses, no streets. There was nothing. Property deeds, carried across the ocean, had no value except that they demonstrated the villainy of smooth-tongued Yankee swindlers. Fortunately, most of the exiles, too exhausted to travel farther, on arriving in Philadelphia chose to settle in lodgings there over winter. So they did not hear about Gallipolis until spring, when a few men who had been sent to examine their place of settlement returned with the calamitous report. Wails of anguish and despair were hushed only by a resolution to lay the matter before the American Congress, the President, if necessary.

Finally, after a second winter of waiting, during which some of the *émigrés*, including Saugrain and Jean Alexandre Michau, had found work according to their skills, while others watched their money disappear in the payment of rent, relief was offered. A new townsite was selected, surveyed, and divided into lots, for sale at a special low price. To buy land a second time at any price was hard, but what else could one do? In February, when the snow began to melt on the mountains, chosen men again set out, meaning this time to engage woodcutters as they went, to begin the building of houses. Families would follow in April.

It was May of 1792 when slightly more than one half of the original two hundred finally reached Gallipolis. Of the remainder, some had risked returning to France, while others, now steadily employed, had elected to remain in the seaboard cities. In the new Gallipolis houses were now waiting and ready. Two parallel lines of one-story barracks, set at right angles to the river, had been partitioned to provide separate family dwellings. At the far end, two large rooms, for eating or meeting or recreation, bound the two rows together. There were no streets. There was no clearing except where trees had been felled for timber.

Nevertheless, spring was at its height, daisies bloomed in the grass, and Mademoiselle Michau, attended by a servant, stood at the threshold of Dr. Saugrain's residence.

"M'sieu le docteur, are you there? Is it permitted. . . ?"

He turned, measuring tape in hand. He had been exploring the possibility of adding a lean-to to his apartment, to provide a room for medical consultation and laboratory experiments. So, there he stood, and here she stood, her brown eyes pleading, the words she wished permission to speak rushing out in a bright stream not to be checked by forbiddance:

"M'sieu, we have arrived. We are here in our own houses. It seem a day for celebrating. M'sieu, on the ship you were very good about directing *fêtes de joie*. The rooms at the end of the avenue are large enough for feasting and dancing. Our good clothes should be shaken out and aired. M'sieu, you know everybody,

especially those who play the violin or the flute. M'sieu, you will
do this for us? Oh, I thank you. We all thank you. Five o'clock
this evening will be a good time to assemble, while there is still
daylight. I go now to give out the news. Also"—a dimple appeared in the cheek nearest him—"I must see where there is wine
and who of the women will make cakes to go with it."

One year later Antoine Frederic Saugrain, aged thirty, and
Genevieve Rosalie Michau, seventeen, accompanied by her parents,
crossed the Ohio to Kanawha County, Virginia, for a wedding
ceremony. A certified Virginia judge heard the vows, stamped all
the papers with the seal of Virginia, then kissed the bride and
handed the bridegroom a jug of Kentucky whiskey for his medicine chest.

"I am well aware," Saugrain, light-headed at this point, told
him, "of the virtues of this draught. I will save it for possible
need."

From that day his rude cabin was glorified by the presence of
brave, charming womanhood. Every light footfall on the puncheon
floor was imprinted on his heart. Life in Gallipolis became endurable. Lean days, when hunger gnawed, became less frequent. The
town, to be sure, grew slowly. The forest, dark and menacing,
crowded close. Swamps behind the town filled with water whenever the river rose. Still, however painfully, enough land was
cleared for gardens. Hens cackled. Roosters announced the coming of each new day. Flatboats and barges tied up at the landing
and traded dry groceries for fresh produce.

Dr. Saugrain's small room at the rear of his house was a pleasing
litter of Leyden jars, medicine bottles, and wires, over which the
medallion portrait of B. Franklin, American, beamed approval.
Patients who visited the den paid for medical care with vegetables, game, or wild honey. This was happiness, but hardly prosperity. Consequently, when his Genevieve announced the promise
of a child, he moved her, such possessions as he had accumulated,
and all his hopes again across the Ohio, this time into Kentucky,
where he settled in a rising town named Lexington. A company of
men operating an iron mine were in need of the advice of a
mineralogist, and offered to pay for the counsel with money.

No Michau accompanied the Saugrains to Lexington. Madame
Michau, the mother, was dead. Soon after settling in Gallipolis

(29)

she had borne a second son, named by her choice Aristide. The birth seemed not to affect her health. At the christening and later at her daughter's wedding, she seemed in the best of spirits; but then, while Saugrain was considering the move to Lexington, it came—complete collapse. One day she was present. The next day she was gone. Her children were grief-stricken; her husband, now generally known as Michau Père, was inconsolable. He blamed himself and America for her death. No, he stormed, he would never move to Kentucky, where only English was spoken. He was glad he had not learned the abominable language. Now he would never learn it. Let the doctor and his Genevieve move to Kentucky, for their own sake and that of the child to come. He, Michau Père, and the others would stay on in Gallipolis, where at least their ears would be at peace.

So, Saugrain and his young wife went to Lexington to live; and, little by little, in spite of the broken family, new surroundings eased their sorrow. Life in Lexington was better than it could ever have been in Gallipolis. They had a whole small house to themselves. The doctor's office and his laboratory were larger. Also there was land around the house, permitting Genevieve Rosalie to plant a garden—for vegetables, flowers, and herbs, some for cooking, some for the doctor's medicines.

The baby arrived safely—a girl child, very small but perfect. There was some argument about whom she resembled, which Madame finally won. Why, even the eyes, as they turned brown, were Saugrain eyes, much darker than the Michau brown. They were almost black finally, and, from the first, lively, noticing everything. There was no argument about her name—Genevieve Rosalie; but she would be called Rosalie only, that being as much name as one so small could carry.

The doctor whistled and sang those days, as he worked over metals, minerals or, occasionally, pharmaceuticals, asking himself how he could most rapidly amass wealth for two women as lovely as his wife and daughter. Would it be through medicine or pure science? He had now perfected several inventions. One was a phosphorus match. In Pittsburgh, that winter of 1787–88 when he had chafed, waiting for the ice to melt in the Ohio so that he could float downstream to what might have been his death, he had learned, among other things, the art of blowing glass. Now, in

Lexington, he made himself a small furnace and amused himself —and visitors—by blowing tubes for thermometers and barometers, also these matches, which were simply small glass tubes with bits of phosphorus sealed inside. One needed only to break off the end of a tube and a flame would shoot out, hot enough to ignite twigs or even wet leaves.

The inventions more than his reputation as a doctor brought many visitors to his office. Some, merely curious, were soon forgotten. Others were exciting people to know. One of the latter was a tall young army officer named Lewis—Colonel Meriwether Lewis. He went away with a thermometer and other samples to show to a friend and neighbor—Mr. Thomas Jefferson, Secretary of State under John Adams, President.

Life, Saugrain sometimes thought, was almost too pleasant in Lexington. One day, after he had been told that a second child was on the way, he took himself to task for his placid contentment. How far, he asked himself, had he advanced along any line of endeavor? He even took his complaint to the image of Dr. Franklin.

"Do not speak to me now of patience," he begged. "I am at present thirty-six years old. It may be that I shall not have your eighty years in which to endure and be patient. . . ." When the round face of the benevolent sage still kept its inscrutable smile, he would have turned the portrait to the wall except that he could not. Instead, he turned his back and strode out of the room—a discourtesy of which he was soon deeply ashamed.

Two days later a letter arrived for him from St. Louis. It had been addressed first to Gallipolis, Ohio, and had arrived there so encrusted with seals, suggesting so much importance, that Michau Père had seen fit to deliver it in person. Without revealing what difficulties he had encountered in finding his way, knowing no English, he reached Lexington finally, trembling with fatigue and sweating profusely—some of that due to continued anxiety.

"Doctor, my son," he said, "do you still have business with the King of Spain?"

Saugrain put out his hand for the letter. "If you will allow me to open this," he suggested, "I can give you a better answer."

The letter was clear enough. Would he consider an appointment as post surgeon of the city of St. Louis? Mention was made of pay—something about *pesos fuertes*—a house and a grant of land. Saugrain saw only the round, benevolent face of B. Franklin, American, beaming with triumph.

"But you do not know this Lieutenant Governor of Upper Louisiana," Michau objected. "He could also die, like that other one, the Viceroy. Antoine, you are considering this offer?"

"My good Bon-père," Saugrain said, "it is not an offer, it is fortune, smiling on me at last."

So now here was Antoine Frederic Saugrain of Paris, France, doctor of medicine, pushing up this river of destiny toward a town of equal significance. Once more everything he owned was aboard a boat—books, notes and formulae, instruments, et cetera, his adored wife, his children, their nurse, his young brother-in-law. In addition, the boat that followed carried the rest of the Michau family. Michau Père had yielded to the pleas of his children and agreed to join this migration for one reason only. He had been assured that French was the language of Louisiana.

Now young Madame Saugrain, having reached the deck, offering a typical ex post facto apology, waited on his pleasure. Over a swelling in his heart, Saugrain put out both hands to welcome her.

"Since you are here," he chided, "let us assume that permission has been granted. That is, if the captain agrees."

When they turned to look, Jacques Cardinal's face was still split by that horrid grin, which might have caused Madame to shudder, if at that moment she had not seen between herself and the captain something still more horrible—her brother.

"Jean!" she cried. "The shoes! Will you arrive in this capital city with bare feet?"

"Annh!" the boy said, drawing the feet up under him.

"Go at once!" his sister commanded. "Odette will find the shoes for you."

"Annh!" The young man rose, then turned to his brother-in-law. "You should have divided us differently. You should have had all men on one boat, and her with the women on the other. Moccasins only," he said from the top of the ladder. "I am to help with the rope when we land." Ignoring the ladder, then, he dropped to the lower deck and disappeared.

Madame Saugrain laid her hand on her husband's arm. "Vigny?" she said.

(32)

Vigny—it was the name of that part of Paris where he had been born. At birth he had been so small—like a crumpled leaf, his mother said—that the family thought he should have a title, to make him worth noticing; so they had christened him Antoine Frederic Saugrain de Vigny, calling him intimately just Vigny. Now, because he had had no other bridal gift to bestow upon her, his Genevieve also enjoyed the family privilege; but with her it had gained new importance. By the way she said it, she could communicate every kind of thought or feeling. Now she was pleading.

"Moccasins will be all right," he said. "Saint Louis is not Paris, you know."

But that was not her present anxiety. "Vigny, all goes well . . . still?"

"All goes very well," he assured her. "Were you arguing about that in the cabin?"

"You heard us, Vigny? That Odette! When she becomes excited, there is no keeping her quiet. It was no argument, just a small disagreement. About a vine. Look, Vigny! But quickly. That large one, very high up. You see it? Odette said it must have roots in earth on top of the bluff. I think it grows from that crack in the rock . . . Vigny?"

"Bravo!" he said. "But you and our nurse are both right. The vine must have its roots in soil, but it has that soil in that crack from which it appears to grow. It is, as you say, a large crack. The strength of the vine helps to widen it; but it could have been a small crack in the beginning."

He went on then to explain how the wind, carrying always some dust, as it blew past such a wall of rock would leave in any opening offered particles of soil, which in time the wind, helped by rain, would push deeper and deeper into the recesses of the crack, until finally there was a pocket of earth ready and waiting for the wind, or perhaps a bird, to drop a seed. In the spring the seed would burst; a plant would emerge, take root, and begin to grow. This vine they were considering had been growing for some time. It was now large enough to bear fruit. The inhabitants of St. Louis, he had been told, made wine. . . .

"Vigny!" What now, he wondered? "We are like that vine, I think. We, too, will take root and grow—in this strange town behind the walls of rock."

(33)

Overcome by sudden emotion, in this public place, with everybody watching, he could only cover her hand on his arm and hold
it. "We shall see," he said finally; but he already was seeing. The
bluffs were no longer a wall. They were a curtain, waiting to be
rolled back. How long? One hour, surely not two.

The oarsmen bent their backs, pulling hard against the brown
water. In unison they raised the blades, dripping water, dipped
them again, pulled again; and another piece of the river rolled by,
but not much. They were now almost in midstream, pulling
against the heaviest current. Moreover, with a change of direction,
the sail had gone slack. One of the oarsmen, lustier than the rest,
began a song. The others tried to join in, but the result was only a
rhythmic groaning. Jacques Cardinal heard, scowled, studied the
bluffs and the water, then cupped his hands around his mouth and
roared an order to the steersmen.

The next minute the boat turned slowly back toward the shore.
Whoa there! Hold! Good! Forward now! Forward! The hand on
Saugrain's arm tightened.

"Vigny, look! The bluffs are breaking away. I see a house. A
chimney, at least. Two chimneys and a roof. It is a house, surely!"

Presently more roofs appeared—and walls, white against the
green of trees. It was the town, set high above the river, although
not so high as the tops of greater bluffs, and it was still some distance ahead. Never mind the distance. The sail was once more
full of wind, and now the oarsmen's chant was strong and hearty:

> *Trois cavaliers bien montés*
> *L'on, ton, laridon, danie!*
> *L' un à cheval, l'autre à pied.*

The bluffs truly had broken away. Between the high ones and
the lesser elevation of the town, a narrow, wooded ravine appeared,
with a little stream running through it down to the great river.
Beyond the little river, below the town, a beach of sand waited to
receive the boats.

Shortly after that a narrow road could be made out, following
the stream down to the beach, and on it a dray of sorts—a boxlike
bed on two long poles, lashed to yoked oxen.

"To carry our possessions to the town," Saugrain explained in haste. "For us—you, the babies, Odette, and me,—there will, of course, be something much more comfortable."

"Not for me," a vibrant young voice rang out behind him. "I choose the oxen." And with that Jean Michau, in moccasins, crouched ready on the coiled rope at the foot of the mast.

"Vigny, I must go now, to be with Odette and the babies."

Saugrain hardly knew when she slipped away. He was composing an entry for the journal he meant to keep from this moment on:

"Today, the second of June, in the year 1800, under the most favorable auspices, after a long and difficult journey, I have arrived at last where I meant to be almost twenty years ago."

PART II

The Village of Pain Court

One ∽

It was now the depth of night. As black a night as anyone would care to see. Between flashes of white lightning dark- ness lay like a pall over the village bearing the noble name of St. Louis. Then the lightning would come again, illuminating every- thing from the proudest mansion to the lowliest cowshed. It seemed to penetrate the very walls, entering boldly, in spite of closed shutters, a large bedroom on the main floor of the stone house of the Widow Chouteau on the Rue Principale. Since there was as yet no tavern of repute in the town, and Madame Chou- teau, living alone, had a room to spare, it was her custom to let out this room to visitors of good name. On this night her guests were the new doctor and his wife and family. A new doctor— another one? On trial? Or, one might ask, was it the town that was on trial?

However that was, the lightning, entering this room like a watchman with a lantern, illuminated briefly but repeatedly, first, a large poster bed on which the doctor and his wife rested, then a trundle bed beside the big one, where a little girl of three slept within reach of her mother's hand, and finally a cradle farther away, holding a baby, also asleep, guarded by a nurse, snoring from a pallet spread against a closed door.

(39)

Resting on the great bed, Dr. Saugrain and young Madame were still wide awake. The doctor lay very quiet, not wishing to disturb Madame; and Madame tried also to be quiet so as not to awaken the weary man. However, her lips moved continually, and occasionally a murmur escaped.

"Don't mutter," Saugrain said finally. "I am not asleep."

"I'm sorry," Madame said. "I was only saying a prayer of thankfulness."

"For what?" Saugrain demanded.

"For being in this good house, Vigny, and not in a boat on that river."

"Cardinal would have had us moored securely somewhere," Saugrain said, then added out of his depth of experience, "There is always a refuge, although I do not recall any landing on our way here that offered shelter equal to this house. So proceed with your prayer, my dear, and add my endorsement. Except for the Governor's indisposition, we might be lodged in his house, which I understand is in need of repair. The polite gentleman who arranged quarters for all of us mentioned a leaking roof."

"Vigny, the Governor is ill? Did you see him?"

"He was sleeping," Saugrain said. "The Honorable Secretary said it was probably another cold coming. I have an appointment with him tomorrow morning before I inspect the garrison. If this trouble is a cold, shall I prescribe repairs for the roof?"

"Vigny, you wouldn't. A nobleman you have not yet seen?"

"As post surgeon," Saugrain said, "I must consider it my duty to offer such advice as seems to be needed."

Before he could say more, a sheet of lightning brighter than any which had gone before illumined the room, followed by deafening thunder; and the bed creaked as his brave, strong, capable wife burrowed under her pillow. The charming idiot! How often had he explained to her that thunder was merely sound that followed an electrical charge occasioned by the meeting of two clouds? If she would count from the flash of light to the thunder, she could judge how far the electric spark was from the planet Earth.

"Vigny?" she was now coming out from under her pillow. "How far must one count to be safe?"

"You are safe at the count of one," he informed her, controlling his laughter. "By then the danger has passed. What has become of your prayer?"

"I am still thankful," she said, "but I am thinking now of Papa and my sisters and Jean and little Aristide. Is the house where they are as good as this one?"

It was another stone house, he reported, even larger than this one—a stone house with a steeply gabled roof extending out over the street, the roof supported there by wooden posts. An Indian woman squatted beside one of the posts, smoking a pipe.

"Vigny, could that roof also leak? Hear how it rains!"

It was his opinion that the roof did not leak. Monsieur Roubidou, the owner, was a dealer in furs. If he stored his peltries in a loft under that roof, he would make sure that water did not come through on his treasure.

"You need have no fears for the comfort of your family," Saugrain concluded. "Monsieur Roubidou, besides dealing in furs, is also a notable baker. When I last saw Jean, he was minding the outdoor oven. He showed me how he could move loaves in and out on a shovel."

"That one," Madame said, softly this time. "I do hope he had his fill of the good bread at supper. He has been hungry so much of his life that I doubt he will ever be satisfied."

Lightning came again into the room, but paler than before, followed by a diminuendo of thunder.

"The storm has now passed," Saugrain said. "It has crossed the river, I think—to the American shore."

Was that a moan he heard from the far side of the bed?

"Vigny, I had forgotten. We are no longer in the United States of America."

"For the present, no," he granted. "But don't let that keep you awake. Sleep, dear. Who knows tonight what may happen tomorrow?"

At last, nestled close to him, as trustful as one of her babies, the dear girl did sleep. The storm drew farther and farther away. At the door Odette's snoring went on and on. Only the doctor lay awake, thinking: What do I know about this town, really? Except that in the past brave men risked everything to establish it? Now my hopes, my fortunes, have been added to theirs. God, what have I undertaken? What have I promised?

(41)

Two ∽

Finally, having told himself, as he had told his wife earlier, that nothing could be known about tomorrow until tomorrow arrived, he too slept, in complete surrender, and knew nothing until daylight, streaming into the room, wakened him. Somewhere there was a sound of bells, not loud, not near, and yet not far.

He lay quiet another minute, analyzing the delicate elusive chiming. Sheep? No. The sound was too heavy to be sheep's bells. But, of course, cows! The morning milking over, they were being driven to pasture. That settled, he studied the room. The children had disappeared. In the open door Odette discussed a matter of importance with her mistress.

"Good morning, mesdames!" he called gaily, and Odette fled.

Laughing, he threw back the covers and hurried to the nearest window.

"Vigny!" his Genevieve cried, her watchful, sensible self now that the sun shone. "Someone could see you!"

"Nobody is there to see," he said. "Have you looked at the street?"

The Rue Principale, which the afternoon before had been deep in dust, was now a sea of brown foaming mud, of pudding consistency. Ridges which had been ruts appeared as islands. Madame Saugrain cried out in horror when she saw this.

"Vigny, how will you reach the Governor now? It is not far, but . . . sabots?"

Saugrain winced. "I hope not," he said. "Surely a way will be provided. Life does not stop in this place, I trust, when it rains."

His trust was justified. Shortly before the hour of his appointment a charette—according to the Widow Chouteau a farm cart, really—drawn by a single horse, mud to the fetlocks, stopped under the overhang of the widow's roof.

"For Monsieur le docteur," the driver announced from a precarious seat at the horse's tail.

The charette in general design resembled an oxcart. Two long poles, smoothly rounded and tapered so that they could be threaded through the harness of the horse, rested the heavier ends on an axle bar connecting two high wheels. These were much lighter than the creaking, solid wooden wheels of an oxcart, being made with spokes radiating from a central hub to the rim. Both rim and spokes were cut and shaped from the tough, pliant wood of the wild orange—the doctor learned later—generally called *bois d'arc* because the Indians of the region made their bows from it. Today he was aware only of wheels and of the driver's seat— a board laid across the shafts, literally at the horse's tail. Behind the driver a large rectangular basket, useful for light hauling or, with a stool or bench added, for carrying people, finished the picture.

Nimbly enough, he mounted the hub of the rear wheel, dropped his medicine case into the basket, and followed it to his seat on such a bench.

"*Allons,*" he said, waving gaily to his wife and the Widow Chouteau, watching from the widow's door. "I am here!"

Obediently the driver whistled to the horse; the horse, without objection or enthusiasm, lifted a heavy forefoot out of one mud-hole, dropped it—*plop*—into another; and they were off.

Three ✺

On the gallery of the House of Government, situated on the southeast corner of the Rue Principale and a so-far name-less and almost obliterated cross street, Monsieur Marie le Duc, Honorable Secretary of the Province of Upper Louisiana and special aide to the Lieutenant Governor, waited. He seemed even more elegant and suave than he had appeared in the confusion of the preceding afternoon. Saugrain would have hesitated to give him the medicine case to hold if he had not put out his hand for it. He set the case down carefully, then held out his hand to the doctor.

"Since you are so kind," Saugrain said, "would you be good enough to lend me the other hand also? I have a foot that does not like to be jumped on."

Also, the wheels of the charette were now plastered with mud. He had already acquired a generous patch on one coattail in mounting the cart and did not wish to add more, but le Duc's arms proved to be muscular, and he had had, no doubt, some experience in handling similar arrivals. A flying leap landed Saugrain safely beside his medicines.

"Thank you, monsieur," he said, a little flustered, then drew back in haste as horse and cart moved past the gallery on their way to some island of safety.

"A useful vehicle that," he suggested, "or so I can imagine."

"Indispensable," le Duc agreed, "considering the state of our boulevards."

Was he amused or contemptuous? It was hard to tell, but when Saugrain looked at him inquiringly, he smiled pleasantly, though still inscrutably.

"If you are ready," he said, "His Excellency is waiting."

"One more minute," Saugrain begged, "if you please."

Why had he asked for that? The surrounding scene rested only too heavily on his consciousness—the mud, the narrow principal street, the uneven lines of hotchpotch buildings on both sides of it. On the corner directly opposite Government House stood the largest, most imposing residence that he had seen so far in the town. A double house of stone, rising two full stories above the ground floor and the mud, it would have been a more fitting seat of government than the long, low stone house at his back—with the leaking roof. The mansion, he had been told the previous afternoon, was the residence of Madame Chouteau's eldest son, Auguste, a merchant.

Merchant he might be, but the location of the house was too strategic to be accidental. A narrow lane, running alongside the Governor's residence, continued westward across the street past the Chouteau mansion, then, dwindling to a mere cart track, up a gentle rise to a rectangular enclosure backed by a circular stone tower. Since Saugrain had been told that there was a fort, he supposed this was it. Low buildings in a line leading off from the tower could be barracks, and he saw now an empty flagpole in the enclosed parade. Because of the mud, no doubt, the flagpole was at present inaccessible.

No flag, no drill, an idle garrison amusing itself at cards—that picture, too, was depressing. In the entire panorama the only bright element was the sun. It was a valiant sun, up early and hard at work, unfurling the leaves of the trees, drying out roofs and whitewashed walls, drawing moisture out of the mud. The sunlit surface of the river, as he saw it from the corner of the gallery, had a silver sheen, and on the far shore houses showed through the mist. Houses? Then there must be a town over there. In the hurry of landing the afternoon before, he had not bothered to look. All alert now, he turned and addressed himself to Monsieur le Duc: "Thank you. I am ready."

Four ᔓ

Don Carlos de Hault de Lassus, commanding, with the rank of captain, at least half of King Charles IV's Royal Stationary Regiment of Louisiana, received Antoine Saugrain with words of welcome, moderated by caution.

Doctor, my son, do you still have business with the King of Spain? Michau Père's remembered outcry overlaid the formal welcome. This was Spain—the handsome man in uniform, the punctilio, the darkened room. To one coming in from the outside, it was very dark. It was a corner room with two windows. One, looking out on the main street, was shadowed by the overhanging roof; the other, looking to the north, caught the sun's rays, but obliquely. Soon that brightness would be gone. No candles had been lighted, and what had been a fire under a broad chimney was now, in June, a bed of ashes.

The furniture was somber. Dark portraits hung upon the walls. Heavy chairs were cushioned in dull leather, with a piece or two done in tapestry. As his eyes adjusted themselves to the semi-darkness, Saugrain was chiefly aware of a richly carved table in the center of the room, with the Lieutenant Governor's chair behind it, like a judgment seat, and in a shadowed corner of the room, opposite the dead fire, a small wooden chest which he might not have seen at all if the wood had not been red mahogany, with hinges and a lock of brass.

The chest had probably no significance. More important was the

(45)

table with the Lieutenant Governor now standing behind it. In this first encounter, with the light at his back, he had the advantage. Saugrain saw only in outline an erect, broad-shouldered man in a high-collared military coat. As for his own appearance, he knew only too well how unimpressive that would be. First would come surprise, then dismay, and finally either rejection or searching inquiry.

But he was wrong about the erect, soldierly Lieutenant Governor. Questions began almost at once. They continued polite but kept an undertone of caution. Had the doctor slept comfortably? Had he found the journey, especially up the Mississippi, exhausting?

He had slept very well, Saugrain assured him. Madame Chouteau had given him and his family the best in her house. As for the journey up the river, it had been neither tedious nor tiring, thanks to the superior boat His Excellency had provided and the skill of the young captain.

"Cardinal?" de Lassus said—warmly enough. "Yes, he is a good man. It is an interesting family."

Originally from Canada, they had settled first in the Illinois country, on a farm near the village of St. Philippe; but, like many Canadians, the men were voyageurs at heart, rather than farmers. The father had eventually come to be in charge of all the boats belonging to Monsieur Gratiot, a wealthy merchant, who also was from Canada and had his home and business in Illinois at that time.

Unhappily in 1780, when there was an attempted Indian attack on St. Louis, this Cardinal, who had been sent to St. Louis on some business for his employer, had been caught outside the fortifications and slain. Monsieur Gratiot had then taken the two sons into his employ, and later, when he married the daughter of the Widow Chouteau and moved his residence and business to the Spanish domain, the Cardinals had moved there also. The sons are still under contract to Gratiot, but I am privileged to borrow Jacques at need."

"Understand," he said then, with an abrupt change of tone, "they are Spanish subjects now. The Mississippi divides two nations, between which there is at present no communication."

Spain, always jealous about frontiers, had spoken there. Well,

(46)

Saugrain had known that in moving to Louisiana he was forsaking, temporarily at least, his American citizenship, but that about communication was absurd. How had His Excellency's letters reached him in Kentucky if communication was impossible? Before he could ask, a servant entered with wine and a plate of small cakes.

"To our friendship!" De Lassus raised his glass. "And our mutual benefit."

The wine was rich and sweet. The cakes were excellent. The interlude allowed Saugrain to look over the room again. Once more his eyes fell on the mahogany chest. A repository certainly, but of what? Secret papers?

"In our correspondence," the Lieutenant Governor interrupted, "you did not ask how we came to know about you."

Dieu! Saugrain had asked himself that often, but let His Excellency answer his own question.

"I believe you have served the King of Spain before this," de Lassus said.

Mexico, Saugrain thought. The Viceroy's palace. "But," he protested, "that was a long time ago."

His Excellency smiled. "As long as you live, and afterwards, if you were only a clerk copying a viceroy's reports, your name will be recorded in the archives of the Spanish Indies and of Spain."

Saugrain did not dispute the assertion. He remembered those reports.

"I am amazed," he said cautiously, and de Lassus laughed outright. "Don't give it that much thought," he begged. "I am sure that anything recorded is in your favor." He paused thoughtfully, then continued. "We have also another source of information. Are you acquainted, Doctor, with a General Wilkinson?"

Wilkinson? He knew the name. The General was both popular and unpopular in Kentucky. A man of intrigue, his detractors said.

"Excellency, I cannot say I know him. I saw him once—some years ago." A large man, loud of voice, wearing buckskin leggings and a blue army coat—with epaulets. . . .

"Where was this encounter, Doctor?"

"At Gallipolis, Excellency."

Gallipolis: there was a barge—a galley longer even than the Lieutenant Governor's. The crew was made up of sailors in uniform. The galley stopped at Gallipolis, for what reason nobody knew, and this big, handsome officer stepped ashore. The people, hearing of the boat, ran to look at it; then, seeing the man, they stopped. The General, too, stood still.

"Excellency," Saugrain said, "these my compatriots were a sorry assemblage. Pale, worn, not by toil or illness—just hunger. The General asked what ailed them, and when he had the answer, he turned back to his boat and gave an order. Excellency, he emptied his galley of all food on board, adding two good guns, with powder and ball, for hunting. When all was done, he had to turn back up the river for fresh supplies."

Don Carlos de Lassus considered this report thoughtfully. So did Saugrain, now that he had delivered it. Kentucky gossip, some of it, said that Wilkinson, while drawing pay as an officer in the United States Army, also took money from the Spanish Governor General at New Orleans. The charge of treason, however, had never been sustained in court, from lack of conclusive evidence, the only known facts being his personal extravagance— out of all proportion to his army pay—and his privilege of cruising the full length of the Mississippi when other boats were turned back or seized as contraband. This privilege, contrariwise, was one reason for his popularity. Using it, he had opened the New Orleans port to other Kentucky boats, raising the value of the leading Kentucky products—tobacco, corn, and whiskey. None of that, Saugrain felt, pertained to this interview.

"Very interesting," de Lassus said of the Gallipolis incident. "Typical. The General, I am told, is a man of impulse. It was he who recommended you to our attention."

With that, he lifted a paper from the table. If it had been there all the while, Saugrain had missed it in his initial survey. He was experiencing the sensation now of standing on the rim of a whirlpool, fascinated, but also dreading the moment when he might be sucked into the eddy.

"I have here," de Lassus continued, "a list of people residing in Gallipolis who might be persuaded to settle in Louisiana. A governor, you see, gains favor by adding citizens to his territory. This list is not a new one. It was discovered among the papers of my predecessor in office. Would you be interested?"

Mutely Saugrain accepted the paper. If the list was an old one,

(48)

this was a fresh copy. The neat, elegant script suggested le Duc. There were twenty names, his at the top: Antoine Frederic Saugrain, Mineralogist.

"But I understood," he protested, "that your need was for a physician."

"That is our need," His Excellency said. "For a year now we have been without a doctor. We survive, I have thought, only because the location is healthy and the inhabitants generally are a hardy breed. You will find plenty to do as a physician, but also have some leisure . . . do you object to being called a mineralogist?"

Naturally Saugrain did not object. It was as a mineralogist that he had been of value to the Viceroy of Mexico. And in Kentucky there had been those iron mines.

"An eminent mineralogist is the way I heard it," de Lassus said.

Now, where and how . . . again Saugrain thought back and so came to the one possible answer—Pittsburgh. That awful winter. That it should be so important afterwards!

"Eminence," he said to the Lieutenant Governor, "is easily come by when one has no rivals."

In Pittsburgh that winter he had been given some samples of lead ore to examine, and had happened, just happened, to discover a trace of silver. "Silver?" He could feel de Lassus' excitement. "But we have rich deposits of lead in this province—some very near Saint Louis."

"Excellency," Saugrain protested, "it was only a trace. I will gladly examine your ore, but I cannot promise to find silver. It happens only rarely."

"Ah-h-h!"

Troubled by the Lieutenant Governor's sigh, Saugrain looked down at the list in his hand. Then it was his turn to sigh. "Excellency," he said "this second name—Michau. That is my father-in-law. When your letter, inviting me to settle in Saint Louis, reached me in Kentucky, I took the liberty. . . ."

"I know, I know!" de Lassus said testily, still disappointed about the silver. "He and his family accompanied you here. That is all right. As I have said, we welcome settlers, especially"—he took the paper from Saugrain and read the name—" 'Jean Michau,

(49)

Farmer. Very large family.' What is wrong with that? Are you trying to tell me he is not a farmer? But we need farmers as much as we need a doctor. Perhaps we need them more. People generally call this town *Pain Court*. Yes, Short of Bread. Do you know why we lack bread? Because it is made with flour, and flour—at first it was thought that the lack of flour was due to the absence of mills. So a dam was built in the Little River—you saw the river yesterday on landing—and a mill was set up below the dam. The mill did very well until the supply of grain gave out. And the town was once more *pain court*. Your father-in-law, I suppose, is a tradesman of a sort?"

"Excellency," Saugrain said with dignity, he hoped, "in Paris he was a worker in leather—a master saddler. He is also good at keeping accounts. He writes a beautiful hand. . . ."

"Ah-h!" de Lassus said, this time mournfully. "Tradesmen also starve in Paris, I hear. Your father-in-law knows nothing about farming—nothing?"

I am doing this very badly, Saugrain thought. All is confusion now. So he tried again.

"Excellency," he said carefully, "in Gallipolis every man who wished his family to eat was forced to acquaint himself with the soil and a farmer's tools. In time my father-in-law became known for his superior vegetables. He also had good luck with poultry."

"No wheat or corn?" de Lassus asked. "What did he feed his poultry?"

"Excellency, the chickens and ducks and geese for the most part also scratched a living from the soil."

"Good!" de Lassus applauded. "We have here the beginning of a very fine farmer. We will give him land to cultivate. If the work is burdensome, perhaps his large family will help with it."

How to tell this determined man that the family included, besides the father, only two males, one a scatterbrain of eighteen, the other a child? But, before more could be said about farmers and farming, de Lassus changed the subject.

"Now to our business," he said next. "Le Duc is here with your commission. Will you please take a chair at the table?"

The secretary placed the chair, then spread a sheet of parchment on the table, smoothing it with his hand and weighting it finally

(50)

with an inkwell and a stand holding several quill pens. The arms of Spain in gold headed the document. The text had been written in firm, black characters, like an engraving: ". . . our trust in the skill and ability . . . and the allegiance he has sworn . . ."

"Do you find the Spanish troublesome?" de Lassus asked. "This being a legal document?"

"I read the Spanish clearly," Saugrain said, and read on: ". . . to serve the garrison and the citizenry of the City of St. Louis. . . ."

What really troubled Saugrain now was the sensation of a hand plucking at his coat sleeve. Madame Saugrain, who had probably been there all along, wished to remind him of something. He fancied that he could hear her plaintive whisper: "Is it permitted. . . ?"

No, it was not permitted. He read some more: ". . . recompense to be thirty pesos in hard money (*pesos fuertes*), to be paid monthly, also a suitable place of residence within the fortified limits. . . ."

"You are sure you have no question?" De Lassus loosened his collar. The plucking at Saugrain's coat sleeve threatened to become frantic.

"Excellency, yes," Saugrain said. "A place of residence is mentioned. A place only?"

"A choice location," de Lassus said with enthusiasm, "on the Catalan Road, the King's Highway South, which continues the town's Street of the Church. In that direction we are able to offer a full square—for grounds and a house."

The plucking was now a pull.

"Excellency," Saugrain asked, "is there a house on that square now?"

De Lassus loosened another button. "For the present, no. The foundations for a house are there. It should not take long to add the house."

There was no house. Little by little the truth appeared. The original owner of this choice location had dug and laid up stone foundations thirty years before this, when the first survey of the town had established a pattern for streets and roads. Then, for some reason, he had built no further. Later another owner had set a couple of wooden buildings on the property, but had added

(51)

nothing to the original structure, probably because the wooden buildings had served his needs.

That was how things stood at present. When Saugrain's arrival had seemed certain in prospect, a stone mason had been sent to examine the foundations, and had pronounced them in excellent condition, even more solid than they had been at first, since they had had thirty years in which to settle. After this report one load of stones had been hauled—for the laying up of walls—but then no more. With the new owner, Saugrain, on his way, it had seemed best to wait and consult him about the plan for the house.

There was no house. How long. . . ? Saugrain could not ask. Now, when he needed a pull or a push, nobody was there. Outside, the sun shone and birds sang. In this room all was dark and still. On the far side of the table His Excellency waited for Saugrain to speak.

"A doctor," he began at last, "with no place to arrange his pharamaceuticals or compound his medicines, or lay out his scientific experiments, no room in which to receive those who come to him for help, is like a captain without a ship."

"Pardon, monsieur." Le Duc, who had left the room after-depositing the contract and the ink and the pens, was now back, in his hands a deerskin pouch. He set this down on the table—softly; but he could not muffle entirely the clink of pieces of metal. The *pesos fuertes*—thirty large silver coins. Saugrain closed his eyes for a few seconds, then had his answer ready.

"Excellency, I am disappointed about the house; but, since, as you say, we have the foundations, surely between us we can manage the rest. The pesos will help. However, please understand. They are not my reason for signing the agreement. Monsieur le Duc, if you will kindly show me where to write my name?"

Five ∿

Oddly, after signing the contract, which in effect bound him to a post he might find difficult to endure, Saugrain's feeling was not only relief, but a mounting exhilaration. By

(52)

signing he had definitely and, in his own mind, irrevocably settled himself in his new position. Difficulties, disappointment, the attitude of the Lieutenant Governor, which he could not read with certainty in one interview, were reduced to obstacles. He was a practiced hand at demolishing those. About to take his leave, with the Governor's permission, he remembered just in time his appointment to meet Jacques Cardinal at the post hospital. Would Monsieur le Duc have time to show him where it was?

His answer was a significant look exchanged between the Governor and the secretary.

The hospital, de Lassus explained, was a mere beginning of an attempt to provide a place where ailing or injured soldiers could be cared for. His company was the usual assemblage of strays and unfortunates who could with discipline and enforced regular habits be turned into fair common soldiers. He thought the garrison at Fort San Carlos in St. Louis was somewhat above the average in quality. If there should be a patient in the hospital, he hoped the doctor would understand that his ailment was probably only a matter of excessive indulgence when on leave—sutler's rum and so on.

Saugrain understood. The men were conscripts, gathered from brothels, low taverns, the streets. Some did eventually find new manhood. Others . . . well, he had not been called to attend those in no need of assistance.

The reality, then, of the hospital was encouraging. A simple stone shed, it stood close to the rear wall of the House of Government. With a high barred door and windows, it suggested a jail and probably was used for that. While Saugrain inspected Cardinal's face, now more richly colored than before in tones of green and purple but plainly healing, a soldier sentinel, at an order from le Duc, turned a ponderous key in the lock on the door, then stood, waiting. Then there was a patient inside.

"So," Saugrain said to Cardinal. "Keep clean and stay out of the sun for another day or two. You are dismissed."

He turned then to the guard. "Open, please. No, do not follow me. I prefer to enter alone. I will call you if I need you."

There was no need. The interior was one large, whitewashed

(53)

room, kept in order by a stalwart Negro attendant. Half of the room was furnished with two stout chairs, a table, a cupboard with tin doors, a stand with a wash-basin and pitcher, and, beside the stand, a bucket for slops. The other half of the room, on the far side of an imaginary line drawn from the barred door to a cold chimney opposite, held two cot beds. One was unoccupied. On the other a soldier in disheveled undress tossed in torment. His face was darkly flushed, and mottled by an eruption. At Saugrain's entry, he pulled himself up to a half crouch, then fell back cursing—in a Spanish dialect which Saugrain had never heard before and of which he made out only a few words, but enough. The soldier thought he was dying and wanted a priest.

"Later," Saugrain said, "when you are well and can make confession and receive absolution. You are not about to die. Not this time. I am here to save you. I will save you if you take my medicines. I will prepare them, but you must swallow them. One will make you a little sick, the other will be bitter on your tongue. No matter. Swallow them and the fever will go away so that you can sleep; and tomorrow you will know you are going to be well again. If you don't take them, before night you will be raving and begging to die . . . but you will take them of course, because I order you to."

He turned his back then on the cursing and addressed himself to the young Negro, who stared at him in awe as he set his medicine case on the table and opened it, then past him to the bed.

"Do you have dishes in that cupboard?" Saugrain asked, calmly selecting a vial of gray powder. "I need two mugs and spoons. Good, that's right. Also a kettle of hot water. Can you obtain that?"

The Negro said shakily that he would have to go to the kitchen of the house. "Well?" Saugrain said, taking out now a bottle of small brown chips. "Are you afraid to leave me alone with that on the bed? I don't understand a word he says, do you? I thought not. Look how he shakes. If he should leave the bed to come at either of us, he would fall in a heap. Go now for the hot water. For an infusion of cinchona bark it should be boiling."

(54)

Six ~

"My brave husband!" Madame Saugrain said when Saugrain finished his report of the morning's adventures, greatly diluted.

Brave? No. His medicines mixed, he had departed at once, leaving the administering of them to the attendant, advising him to have pail and mop waiting within reach when he gave the emetic.

Saugrain opened his watch. It was now two o'clock in the afternoon. Both the emetic and the fever brew had been either swallowed or rejected. He hoped the poor brute had taken them. There was nothing men like that feared half so much as dying. Tomorrow he should have a more peaceful patient.

With a sigh he put the watch away. The June afternoon was tender as a woman's caress. Sun and wind had dried the mud in wide streaks. The crust was still not to be trusted, but here and there islands of green emerged, firm enough to hold a person if he did not stop too long. Under these circumstances, the doctor and Madame, his wife, once more leaving the children in the care of their nurse, now reinforced by a completely captivated Madame Chouteau, bounced along happily, side by side in the charette, on their way to inspect the hole in the ground, framed in stone, which would some day be the base of their house. They felt it was most important to study the old foundation before they began a reluctant search for a smaller house that they could rent.

Madame Saugrain had accepted calmly the information that the promised official residence was not waiting to receive them. Perhaps Madame Chouteau had prepared her for disappointment. Saugrain then had made a gay story out of his morning. There was le Duc, for instance. Like them, he too was a refugee from the Revolution. He had lived in St. Louis only two years, but there he was now, Secretary of the Province.

And there was the Teniente Gobernador, another Frenchman. His family in Paris had been high in the court circle surrounding Louis XVI. He meantime had taken service in the armies of

Spain and had risen to be captain of the palace guard in Madrid. However, on hearing that his family had escaped to America, he had asked to be transferred to the Royal Louisiana Regiment, so that he could be near his people if they needed him. A brave gentleman, filling now what Saugrain thought must be a most difficult position. His family lived at Bourbon, a town not far from Ste. Genevieve; and between that place and St. Louis there were other royalist exiles, some of them with homes on the same road where the Saugrains hoped to build their house.

"Vigny," his Genevieve said now, "when we have that house, a charette might be very convenient. Not right away, perhaps. . . ."

Why not right away, Saugrain asked? With thirty pesos coming to them every month, in addition to such fees as he might collect from the townspeople, surely they could afford a cart.

Twenty-nine of the first pesos were now in the trustworthy le Duc's keeping—until Saugrain had a strongbox in which to store them—a chest, perhaps, like that one of the Teniente. The thirtieth coin reposed in a small silken sack on Madame Saugrain's bosom, her dress buttoned tightly over it. It had been offered first to the Widow Chouteau. She had taken the good coin, held it for a moment in one hand with the other clasped over it, in the way of one who had learned the value of minted dollars, then, still with reluctance, had given it back to Madame Saugrain, saying that she could not accept pay for the pleasure of making the acquaintance of the doctor and his charming family. Young Madame Saugrain must keep it for a souvenir and a talisman. Then she had hurried off to find the little sack and a cord to tie around its opening. Saugrain, noting now that his wife's hand rested lovingly upon the treasure, knew that it would indeed be hard to separate her from it.

He also noted that her dreaming eyes were now directed forward over the driver's back to the not-very-proud head of the horse.

"I am thinking," she said. "Even if the Governor must pay for erecting our house, we shall have other expenses. For the present some money must go for rent. Also of what use would a charette be without a horse to draw it?"

"Her name is Hortense," Saugrain said. "She is a good horse for hauling, but unfortunately she belongs to Gabriel."

"Gabriel?" Madame inquired.

That was their driver's name, Saugrain explained, and watched her dreaming eyes return to dwell on Gabriel's back and Hortense's rump. This was as good a view as any other of the mare, and the very best to be had of the man. If Gabriel had been endowed at birth with clear, pleasing features, toil and disregard through the years had swollen them out of all comeliness. Also at some time in the past his weathered face had been further decorated with smallpox scars—*la petite vérole* in Parisian French, *la picotée* in Louisiana. Gabriel, however, though robbed of manly beauty, had still his pride. In the interval between his morning duties and the afternoon he had knocked most of the dried mud off the wheels of the cart and as much more off Hortense's coat and his own moccasins and leggings. These efforts at respectability were not overlooked by Madame Saugrain. She contemplated Gabriel's rear with obvious approval—and what else?

It pleased her adoring husband to imagine that she was alternately entertaining and renouncing the thought that it would be nice, when they were settled in their prospective home, to possess charette, Hortense, and Gabriel. They had now crossed the weedy cart track leading from the Rue Principale to the fort and were continuing along the Street of the Church, a boulevard overgrown with weeds, like all the others. At this rate they would need a cart and horse to convey them to and from the center of the town. He would need them in pursuit of those extra fees. Cart, horse, the man to care for both. . . .

Plop!

Hortense, perhaps also a dreamer, had stepped into a deep mudhole, scattering everyone's thoughts including her own, splashing herself with fresh mud and the cart wheels with more. Gabriel cried out at her in pain and fury and picked up his whip but did not use it, judging his screams of anguish to be sufficient reproach. Hortense twitched an ear, lowered her head slightly, and plodded on.

Madame Saugrain looked at her husband with shining eyes and smiling lips. "Those two," she whispered, "understand each other."

Saugrain, who had come near being thrown out of the cart into the mud, smiled back at her. "Plainly," he agreed, "they are inseparable."

Minutes later Gabriel and Hortense placed the charette closely alongside a stretch of barely exposed masonry, Gabriel still scowling.

"I would sell the beast," he said in an undertone to the doctor, "except that she and the cart are all I have to live by." Then, misinterpreting a question in Saugrain's eyes, he added, "You and Madame can step on the stones safely, m'sieu. I know the strength of these foundations. I helped to lay them. Today they will do for a promenade. Monsieur and Madame can walk all around on them without need to step off into the weeds and mud."

Saugrain saw that Gabriel spoke the truth, and for himself he welcomed the suggestion of an elevated promenade, but that dreamy look had settled once more on Madame's face. There were sabots in the cart, and here and there among the weeds flowers raised parasols of blue, white, or yellow. It would be hard to restrain her from plunging into the tangle.

"Vigny, do you see that pinkish lavender flower yonder? Not the wild clover. This is taller, a larger bloom, the petals making a pincushion of the center. That is bergamot surely, and the blue spike near it is vervain, and, oh-h! That monster plant with purple stems and purple veins to its leaves is nightshade. Vigny! I must see those plants close by. I will put on sabots. . . ."

Saugrain stiffened. "No!" he said. "Today there is time only for measuring the foundations. We don't know yet whether they are right for the kind of house. . . ."

"Vigny, it would not take me a minute."

"No!" he said. "I forbid you. Look at those weeds. You do not know what besides flowers lives among them."

"What could live there that is harmful?" she demanded.

"Serpents," he suggested. "They like such cover. And, at this time of year, they are most venomous. You may ask Gabriel."

Gabriel would not say there were no snakes, venomous or no, in the grass. They measured the foundations. The length of the rectangle, as it paralleled the road, was forty feet. The depth was thirty.

"It will be a palace," Madame declared, disappointment over the flowering herbs fleeing before a new vision—their house, their very own house.

The wall facing the road would be the front of the house, with

(58)

a door and steps in the middle, and windows looking out over the road and a steep embankment, now also overgrown with weeds, to the great river.

"I do not recall a bluff so low or so gentle," Madame said.

She must remember, Saugrain thought. It could not have been much farther south than this that the bluffs had parted on a ravine with a little river....

Madame remembered the little river—charming—but then they had got into a carriage and driven up the hill to this road and along it into town without seeing so much as one stone of these foundations, now their property. It was incredible. She sighed, then went on planning.

The picture she had in mind was of an American-style house, such as they had seen and admired in Lexington—a double house with a central hall running from the front door to the back and rooms on both sides. Two large square rooms in front would be their parlors—one for receiving company, the other, not quite so elegant, for more general use. The doctor, for instance, could have his writing desk there and, since he was always buying books to read, a bookshelf. There would be comfortable chairs and a sofa and pictures on the walls. Of the two rooms to the rear, one would be their bedroom; the children would sleep upstairs with Odette. The first mention he had heard, the doctor thought, of a second story, but he did not interrupt. The other would be a kitchen—a French kitchen, with a pot of soup always hot. There must be double chimneys at both ends of the house, to provide an open fireplace in each room. Had she mentioned that? Finally she hoped that, in addition to the main house of stone and apart from it, there would be a second smaller building, also stone, half of which could be an American-style summer kitchen, and the other half could be a special place reserved for the doctor's medicines and his scientific experiments.

"Ole!" Saugrain cried. "I was beginning to wonder." Then, in answer to Madame's look of reproach, he added, "But why the separation of the two buildings?"

"Vigny, you know why! You raise at times the most dreadful smells and you build such hot fires; and, as for electricity, one spark from your wires could burn our house to the ground."

"I have yet to generate heat with an electric spark," he said, "I merely hope . . . but no matter. I thank you, dear, for your thoughtfulness. I had thought I might need to share one of the wooden buildings with Gabriel and Hortense."

Before that discussion could be prolonged, Hortense nickered. "Someone approaches," Saugrain said. "Along the road from the south, I think."

Someone known to Hortense. A second nicker, longer and louder, greeted the emergence of a man mounted on a horse which could be sister or brother to the mare. There was a similarity of color and more of temperament. The second horse had to be placid or the rider could not have balanced before him the huge, flat basket, filled to the edges with garden vegetables. Giving commands by word of mouth and a kick here and there, he brought his steed up to the foundations, facing Hortense and close enough for the two animals to rub noses. Then, with Gabriel's help, he stepped down, landing himself upright with no loss of dignity or produce.

"Monsieur the doctor! Madame!" He bowed low and rose, a bouquet of radishes in his hand. "For you, madame. Please regard them as roses." Then he addressed himself to Saugrain. "Have you decided to complete the house here? Bravo! We shall be neighbors."

His name was Soulard, Antoine Soulard. He had a house in St. Louis, but also a modest farm place farther down the road, on the far side of the Little River.

From that point onward, conversation raced. Sentences tumbled and collided. Madame Saugrain was the first to withdraw from the Babel. Walking to another corner of the foundations, she studied once more, and minutely, her husband's new estate—with the result that suddenly she was back before the men, breathless with inspiration: "Vigny . . . Monsieur Soulard, is it permitted? Excuse, please. I am thinking of the wooden buildings still standing. Are they habitable?"

Soulard studied the question. "Hmm!" he said. "Yes and no, madame."

The smaller one, he explained, as she could see, was a mere shed. It might shelter a horse, a cart, but not people. As for the larger house, people had lived in it once—some years ago. The floor had probably rotted. The roof might leak.

"Is it permitted," she asked then, "that we see the interior?"

"You, madame? No. Not until we at least organize a rat hunt. I have a dog," he added quickly, as Madame paled, "who is very good at hunting rats. We need, besides, three or four strong men with clubs and at least one lantern. Evening is the best time. Doctor?"

"I should be proud," Saugrain said happily, "to carry the lantern, and I know a young man who would do valiant work with a club."

A half hour later, with a sample of every vegetable in Antoine Soulard's basket—radishes, carrots, onions, peas in the pod, beans, beets, all young and tender, with salad greens and a head of cabbage—piled on the floor of the charette between them, Dr. Saugrain and his wife were on the way back to their lodging. The rat hunt had been set for the following evening. After that there would be a cleaning.

"Vigny," Madame said, "it will be nice to live in the old house on our own land. We will not need to pay rent on other lodgings. We can watch our fine house being built. Vigny?"

Saugrain had no answer ready; if it had not been for those tender vegetables between them, he would have crushed his wife in such an embrace! Had he thought of favorable auspices yesterday? How, then, would he describe today?

PART III

"To every thing
there is a season...."

Ecclesiastes 3:1

One ∽

They—the villagers—called it the Year of the Great Winter. St. Louis—Pain Court—had at this time, counting everybody, black or white, slave or free, male or female, nine hundred inhabitants. Of these, only a small number were people of means, some education, breeding, and a surprisingly elegant manner of living, which they could not have maintained without the services of those whose lives were as humble as the lives of the rich were splendid. Having no schooling, the poor could neither read nor write, and when one of them had to sign a paper, he made a mark, then trusted another to write out the name.

When Saugrain first made the acquaintance of these simple folk, who, being more subject to misadventure than their superiors, were his first patients, he discovered that they had no sense of the divisions of time. They knew day from night and summer from winter by the amount of light and the feel of the air. But hours? No. Why would one bother with those? If he left a bottle of cough syrup for an old mother, for instance, he could not say to those caring for her that she must have a spoonful every three or four hours. The dosage must be administered early in the morning, again after the midday soup, and in the evening before sleep, with an extra spoonful between times if the coughing was very bad. Well, it worked, did it not? Yes, usually. Most of the sick, endowed naturally with good health, recovered in time, although some required a second or even a third bottle.

Now, with such people, to give a year a number, like 1800, was foolishness. They would not remember; but when winter brought the first snow, to be followed by more and more, never loosening its grip beyond a day or two until spring arrived, that was different. So, this was the Year of the Great Winter.

From the beginning Saugrain found these simple folk interesting, amusing, sometimes even admirable. They had many virtues. They were cheerfully content with their lot; poor, but with no envy of those born to be rich. They were in a sense industrious. They would work hard all day if that was necessary, then dance away half the night. That they called resting.

They were honest folk, as trusting as they were trustworthy. The first test of Saugrain's skill as a surgeon was a summons to the public wood lot to take care of a young man whose axe had turned in his hand and cut a deep gash in the flesh of his thigh. Baptiste would have bled to death, his friends said afterwards, if the doctor had not come quickly and known what to do. He had tied Baptiste's head kerchief around the leg and glued the skin together over the cut. Yes, truly. They had seen him do this.

So they had. The kerchief had supplied a tourniquet to check the bleeding, enabling Saugrain to cleanse the wound and examine it. It was an ugly gash, but the axe had struck obliquely, injuring neither tendon nor bone. As for the glue, it was a mucilaginous salve made from the pithy stems of the wild mallow, which he carried with him always for cuts. Drawing the edges of the cut together and holding them with one hand, he had applied the salve. Hardly a glue, it kept the wound closed while he added a pad and bandage. Two days later, when he went to Baptiste's house to change the bandage, healing had already begun. At the end of a week, by using a stick to keep his weight off the wounded leg, Baptiste could walk. At the end of a second week he was back in the woods, wielding his axe—with some caution, however.

The wood Baptiste cut that day he delivered to the Saugrain place, as payment for his cure.

"Baptiste," Saugrain objected, "there is no hurry about the pay. You should be cutting the winter wood for your own house. You have been idle now for two weeks."

(66)

"M'sieu Docteur," Baptiste argued, "what are weeks? I am alive and I have two legs. Besides, my house has only one chimney, while yours. . . ."

Looking around, he could count two chimneys and see the possibility of at least one more. That meant a fearful amount of wood; and yet, after the young man had stacked a winter's supply against his own small house, Saugrain had difficulty in persuading him to cut wood for pay.

This showed the character of the people whose health and well-being Saugrain knew he must study and understand. He did understand, he thought, but finally there came a day when one of their leading virtues—their refusal to be harried by hours spent or hours wasted—seemed to him open to question.

October arrived; and his house, the house which he had been promised before he left Kentucky and which then was to have taken only a few weeks to build, was less than halfway toward being a house in fact. For this there were reasons, to be sure—many reasons.

To begin with, the land inside and outside the old foundations had to be cleared. Thoroughly. After the tumult and fury of the rat hunts—three, not one—snakes had to be exterminated. For this Monsieur Soulard recommended pigs. A pig, he said, liked nothing better than to root out a snake and destroy it. For a week, Jean Michau joyfully herded four squealing porkers up the road and turned them into the Saugrain lot, and in the evening drove them back again to their Soulard pen.

After the pigs came a pair of goats—to deal with the underbrush. Goats, Antoine Soulard said, ate everything. They did indeed. Gabriel, in what he called a frenzy of haste, barely kept out of reach of their munching as he dug out plants which Madame Saugrain wanted saved to make a showing in the garden she now had ready—on paper.

After the goats, sheep were borrowed—to graze off the weeds and wild grass among the stubble. June was now gone, and the Saugrains were planning to move into the large wooden house in order to be present when the walls of their permanent home began to rise. Alas, that was not to come immediately. In preparation for the move, Madame Saugrain devoted two days to a thorough cleaning of what were to be their summer quarters.

Alas, with the help of a strong Negro woman hired in the town, she exposed a few faults which had been overlooked before. The puncheon floor had held up well, but now there were damp spots directing the eye to rivulets on the walls, which in turn suggested that water leaked in somewhere when it rained.

A carpenter, recommended by the stone mason who was to build the stone house when the time came, examined the water marks and acknowledged that there were leaks, but not in the walls. Rather, they were in the roof, he thought, probably around the chimney. It would be best for the stone mason to examine the chimney before any other repairs were made.

The stone mason obliged. The chimney was a large square stack of stone with two opposite openings serving the two large rooms into which the old house was divided. It needed repair. The mason thought the old pile of stones on the ground would be just about enough to fill the worst gaps. Again he was right. He used all but one stone block. With the chimney weathertight, the carpenter went to work on the roof. A coat of whitewash was then spread over the stained walls, and the Saugrains moved in with all their belongings.

Meanwhile the Michaus had rented a plain little house in the square north of the Saugrain property and agreed to store some of the Saugrain furniture until their stone house was finished. Just to be settled seemed such an advance to both families that it called for a proper celebration, with cake and wine and invitation to all their new neighbors on the same road. It was such a gay party that nobody bothered to study the calendar until the following day, and then nobody believed what he saw.

One week remained of July. But that was not possible. It was true. Oh well, nothing now stood in the way of building the stone house. Michau Père, not having so far obtained any orders for saddles, had busied himself with drawing a plan according to the wishes of his daughter and her husband.

The stone mason took the plan into his rough hands and, not being able to read even Michau's clear script, turned it around every which way until he thought he knew the front of the house from the rear, and gave his approval—with a reservation. Would the doctor and Madame want the frame of the house set on the foundations as they stood, or would they prefer to add a few layers of stone, to elevate the level of the floor? For a house as fine as this one a cellar was a thing to consider. Saugrain wasted no time in considering. A higher elevation would provide a better view from the front windows, looking out over the road and the river.

"Good!" the mason said. "Have you then, Monsieur Docteur, obtained permission to quarry the stone we shall need?"

"Permission?" Something in Saugrain's throat threatened to choke him. "The Teniente is building this house, not I. He has the right. . . ."

That was true, the mason agreed. Still, it might be well to have a paper to hold when it came to taking the stone. Saugrain swallowed the thing in his throat.

"All right," he said. " I will see about it at once—today." *Dieu!* He had been on the edge of saying "Tomorrow."

So. obtaining permission, and marking the area on the bluffs from which the stone could be taken, and cutting the stone from the bluff, then into blocks suitable for building, and trimming those with a chisel so that they would lie securely one upon another, naturally took time; but Madame, now busily preparing, with the help of Gabriel and her brother Jean, two garden plots —one to the front of the house for flowers, and one to the rear for homelier herbs and vegetables—filled the time of waiting.

From the beginning he had been troubled about water—clear, pure water for drinking and cooking. Vainly Saugrain tried to convince her that it was absurd for people with the Mississippi flowing practically past their front door to be anxious about water. The inhabitants of St. Louis drank Mississippi River water. Ox-carts hauled it in barrels up the road past the Saugrain place and distributed it where needed. When it had stood in a jar for a time, the water above the sediment was clear and sweet and apparently healthful. To prove his point, he put some to settle in a stone jar, then examined both the clear water and the sediment. And what did he find?

"Animals," Madame said scornfully.

"Organisms," Saugrain corrected, "too small to be seen by the naked eye, but all alive and healthy. None of them dead."

But Madame would drink no water with animals in it—alive or dead.

So Gabriel for a while hauled water every day from the Soulard well for Madame's satisfaction. But that could not continue indefinitely. Why should it continue, Madame reasoned? If Monsieur Soulard could find good water by digging a well, why could they not do the same, having a whole square of ground at their disposal, much of it not needed for any other purpose?

The well was dug. They were lucky, the hired diggers said, to find water so close to the top of the ground. The hole they had made looked like a deep, dark pit to Saugrain; but the water was there all right, at the bottom of the pit still but rising—clear, beautiful water. If later he found organisms in it, he knew better than to mention them. Madame was enchanted with the well.

But digging, it seemed, was not all of having a well. It must be faced with stone, and a curb must be set at the top to support the machinery for drawing water and posts for holding a roof. Half of the first load of new stone went to completing the well. The other half Saugrain—grimly—reserved for himself. In the interim, while these other businesses were in progress, Gabriel had devoted what time he could spare from driving the doctor around and helping Madame with her garden to making repairs on the small shed house at the rear of the lot. Eventually this was to be Gabriel's house—comfortable quarters for himself and a stall for Hortense. This arrangement had been planned when the doctor was counting on having an office and a laboratory in a separate building of stone adjacent to the main stone house. Now, with the family residence hardly begun, it seemed probable that the doctor would not have his quarters for another year, and the plan had to be changed. The main part of the small shed house was to be made ready for the doctor's temporary use, with Gabriel sharing meanwhile Hortense's stable. Gabriel himself had made the suggestion. He had been sleeping beside Hortense for years, so that was no hardship. Besides, was it not right that someone should stand guard in that little house over the doctor's beautiful tools and other treasures? He could do that. He could also keep a fire going so that in the wintertime the house would always be warm for the doctor's use.

More industriously than before he toiled at the repairs. By the time the well was finished he had completed floor, roof, and walls —except the east wall, which was to accommodate a new chimney. The old one being in ruins and much too small for his needs, Saugrain had ordered a stone chimney large enough to give him room for a small furnace for blowing glass. He needed bottles for dispensing medicine and, since he knew how to blow glass, it seemed easier for him to make them than to search for another source of supply nearer than the head of navigation on the Ohio. While looking over the Teniente's samples of lead ore, he had made note of some very interesting beds of sand, but they were of no use to him until he had his chimney and his furnace.

This was behind his determination that, for every stone that went into the work on the well, one should be put aside for his needs. If stone was on hand when the well was finished, the stone mason could set up an extra chimney very quickly.

"Vigny," Madame said to him one summer evening, as they walked the paths of a now green and growing garden, "it all consumes too much time, does it not? It is now August, and the stone mason is only beginning to raise the walls of our house."

"He had to wait," Saugrain explained, "for the carpenter to set the wooden frame for the house, and mark the spaces for doors and windows. Never mind. All will go better now. And faster. You will see."

"And you are not afraid of the cost?" Madame said then. "We have used so much stone. Every day more must be brought. I know His Excellency the Governor is building the house for us with money from New Orleans, but the agreement mentioned only one hundred dollars for the building. With everything extra that we have wanted, Papa thinks we have spent another hundred. Do we have that much money, Vigny?"

"Not in *pesos fuertes*," Saugrain answered. "We have not lived here that long. However, in the usual currency of Louisiana, it is just possible that I do have that sum, one hundred dollars being equal to two hundred fifty deerskins."

"Do you have that many deerskins. Vigny? Where do you keep them?"

"In a tin box," he said. Then seeing that Madame was not in a mood for a jest, he had to make more explanations.

In Louisiana, he said, a money debt was paid like this. Say a man named Prudhomme owed Dr. Saugrain a sum for medical treatment. He would give the doctor a note good for, say, fifty dressed deerskins, which, or the value thereof, would be delivered at some future date—in St. Louis, usually the first of May in the coming year. This note, called a *bon*, the doctor would deposit in his tin box. As for the skins, either Monsieur Prudhomme had them himself or he had deposited them with a merchant like the Chouteaus or Monsieur Roubidou, someone with a dry cellar or loft for storing furs.

In the spring of the year all the furs taken in St. Louis were carried in boats to New Orleans, the merchants accompanying them to make sure that they brought a good price, and sold either for real money or for goods that would be in demand at St. Louis. On their return, then, the merchants would call in everyone on their account books and pay them. Monsieur Prudhomme would then be in a position to redeem all the *bons* he had signed.

"It works, I am told," Saugrain concluded. "One must believe. . . ."

"I understand, I think," Madame said, "but now about the tin box. Where do you keep that?"

He kept it with his other papers, naturally, on a shelf in his little house.

Madame was horrified. In that rough little shed with its great chimney and a fire burning night and day? The box might be of tin, but the notes were paper. Had he counted the money they were good for?

No, Saugrain confessed. He left all that now to her father. Michau Père, having still no business of his own to handle, had been glad to take over Saugrain's accounts, freeing Saugrain for his professional duties. Michau Père had an account book in which he entered every sum that Saugrain owed and every sum scribbled on a *bon* to his credit. As for the balance, Saugrain, not having worked out the figure himself, was afraid to repeat it. It was not wealth Michau Père said, but it was more than Saugrain had ever earned before in three months' time.

And the walls of their house were now rising, he reminded his wife—their beautiful, solid house, their assurance of the fulfillment of hope. They rose slowly but steadily, the mason setting each stone with precision. Early in September they enclosed every door and window. By the end of the month, they had almost

(72)

reached the top. One more week would see them ready for the timbers that were to hold the roof. Now watch. One must not be too sure. Why? What could happen in a week?

Everything. One cold, clear night, following two days of a north wind and chilling rain, was enough. In the morning, everything —forest, meadow, garden beds—was white with hoarfrost. Vegetation shrank under it and, when the sun shone, drooped and died. Only one crop benefited. The wild grapes in woods and on the bluffs ripened. Filled with juice and flavor, they must be harvested at once. They could not wait. They would spoil.

So, every other duty was laid aside for the gathering of the grapes and the making of the wine. The stone mason took leave, among others. He and his father before him had always directed the harvesting of the grapes and the making of the wine. Stones, the building of a house, would wait. Not the grapes.

"Well?" Saugrain said to him on the day of his return from the bacchanalia, "What do you think now? Shall we finish the house before winter?"

The mason trudged around the house, muttering dolefully. "A house of posts," he said finally, "would have been finished long ago."

"I live in one of those," Saugrain reminded him. "I am waiting now for one of stone. How long?"

"A month?" the mason said, his rough face creased with the effort of calculation. "Two months?"

"Six months is more probable," Saugrain said. "Or a year."

Either figure seems possible to the mason. Not much laying of stone remained—two or three courses around the house—but then the gable ends must be faced with stone. The stones there must be set very carefully—to meet the slant of the roof.

"The stones are waiting for you," Saugrain said. "Get to work, then, and tomorrow, when you come, bring the carpenter with you. Besides the roof I want to ask about covering the doors and windows. My right foot tells me winter is not far off."

What wonder was it, then, that dismay swept over Saugrain afresh when, on a fine October morning, as he was on his way to his shed house, he stopped to examine the building operations and found nobody at work there except Gabriel, who was moving a heavy object in a wheelbarrow from the direction of the Michau house to the Saugrain place. It was the last piece of Saugrain freight which had burdened the Teniente's galley in June—and the heaviest. Meeting Saugrain, Gabriel respectfully and willingly set the wheelbarrow down on its legs. Saugrain had now taken his silver watch from his waistcoat pocket and was studying it.

"What is it with our stone mason today, Gabriel?" he asked. "It is now past eight o'clock. Much of the morning is gone. Does he come to work this late every day?"

"No, m'sieu," Gabriel said. "Today he is in need of more stone. When that happens, he waits in town for the oxcart, which carries the stone."

Only one cart in town was so constructed that it would bear stone. It was the same cart that delivered water to the village. It went out with empty barrels first thing in the morning, returned, and delivered the water where needed; then the barrels were removed and it was ready for other hauling. One morning Saugrain had heard it pass with the empty barrels while he was dressing and return with the barrels filled while he finished his breakfast. So the stone mason, Gabriel explained, on days when he had to wait for more stone before he could work, remained in bed until he heard the wagon return to town, then rose and was ready to ride to the Saugrain place when it went for the stone.

"I see," Saugrain said, frowning at his watch. "Are there no timepieces in town but mine?"

Watches? Gabriel questioned. There were not many, none so fine or so big as the doctor's. No clocks, no bells—Saugrain had missed the ringing of bells. Oh, but there was a bell, Gabriel said, a very fine one. An early governor, Cruzat by name, had ordered one from Spain. Silver, it was said, was mixed with other metals to give it a beautiful sound. Where was it now? Alas, it stood on the ground behind the church. The bell tower on the roof of the church would not support it. It was heavier even than the object Gabriel had in his barrow. For the first time Saugrain turned his attention to that object. His face brightened. He put away his watch.

"My mortar and pestle!" he said joyfully. "I wondered where they were."

(74)

A mortar? This iron pot with a stick of iron in its mouth? True, it had something of the shape of a small china dish the doctor had in the little house, but. . . .

"Idiot!" Saugrain said. "I do not grind medicines in the big fellow. It is a symbol only. In Paris such a mortar set in the street beside one's door says to the passer-by that a doctor is within, who is licensed to compound medicines. So! Let us move on with the mortar at least. We will set it at the corner of the little house . . . wait, I will take away some of the weight." He laid hold of the pestle, but it, too, was heavy. Lifting it from the mortar, he brushed the iron lip, producing, not a loud noise, but certainly a muffled boom of promise. If he were to give the pestle a good swing . . . looking up he saw consternation, even terror, on Gabriel's face. The poor man could not know the doctor's intentions, but was sure he had some.

"M'sieu," he stammered, "I have a thought about this mortar. Of what use will it be where the little house sits? Nobody passes there."

"That, too," Saugrain said happily, "could change—after tomorrow."

Two ✎

So it happened that on the following day, when most of the people in town were still snug in their beds, a blast of sound—metal against metal—tumbled them all out and sent them on a run for their doors, to discover if possible what the hideous noise might mean. Five times—the fingers on one hand—the alarm was repeated; six times in all. Then everything went fearfully quiet even though by then the streets were full of people, listening, looking, wondering. There was no smoke from a fire. It was not Indians or the English across the river. In either case the cannon from the fort would have spoken. One minute after the noise ceased, a chitter-chatter as of a thousand birds broke the stillness as one villager turned to another, and none had an answer ready until one found the explanation in his own mind.

The noise came from the south, did it not? Where the new doctor lived—beside the Catalan Road?

Yes, the little doctor from Paris. Everyone knew about him now. He was a good doctor, but he had his notions. He did not bleed a person sick with a fever. He gave bitter medicine instead. Very bitter; fever fled before it. His plasters and liniments burned like hell's fire, but they drew out pain and cured the swelling. Nobody put together the ends of a broken bone so neatly or strapped leg or arm more securely to a board. Still, he had notions. Had anyone before him ever raised such a sound? That settled it. It was the doctor.

But how had he made the noise? What did it mean? Finally a guard detail from the fort marched through the streets, to answer questions. The noise, the corporal in command said, was a sort of reveille, an awakening. The six bangs indicated the hour. It was now six o'clock in the morning. The commandant at the fort was preparing to visit the Teniente, to consult him about the reveille; but now, since everyone was up and out, why should they not begin their day's work?

Meanwhile, at his home on the Catalan Road, Saugrain settled the iron pestle in the iron mortar, rubbed his arms reflectively, and ventured a glance at the open door of the shed house, where stood his man of all work, his eyes bulging, his hair full of straw and his hands closing his ears.

"Well, Gabriel," he called cheerfully, "how did it go?"

Shuddering, Gabriel dropped his hands, and opened his mouth to answer, but a plaintive neigh from the stable turned him that way instead, and he ran.

"Success!" Saugrain called after him. "Success!"

Others might not agree, among them Madame, his charming wife, who stood at the door of the larger wooden house, pale, wide-eyed, shocked from her lace cap to her shoes. He blew her a kiss.

"I'm coming," he said, "presently. I want to look first at the new house."

Faint, still far away, he thought he heard the shrieking of wood wheels—the water cart. When it appeared, he hoped to see on it, besides empty barrels, a stone mason. It just might carry, in addition, a carpenter.

(76)

Three ∽

To Saugrain's surprise, Governor de Lassus did not forbid him to strike the hour of six on the iron mortar mornings and evenings. Rather, he was at first amused, then, on second thought, pleased. Reveille at dawn and retreat at the other end of the day were correct military practice. Reasonably, but perhaps regrettably, at this remote post, such formalities had been allowed to lapse. For one thing, a bugler was not usually on the roll of the garrison; and to fire a cannon or even a fusillade of muskets meant extravagant waste of powder.

"So," he said, "even though some complain that their sleep is broken too early in the morning, amuse yourself this way if you will. But I warn you—once you establish the custom, you must keep it up. Already there are some who wait for you to tell them when to work and when to lay up their tools."

Saugrain had no intention of failing at his self-imposed morning and evening exercise. Through the hard winter he kept his promise. It was not always easy. There were mornings where he was as much tempted as any other to keep to the warmth of his bed; but the evening before he had told his silver watch and himself that he must not yield to temptation. Shortly before six he was up, wrapping himself in layers of clothing, preparing to rush out into the cold to sound his matins. When the exercise was over, warmed thoroughly inside and out, he found his spirits soaring. Soon he began to hear from people in the town who waited for his morning alarm. When it came, they said to their wives and their children, "Our doctor, thank God, is alive and stirring. He does not forget us."

How could he forget? After the first snow came a succession of arctic storms, each driven by a howling wind, carrying more snow and more bitter cold. Snow piled up to a depth greater than the height of any doorstep. If the sun shone briefly, it melted only the surface, and the water froze to ice overnight, providing a white pavement as hard as stone. Icicles hung from every roof. The ground disappeared. To reach it called for a pickaxe in the hands of a man of muscle. Finally digging, even for a grave to bury the dead, became impossible. Coffins had to be covered and left beside the church wall, to wait for a general thaw. Passing the church on one bleak day, on his round of visits in the town, Saugrain saw a young man enter the churchyard carrying a bundle and hailed him, to ask what he had there.

"A blanket for *Grand'mère*," the young man said. "She chills so easily."

That evening the iron pestle was heavy in Saugrain's hands, and the noise it made sounded like a dirge; but the next day his blows on the iron mortar had their usual vigor. Overnight he had reasoned things out. It was by his own wish that he lived in this place. It had taken him many years to reach this vantage point, if it was that, on the great Mississippi. In return, while he waited for his appointed destiny to reveal itself, he had agreed to care for the illnesses and the injuries of the nine hundred inhabitants and the soldiers of the garrison. He would keep his promise and . . . well, he would see what he would see.

Fortunately for all, there was less illness in the town than the inhabitants recalled from much milder winters. This, Saugrain thought, might be due to the destruction of impurities in the air by freezing, and to a state of health induced by the labor a man had to perform to keep his family fed and warmed—stalking deer, for example, and setting traps for fur and meat.

This robust theory, however, did not apply to the very young or the old and infirm. Chest colds were prevalent, and rheumatism. With the old, rheumatism was expected and accepted. Lung fever, attacking both young and old, was more frightening. Saugrain fought it with poultices, fever brews, both gentle and strong, and much counsel: "Eat the hot soup. Drink water, much water. Keep close to the fire. Tell your good man to pile on more wood, even if he must cut down another tree."

He fought the cold and the chill with all the skill he possessed, and what medicine he had at his command. If he lost a battle . . . well, what could he do but fight on? Determination not to lose another showed on such days in his fierce attacks on the mortar.

On one particularly bitter day in December, as he turned from

(78)

his rousing exercise to speak to Gabriel about going to town, he was surprised to find the door of the little house still tightly closed and no Gabriel in evidence. Was Gabriel down, for a change? Or could it be Hortense? Either collapse could be calamitous. He had in his pocket, under his outer wraps, a list of people in town whom he felt he must see this day in spite of wind or weather. So, still apprehensive, he knocked on the door, then opened it.

Inside the house, before a grand fire, Gabriel waited. Saugrain had never seen his scarred face so set, so solemn. He listened stoically to Saugrain's plan for the morning, but then. . . .

"M'sieu," he said, "you cannot go to town today. It is too cold. It is the coldest day of the winter until now. I watched you outside. Your breath froze. That could happen to Hortense. The air could freeze in her nose. That is very painful, m'sieu. The poor animal could die."

The good man's face was becoming more set by the minute. From other encounters Saugrain knew it was useless to argue. Still, he tried.

"These people are old," he said, bringing out his list. "They need me."

"M'sieu," Gabriel said, "if they are very old and they die, it will be because they cannot fight against the cold. You can help them a little, but you cannot save them. They know, these old ones, that their lives are spent, that their lives are not worth to the people of this town, to their families, to your family, to me, what your life is worth. M'sieu, if you will prepare the medicines and mark on each bottle and tell me where it is to be left, I will take it for you."

"But, Gabriel . . ."

"I know, m'sieu. I cannot read the names, but I can read numbers printed plainly like one, two, three and so on. I will go into town over the Rue Principale and return by the Street of the Church. If you will number the bottles and say whose house each number stands for, if they are not too many, I can remember."

"Gabriel, will you be still a minute and let me speak? How will you go into the town except in the cart?"

"M'sieu, on snowshoes. It is not far on those."

(79)

Saugrain had seen men and boys go into the woods on these webbed rafts, but he had never thought of Gabriel doing the same.

"M'sieu," Gabriel said, "I have lived a long time. We have had other bad winters. I learned as a boy to walk on snowshoes."

He ducked into the stable and returned with a pair as scarred as he was, also as strong—frames of the tough bois d'arc and webbing of deer sinews.

"Who made these for you?" Saugrain asked. "You—yourself? Then you can make me a pair. You will prepare the material at once."

"M'sieu?"

"What now?" Saugrain said.

"M'sieur Docteur, you will have to learn how to walk on them. It is not easy."

"I will learn," Saugrain promised. "You will show me. Agreed? Good! In return, I will permit you to run to town today with a few bottles—after I have breakfasted. Have you eaten? Good! Then I will be off, to satisfy Madame that I am not lying somewhere in the snow, frozen stiff. *Au revoir!*"

Four ✍

It was now the middle of December. On the Saugrain land the stone house stood—silent, empty, but strong against the assault of winter. A roof that did not leak rested securely on completed walls, letting no snow touch the hollow interior. Boards over what would be windows and doors were, to be sure, like patches over the eyes of the blind. Still, there the house stood, a bastion of hope. Each morning Saugrain saluted it as he went out to strike the hour of six. Not once, the villagers boasted afterwards, did he fail to perform this duty. This was of benefit to all. If, as the doctor said, the exercise made his blood run faster, who in town, after those ringing blows, could think of sleeping? *Dieu!* The cows in the barns knew what the alarm meant. Before the last echo was silenced, they bawled for attention. After this rousing beginning, a day seemed to hold an extra measure of time, to be used as one pleased instead of as one must. A person could go for a look at the river, for example.

The Mississippi was filling fast with ice. Great cakes, like rafts torn from their moorings, floated past St. Louis. Before the month was over, hunters and fishermen reported that, above the point where the Missouri poured in its waters, the Mississippi was closed from shore to shore. Below that, until the Missouri was blocked, the ice in the Mississippi would continue to toss and tumble. It took a while to close both rivers.

The year ended with great blocks crashing against one another, sometimes turning over and sinking, only to rise again and go racing onward, but the channels narrowed steadily. As they shrank, the ice coalesced into a rumpled, billowing sheet, the process accompanied by a fearsome crashing and groaning. Even after bold men, irresistibly drawn to the river, ventured out on the ice, repeatedly there would come a rending sound underfoot which made them retreat, to wait a day or two longer. The river, men said after such a scare, did not like its prison. It wanted to be free.

The tales, these manifestations of power, pigmy men battling a great river, were to Saugrain a source of new enchantment. Mentally he shook his fist at the elements for blowing up a storm, which kept him from his daily view of the panorama. Threatening noises did not keep pigmy man off the frozen surface. Fishermen chopped holes in it and drew out fine, hungry fish, their meat especially succulent; and a fisherman, after a good catch, would not leave that hole without planting a stick in it, tied with a bright rag. Unless so marked, that fruitful hole would freeze over during the night and he would never find it again. Finally the river bristled with markers like the darts in the neck of a baited bull.

The next phenomenon was the appearance of a path crossing the river. Whose feet first made it nobody knew. Once the way was shown, so many used it that footprints were impossible to identify. Slowly the trace widened and became a kind of avenue in and out around the ice hummocks. A guard set at the St. Louis end proved ineffectual for halting either travel or trade.

"Smuggling," Don Carlos de Lassus said. "There is a law on the books against such trade. The punishment is heavy, but

(81)

nobody stops for that. I am told that sleds are used now to carry the contraband.

Besides the Teniente, four good friends, French expatriates like himself—le Duc, Saugrain, Soulard and another with a home on the Catalan Road, Monsieur du Breuille—toasted themselves before the Soulard hearth and said nothing. They knew about the sleds. The tracks of the runners began where the light of the fire at the St. Louis guard station illumined the path for a considerable distance. After that the men set their course by a fire on the Illinois shore.

"Well?" de Lassus said, when he was given neither sympathy nor counsel, "are you afraid to speak? Doctor?"

"Contraband," Saugrain suggested, "seems a harsh term under the circumstances. Illinois is natural farm country. There is wheat flour to spare on that side of the river. We, on our part, have the best hunters. So, we have meat to exchange."

"Also," Monsieur du Breuille added, "the people on the two sides of the river are often related. I am told that the first families who settled Saint Louis came from over there. Most of them, no doubt, left sisters and brothers when they departed. In this distressing winter, may we not relax our vigilance a little?"

"How can anyone relax vigilance?" de Lassus questioned. "Am I to disregard my orders, lift all restrictions, take away my guard? That would please our doctor, I am sure, who is always finding new chilblains at the fort. If I do this, what shall I plead as an excuse? The winter? Who in New Orleans will believe that story?"

"Excellency," le Duc said, "let me write the plea for you. Those who read my description may not have chilblains as a result, but I promise you they will shiver."

Nothing more was said to influence the Teniente, but the next day restrictions were at least loosened. A small number of people were given passports to visit friends and kinfolk in the land of the Illinois, and an equal number from that side were permitted to cross to St. Louis, to visit or to trade. In consequence, on the following Sunday, when a priest happened to be present to say Mass, prayers of thanksgiving were offered in the rickety little wooden church. Just as thankfully, as a matter of custom rather than for a specific reason, the Michau family joined the Saugrains for *déjeuner* after church. The Michau house was too small to hold both groups, but the barnlike temporary residence of the Saugrains seemed to accommodate any number.

"Besides," pert, fourteen-year-old Sophie Michau said, "I think the doctor likes to have us where he can count us."

There was truth in her remark. Feeling with each passing day more rather than less responsible for the well-being of this second family which had followed him to this wilderness post, Saugrain took advantage of every opportunity for a general inspection. He had now perhaps an hour for observation while Madame Saugrain in the kitchen tasted, seasoned, basted, and stirred the contents of pans and kettles, completing the preparations for the meal to follow.

Meaning to make the most of his hour, he began with a silent study of his father-in-law. A handsome man in his middle years, as sturdy as an oak, Michau Père was never ill, only difficult. He grieved for his dead wife. He would grieve always, because that was his nature. Today he sat in one of two armchairs, his able hands empty. He still had found no demand for hand-tooled leather, but before the winter set in, he had begun making chairs and tables of native woods—cherry, maple, walnut. Alas, right now the only wood cut was firewood. So, since keeping Saugrain's accounts did not fill his days, he was often idle; and, being idle, he brooded. So far, for one reason or another, de Lassus had not renewed his suggestion that he be given a farm to cultivate, which was good. Still, Michau Père brooded. Over what? The past, the present, or the future? His children, perhaps.

He had cause for concern there. Saugrain's eyes, following the father's, rested on Elinor, the daughter nearest in years to Madame. He would have preferred to see a little more meat on her bones. Considered the beauty of the family, she was too pale, too slender for what he thought of as health. He felt great compassion for this sad young person. He would have liked to help her, but he was baffled. It was at times like this that he missed—not Paris, but the resources of Paris. His books, for example. He remembered one in particular, entitled *La Système Physique et Morale de la Femme*. He had no doubt that this book contained all the wisdom he lacked on that subject; but alas, that volume was part of a

(83)

personal collection made during his student years and later, which he had stored in a closet in his uncle's Library of the Arsenal, when he left France finally for America. He had been able to carry with him his instruments, scientific and professional, even the clumsy mortar, but books he had understood he could replace in Philadelphia or Boston. However, in the confusion that attended his arrival in America, he had seen little of Philadelphia and nothing of Boston.

Madame Saugrain said he was foolish to worry about Elinor. She had always been thin and pale. She did not eat enough. Now she missed Maman more than anyone else except Papa. Saugrain thought she missed most a husband and children. There had been nobody for her in Gallipolis. Now twenty-three years old, how should she find a husband in Louisiana? Young men there either had marriages arranged for them or they chose heartier mates—such as young Sophie, for example.

Sophie would have no trouble in finding a husband when the time came. She had velvet eyes like Madame's, and the same charm. At present, while Elinor stood talking to Odette, she had placed herself on the hearth between the two little Saugrain girls and her brother Aristide—to keep Aristide from pulling the little nieces' hair to hear them scream.

Aristide—Saugrain as brother-in-law had a plan for him: school. There was a school for boys in town, directed by a man of some learning named Trudeau. He would speak to Michau Père about entering Aristide there, but . . . later.

So`there were his family problems: school for Aristide and a husband for Elinor—a widower, perhaps, with a family already begun. He had no such widower in mind, but he had not really searched for one. As for the other two Michau offspring, Sophie and Jean, they could be trusted to provide their own futures. Only that morning Madame had said that she was sure Jean had something on his mind. She knew the signs. So would Vigny, please, try to find out what it was?

As if summoned, Jean now entered the room, bearing a log almost as long as he was; his present duty was to keep the fires burning well in the common room and in the kitchen. He scattered the fire worshipers clustered around the hearth and gently, with beautiful muscular control, added his log, then stood

(84)

up, dusting his hands, and smiled triumphantly at Madame sister, watching from the kitchen door. "You see, no sparks! seemed to say.

For the past hour odors from the kitchen had been tantalizing. Now a richer aroma of meat and seasonings was enough to make one's head swim.

One early morning in the week just finished, Saugrain had discovered the frozen carcass of a deer hanging from a tree limb near Gabriel's quarters—payment, no doubt, for some medical service, although no name was attached. On Saturday Gabriel, standing on his cart and using hatchet and saw, had been able to hack off enough of one hind quarter to provide Madame with meat to roast and a joint for soup. This morning Gabriel had remained at home, to keep the soup in its kettle bubbling and to turn the spit holding the roast above a pan set for drippings. All Madame had to do on her return from church was to taste, add seasoning, and prepare salad from a window garden. Success was plain to read in her flushed cheeks and bright eyes. All was ready now, she said, and would they take their places at the table quickly, please? Soup in bowls cooled very fast.

For some time after that nobody said anything. All were too busy eating the hot soup, the roast venison, the fresh, homemade bread, sipping the sparkling grape wine—all but Madame. Still flushed and, one would have said, anxious, she looked around the table at the others, eating, and from them to walls, the rough wood already showing through the coat of whitewash. Suddenly she sighed.

"I cannot help thinking," she said, "we are all refugees still, in a sense. Are we not?" Then, when all had stopped eating to stare at her, she added, "I know. It is not exactly like Gallipolis. . . ."

She got no farther. Young Jean shouted irreverent laughter, and that set off the others. Madame Saugrain laughed with them. She was ridiculous, was she not? Only her husband seemed to disagree, but when even his father-in-law continued to be amused, he kept his dissent to himself. However, once the feasting was over, and Michau Père had wrapped himself and Aristide and made off for the shed house to review an account which puzzled him, Saugrain turned at once to young Jean.

"What do you say?" he said. "Shall we leave the women in

(85)

command here? I feel the need of exercise—a practice run on the snowshoes, perhaps—and I have not seen the river at this point for days. Add some wood to the fires and come with me."

Ten minutes later, bundled in wraps except for their eyes, they stood at the edge of the embankment leading steeply down to the river.

"You do very well on the snowshoes," Jean said.

"I wanted to hear you say so," Saugrain admitted. "I am proud of the accomplishment myself. I can now go as far as the town on them. I am not sure that I could return home afterwards, but I find that Gabriel, having watched me float away, counts the time until he thinks I should have my business finished, and then hitches poor Hortense to the cart and comes after me.

"Brrr!" he shivered on his next breath. "Can we find a spot here less open to the wind? I still have not looked at the river. How about that ledge of rock below us?"

"Let me go first," Jean said, and took the descent easily, then lifted Saugrain safely to a spot beside him. The ledge was an excellent vantage point, perhaps the only one on the face of the bluff. The rock behind them cut off the wind. They could breathe more easily and take time to look about. Not much time, but some. The air carried a forbidding chill. The view, while impressive, was not inspiring.

The river was still a distance below. In its struggle against imprisonment, it had piled against the bluff a barricade of ice that reached almost to the ledge. Below that, the frozen watercourse was like poured metal, now hardened. The Illinois shore was barely visible; the sun had raised enough vapor to form a curtain which hid entirely the small settlement across from St. Louis —Caos, Cohos—Cahokia, the Americans there called it. It was on that obscurity, however, that Jean's attention seemed fixed. Saugrain wasted no more time in preliminaries.

"Jean," he said, "what is it you see over there in the mist? I know you have crossed the river on the ice. Did you find something to your liking?" Jean did not answer at once; and when he turned, he threw back his head in a sort of defiance.

"The richest farmland in America," he said.

(86)

He spoke so fervently, so tenderly, with such yearning that at first it seemed preposterous—mere youthful exaggeration.

"Jean," Saugrain said, "are you speaking of those mud flats over there? Every year they are drowned by the river in flood."

"Not every year," Jean objected; "and when a flood comes the water going down leaves a layer of new, fresh soil. Anything will grow on it or in it. That is what I want more than anything else —good ground that I can call mine. I want to clear it, break it up, sow seed in it, watch the seed grow, gather a harvest . . . maybe it is because I was hungry back in Ohio, but that is what I want to do now—farm a piece of land. You don't believe me?"

Saugrain did believe him. In his mind it was last summer. Jean and Gabriel were preparing a seed bed for Madame Saugrain. Jean stood in the middle of it, cooling his body, resting. Suddenly he stooped, picked up a clod of the freshly broken ground, fondled it in his hands, brought it to his face, and sniffed at it as if it had a fragrance. Saugrain understood, but now he also perceived why Spain forbade communication between her provincials and foreigners beyond a boundary line.

"Jean," he said anxiously, "you are not thinking of leaving us, to settle in Illinois?"

"No," Jean said tensely. "I can't do that. I can't leave my father or the sisters or the little brother. But what, then, can I do? I will be twenty this summer."

"Anchor your dreams to reality," Saugrain advised, "even though they suffer some loss in the process. Would you, for instance, accept a piece of land on this side of the river—perhaps not so rich as the Illinois bottoms, but good land, like the farm of Monsieur Soulard?"

"Don't laugh at me," Jean begged. "How can I have that?"

Saugrain was not laughing. He felt more like shouting. Again it was June—early June of the year before. In the presence of Don Carlos de Lassus, he studied a list of desirable settlers from Ohio with his name, "Antoine Frederic Saugrain, Mineralogist," at the top, followed by "Jean Michau, Farmer." Now he had only to call on the Teniente again, saying, "Excellency, I have been all this time locating the Jean Michau you wished to see. I have been blind. It is Jean Michau the Younger who wishes to have a farm.

(87)

Will it please you now to consult with Antoine Soulard, His Majesty's Surveyor General, about a farm for the young man? He is most anxious to plow the land and build a cabin this spring."

To his dismay, Jean's eyes were now glazed with tears.

"Would you do that for me?" he asked. "Why?"

"I am your brother-in-law," Saugrain answered. "It is my privilege. Some day I will explain that to you, but not now. I am beginning to chill even in this niche. My leg aches. I have a longing for an armchair by the fire and a pillow for my foot. Let us take one more look at the river."

"Why?" Jean asked. "It has not changed."

"You may be wrong." Saugrain said. "I think it may have something to say to us now. It says to me, 'Wait. Spring is on the way.' Another spring, another year. . . . Come, Jean, come."

Five ⌒

Spring came, as promised. The ice in the Mississippi went out with a roar, grinding, crushing everything that had been caught by the big freeze. The ice went out too fast, Gabriel said. The warm south wind blew all over the land from the Gulf of Mexico to Canada, melting the ice on the rivers to the north as well as those to the south. Consequently, while the lower rivers were still rising, icy water from above added to their volume, creating a winter flood—the worst of all, according to Gabriel, who had lived through many floods. He and others his age also remembered that it had been through such high water that young General Clark in the month of February had marched his Long Knives across Illinois to surprise the British and capture their fort at Vincennes in Indiana. Under any circumstances a flood in February was bad, because winter was not over. There would be more freezing, more snow. However, few shared Gabriel's gloomy apprehensions. After the dark and bitter winter, the sun and a wind that did not chill were welcome. There might be more freezing, more snow, but with spring on the way, neither could last very long.

Young Jean Michau was one of the most impatient. He now held title, under his father's guardianship, to fifty acres of good land, three fourths forest, one fourth clear. Saugrain could have obtained for him more acres—in back country—but Jean chose the smaller piece of land. It was as much as he could handle by himself, which he wanted to do. The cleared area offered space for his first fields and for necessary building; and the location—south of the Little River on the Catalan Road and halfway to Ste. Genevieve—was perfect, he declared happily, after he had walked that far and back the first time.

Saugrain was sure it was another feature of the location that had decided Jean's choice. From his property he could look across the Catalan Road and the Mississippi at a settlement in Illinois named Kaskaskia. Over there, south of the village, a sparkling river of the same name emptied into the Mississippi. North of it, a rounded hill rose from the Illinois flood plain. Jean had by no means abandoned his initial dream. Wanting to hold him, Saugrain thought, I have given him wings to take him away from us. But that, he also knew, was right. At twenty a strong young man must think of flight. Meanwhile, preparations for the near future would hold him.

In tacit acceptance, after assisting Antoine Soulard with the surveying of his land, Jean settled down with paper and pen to plan sensibly the first use he would make of it, what acres he would plow, what he would sow in those first fields, what trees he would fell to supply wood for a shelter he must erect for himself and any animals he might acquire. The shelter this summer would be no more than an open shed, which before winter could be made over into a barn. A house was not to be thought of before the second year.

This sensible planning lasted as long as the winter weather. On the first day of what could be real spring, his control snapped.

"I am going to look at the farm," he said. "I must."

He took off on foot. On each of five days he made the journey, accepting a lift when one was offered, but walking most of the way. He returned each evening, bone-weary but exalted. Asked what he had found to do at the farm, he repeated the same answer: "I was looking around—just looking around."

On the fifth day, homeward bound, he was stuck in the mud.

Hunting bottom, his father suggested. With great difficulty he pulled himself out first and then his boots. He came home, caked with mud, his hair full of brush. The next day the wind blew from the north with snow on its breath, and madness subsided.

Saugrain, through every paroxysm, gave him scant attention and no interference. He was involved now in problems of his own. During the recent warm spell, both the stone mason and the carpenter had visited the Saugrain lot, also to look around, the mason to mark and estimate the foundations needed for the additional stone building to the rear of the main house, which was to be Saugrain's private, professional domain, and the carpenter to plan floors, doors and windows in the family residence. He could do nothing about windows, however, he explained, until he had glass for the panes. Had the doctor ordered that glass from Pittsburgh, as promised? Saugrain had ordered the glass from the same glassworks where he had learned to blow glass. Michau Père had written the order and the promise to pay. The letter with the order had gone down the Mississippi with the first melting of the ice. Now, after the renewal of winter, followed by a better promise of spring, Michau had made a second copy of the order, which, with other mail, was to leave St. Louis on the boats carrying the winter furs to the New Orleans market. Saugrain had cautioned his father-in-law to be especially careful in addressing the order for glass, so that it could be sent up the Ohio from New Madrid to Pittsburgh and not be taken on to New Orleans.

M. Pierre Chouteau, the younger of the two Chouteau brothers, who was to command this year's expedition, had also promised to give his personal attention to the mail for Pittsburgh. So if by chance the first order had gone astray, the second would surely arrive at the Pennsylvania glassworks. By the grace of God, the window glass might be waiting at New Madrid for Monsieur Chouteau to pick it up on his return voyage.

The barges with the winter furs, the richest loading that the town had ever known, with the Chouteau galley and the Teniente's leading the way, left for New Orleans in March. The galleys and the best of the barges returned in April, carrying the treasure taken in return for the furs—everything from boots and shoes to sugar and salt—and the Saugrain glass. Saugrain's Pittsburgh friends

(90)

had filled his first order in time to send it off when the second copy arrived.

Also on the boats was a supply of pharmaceuticals which Saugrain had ordered from New Orleans—oil of vitriol, capsicum pods, Peruvian bark, mercury—everything. Almost surfeited with good fortune, he could at first hardly take in the printing on a scrap of newspaper which Cardinal had picked up on the way home, although finally the news was such that the paper was possibly the best gift of all.

The United States of America had a new president—Thomas Jefferson, scientist, scholar, patriot, composer of the American Colonies' Declaration of Independence—the same Mr. Jefferson for whom the young army officer, Colonel Lewis, had bought a thermometer from Saugrain in Lexington, Kentucky.

"You say he is the third President?" Michau Père said, interrupting Saugrain's inspired interpretation of the news. "That seems many for so short a time."

Elections, Saugrain informed him, were held every four years. So, if a president found favor with the people, he continued in office; or, if he seemed unworthy, he could be turned out before more harm was done.

"The people?" Michau questioned. "They can do this? The people vote?"

"Yes," Saugrain said. "Every male citizen twenty-one years old or more. That is my understanding of a democracy."

"It looks dangerous to me." Michau muttered. "What if the elected President should die while in office? Do they vote again?"

Saugrain explained then about the vice presidency. A new vice president had also taken office now, but that name was one he had not heard before—Burr—Aaron Burr.

Before they could conclude this interesting discussion, the carpenter appeared. He had fitted the glass into one window and he wanted the doctor to see. By late summer the stone house was practically finished. The carpenter was making shutters for the windows and fitting latches and locks to the doors. The stone mason's final touch had been iron railings, guarding broad stone steps leading from the front door and the rear door to the ground. He was now laying up the walls of the doctor's sanctum. It seemed certain that the family would be living in the stone house before

(91)

another grape harvest could halt proceedings, and Saugrain was counting on being in his den before the first snow.

In the humming peace of an August afternoon, he sat on a stool beside the well in the rear garden, enjoying the shade of the trees and studying a list of medicines administered to a chronic malingerer who refused to get well and would not pay for treatment. Oil of vitriol, tartar emetic, Glauber's salts, tincture of iron. . . . *Dieu!* a man who had swallowed all that should have been dead long ago. Madame meanwhile was in her flower garden, snipping off dried blooms and letting them fall into a pouch she had made of her apron, sometimes going down on her knees to pull an intruding weed, but remaining alert to hear the chatter of four-year-old Rosalie, playing on the front steps with a puppy given her by Monsieur Soulard. Everyone else was asleep—Odette in the old wooden house minding little Elise. Gabriel snoring beside Hortense in her stall. One minute there was this utter peace; in the next came sound of feet running down the road. The running stopped. A moment of silence followed, but was broken at once by a fiendish yell. Rosalie screamed.

Saugrain was already on his feet, his stool overturned, his paper blowing, it did not matter where. He was the first to reach the front steps. Madame, caught kneeling, had shaken so, she said, still trembling, that she could hardly raise herself to stand. Saugrain nodded. He had Rosalie in his arms now. Gabriel came, followed closely by the stone mason and the carpenter. Somewhere near the puppy whimpered.

Out in the road two Indians seemed locked in a fierce embrace. No, one of them crouched above the other. Sun shone on the blade of a knife. In another minute the Indian broke free, brandishing a bit of skin covered with hair and blood. Madame Saugrain cried out softly, then closed her eyes. Rosalie buried her head in Saugrain's shirt front and clung to him like a bird in terror of a snake.

Saugrain's knees were shaking now, but he strengthened his hold on the child, murmured meaningless words over her, and tried to think.

"Do not be frightened," he heard himself saying, the sound muffled by a thickness in his ears. "It is all over now. The wicked men are gone." One of them at least had left. "We must take care of the little one now, Maman. Bed, I think. Yes, bed. No, I will carry her while you go ahead to make her bed ready. Bed and a soothing tisane—camomile, peppermint, something with a nice taste."

"Wait here," he said to Gabriel. "I will be back soon."

Arrived safely at the wooden house, as he stood beside the bed, he thought he would not be able to free the small hands that still clung to him; but then Rosalie opened her eyes, saw him, then the ugly walls, and freed him of her own will. Later she sat up obediently to take the tisane, but her teeth rattled against the cup. Saugrain stumbled then, leaving the house, and had trouble keeping his feet on the path back to the steps, where the three men waited. Gabriel had been out to the road.

"It will not be necessary for you to go, m'sieu," he said. "The Indian is dead. His head is very bloody."

"Don't be foolish," Saugrain said sharply. "As a doctor, I am not afraid of a little blood, I hope."

Still, he shuddered when he stood near the twisted body of the Indian. The head was a bloody mess. The eyes bulged. . . .

"Close," he said to Gabriel, then changed his command. "No. Do not touch him. The Teniente—someone in authority—must see him first. Gabriel, my friend, if you will stand guard here so that nothing may disturb the corpse, I will send a messsenger— the carpenter, perhaps. He is the youngest among us. He walks the fastest."

It was not long before the carpenter returned, with a military escort—four soldiers, a sergeant and a cart. The soldiers lifted the dead Indian into the cart and covered him with sacking while the sergeant gave his explanation of the affair to Saugrain. The Indian was a Shawnee, he thought, one of a settlement near Cape Girardot. He must be taken back to his people, and the happening reported to the commandant at the Cape. The whole matter was a personal feud between two braves. These occurred—not frequently, but once in a while. Never before, however, had one angry warrior pursued his enemy so far as this, to settle an argument. The teniente at Cape Girardot would know how to deal with the affair. He would report to the Teniente Gobernador. Meanwhile the Teniente Gobernador had ordered two soldiers to

(93)

stand guard before the doctor's property tonight, tomorrow, as long as Saugrain wished a sentinel to be there.

With that, the sergeant, having given the two chosen guards final orders, mounted the cart with the other two and drove off southward.

That night, as Saugrain and Madame walked in the garden because neither could sleep, all was so peaceful and so quiet that the steps of soldiers patrolling the road could be heard from any corner of the grounds.

"But it is a pleasant sound," Madame pleaded. "Don't you think so, Vigny?"

"I do, and I do not," Saugrain said. "My dear, I am sorry."

"Sorry, Vigny?"

"How could I fail to remember Indians?" he lamented. "I knew they would be here. They are all around us—on both sides of the river—everywhere."

"Friendly Indians, Vigny. The Sergeant said so. His Excellency the Teniente says so. Those in the road today did not threaten us."

"Savages," Saugrain said. "Cruel, murderous—and I brought you and the children into the midst of them to live."

"You are thinking of Rosalie?" Madame at that point had been nearly distracted, she confessed afterwards. "But she is sleeping quietly now. She twitches only once in a while. She will have bad dreams, as you said, but they will fade. She is young. She will forget."

"She will never forget," Saugrain said. "I know. My neck, where the Indian's bullet scratched it—years ago—throbs tonight. And my lost toe shoots pain up my leg."

"My poor Vigny! Try to forget, for a little while at least. Turn your back to the road, and look at the house, the garden. Are they not beautiful?"

"More than beautiful," he agreed. "When I think how long it has taken for me to come this far, I ask myself how could I possibly close my eyes and go away now."

"Vigny, what are you saying?"

"It would be like tearing my heart out by the roots," he continued, as if she had not spoken.

But then Madame saw light in the darkness if he did not.

"Vigny," she cried, "do you remember—that afternoon a year

ago on the boat? That vine growing out of the bluff? Vigny, if you pull that vine out, with its roots, it will die. So, let us talk no more about . . . about anything. Let us return to the ugly old house. I will make us a tisane now. We will drink it and we will sleep. In the morning everything will look different. Vigny, do you know? You did not strike the hour this evening. For the first time, you forgot."

"No!" he said, and made a movement as if he meant to run for the pestle and mortar, but Madame restrained him. It was late. The town was asleep. In the morning she would see to it that he did not sleep past the hour.

As usual, Madame was right. In the morning Saugrain awoke in good time with a clear head and clearer vision. He struck six ringing blows on the mortar, ate a little breakfast, then placed himself on the front steps of his new house to wait for the mason and the carpenter.

Naturally, they were late, but no matter. He stood there. While they were still some distance away he began telling them about his new idea. He wanted a wall built around his property—such a wall as surrounded the Chouteau residences, only higher. It must hide the road from the house.

"Of stone, M'sieu Docteur?" the mason rubbed his forehead. "Around the whole square? That would mean more stone than we have used on both houses. It would take time. . . ."

"A fence would serve as well," the carpenter suggested. "It could be of walnut posts, as high as you want, sharpened to points at the top, and set closely together. The wood can be green. Once the posts are cut, it will go up fast."

The one word—fast—persuaded Saugrain to alter his vision. He wanted the fence as soon as possible. Every other work must be put aside.

"Vigny," Madame said, when the first posts—those along the road—were ready for her inspection, "I do not like it. It is very ugly."

It was not ugly. The smooth posts, eight feet high, eight inches wide, symmetrically pointed at the top, hid the road absolutely.

"But it is not good." Madame argued, "to shut out everything and everybody that way. It is not good even for Rosalie. She

(95)

must learn not to be afraid of the road. What will our friends think? Or the sick who come to find you?"

Saugrain had thought of that. Two gates, latched but not locked, would be set in the fence, the one in front for formal callers, the one to the rear for those who wanted only to see him. People would learn. Those who had a reason for coming would be as welcome as ever. Others could stay away.

Six

Against all objection, Madame's the most potent, the fence was completed. The enclosure, Saugrain allowed, had some resemblance to a medieval castle keep, but he liked it. It held the property together; he had more assurance of possession; and the children, watched by Odette or their mother, were out in the sunshine again. Another spring might be expected to wash away remembrance of the Indian scuffle, and the whole enclosure could be their playground.

The building of the fence, with everyone lending a hand, went fast enough but caused some delay in finishing the stone house. It was October when the Saugrains moved their furniture into it. The barnlike wooden house would now be a place where Madame could dry herbs. Saugrain's addition was finished a month later; but, at the stone mason's advice, reinforced by his own inclination, Saugrain put off moving his professional paraphernalia there until spring. It would be better to let the stones rest as they were until the sun outside could help the fire in the chimney to warm them.

In March a fire was laid and lighted. In April Saugrain and Gabriel moved the furnishings, Saugrain himself carrying his delicately balanced scales and his microscope, Gabriel moving the rest as Saugrain called for each item. There were so many shelves, so many cabinets with doors, that he had to study at times where to put things. He had promised himself, Madame and Michau Père to keep order here as never before anywhere. Finally Gabriel had his wheelbarrow ready to move the last piece—the iron mortar and pestle. Hearing a rustle of movement outside,

(96)

Saugrain thought Gabriel was coming; but when no scolding accompanied the rustle, he knew he was mistaken.

What then? The post. During the winter—an open one, thank God—Governor de Lassus had asked a favor of him. Since he knew most of the villagers, and all of them knew him, would he take charge of receiving and giving out the general mail? Saugrain was happy to oblige. The letters were usually few. A window sill provided space for laying out those that came. Anyone hoping for a letter could look over what was there, and find or not find what he expected.

Now, in the new building, another window sill, as deep as the stone walls were thick, provided even more space—a good thing at this time, when the merchants' boats from New Orleans were overdue. So, thinking only of the mail, Saugrain looked expectantly at the window opening on the path which led to the rear gate, sure that he would see Jacques Cardinal with the letters in his blue head kerchief.

The window was empty. The shuffle of feet drew nearer. The door latch rattled. Then it was lifted; and, pushing the door open, a near-naked Indian strode arrogantly into the room.

Gigantic, he seemed to Saugrain, a true aborigine. Moccasins, a breech clout held by a strip of rawhide, loops of beads, one loop ending in a medal, were his clothing. Scars and ceremonial paint masked his face, setting on it a ferocious scowl. Desperately Saugrain tried to remember advice given him by friends on how to deal with a strange Indian. "Never show fear," they said. "Make no hostile movement. Assume that the Indian is friendly." Friendly— the word buzzed in his head. With great effort he put out his hands, palms up, and said, "Amigo?"

The effect was magic. "Amigo," the Indian repeated; but then he took his first good look at Saugrain, and he laughed. The laughter was relief, not contempt, Saugrain was told—afterwards. At the time contempt stung, but it cleared Saugrain's senses. With a shrug, he turned away.

That, alas, did not remove the Indian. More at ease now, he stalked around the room, looking at everything, Saugrain watching to see that he touched nothing. Curiosity moved the savage, possibly something more. Could it be awe? Had arrogance been meant to conceal fear? If so . . . Saugrain made a hasty survey of his own.

In the center of the room stood a long work table, designed to hold electrical apparatus—Leyden jars, a handful of wires, scrap metal, and a dish half full of water. He used it often to amuse children. If he dropped a strip of paper cut into a sort of fringe into the water, charged the water and covered the dish, the paper would fly up against the lid, the fringe dancing like a dolls' ballet. Unobtrusively, Saugrain approached the dish, removed the cover, inserted the end of a wire, took a silver dollar from his pocket and dropped it into the water. When the Indian turned to see what he was doing, he stepped aside. The dollar was the Indian's—for the taking.

The Indian was wary. He suspected a trick, but he also recognized the dollar. After a few feints and withdrawals, he plunged his hand into the dish and touched the coin—only to find his hand held fast to the dollar and the dollar to the dish by the magic of electricity. Hand, arm and shoulder tingled with a charge of the same current until with a final frantic pull he won free, and fled, howling.

"Bravo, Señor Medico! Bravo!"

In the door now stood a white man, swarthy enough to be an Indian but plainly a paleface. He wore a black coat, breeches, hosiery and shoes with the ease of custom. His white shirt had been freshly laundered. In his left hand he carried a high-crowned hat of beaver, in his right a silver-headed ebony cane. Like Saugrain, he was a small man—only a few inches taller—and he looked to be of approximately the same age. His black hair, short, brushed back from a high forehead and oiled until with a little more pomade it could have been pulled up into a crest, showed no trace of gray. His black eyes sparkled with amusement, appreciation and interest.

"My name is Lisa," he said, speaking English now. "I am sorry that one of my Indians called before I could prepare you. Were you frightened?"

So—there had been more than one Indian!

"A little," Saugrain confessed, also choosing English. "You say he was one of yours? If I had known . . . but enter, please. I hoped to have the pleasure . . . I have heard about you."

(98)

"Nothing good, I am sure," Lisa said, coming into the shop, his curiosity as lively as that of the Indian, but more knowing.

Little good, it was true, but nothing altogether bad. "A scoundrel named Lisa," le Duc had said, more deprecating than condemning. "His Excellency hardly knows what to make of him." "Captain Manuel," Gabriel said, gathering his information from here and there. "He will stir things up. You will see." Manuel Lisa, it seemed, was a Spaniard from New Orleans. He called himself a merchant—an independent merchant. Up to this time his trading had been restricted to the lower Mississippi and the Ohio Rivers. Now he had settled himself and his family and his business in St. Louis, where his welcome had not been exactly cordial, independence being a questionable virtue under a monarchy. However, since he was a Spaniard, born in New Orleans, de Lassus could not refuse him entry.

"The Teniente Gobernador," Saugrain explained to his visitor, "has a difficult post here. He must please his superiors at New Orleans and Madrid. His success depends on the prosperity of the established merchants. . . ."

"Ah!" Lisa interrupted, his eyes snapping. "The merchants! I have dared to dip my paddle into a river which, by a franchise given an ancestor of theirs years ago, they have come to look upon as their exclusive property. As if God ever meant a great river to belong to one man or one tribe. I have presented my petition, asking official permission to trade on the Missouri in regions which the established merchants have not yet explored. The petition, I am promised, will be sent on to New Orleans, where it will be reviewed and possibly sent on to Madrid. In the course of time, if I live that long and the ship carrying the answer of the king's council is not waylaid and sunk, I shall become a licensed trader, or I shall be rejected and turned away—the merchants hope. But why do I burden you with all this? Why do you listen, endangering the favor you now enjoy?"

"How do you know I am in favor?" Saugrain countered, wanting only to hear more.

"You are here, are you not?" Lisa replied. "I have heard about you also. *Dios!* Your reputation will spread in another direction now. Those were Kansas chiefs from up the Missouri whom you frightened away with your medicine, and I must go in pursuit of

(99)

them. I promised to show them a few wonders in the white man's village, but also to return them unharmed to their own people. I must overtake them before they steal a canoe and start off on their own. You understand, I hope."

He was gone before Saugrain could speak. Then in the same moment he was back. "Señor Medico, I had another reason for calling on you. I have a wife and child in town. You know?"

Saugrain knew. Again, this was a story pieced from scraps of information. Captain Manuel's wife and child were English, meaning, in this case, American. Knowing no French, they could not communicate with anyone in town except each other, and Lisa when he was at home. The child in talking to her mother spoke a gibberish, and the mother answered in kind. The Negro woman whom Lisa engaged to keep house for all of them in his absence said it was Indian talk. It could have been that, because that was part of the story.

Captain Manuel had not married the woman in the usual way. He had paid ransom money for her and the child at Fort Vincennes in Indiana. He had just happened to be there on a day when some Miami Indians, according to a treaty made with Governor Harrison, were delivering captives whom they had taken three years before in a raid on a town in Ohio. Many of the captives had people at Vincennes to claim them, but not these two—until Lisa stepped forward. He not only paid money for them; he also gave notice of his good intentions by marrying the woman and adopting the child as his own. Surely he had not been obliged to do that. He wished to do it that way.

Now this good man was addressing Saugrain in a tone of apology: "I am away from home much of the time. The Negress will be good to them, but, if you will see them once in a while . . . you will? Señor Medico, I am yours to command—always."

The door closed. The room, except for Saugrain, was empty. He still tingled from the encounter. Life on the edge of the wilderness was like that, it seemed. Days went by, one very like another. Then suddenly a stranger. . . .

"M'sieu Docteur?" That was Gabriel now, breathless from exertion. "Where shall I deposit the iron monster? I have it here in the barrow, standing on its head. It fell that way when I loaded it. Now, if I tip the barrow again, it may oblige by rolling out on its bottom. But where?"

"I am coming, *mon ami*," Saugrain called. "Only wait."

Seven ∽

So a year of days, filled with incident and accident, sorrow and joy, gain and loss, passed. Another year began, 1803. Another spring arrived, the third since Saugrain had thrown in his lot with that of the village of Pain Court. Again, on a balmy April afternoon, he stepped briskly about his laboratory, pursuing this time some conclusion to be derived from the perplexities of the magnetic field.

Today he was not alone. Rosalie, now nearly six years old, had chosen to spend the afternoon helping him. Friends outside the family, seeing her these days, often remarked on her complete recovery from the shock of the Indian scalping. Only those close to her knew that recovery was still not complete. A laughing, chattering, artless baby had changed into a much too thoughtful little girl. Her health generally was good. Thanks to the enclosure of the fence, she could respond to the pleading of her dog or her mother, busy in the garden, by going outside to play; but her preference was her father's sanctum, where her presence was generally welcome. She was a quiet child, never in the way, and it delighted Saugrain to provide amusement for her. Today it was drawing pictures on a slate with some chalk that Saugrain had colored for her.

The laboratory was very quiet. Saugrain sat at his table, surrounded by three types of batteries, wires and scraps of paper—notes he had made on previous experiments, which now he could not decipher. Suddenly the quiet was too much. His head dropped forward. He caught it just in time to keep it from striking the table. Everybody on the place except him and Rosalie was probably sound asleep—Gabriel in his shed, Odette in one room of the big house minding Elise, still a baby at three and a half, and

Madame in another room, in bed he hoped, cradling a new baby, her third—and a son. So he, too, had drowsed.

Ridiculous! He shook himself awake; then, fearing that this was not enough, stood up and began to walk the floor. Since he could not read his notes, and must think through the whole process again, it might help a new approach to turn his thoughts elsewhere for a change.

There was this matter, for instance, of being father to a son. At the time of the birth Madame had been more than a little displeased with him for seeming to take the event so calmly. Was he not, she had demanded, even a little proud? When he said—wanting only to cover a kind of fright—that he could take no credit for the phenomenon, instead of scolding him she had commiserated with little Alphonse Alfred—her first mention of the name she had chosen.

Alphonse Alfred, she said, was not to pay any attention to the wicked teasing of his papa. He was a good, kind papa, really, as Alphonse Alfred would come to know. Papa, she called her husband more frequently now than the endearing, respectful Vigny. Saugrain was sure he did not like that.

Today, before he could go more deeply into this evidence of a woman's pride in a son who, as soon as he reached manhood, would probably leave her to enter a life apart from her, breaking her heart, his thoughts were arrested by footfalls on the path outside, and Jacques Cardinal appeared at the window, his blue kerchief filled with mail. There was even a separate piece for Saugrain, although how anyone knew it was for him was a mystery. The cover was a tangle of pen scratches and seals in the midst of which a name was almost hidden. But there it was, finally—"Antoine Saugrain. United States of America."

"I have someone to thank in New Orleans for knowing that I live in Saint Louis," Saugrain said.

"M'sieu," Cardinal said, "the letter did not come with the mail from New Orleans. It was with that which Captain Manuel brought from Fort Massac on the Ohio."

His tone was solemn, even portentous. But why? This was how mail traveled in the unsettled portions of America. Studying once more the scratches on the letter from Paris, Saugrain saw that it had arrived first at New York and from there had been carried in turn to Philadelphia, to Gallipolis, to Lexington, to Louisville, to Fort Massac, where Lisa had picked it up, guaranteeing delivery. How had he happened to be at Fort Massac? The answer to that was simple.

Before settling in St. Louis, Lisa had conducted a flourishing trade on the Ohio in partnership with another Spanish merchant by the name of Vigo—Colonel Francis Vigo. The partnership was still in effect, Vigo handling the business along the Ohio while Manuel gave his attention to the richer and more venturesome prospect of sharing in the fur trade on the Missouri. The arrangement was that each should work independently of the other, but once a year, at least, they would meet at some intermediate point to settle their accounts. Often the place was Fort Massac, a minor fort on the Ohio between New Madrid and Louisville. Plainly they had met there this year; but then Saugrain would have had other mail in addition to the letter from France.

In the spring, when the St. Louis boats set out for the fur markets, Lisa with them, Saugrain, who had already given Pierre Chouteau an order for pharmaceuticals to be filled at New Orleans, had written a similar order for Lisa to give Vigo, if they should meet, to be filled at some eastern source, and with it a letter to his army friend, the surgeon at Fort Louisville, asking for information on another matter. Surely Lisa would have some report on one or the other of these two commissions, if not both. Anxiety, for no real reason, suddenly seized Saugrain.

"Jacques," he said, "you spoke of other mail from Massac. Some of it is for me. I am expecting . . . Jacques, Lisa knows. You are hiding something from me. Where is Manuel Lisa? You must know since you traveled together. You arrived here together. . . ."

"No, m'sieu," Jacques said, finding his tongue. "We did not arrive together. We did not ever travel together, really. We were too slow and careful for Captain Manuel. Going down the river, we lost him before we reached New Madrid. Somebody said he had gone up the Ohio. I don't know. We saw him again at New Orleans. We started away from there together; but those oarsmen of his row like devils escaping from hell. At New Madrid again he was waiting for us, but then again, he went too fast for us. He arrived in Saint Louis early this morning. M'sieu, the Teniente's soldiers were waiting for him at the landing. They took the mail. They took him. M'sieu, Captain Manuel is now in the calaboose."

"No!" Saugrain said, refusing to believe it. "On what charges . . . no, do not answer, I will take my questions where the true answers are. You may go now, Jacques. Thank you for coming so promptly. Rosalie, have you finished your picture? Why are you hiding it? Oh, I see now. It is of me. But do I really look like that? that—my hair flying, the coattails also? Only when I move fast? I will try to remember. Shall we put the slate aside now until tomorrow? I will take you to the house then to be with Maman and sister Elise and the baby brother while I go to town on business. You will take her, Jacques? Good! But hold! Do you ride her on your shoulder still, a young lady of six years?"

A small incident, but it warmed his heart as he went to rouse Gabriel.

Town still dozed in its midafternoon torpor as he drew near Government House in the still useful but much used charette, drawn by the patient, but more and more deliberate Hortense, coaxed along by Gabriel, who grumbled in sympathy with her over this second expedition of the day.

"She grows older, Gabriel?" Saugrain remarked placatingly.

"Who does not, m'sieu?" Gabriel responded.

I must really do something about replacing this horse and equipage, Saugrain thought, as he had been thinking for the past year. He should have a carriage—professional man with a fair practice, an official besides, living in a fine house which, together with Madame Saugrain's garden, was a matter of pride for the whole town, now approaching the thousand mark in population. Yes—he should have a carriage for general use and a horse for himself, to ride on his rounds. Without delay or further indulgence in cowardice, he must learn to ride a horse. For the cost of this display he must consult his father-in-law, who would promptly and with pleasure sue the necessary number of people for payment of their accounts. He himself did not relish instituting these law suits, but Michau Père said it was the only way he could collect what was owed him. He still wanted the carriage.

But now for the business of the afternoon. How should he approach it? The indirect method might be best, since de Lassus would surely know why he had come. He could begin by expressing gratitude for the letter from France. Ahh! In leaving his laboratory what had he done with that letter? He remembered thinking that he would not open it for a hasty reading. He would wait . . . beyond that he had no recollection. Truly he had the brain of a lizard.

As it happened, the Lieutenant Governor opened the interview, speaking very directly. "You have come to inquire about your friend, Señor Lisa."

"I am shocked to hear of his arrest," Saugrain confessed. "May I ask why this was done?"

"Certainly you may ask," de Lassus said. "Charges have been made against him, some of them serious."

It was hard to say whether His Excellency was annoyed or amused. Saugrain did not need to ask who had preferred charges. It would be one of the rival merchants, but what had been their grievance?

"That he prospers from the sale of contraband," de Lassus answered. "His merchandise is contraband, you know. Sugar, spices, perfumery, lace may come from New Orleans, but most of his goods comes by way of the Ohio from cities on the eastern coast. Have you heard about the clocks?"

Saugrain knew that Lisa had an American clock in his house. A handsome affair with a pendulum and chimes, it stood on the mantel of the principal room, visibly and audibly ticking off the seconds—provided that someone remembered to wind its mechanism regularly with a key.

"There is a second clock," de Lassus said.

Saugrain also knew about that one. Lisa had sold it to a Monsieur Bisonette in exchange for the purchaser's agreement to provide the Lisa household with milk and eggs, and a chicken as needed, for one year. Bisonette wound his clock without fail, being reminded daily by Saugrain's alarums.

"Do you think," Saugrain asked, "since we have two Yanqui clocks in the village, that I should abandon my morning and evening exercise?"

The Teniente's sharp reply betrayed harassment. The clocks had been merely an example, as he said. Lisa, on his first arrival

(105)

in St. Louis, had brought with him a considerable amount of goods from his Ohio trading, and had asked to be allowed to dispose of it in St. Louis, since he had left Ohio in great haste, being anxious to settle his wife and child in their new home. By the time he had them settled, it was too late for him to go in search of other goods.

Looking at the situation from all sides, de Lassus had given Lisa the license he desired, only to bring trouble on himself. From all sides now he had heard the same complaint. The merchandise from the East was better than that which had been bought at New Orleans. Even the Osage chiefs, long-time friends of the established merchants, discovered that the copper kettles Lisa traded to the Kansa Indians surpassed theirs.

"The man creates unrest," de Lassus finished.

"But, Excellency," Saugrain argued, suppressing a desire to applaud, "an infusion of unrest may be what this town needs."

"It may be that," de Lassus admitted, his generally good-humored face now furrowed with thought, "but if it has to come like this . . . wait. Let me tell you the rest of the story."

Exceeding his authority, he had granted Lisa permission to dispose of his Ohio merchandise. With what reward? This year Lisa had returned to the Ohio to buy more merchandise. "You think he did not do that?" he asked when Saugrain protested. "How then did he come to have mail from Fort Massac?"

"Excellency, if you will let me speak now," Saugrain begged, "I can explain everything."

He began with the projected meeting between Lisa and his partner, Vigo. De Lassus, his face clearing a little, agreed that it was natural that Lisa, having left a good business in the hands of a partner, should have arranged for an accounting at the fort on the Ohio. Well?

Saugrain described then his order for pharmaceuticals.

"But those," de Lassus objected, "you could have ordered from New Orleans."

"Excellency, I did," Saugrain said. "My stock of medicines was so depleted that I sent two orders, one to the Ohio and one to New Orleans. My thought was that from one place or the other I might obtain a few items that I desperately needed. Why do you laugh? Am I so fortunate as to have had both orders filled?"

His Excellency's reply was to send for le Duc, who came bearing two cartons, well-wrapped and of practically the same dimensions.

"And is that all now?" de Lassus asked, his good humor fully restored.

"Excellency, no. There was a letter—from France. I wish to thank you for sending it to me at once. It is the first word I have had from my people in many years, but there should have been another letter—from Kentucky, from the fort at Louisville. I am acquainted with the post surgeon there." Briefly he explained the nature of that acquaintance. "So, when I sent an order for medicines to Captain Manuel's partner, I also asked him to deliver a letter from me to my friend at Louisville. It was only a request for information, Excellency, about smallpox vaccine."

De Lassus' smile disappeared. Even le Duc seemed startled.

"But why?" de Lassus said. "We have no smallpox. We have not had any since my coming here."

"There have been other years," Saugrain reminded him. "Surely you have heard of the *Année de la Picotée*. The epidemic began with someone taken off a boat, with a high fever. It could happen again. Our Gabriel is a survivor. He can tell you how terrible it was."

"But you spoke just now of vaccine," de Lassus said. "One of these packages is from Louisville. Could it possibly contain vaccine?" That was not probable, Saugrain assured him, since the difficulty about vaccine was keeping it fresh if it was to be used farther than a day's travel from its source. He had not asked for the vaccine, only for information and advice. Surely to ask a few questions of a friend was a small and harmless beginning for an experiment which he, as doctor and scientist, wanted to pursue.

Harmless enough, de Lassus said, and thanked him for his frank statement of intentions. He hoped Saugrain would be good enough to inform him of any progress he made in the experiment. Inoculation was, as the doctor knew, not favored by some people. He was also grateful for a good explanation of Lisa's movements on the Ohio.

"Now I am sure you would like to take your double order of pharmaceuticals and the remainder of the mail from Fort Massac and be gone. Meanwhile I will interview Captain Manuel further with regard to his trading rights from this place."

Eight ⌒

"So you put your head into the lion's mouth in my behalf? Was that wise?"

In the cool of early evening, Lisa sat on a chair placed conveniently to receive a gentle warmth but not the full heat of the fire in Saugrain's workshop, a glass of Madeira in his hand, his black eyes phosphorescent in the shadows. Saugrain, at ease for him, perched on a high stool beside the table, now decorated with an assortment of small paper packets and sealed vials, each labeled with hieroglyphics intelligible only to himself.

"I did not consult wisdom," he said to Lisa's question. "As it turned out my audience with the Teniente was generally pleasant. He is not really difficult."

"Not to you, perhaps," Lisa allowed. "He was kind to me, too, at our first meeting. That was before the other merchants found reason to complain. He must listen to them, too, you know. They have influence—but then, so have you, it seems. You must have offered some potent arguments in my favor."

Saugrain sipped his wine thoughtfully. "I think," he said, "it was not so much what I said as that he wanted to be persuaded. He was annoyed with you for giving him a reason for putting you under arrest. Either it was that, or something happened immediately afterwards that caused him to regret the act. He also received mail on the boats, you know. He had some word or he read something in a newspaper. I don't pretend to understand this man, but I have always felt that he knows more than he is permitted or willing to reveal, that he has some secret source of information. There is that small mahogany chest in the audience chamber. It was there today. Did you notice it?"

Lisa had noticed it. "But every man has his secrets," he said, "even Bonaparte, who now rules France and most of Europe, besides, including Spain. Have you read the paper that came with the mail? Good! Then you know that President Jefferson has sent

(108)

a second ambassador to Paris, to strengthen the power of the one already there. But why? Is Bonaparte planning something concerning Spain's empire in America? Only Bonaparte or Jefferson can say. We will know after everything is accomplished and done. Unless . . . did your letter from Paris give you any information?"

No. The letter had been written by Saugrain's mother and contained chiefly news of the family. They had all returned to Paris under an amnesty granted by Napoleon. They had lost, of course, most of their money and all of their property. His mother lived in a between-the-floors apartment, one of those provided by stealing some space from the height of the story below and raising the floor of the one next above. A married daughter, Saugrain's sister, lived in the apartment below, so his mother felt quite safe.

France, she said, was in a state of armed peace, whatever that meant, but her sons-in-law, Saugrain's brothers-in-law, had obtained employment in civil posts. Even an uncle, a librarian, in charge before the Revolution of the Library of the Arsenal, had been restored to that post, the library having miraculously escaped destruction.

"So now," Saugrain said, mellowed by the wine and memories, "she has only me to worry about. Am I safe? Am I well? Prosperous? Have I married? Are there children? And so on. Even— now listen. You won't believe this."

The letter also mentioned the box of books which he had abandoned when he left France for Gallipolis. They were safe where he had hidden them, in his uncle's library. Now the family asked if he would like to have them. They would pack them carefully and put them on a boat, but he must write clear directions on how to send them so that they would surely reach him.

"What kind of books?" Lisa asked. "How many?"

Two, three, four hundred, Saugrain guessed. Some were schoolbooks—arithmetic, geography, covering the known world for both the younger and the older reader. There were books on philosophy, all the sciences—chemistry, physics, botany, practical books on surgery—he wanted them all. He could use them.

"My good Bon-père," Saugrain said, "has offered to write the directions for shipping; but he wants everything to be clear and

(109)

correct beyond question. Should they be sent to Saint Louis by way of New Orleans—on a French ship?"

Lisa elevated his eyebrows. "As safe as any other," he said. "The captain should know enough to keep islands in mind on the way over. He may have to make port suddenly and quickly before completing the passage. Don't count on seeing the books before this time next year."

"I will be fortunate to see them then," Saugrain said ruefully.

He turned the talk from that to the letter he had sent to Louisville inquiring about smallpox vaccine. The post surgeon at Louisville had said in reply that there was no practical way at present for sending vaccine to St. Louis, but he had promised to study the problem. Naturally, Saugrain was disappointed, but hardly surprised. He spoke of the matter now only because his mother had mentioned an epidemic in Paris. Only those who had been inoculated, Saugrain's kin among them, had escaped the disease.

"I know you are disappointed," Lisa said. "I too will give the matter some thought, and will ask a few questions. Meantime, since sorrow won't change anything, will you listen to another story—one I brought with me this evening for your pleasure? Are you acquainted with my compatriot, Don Miguel de Cervantes? My favorite work of his tells of a hero to whom I think you and I bear a certain resemblance. We defy the authority of Spain; and he, Don Quixote de la Mancha, girds on a knight's armor and rides out to defend the lady of his heart against the powers of evil that threaten her."

"What a man!" Saugrain said. "And you have brought that book to share with me? You are truly a friend. Wait! I will make a light."

The light was a fat candle in a dish, to which was fastened a shield of bright tin that acted as a reflector.

"An invention of mine," Saugrain said modestly. "Well, commence! It is true we have the night before us, but is that a reason for delay?"

"You think I will read you the whole book?" Lisa protested. "I will do one chapter only. In it our hero challenges and fights to the death what ordinary men might call a windmill. To Don

(110)

Quixote it is a monster astride his path. He calls to it to surrender, to stand aside. When the windmill does neither, he rides at it with his spear. . . . But let us hear the tale as Cervantes tells it. There is just one thing. He writes in his mother tongue, which is Spanish."

"My Spanish," Saugrain said, "is at least as good as your English. Proceed."

PART IV

*"... and a time
to every purpose...."*

Ecclesiastes 3:1

One ✍

The summer of 1803 was what one might call uneasy. Too much of this, too little of that. In particular, there was too much heat. May was unduly warm, June much warmer, but mild compared to July. A July day was a blazing torch from sunrise to sunset. The flame smoldered overnight, only to burst with renewed fire the next morning. Afterward, however, this first half of summer was remembered as much more endurable than the second half. Periodically, thunderstorms exploded in the sky, drenching the suffering land with rain and cooling it, if only for a night and a day; but in mid-July the rains ceased. Everything went dry. Corn lost its juice where it grew, the leaf blades rattling in the hot wind. Every bare piece of ground acquired a crust, seamed with deep cracks. Living water shrank. Creeks disappeared. Small rivers dwindled. Even the great Mississippi dropped alarmingly. If the Mississippi should go dry, surely the end of the world would be at hand.

Saugrain, faced with this proposition more and more frequently as the dry weather persisted, puckered his face in the semblance of deep thought each time he was approached, then said with authority that he was sure this would not happen. He had read in books the stories of great rivers and could not remember one instance when a river of consequence had ceased to flow. The dry weather would end and the rains return—not next week, perhaps, or the week following, but some time, before every living thing perished.

However, since the rivers were low, even those under the earth, which supplied springs and wells, he had a few recommendations. Water was essential to all life—plant or animal. Besides having in it chemicals helpful in the digestion of food, it was also the great lubricant and cleanser, internal and external. Having from the first hot weather recommended frequent bathing, with soap and, in case of heat rash, the addition of salt or soda, he did not now say, "Don't wash so often." Rather, he said, "Don't waste wash water. When you are through with it, empty the basin around the roots of a thirsty plant or two." Madame Saugrain had been doing that ever since the day she had been told that the water in their fine well was falling. Also, while the doctor said still, "Drink plenty of water," he added, "but only after it has been boiled." This was to destroy possible impurities, but it produced complaint. Nobody liked boiled water. Could one drink a little wine instead? After that the wonder was that the supply of last year's wine survived the drought.

Added to the heat and the resulting unease of that summer was another thing—the prevalence of strange new rumors. These grew, Saugrain said afterward, out of natural causes. Through the hot weather, only the early morning hours permitted outdoor labor, such as gathering hay—dried where it grew—or building or plowing or cutting wood. The sun at midday could fell a man as if he had been hit in the head with a club. So people remained indoors. Even a small tight house of wooden posts was cooler than the air outside.

But what was a healthy man to do with all those hours of idleness? He could not sleep all day as well as all night. So, when one grew tired of quarreling with his wife or children, he sought out a public room, perhaps, where there were several other men, idle like himself, and a billiard table, or he visited a particular friend. The friend's wife knew enough to keep quiet when her husband had a visitor.

Having come together then somewhere, the men played at billiards or cards, or they sat and talked. About what? The weather, the probability of poor hunting in the coming autumn, and whatever news they could glean from an almost empty storehouse.

(116)

Almost, but not quite. Two men could not meet but what one of them had heard something which had not reached the ears of the other. When they parted, each had a story to carry. Some of the tales had no truth in them, but with a little embellishment they sounded true enough.

In August, for instance, the story most often repeated was that Louisiana, both Upper and Lower, no longer was ruled by the King of Spain. It had been sold or given back to the King of France. But there was no king of France now. There was only Napoleon. Was it good to exchange the kindly King of Spain for Napoleon? He was not even a true Frenchman, having been born on some island, the name of which had escaped the memory of the informer. When Saugrain asked where his friends had obtained such information, that, too, seemed to have been forgotten. The Teniente had visited his family at New Bourbon during the hot weather. They could have had a letter from France. Someone in attendance upon the Teniente could have heard something. What did the doctor think?

Saugrain thought they were making much out of very little, and said so. The heat seemed to have gone to their brains. Nevertheless, he took what he had heard to town for examination.

"Bonaparte?" le Duc said. "That Corsican pirate would sell his grandmother if he wanted money . . . or thought it would help him crush England."

Which was not information exactly; but, added to the gossip and the fact of two envoys representing the United States in Paris, provided a neat pattern for study. That remark about Napoleon selling his grandmother suggested a purchaser. For New Orleans? Possession of that port city had been the aim of the conspirators in Kentucky when Saugrain had lived there. But they had said nothing about buying it. "Take New Orleans!" had been their cry.

This was August. In September—but that was when the rains came. One morning the sun burned in a glassy, cloudless sky; but early in the afternoon a pale gray mass crept above the western horizon. As the mass advanced, it darkened and thickened. Suddenly a spear of lightning pierced it. Then came thunder, still far away, but unmistakable. Many were out of their houses by then, watching. At the first loud thunder, some ran for cover, but others stood where they were, waiting for the rain—if there should be rain.

The first rain fell in large, warm drops, which, as they multiplied, sounded like lead pellets, striking roofs, walks, the hard, dry ground. But it was water, blessed water, a curtain of water finally, advancing upon the town, driven by a roaring wind. What a roar! Few had ever heard anything like it. All ran now for the nearest cover—his own house or another's. Saugrain at his home south of the town took time only to make sure that the latch on the door of his office held against the wind, then ran to the main house, crying as he went, "Maman! Odette? Where is the baby? Rosalie? Elise?"

All, praise God, were soon known to be safe, even Gabriel, who had fled to his own place to guard and comfort Hortense. In the big house as Saugrain entered it the baby was crying lustily in his mother's arms. Elise was also screaming somewhere. Odette, it developed, had pushed her and Rosalie under a bed and crawled in after them to make sure that they would remain in the smothering dark. By the time Saugrain had located them and rescued the little girls, the wind had passed, and torrents of rain were falling.

How it rained! It was evening when birds fussing outside gave notice that the rain had stopped. Cautiously Saugrain opened a window. How sweet the cool night air! How gentle the wind! He could have remained at the open window for hours, if the birds had permitted. But they were fussing again, and at him. Would he please go away, they asked, while there was still enough light for them to find their nests? Poor helpless creatures! Many nests could have been torn from eaves and trees by the wind of the afternoon. But knowing that he could not help them settle for the night he closed the window softly—so softly that a loud knocking at the back door of the house sounded like a fresh alarm.

It was only Gabriel, with a lantern. He could not sleep until he knew his family was safe. Asked about his supper, he said he had not given that a thought. Hortense had been very nervous during the storm.

"Perhaps she smelled the water," Saugrain suggested. "She can have a good drink now. What a pity we did not set out pails and basins to catch the water as it fell!"

(118)

"M'sieu," Gabriel said, "there is always one basin—the monster mortar. It should be full. I will fetch a pail."

"Nonsense!" Saugrain said. "I will give you something from the kitchen. You can take Hortense a drink, then return here for a little something to eat. I can eat a little myself, now that I have cooled off. I forgot to be hungry before."

"M'sieu." Gabriel said, now with some hesitation, "you forgot another thing this evening. The mortar was full of water, I know. . . ."

"Gabriel!" Once more Saugrain had failed to strike the hour of six, but according to Gabriel this evening's lapse did not matter much, because about that time nobody would have been listening. It was still raining. Tomorrow would be different. Everybody from the Teniente on would be awake and waiting. Gabriel too would be awake in time. If he did not see the doctor come out. . . .

"In that case, don't keep me up any later tonight," Saugrain said. "Go water Hortense and hurry back for your supper. I want to go to bed."

Two ∽

If forced idleness had been a reason for rumors rising, the September rain did not quench them. Whereas before this prominent men and affairs had helped to pass the time, now certain activities close at hand demanded one's attention. There seemed, for one thing, to be more movement on the far shore of the Mississippi. They asked Saugrain if he had noticed. Saugrain laughed. People were coming to life over there, he thought, as they were on the near shore, with good reason. The land, refreshed now, needed to be restored, the parched corn harvested for what it was worth, the stubble cleared away so that fields would be ready for plowing in the spring. Meanwhile, field and pasture had a new growth of grasses. Cows could be driven out to graze on the sweet wild clover, so that, when calves came on later, there would be good, rich milk for all.

(119)

But that was not what his questioners meant by activity. That was work. They were asking about the people traveling up and down the Illinois shore—from south to north, then back again, on foot or riding horses. Some looked like soldiers. American soldiers? There were strange boats.

Some were soldiers, young Jean Michau affirmed. Compelled to rest occasionally from the labors of restoring his farm, he too had been watching the Illinois shore. Soldiers, he said, had been added to the garrison at Fort Kaskaskia, and they had arrived in boats. As it happened, the Kaskaskia River had overflowed its banks during the rainstorm, so Jean supposed the added soldiers had been sent to help repair the entrenchments around the fort. If they were lasting additions to the garrison, their work could also be the building of new barracks.

"Thank you, m'sieu," Saugrain's friends in town said, when he gave them this report, "but we do not believe they are here to strengthen Kaskaskia. The Americans are planning a new fort across the river in addition to Kaskaskia."

They knew exactly where the new fort would stand. On the Illinois shore, across from the point where the Missouri River emptied into the Mississippi, there was a small stream, hardly more than a branch, known as the River Du Bois. The new fort would be built near the mouth of that little river. But it was the Americans' privilege, Saugrain pointed out, to build whatever they wished on their own ground, was it not?

"That is true, m'sieu," it was agreed, "but the Americans are a pushing people. If they should decide to cross the Mississippi, what defense have we against invasion?"

"You have the Mississippi," Saugrain answered. "Consider how many boats would be needed to transport even a small army across the river, also how few places there are on this side where one can climb the bluffs. Mind you, I do not believe that any hostile purpose lies behind the movements which seem to alarm you. My advice is: look on, if you must, but do not make more of what you see than the facts support. September is passing, and you have still many preparations to make for winter. Have you looked at the grapes on the bluffs, for instance? Will there be a harvest for the wine?"

The grapes, when examined, seemed to have done very well.

The vines must have found both moisture and nourishment deep in the rock walls. Yes, there would be wine-making in October, that is, if. . . .

"If what?" Saugrain demanded. Were there new threats of an American invasion? Not at present, it seemed. All was calm on the Illinois shore, but now it was the Teniente. He had made another voyage down the river in his galley, not to visit his family again at New Bourbon; he was going all the way to New Madrid this time. The militia at all the capitals on the river—New Bourbon, Ste. Genevieve, Cape Girardot, New Madrid—had been summoned. He wished to hold a review.

"But he does that every year," Saugrain said. "It is to keep the Indians quiet."

An old alarm troubled his breathing briefly but gave way before a newer, greater excitement, which he was again bold enough to take to the Government House, presided over by his friend le Duc in de Lassus' absence.

"I am consumed with curiosity," he apologized, "which you are not obliged to satisfy; but I am also victimized by a much disturbed populace. I do not expect you to share any official secrets, but if you could answer some of the questions, it would help."

"I am sorry," le Duc said, "but I have no information to share with you." Then, as if he realized the stiffness of his answer, he smiled and added, "You would like to hear, I am sure, the result of those negotiations in Paris. So would we like to hear—Don Carlos in particular, since his future may depend on the result; but so far there is nothing. Our latest correspondence with New Orleans was an exchange with Spanish officialdom. Does that mean anything to you?"

It would have meant more if Saugrain had known the contents of that correspondence, but all he said was, "It suggests only that His Excellency, expecting news, felt that he would receive it sooner if he went to New Madrid to meet the bearer."

Le Duc laughed aloud.

"There will be no news," he said. "You know how those things go. If an agreement should be reached in Paris between Napoleon's representative and the American ministers, the treaty must be brought over the sea to the French ambassador in Wash-

(121)

ington, who will deliver it to the American Secretary of State, who will lay it before the President. If the President approves the treaty and signs it, all that remains is ratification by the American Senate. Each step takes time. . . ."

"I see what you mean," Saugrain said, preparing to leave. "You are a perfect secretary to a public official. Having listened to your eloquent concealment, I am much better prepared for tomorrow's inquiries."

"But I have told you nothing," le Duc said.

"Exactly nothing," Saugrain agreed. "And yet in my heart there is a singing. All right, I will keep it there, if you say so. Adieu, my friend, adieu!"

Three ◡

Two days later Governor de Lassus returned from his southern journey, rested and refreshed, agreeable as always, but with nothing to report. A few days after that, however, on the twenty-ninth day of September, to be exact, an American keelboat was beached on the Illinois shore at the mouth of the River Du Bois. From it men disembarked, the number varying from a half dozen to twenty, as the story was repeated. At least some of the men wore uniforms. That item was constant.

Saugrain, hearing this astounding news at one house and knowing what he might expect at every succeeding call, also sensing an inner tumult threatening his discretion, hurried through his other visits and fled to the fortified calm of his stone citadel.

Hurry between the town and home was now quite possible. Recently, after the cooling rain, with the help and advice of his good friend Manuel Lisa, he had purchased a small, sturdy brougham and a pair of young horses. To handle this elegance, which would have been beyond him or Gabriel, he had also contracted for a young Negro driver, purchasing his service from a gentleman in town who had more slaves than he could keep busy.

To Saugrain's delight and relief, nobody in his household

thought he had been too wildly extravagant. Madame Saugrain had been happy to surrender half of her drying house for a stable. Michau Père found money or credit to cover the purchase. Finally, only Gabriel could have been put out, but when he found that he, the charette and Hortense were to be retained to serve Madame and the children, he was only humbly grateful for a solution to his own problem. He had thought often and anxiously over Hortense's retirement, but it seemed now that she as well as he could still be of use.

Certainly Gabriel was still useful. He was busy any time that Saugrain saw him. If he had a little time now for his own pleasure, so much the better. Or, was it better?

On reaching his home that twenty-ninth of September, Saugrain found Gabriel waiting for him in a state of excitement equal to any in the town. He waited only to tell the doctor about the American keelboat.

"How do you know it is American?" Saugrain suppressed a sigh.

"M'sieu, I saw it with my own eyes," Gabriel said. He had gone with the stone mason to examine the grapes on the bluffs north of the town. So much for leisure time. "It is not one of ours. It is very long—longer even than the Teniente's galley, although it does not make such a long point at the bow. The whole middle of it is a cabin, with walls and a roof and windows. It is a stout boat, made of oak, I should say."

"No portholes for cannon?" Saugrain said, half in jest.

"M'sieu, no!" Gabriel said reproachfully. "I know it is not a warship. It is a ship for trading, but. . . ."

"Vigny," Madame said to Saugrain that evening, as they walked in what she still called her ruined garden, "you are not hearing a word I say. You are not listening."

"I am listening," Saugrain declared, but that was not true. His thoughts were far away. "We were talking about the flowers that survived the dry weather—lavender, roses—and how sweet they smell."

"Their fragrance is not half what it should be," Madame said; "and we finished about that a half hour ago, before the children began to sing. Do listen, Vigny!"

"I am listening," he said again, and now it was true. "But what

I hear is not a child singing. This is an older voice, very clear and strong and true."

"You do hear now," Madame said, with approval. "That is Elinor singing. She is teaching the children the songs children sing in France."

"I remember now," Saugrain said, and he did. Elinor was said to have a talent for music. In Paris she had studied the piano. But of course she could not move her piano to America. It weighed more than several boxes of books. What had become of it, he asked now? They had sold it. The money had paid over half the cost of the Michaus' passage to America. Ah, poor Elinor!

"Why did you not remind me of the piano," Saugrain demanded, "when I talked of buying the carriage? A piano is not impossible in Saint Louis. I know of two—and a half-dozen harpsichords."

"Vigny," Madame said in horror, "you would have bought a piano for Elinor in place of the beautiful little carriage? We would never have permitted it."

"I could have waited another year," he said ruefully. "Now Elinor must wait. I am truly sorry, but . . . listen. The music has stopped. Elinor is probably tired. She will be wanting to go home. If you will present my compliments to the singers, I will call your father. He has spent another long evening going over what I owe—not counting himself, to whom I owe most."

Before he finished speaking, Michau Père appeared, looking for him.

"Antoine," Michau said, "you have a visitor. In your shop. A military gentleman, American, I think. His French is terrible. Of all he said I understood only two words: Lexington and Kentucky. I did not hear his name. I had a lamp burning—for the account books. He must have seen the light from the road. Aristide is still there, doing his lessons. If you will send him. . . ."

Aristide! Saugrain deposited a hasty kiss on his wife's forehead and hurried off.

It must have been warm, working in the laboratory. Michau had opened the door wide, to let in the cool night air, and had had not thought to close it when he went to summon Saugrain. The circle of radiance outside was enough to attract a stranger's notice. It had attracted a number of other things. As Saugrain

(124)

reached the door, insects of every species whirled about the lamp. Aristide, still a gamin at eleven, was absorbedly studying their gyrations.

The visitor, meanwhile, had sensibly withdrawn to the shadowed rear of the room. Saugrain snatched a cloth, whisked it indiscriminately at Aristide and the insects, driving the boy and most of the bugs out of the house, and closed the door. When he turned to face the room, some bugs were still flirting with death by burning, and the visitor was laughing.

"Dr. Saugrain," he said, "I would know you anywhere, but you have forgotten me, I see."

Not exactly. The tall man in the dark uniform, still standing in the shadows, was strange, but the rich, soft burr of Virginia one could not forget.

"I remember you perfectly," Saugrain declared. "You are Colonel Lewis. Colonel Meriwether Lewis. You bought a thermometer—a gift for your friend and neighbor, Mr. Jefferson, who is now President."

Four ∽

What an evening that was! Pity the guide, waiting at the gate! Probably asleep, Lewis said. The Governor had wakened him from sleep, he was sure, with this duty.

In the late afternoon, Lewis had crossed the river to pay his respects to de Lassus and to deliver a letter written by President Jefferson. De Lassus had received him very politely and insisted on Lewis's having supper with him. While they were at the table Lewis had mentioned knowing Dr. Saugrain, who, he had been told, was now living in St. Louis. So His Excellency had suggested that he call on Dr. Saugrain and had furnished the guide.

"I think His Excellency," Lewis said, "was glad to be rid of me."

So the Teniente's loss was Saugrain's gain. How they talked, these two, the soldier and the man of science! They talked of the Indian wars in Ohio, where the soldier had won his spurs and the rank of colonel. But that was all in the past now. The

Indians were at peace, and the soldier, feeling that his energies and his years were being wasted, had surrendered his commission and his rank and returned to Virginia.

They talked then of Virginia, land of a boy's remembering; but the man, returning, after a certain amount of hunting and farming and visiting had once more become restless. So, he had welcomed an invitation from Mr. Jefferson to accompany him to Washington as his personal secretary.

The talk then moved to Washington, the raw new capital city, but dealt even more with the bewilderment of serving Thomas Jefferson. Almost from the first, Lewis had found himself closeted in a small room with piles of notes and sketches, pertaining to a special project which the President hoped to see realized in action. He was to sort the notes and embody them in a chart and a detailed statement of purpose, to be presented finally to the Congress for approval.

Briefly, the project was a dream, based on a familiar legend, namely that somewhere south of the Arctic Circle there must be a waterway crossing the American continent and joining the two oceans—the Atlantic and the Pacific. Mr. Jefferson had tried several beginnings, only to be turned back, defeated. Now, he thought he had a plan that must end in success. The waterway was there, as it had been all the time, provided by a network of rivers—the Ohio to the Mississippi, the Mississippi to the Missouri, the Missouri westward to mountains more formidable than the Alleghenies, but no barrier to Thomas Jefferson. Mountains, he said, always had passes. In one of these the Missouri would have its source; and nearby, there would be the beginnings of another system of rivers, leading onward to the Pacific.

"But I am tiring you with all this talk," Lewis said abruptly. "You encourage me by listening."

"I am enthralled," Saugrain said. "Please continue. I take it for granted that you finished sorting the President's notes and were ready in good time to hear what Congress might have to say. I am anxious now to hear the outcome, although I know it must have been propitious, or you would not be here."

It had been an anxious period for everybody, Lewis confessed. Congress had his chart and his estimate of costs in December. The deliberations went on after that into spring. Finally, in May, as if there had been no opposition, everything was approved and a sum of money appropriated to cover costs. "Two thousand, five hundred dollars," Lewis said, still awed by the sum.

Saugrain was equally impressed. That was more than he had spent in Paris on the credit of a dead viceroy. He lightened the tension of this fine young man with that story, and was rewarded by an uncertain smile.

"You had wonderful kinfolk," Lewis said. "I have a few, but I could not expect them—my mother, for instance—to rescue me if I failed."

"You have the President," Saugrain reminded him.

"Yes, sir, I know. He has been very kind to me. I asked him soon after he laid out the work I had to do if he would consider giving me command of the expedition to the West. He said yes, if I still wanted it when the time came."

"Ah!" Saugrain said. "He had you in mind for the command before he asked you to join him in Washington. Now, with the approval of Congress and money in the hand, the time had come, as he said, and he offered you the command. I know you accepted it."

"Yes," Lewis said—thoughtfully, omitting the polite "sir." "I wanted it, of course, but by then I knew I had a few deficiencies. I said I would take the command, if I could have help—a co-captain preferably. The distance, you see, began to look very great and the way very lonely—until the President asked me to choose my partner. I named him at once—my old friend of the Indian wars—Bill Clark. Having lived in Kentucky, surely you have heard of the Clarks."

Saugrain knew about the family. He had even been privileged to spend a whole afternoon with the great General George Rogers Clark—a fiery, outspoken man, swearing at the gangrene that had robbed him of a leg and bound him to a wheel chair.

"Bill is eighteen years younger, I think," Lewis said. "His hair is just as red and his eyes the same bright, clear blue. He gets on with everybody—black, white and Indian."

Clark had accepted his appointment without reservation and was instantly ready to assemble a detail of soldiers, also hunters, and have them waiting at Louisville when Lewis came down the Ohio.

But Lewis was back in school again, he admitted ruefully, in Philadelphia. The great expedition was to have scientific importance, along with everything else. The President wanted a journal kept of every day's features—plant, animal, climate and, if you please, longitude and latitude.

"I did not know how to use a sextant," Lewis confessed.

So he learned to sight by the sun and the stars, and he had listened to the learning of great men—Dr. Rush among them.

"A doctor of great repute," Saugrain said politely, keeping quiet about his opposition to some of the great man's medicines—strong chemical compounds which he considered poisonous. He made up his mind then and there to pack a case of simples that Lewis and his co-captain could understand. Leaving Dr. Rush on his pinnacle, he described for Lewis the sage Dr. Franklin, with his foot on a pillow, bolstering the courage of a young Frenchman, grievously wounded on his first visit to the United States of America.

"I have attained neither the years nor the dignity of Dr. Franklin," he said, "nor his gout, but I give advice just as generously, I hope."

Time passed rapidly in the Saugrain citadel while Saugrain listened and Lewis finished his adventures in Pennsylvania, culminating in the building of a keelboat at Pittsburgh, where Lewis, for companionship, had bought himself a dog.

"A Newfoundland," Lewis said. "Good company and a great retriever."

"I am glad to hear about the dog," Saugrain said. "He will enjoy the journey more than anyone else, having no worries about longitude or latitude."

He was also a good sailor, it appeared. When the boat was launched, Lewis had taken it down the Ohio alone, except for the dog. The voyage was uneventful—no Indians. At Louisville Captain Clark was waiting with his hunters and soldiers.

Captain Clark? The rank puzzled Saugrain. Lewis had been a colonel in the army. Militia, Lewis said; and naturally, if he and Clark were to command on equal terms, they must have the same rank. So it was Captain Lewis and Captain Clark, on special service to the President.

(128)

Now the keelboat was beached on the Illinois shore. The captains with the men, in so far as they had been gathered, were bivouacked there, pending the establishing of a camp; and it was midnight by Lewis's watch. Horrified, Lewis apologized again for wearying the doctor with his confidences, and was in a hurry to depart.

"Wait," Saugrain said, opening the door. "I hear voices. My man Gabriel has been passing the time with your guide. Yes, there he comes with a lantern. I will see you again—here or over in Illinois, I trust."

"You must come over," Lewis said. "We shall be there until spring. So many preparations remain . . . we couldn't possibly leave any sooner."

Now he was gone, and nothing had been said about the letter he had delivered to de Lassus. Saugrain had had no thought of asking about it. He did not need to ask. While Lewis was talking out his excitement, his enthusiasm, his doubts, Saugrain had been reviewing calendar dates. If it had taken Lewis a year to arrange the President's notes in order and organize a report to lay before Congress, and the report had been presented in December of 1802, Lewis had gone to work for the President in 1801. Something must have been brewing in France or Spain or both even then.

By May of the following year—this year, 1803—Congress was in full accord with Jefferson's voyage of exploration. The negotiations in Europe must have been completed by then, and they must have gone very well. Only the formalities of an exchange of government remained. The letter to de Lassus was a formality. Outwardly he represented Spain in America, and the Missouri River watered Spanish territory. It was only civil to announce the American intentions to the Teniente at St. Louis. Mr. Jefferson might even have gone so far as to ask Spain's permission for the exploration. Ah, if that meant consulting New Orleans, most assuredly the voyage would not get under way before spring.

In the stone-walled workshop Gabriel fussed now over a fire allowed to burn so low that keeping it for another day seemed doubtful. On the mantel Dr. Franklin's eyes twinkled and his fat cheeks shone in the light from the lamp and the fire.

(129)

"M'sieu," Gabriel said, "I know it was the captain of the keel-boat who came to see you tonight. Do you know where he expects to go in it?"

"Yes, I do," Saugrain said. "Soon everybody will know, but you are not to spread the news as I give it to you. He and another captain will take the boat up the Missouri. Exploring, they call it."

"Oh, but the Missouri is a rough river, m'sieu. With fierce Indians."

"He goes armed, Gabriel, but hopes to make peace with the Indians."

"How far will he go, m'sieu? To the Great Stony Mountains?"

"Farther, perhaps. Beyond the Stony Mountains there is another sea; but the night is half gone. Morning will come too soon, and I do not wish to omit giving the alarm tomorrow. Good night, Gabriel. We will talk about the great western sea tomorrow. Good night."

"Good night, m'sieu, I will hold the lantern until you reach the door."

"Thank you, Gabriel."

Five ✍

A winter overcharged with excitement followed. It seemed to Saugrain that his friends, the simple folk of St. Louis, went about their preparations for cold weather at double their usual comfortable pace. He laughed to see them. He halted them when time permitted, asking why they ran from their homes to wood lot or pasture, when always before this they had walked? Would running bring winter any sooner or keep it away?

The villagers looked at him in surprise when he put this question. Was this the doctor speaking? To tell the truth, Saugrain was surprised at himself. He, too, walked faster these days, especially after a visit to the camp across the river. He soon formed the habit of paying this visit once a week, if he could find a boat and a man to row it. The only difficulty about that was choosing one man from the number who volunteered. He had to name a new man each time, to keep the peace.

No matter who manned the boat, the result was the same. Both Saugrain and the boatman, after an inspection which usually took about an hour, came back with a tale of wonders that lasted until the following week—but no longer. If for some reason Saugrain omitted the weekly visit, everyone experienced a sense of loss. There were the boats, for instance—three in all, the captains' keelboat first. It was, according to Saugrain's boatman, enormous, very large by the doctor's estimate. Empty of men or cargo, it floated lightly enough at its mooring; but, if it should ever be loaded with all it could carry, fifty men would be needed to move it upstream. The cabin amidships was a small house. A piece of it at the stern was walled off for the two captains' use. The rest of the space was for cargo. Loading would be done through a hole in the roof, fitted with a tight cover. Ah, that loading would be something, would it not?

The other two boats were incomprehensible only because of their size. Two giant cottonwood trees were felled, and men were set to work at stripping small branches and bark from the trunks and hollowing out pith and wood within, to shape two stout pirogues, each equal to carrying twenty men and more supplies. By this time, with the approval of de Lassus, Saugrain had revealed to others besides Gabriel the purpose of the camp and the gathering of men and boats: there was to be a voyage of exploration—up the Missouri. But of course, up the Missouri, everyone said. Anyone should have known that. The Missouri was a river that laughed at little boats and bark canoes. But when houses began to appear on the campsite—a large double house for the captains, smaller ones but equally solid for the men, American-style houses with the logs laid endways instead of as up-and-down posts, doubt settled once more on the watchers from across the Mississippi.

"This is no camp," they said. "Nobody builds such houses meaning to use them only a few months and then leave them. This is a town—a settlement, at the very least." And when a high stockade was set up all around the buildings except on the side of the river, with the keelboat and the pirogues beached inside the walls, they changed again. This was not a camp, or a town. It was a fort.

"No!" Saugrain reasoned, except in the sense that a station set up by a merchant for trading with the Indians was sometimes called a fort.

And the marching, the villagers asked then? Every day there was marching at Camp Du Bois. Surely men did not march on a voyage.

The time might come, Saugrain said, when they must march. So, the houses were stout, to protect the men from winter's cold; and the marching was to keep them active so that their blood ran freely. "Wait until spring," he urged. "You will see."

They knew what they would see. In the spring would come the Yanqui invasion. The boats? With them they would take command of the Mississippi, then go on to conquer the Missouri as well.

Winter settled down, then, and with less crossing of the river, the inhabitants of St. Louis grumbled less, having other concerns to consider, such as rheumatism and coughs. Saugrain worked long hours in his laboratory, muttering at times as he moved about but more often singing—not tunefully, but cheerily. He was now ready to fill that medicine chest which he had promised himself to send with the captains—a very small chest. A box, Michau Père called it; but it must be small, Lewis had said, so that he could tuck it away in his cabin. He knew now that there would be no room for extras in the cargo hold. So Michau Père had fashioned the box according to directions, and Saugrain had heated up his glass furnace and blown an assortment of vials for concentrated solutions, ticketing each with directions for diluting, while Madame made small flat packets of herbs from her collection in the barn. No strong medicine in either vial or packet. The great Doctor Rush had provided enough of those.

"The captains will use our chest more often, I hope," Saugrain said to Madame. "They grew up as Virginia farm boys and know many simple remedies, and how to identify the plants. There is that root called pocono, which Captain Redhead swears will cure snakebite. But there will be times when what they need may be lacking. Then our little cupboard may save the day."

(132)

While Madame emptied her apron of her carefully tied and labeled packets, he recited the list: hot peppers ground, ready to mix with grease—bear, buffalo or pig—for a salve to break up congestion; a medicine for poison rash—equal parts of tincture of lobelia, arnica and ammonia water; rhubarb pills, anise for colic, plant mucilage for cuts. . . .

"The chest," he said to Madame, "with the new thermometer and some phosphorus matches, will be our contribution to the great American adventure."

The door of the shop opened and closed. Michau Père had departed.

"Now what did I say?" Saugrain asked.

"Nothing," Madame answered. "In the summer, when people were believing that Louisiana had been given back to France, he was very happy; but now . . . you know how he regards America—because of our dear Maman. I often wonder how he has lived this long, still grieving."

"Your papa," Saugrain said, "lives because he is strong as an oak. That is how he is made. He will live longer being sad than I shall being happy."

"Vigny!" Madame said—in horror.

"Wait!" Saugrain rebuked. "I was not setting a time of departure for either of us. I was making a biological comparison. Look! I would not leave now if I were summoned. There are too many things I want to see happen."

Six ✍

Happily, the winter of 1803–1804 was an open one, meaning that there was never enough ice to close the rivers. If a gorge formed above or below St. Louis, within a week a thaw would open it.

Consequently, on the nineteenth day of February, a messenger in the dark blue uniform with white facings of an American infantryman, in this case a sergeant, by the braid on his sleeve, experienced no great difficulty in crossing the Mississippi from

Cahokia to the St. Louis landing. There, as he stepped out of the boat, carrying with ease a bulging leather satchel, he met his first obstacle. Saugrain, as post surgeon, heard the story right after it happened.

The sentinel on guard at the landing met the American soldier properly by presenting his rifle with bayonet fixed and demanding his name and business—in Spanish, of which the stranger knew only two words; but he recognized the rifle and the bayonet. With the help of his boatman, who understood English and addressed the Spanish guard in French, which the guard understood, he made it known that he carried dispatches for Governor de Lassus from New Orleans, which he wished to deliver *muy pronto*.

Pronto then, if not *muy*, the sentinel laid aside his gun, motioned to the soldier to follow him and set off up a steep slope, which he knew to be the most direct approach to the top of the bluff. The path led over loose rubble, around immovable boulders and over deep crevasses, but the American, in spite of his burden, kept close behind his guide, and the two of them arrived together at the entrance to the House of Government. From there the sergeant commanding the Teniente's guard would have carried the dispatches into the house, but the messenger refused to surrender the satchel. Nor would he give it to Monsieur le Duc, who held out his hand for it at the door. The sergeant's orders were to deliver the satchel only to Governor de Lassus, to whom the dispatches were addressed. Le Duc, who handled all the Teniente's mail, seemed surprised, but he smiled and ordered the sentinel fom the river front to wait where he was, then opened the door and motioned the American inside.

In a very few minutes—hardly time enough for the sentinel from below to exchange opinions with the corporal commanding the Teniente's guard—the American reappeared, his satchel flabby with emptiness. he himself in a great hurry to get back to the river and his boat.

"Now, what do you make of all that?" asked the first patient on Saugrain's list the following morning.

"Nothing," Saugrain said, with fine nonchalance," although it is an interesting story. It might pay one to watch, perhaps, from day to day, so as not to miss whatever comes of the Teniente's important mail."

(134)

With that, he made each succeeding visit in town shorter than the one before, and so at the end of the morning he had almost an hour to spend at the House of Government. Le Duc opened the door for him.

"We were expecting you," le Duc said, in welcome. "In fact, if you had not come when you did, we contemplated sending someone in search of you." Then, closing the door, he lowered his voice. "The official documents are here."

The documents—pages of writing, all with a flourish of signatures, some with seals affixed—were spread across the wide table in the half light of the audience chamber. Not haphazardly. They made a sort of pattern, but Saugrain addressed himself first to the Lieutenant Governor. De Lassus, he felt sure, had read all the papers. His color was high; his hands were restless.

"Excellency," Saugrain said solemnly, "it has come, has it not— the change of government?"

"Forgive me," de Lassus said. "I am not ready to speak of it just now. Read the papers. They tell the story better than I can— or even le Duc. Be seated, please. The reading will take a while. Do not mind me. I will sit or I will walk, when I feel I must. Read."

Le Duc brought a candle as Saugrain placed himself in a chair before the table.

"This paper here," the matchless one said, "is perhaps not the most significant, but it opens the story. It will add to your understanding of the rest."

Saugrain began reading:

Don Manuel de Salcedo; Marquis of Casa Calvo,
to Don Carlos de Lassus, Commander of the Illinois:

The King our Sovereign, having determined to retrocede the Province of Louisiana to the French Republic, according to the announcement of the royal order, issued at Barcelona on the 15th of October, 1802. . . .

Saugrain marked the date with his hand and looked up from the paper. "Eighteen-oh-two?" he questioned. "Was it so long ago as that?"

"That was the year, I believe," de Lassus said, "when the King of Spain made the formal acknowledgment. The agreement had been made at least a year before that."

"And you knew nothing of it, Excellency?"

De Lassus smiled—indulgently.

"It was a secret treaty," he said, "and, as you have remarked on more than one occasion, Doctor, Spain and this post are a great distance apart."

"Excellency. . . ."

"It does not matter now. Please continue with the letter of the commissioners."

Commissioners? What commissioners? Oh, yes, Señores Salcedo and Casa Calvo; but now Saugrain had lost his place in the letter. No, here it was, right after the retroceding:

> and having commissioned us to carry into effect the royal order given at Madrid the eighteenth day of January, 1803, we have put into execution the intentions of the Sovereign by delivering up the governorship of this place and the command of the province to the Colonial prefect Pedro Clement Laussat, Commissioner of the French. . . .

The room seemed to Saugrain now to be oversupplied with commissioners, two for Spain, one for France. . . .

"This Laussat . . ." he closed his eyes to rest them from the reading, "what was he doing at New Orleans?"

Le Duc answered for the Teniente. Pierre Laussat was merely a necessary link in the chain of events. Since Spain had ceded the province of Louisiana to France, which was to say, Bonaparte, a representative of France must receive it officially, even though Napoleon had already disposed of it.

"In which case," Saugrain said, "we shall have a fourth commissioner. American? And this Laussat will deliver up what in fact he does not possess . . . I regard him as an intruder. But I will read on. I am anxious to learn how the Spanish commissioners extricated themselves from their not too noble situation . . . ah! Here we have it. . . ."

> the surrender of the post to be made under the formalities of an inventory and valuation made by two skillful persons in that post. . . .

Saugrain had their names ready; Marie le Duc and Antoine Soulard.

both to act with impartiality, of the buildings which belong to the King. . . .

Bravo, Señores! Saugrain thought. To reserve something for His Catholic Majesty and Spain! The final paragraph of the letter was even more in character:

under the same formality of an inventory, the archives, the papers and documents which concern only the inhabitants of the district and their property, shall be delivered, taking for the whole a receipt, in order that there always may be evidence of what has been delivered upon our part to the French Republic.

"Excellency," Saugrain said, "this matter of a receipt stirs memories in me. It cannot have been pleasant to deliver up a province which was until that day a proud possession of a proud monarchy. To have done all so carefully, so correctly!"

De Lassus agreed, but said then that the French commissioner had been equally punctilious and correct in his behavior. Chiefly, Saugrain thought, his punctilio had consisted in his avoiding a long and tedious journey to St. Louis by giving the American commissioner, when he presented himself in New Orleans, full authority to act as agent for the French Republic, to take possession of the territory and all the establishments commanded by de Lassus for His Catholic Majesty, the King of Spain. Laussat's letter of authority was included among the dispatches outlining the surrender of New Orleans, which he was forwarding that day, with a letter to Governor de Lassus, and another to a Mr. Stoddard, Captain of Artillery in the United States Army. He signed each letter with a flourish: "I have the honor to salute you, Laussat," and with that took his departure. He had done all that was required of him in the business of "delivering up" and was, no doubt, thankful.

That left finally only Mr. Stoddard of the Artillery. Amos Stoddard, he signed his name—Amos, a Biblical prophet, Saugrain recalled. His letter was brief, even terse, but sharply clear, written in academic French. He had received the dispatches at Kaskaskia the day before he wrote:

> I do myself the honor to forward them by a sergeant of our army, who is bound on business to Capt. Lewis.
> In a few days the troops under my command will ascend the Mississippi in public boats. I shall proceed before them by land and concert with you the necessary arrangements before their arrival in St. Louis.
> Please accept the assurances of my respectful consideration,
>> Amos Stoddard, Captain, U. S. Artillerists,
>> Agent and Commissioner for the French Republic.

The letter, although quite correct, had a certain tone—abrupt, dictatorial. Saugrain read it twice and was still at a loss for comment. "Excellency," he said finally, "Kaskaskia is very near. What will you say to this captain of Artillerists?"

"I will have my answer ready," de Lassus said, "when his messenger stops here tomorrow. I will promise him a most gracious reception and my assistance in arranging the necessary formalities for the surrender of Upper Louisiana, asking only that he notify me in advance of the exact day of his coming."

"Excellency, he may consider that a waste of time."

"I know," de Lassus granted, "but he spoke of coming ahead of the troops. There must be a suitable interval of time to arrange . . . come, come, my friend. Your face is longer than I remember ever seeing it. We looked for some rejoicing on your part."

"Excellency," Saugrain said—loudly for him, "I am sorry—for many reasons. I am sorry for things I have said in a moment of despair or impatience. You know why I came here to live. Not for thirty pesos a month, but because long ago I had been led to believe that this part of America would be the place where the new republic would show its first real growth. In the four years I have lived here I have hoped and feared and prayed and despaired, but always I have come back to that belief, that promise. Now fulfillment is at hand; but it comes too suddenly. I am not ready. I have a sad face because my thoughts are sad. Only once before in my life have I known a sadness so deep. That was when I left France fourteen years ago, knowing that I would never return.

(138)

Excellency, this odd little village will never be the same again, will it? I am thinking of the people. They sense a change in the air, and they are afraid. I am afraid with them. I think of you. I am not the only one who will ask what is to become of you? Well?"

De Lassus stood up to answer. No man could look nobler than he did when he stood straight like that, his chin not even touching the stiff, high collar of his coat. "Dr. Saugrain," he said, "I am still captain in His Majesty's Stationary Louisiana Regiment. I shall await orders." Then he smiled. "Until they come, perhaps I may be of some help with that inventory which we have been directed to make."

If the room had been quiet before, it was now a vacuum.

"Excellency," Saugrain said, suffering another shiver, "I can only borrow the words of Monsieur Laussat! I salute you. Have I your permission to withdraw?"

Seven ∽

Saugrain's melancholy, although genuine, proved to be only temporary. An hour in his own domain, the combination of a brisk fire and the terra cotta portrait of Dr. Franklin beaming at him from the mantelpiece, enabled him to put sadness at least in its proper place among other emotions. It was the natural, belated reluctance of any human being, jumping from the known —often undesirable—into the unknown, which would be in every way an improvement over the past, but still hazardous because it was unfamiliar.

Meanwhile, the inhabitants of St. Louis had made up their own minds about the significance of the dispatches delivered by the American army sergeant. By some sleight of hand known only to rulers of states, all of Louisiana had been delivered to America. At any time the invasion might begin. What did that mean to them? Would they be driven out, along with the Teniente and the Spanish soldiers?

To still their fears, Saugrain told his friends in town about the inventory ordered by the Spanish commissioners before they released their hold on the territory. His friends listened respectfully, but with some doubt. The invaders were American, were they not? Which was the same as Anglais? They could tear up that list of people and properties, which, after all, would be only another paper.

Americans, Saugrain said, were English only in the sense that their forefathers had once lived in England. Then he improvised a short history of the United States. These forefathers, not liking some of the laws of their native England, had crossed the ocean and settled in a strange land where, after a hundred years or so and a war for independence, they had formed a new nation, the United States of America, which was in no way like England except that the people spoke the same language.

"Do not try to understand everything at once," he begged. "Do not be afraid. I have lived among the Americans. They are good people, for the most part. You will get on well with them, I am sure."

How was that possible, some asked, when the Yanqui spoke no French and the French spoke no English? But some did, he said, thinking of Amos Stoddard. They learned it in school. As for the rest, "Look," he said. "You speak no English now and the strangers speak no French, but that will change. A few words at a time, you will learn a little English and the Americans will learn a little French. . . ."

"Monsieur Docteur," one grandfather said, "I am too old to learn a foreign way of speaking."

"You think so, Baptiste?" Saugrain chided. "Listen. An American wishes to buy a cow. Having seen your cows, he thinks he would like one of those. So he comes here with a small sack of money in his hand. He rattles the money and points to a cow. You understand at once, I see. You say, 'Ah! *Une vache.*' He says, 'No, a cow.' '*Qui*,' you say, '*une vache.*' Before this goes on much longer, you reach an understanding. What is a cow to the American is a *vache* to you, and what is a *vache* to you is a cow to him. Each has learned one word of the other's speech. If you will take a small dose like this each morning and each afternoon and repeat the lesson at bedtime. . . ."

"Monsieur Docteur," Baptiste said, "you will always have the little joke. Tell me this. Are you remaining here with us?"

(140)

"Why not?" Saugrain asked. "Where would I go? I have my home here—my family, my house, my land, sick people who need me. Listen. I will tell you a secret. I think what is about to happen is a very good thing for everybody. Shall we wait now and see how it goes? Good!"

He came away from such encounters with his spirits high, his hope renewed, his faith strengthened simply by letting it speak for itself; but his true, deep exultation did not take full possession until the day when the captain of Artillerists first set foot on the St. Louis waterfront.

On the twenty-first of February de Lassus gave the American sergeant, returning down river from Camp Du Bois, a letter to deliver to the captain at Fort Kaskaskia. The letter contained the Lieutenant Governor's promise of a gracious welcome, also his request for suitable notice in advance of the captain's arrival.

Apparently Captain Stoddard found letter-writing difficult, or, perhaps, a waste of time, and the use of an orderly to deliver the letters further waste. On the twenty-fifth of February, word came from the watchers on the bluffs at St. Louis that many boats loaded with soldiers were on the way up the Mississippi from Kaskaskia. The next word was that the boats were stopping at Cahokia.

These were, Saugrain felt sure, the "public boats" mentioned in Captain Stoddard's one and only letter. Since Cahokia, on the Illinois shore, was only a little below his place, he took his spyglass across the road and trained it on the scene, hoping to add something to what the others had reported.

Something, but not very much. As was often the case, haze covered the Illinois country back from the water's edge. He made out that the soldiers were infantrymen from being able to distinguish white trimming against dark blue uniforms. Two officers were in command at the time of landing. One, from the white on his uniform, was also of the infantry, but patches of bright scarlet decorated the coat of the other. Captain Stoddard? But certainly; red was always the color for artillery. Excitement began to squirm deep in the doctor's chest cavity.

Meanwhile the soldiers had been busy unloading the boats and carrying a miscellany of filled sacks, small kegs and boxes into the obscurity. Only one object was immediately identifiable—a small

(141)

bright brass cannon on wheels. Saugrain's excitement mounted. The captain, having no positive information about the armament of Fort San Carlos in St. Louis, had seen fit to provide himself with at least one field piece. After all, an artillery officer must command one gun that could be fired.

The cannon also disappeared presently into the background haze, whereupon the captain spoke briefly to the infantry officer, then turned and marched quickly to the first of the hired boats, the one farthest upstream, stepped aboard, and took his seat in the stern. In the middle of the boat two oarsmen, in place and ready, faced him. Beyond them, a soldier sat on what could be the captain's trunk, and a bossman on shore had his hands on the mooring rope.

The oarsmen held the boat against the shore until the bossman freed the rope and held it as he stepped aboard. Seconds later the pirogue was heading for midstream.

Saugrain closed his spyglass. He could not see the landing at St. Louis from where he stood. If he wanted to see it, either he must hurry into town and scramble down the rocky incline to the official landing, or he must travel even faster southward over the road on which he and his house stood until he came to the Little River, then follow the usual—in fact the only—road to the boat landing. By now de Lassus would have had ample warning of Captain Stoddard's approach and would have ordered a carriage to the landing to meet him. In fact, Saugrain thought he remembered more than one set of wheels rolling south over the road while he had his eyes fastened on the Illinois shore.

Now he had a better idea. The carriage conveying Captain Stoddard to the town must use this same road, passing right by him, and now by Madame as well, where they stood.

"Vigny, no!" Madame said to that. "We must not be here. We must hurry back to the house. How would it look for us to be standing on the road, staring, when the carriage goes by?"

It would look very bad, Saugrain confessed. The only thing worse would have been for the carriage to meet him running down the hill, red-faced and breathless.

So he watched the passing through a front window. The result was a more comprehensive portrait, but still not very clear. Le Duc had gone with the carriage to meet the captain; and on the

(142)

way back, as Saugrain learned later, as soon as residences bordered the road, he had ordered the driver to hold the horses to a walk, so that he could name the owners. Then it might be easier for Stoddard to catch the names when he heard them again, as he was certain to do, all these being people of consequence.

The carriage all but stopped at the Saugrain gate. Stoddard, le Duc said afterwards, was much impressed by the stone house. He called it handsome. Saugrain saw from his window an alert face with no extraordinary feature except possibly intent blue eyes. Or they could have been gray. Certainly they were not brown. Red trim on the dark blue uniform included a cockade and a short plume on a chapeau bras, and the deep cuffs of the coat, and there was also gilt buttons here and there and some gold lace.

Further details of the captain's arrival and his subsequent conduct of a difficult assignment Saugrain pieced together out of village gossip, his own interested observations, and a few direct encounters. In town a room had been made ready for the American captain in the house of Monsieur Charles Gratiot. For that Stoddard was especially grateful. Gratiot, of all the Chouteau connections, of all the local gentry really, spoke the most English. Also there were many Gratiot servants, one ready always to supply what he might need.

"But he asks for very little," Madame Gratiot said later. "He is no trouble whatever. Very neat—one seldom sees a man so neat."

Neat, precise, correct, Saugrain thought, able to make decisions, strong to insist that his orders be carried out—a thoroughly disciplined soldier, trained to command. President Jefferson could not have named a better man to be the first to represent American authority here.

With his orderly, who turned out to be the sergeant who had carried the first dispatches, he moved into the Gratiot house and, according to some, seldom left it between that day and the day of changing the government. What did he do there all that time? He wrote. Rather, for the most part he told the orderly what to write. Then he signed his name.

This was exaggeration. Captain Stoddard busied himself in many ways besides writing. He inspected the fort. He visited the nearby smaller towns. At a public reception given for him by de Lassus, he appeared for the first time in his full-dress uniform:

(143)

white gaiters in place of the usual black ones that covered the meeting of his trousers with his shining boots, white cross belts three inches wide, fastened with gold buckles, gold buttons and gold lace on his red collar. He wore his brown hair sleek and short. On any state occasion he presented a handsome and very military image.

To be sure, there was considerable writing. The situation seemed to require it. On the day of his arrival, hardly waiting to unbutton his coat, he composed and dispatched a letter to the Lieutenant Governor, (1) stating his plenary powers to receive possession of Upper Louisiana and its posts, (2) demanding the immediate, formal surrender of the same, and (3) repeating assurances of his respectful consideration.

As he saw it, that was his business here, and the sooner he got it under way, preferably on a basis of good understanding, the better.

His letter, however, created some hysteria at the House of Government. De Lassus had about completed his plan for the ceremony of surrender but had scarcely begun work on that inventory demanded by the Spanish commissioners. Le Duc and Soulard, on opening the first storage place for records, had encountered such heaps and bundles of papers, to say nothing of record books, that they had closed the door in consternation. Forty years of history were entombed in that room. The next day they had been bold enough to open a few books. They were not impossible. Their information was clear and legible. They might serve as guides for classifying the miscellaneous papers, but. . . .

"There it is, Captain," de Lassus said. "It will take a year, maybe more."

A year was out of the question, Stoddard thought. There must be a solution. Presently he offered one. He would give de Lassus a receipt in toto in exchange for a written promise that the inventory would be made . . . post facto.

That removed the obstacle of the archives for the time being. The Teniente and the captain were now ready to discuss a program for the day of delivering the territory.

"Shall we begin with the date?" Stoddard suggested, viewing with suspicion the writing that de Lassus had done in preparation.

"How about tomorrow or the day after? Nothing will be changed by delay now."

De Lassus objected. A great deal could be changed. The people of this territory were not used to so much haste. If a proper ceremony could be arranged, something of a spectacle which they could remember and talk about later, it would go far toward quieting their fears and removing their unwillingness. To begin, a notice should be fastened to the church door. Well in advance, please. Then he, personally, would like to invite a few prominent citizens to gather as witnesses of the act of transfer. There could be a few speeches, a marching of soldiers, the firing of cannon when the flag was changed. A month would take care of these and other details.

A week at the outside. Stoddard said. Finally, retreating and advancing, they agreed on the ninth of March. Once the date for the transfer was settled, they adjusted everything else harmoniously.

Eight

The ninth of March was too soon for just one reason. It was a cold, gray day, with a bone-chilling wind blowing from the northeast. What a person wore was of no significance, since hooded blanket coats and shawls covered broadcloth and silk as well as homespun. Dr. Saugrain, dressing before a blazing fire at fifteen minutes before six, with his silver watch on a stand before him, was grateful for warm hand-knit hose of gray wool, long enough to garter above his skinny knees. Now the breeches. . . .

"Long ones," a sweetly husky voice said from the far side of the room, "such as Captain Stoddard wears, would be warmer, I should think."

"I hope I do not have to experiment with them," Saugrain said. "I am afraid of entangling my feet and taking a fall. In any case, knee breeches, I am told, are still court dress . . . heavens, do not speak to me now! Where is my coat? I shall be late with my morning chimes."

Today of all days! Pulling on a warm sheepskin jacket, the gift of young Jean Michau, and wool mittens, he went outside.

Wrapped as he was, he felt no discomfort from the sharp wind. It was only when he hefted the iron pestle that he knew he had appraised the weather correctly. The chill of the cold metal penetrated his mittens as if March were still part of the winter. He dropped the pestle cautiously back in place. He had still one minute remaining—time enough for him to shake his hands and arms vigorously and loosen his shoulders. Then he braced his legs, lifted the pestle again, swung it back far enough to provide the desired momentum, and let it carry itself forward against the iron, raising the usual reverberations.

The same force also caused the pestle to rebound—enough to enable Saugrain to swing it back to the apex of the striking arc with no sense of labor. Six blows in all were executed. On the last —and loudest—he held the pestle against the rim of the mortar. His arm quivered if the iron did not. When the quivering passed, he lifted the pestle and dropped it in place inside the mortar, beat his hands together to quicken the flow of blood, then turned to see if the usual audience was present.

It was. On the path to the small shed house Gabriel stood, his legs a little more bowed, his shoulders more bent than on first acquaintance; but his ears were covered as always, and the expression on his scarred face indicated still a stifled remonstrance. In the other direction, on the way to the carriage house, he saw Guillaume, the young Negro coachman. Guillaume was very young. He smiled broadly, his teeth gleaming against the ebony of his face. Understanding that both faces sent the same message —"Good morning, M'sieu Doctor, we are pleased to see you in continued good health"—he said, "Good morning, William," to the coachman, then turned to Gabriel, who had now dropped his hands from his ears but otherwise looked the same.

"Well, Gabriel," Saugrain said, "have you changed your mind? Will you ride to town with William and me? We shall be early, but you can take a stool to sit upon if you have too long to wait before the ceremonies begin."

"Thank you, m'sieu," Gabriel said. "I hope you will excuse. I

(146)

still think it best to stay at home—with Hortense—and keep warm. I begin to know what it is like to ache with rheumatism."

"Ts, ts!" Saugrain said compassionately. "Well, do as you think best. I can go over it all with you later—this evening, perhaps."

He turned again toward the barn, to repeat the carriage orders for the morning.

"Well, William?" he began gaily, and the coachman broke into open laughter.

"I can't say it so, M'sieu Docteur," he pleaded. "It comes out always the same—Guillaume."

"Never mind," the doctor said. "It is others who will be calling you William, no matter how you say it. Have you had breakfast? No? Then come along with me to the house and get some. I will fill your plate. You must eat plenty so that you will not feel chilly or hungry. When you have eaten, bring out the carriage. I will be waiting. You will have ample time to take me to the Government House and return for the ladies, but we must not waste any of it. When you bring the ladies to town, you will want a good place for them. Monsieur Michau and Monsieur Jean will be there to help you. They will remain near the carriage, to help hold the horses in case a sudden noise should frighten them."

"They won't take fright, M'sieu Docteur. They. . . ."

"Their behavior will be the very best, I am sure," Saugrain said. "Well, here we are at the house."

Slipping out of the sheepskin coat then, in the warmth of Madame's kitchen, he laid it aside with misgiving. His dress coat, however long and full-skirted, would not be as warm. Then he laughed at himself for his concern. His dear wife had taken care of all that. She had added an extra lining of flannel to his waistcoat, and she would insist on his wearing a hat.

As he might have expected, he arrived early at Government House, but that was how he wanted it. The vacant square north of the mansion, known in spite of disuse as the Place d'Armes, had been cleared of undergrowth, and people were already gathering there, although none of the nine carriages which the town boasted had appeared in the space reserved for them.

Le Duc, all smiles, opened the door of the house as Saugrain left his carriage, but Saugrain, hurrying to greet him, spoke first.

"Good day, my friend," he cried. "I would embrace you, but you see I am encumbered."

"I see," le Duc said, his smile even broader. "The hat is very becoming as you wear it."

"You think it looks better in my hand than on my head?" Saugrain asked. "So do I. The head was measured, hair and all, when the hat was ordered, but it still will not sit on the hair. Madame Saugrain has threatened to fasten strings to it, but I prefer to carry it."

"If you are ever tempted to part with it," le Duc said then, pretending envy, but Saugrain did not let him finish.

"Tempted?" he said. "I have been tempted since before it arrived at our house, but, you see, a hat like this, of the best beaver, with a silver buckle added, is costly. It looks handsome on a peg in our hall, where it hangs most of the time, unless Madame mistrusts a caller and whisks it out of sight. But enough of that. I see we are going to have a full assembly today."

Le Duc agreed, and asked whether, being the first of the chosen prominent citizens to arrive, he did not wish to select now a spot on the gallery from which to view the ceremonies, but Saugrain said no, he had rather be the first to pay his respects to His Excellency. He was sure to have his choice of vantage points later. Because of his height, anyone would stand back and make room for him. He could not possibly obscure one's view.

He was right. When he stepped outside again after a half hour of felicitations and toasts indoors, the gallery was filling rapidly, but he found no difficulty in reaching the edge facing the Square. With cheerful greeting, everyone made room for him: "Good day to you, Doctor! Good day to you, sir!" Finally he stood in front, only the width of one person separating him from a sort of corridor being kept clear from the steps to the door. The one person was Monsieur du Breuille, his neighbor from the Catalan Road. He would have given Saugrain his place, but Saugrain thanked him and refused. His position was perfect. He had a clear view of the streets and the square and was surrounded on three sides by good friends of bulk, who kept off the wind. What more could a man ask?

He looked out over a sea of head kerchiefs, hoods, shawls, and his eyes misted with sudden emotion. Few of the thousand inhabitants were missing. That this should be happening today and he should have a part in it! Remembering the picture as he had seen it on a morning four years before, he blinked away his mist and looked the scene over again—the Square filling with people; the line of glistening carriages on the far side, his marked by two tall men, his father-in-law and his brother-in-law, standing guard; across the street to the weathered stone mansion of the elder Chouteau brother; past that, then, to the fort and the lane leading to it—the Street of the Tower.

Here, too, underbrush had been cleared away. From the top of the flagpole on the parade the royal green and white banner of Spain stood out stiffly in the wind, and a double line of soldiers waited, their arms temporarily at rest but ready to be shouldered at a word of command. He knew most of the men now. Some were friends. Two, His Excellency had said, had asked leave to remain in St. Louis when the order came to move on. They wanted to settle in the town or some place nearby, where there was hope. . . .

Having trouble with his eyes again, Saugrain turned halfway around to look at the river. After viewing it once a day all this time, what difference did he expect to find now? He did not expect. He knew. Every day there was something. He was right. As he watched, the sun found a hole in the clouds and sent a shaft of light down to the water, touching every ripple with gold. A murmur from the square told him that the people there had noticed the phenomenon and wondered. Was it a sign? Assuredly, he would have said, it was a sign; and before the day ended, there would be more.

The next minute the beat of drums came from the south muffled by distance. The volume of sound increased steadily. Presently it was accompanied by an obbligato of marching feet. Then, approaching over the Rue Principale, the company of American infantry appeared. Only that. When they reached Government House, the officer in command turned them smartly to the left and led them up the Street of the Tower to the fort.

At the same time the Spanish line had formed another column and marched forward. The two columns met on the parade, separated, reformed in line, and halted, facing each other, with the flagpole between them.

(149)

The Teniente had now come out of Government House. He stood at the edge of the gallery, waiting for the attention of those in the Square to deliver an appropriate speech. Finally, although his address was brief, only those near him heard the words as he spoke them and had to have them repeated later:

"Inhabitants of Upper Louisiana:

"By the King's command I am about to deliver up this post and its dependencies.

"The flag under which you have been protected for so many years is to be withdrawn. . . .

"The fidelity and courage with which you have guarded and defended it will never be forgotten. In my character of representative, I entertain the most sincere wishes for your perfect prosperity."

With that, he offered the key to the house as a symbol of possession to Captain Stoddard, who, accompanied by Charles Gratiot and Captain Meriwether Lewis, had arrived almost unnoticed and stood now at the foot of the steps.

Captain Stoddard saluted and took the key. Then it was his turn to speak, which he did—in French—but again only those on the gallery heard what he said, and they not quite all. As he took the key, a soldier stationed on the gallery, facing the fort, waved a large white handkerchief in that direction, and a roar of cannon swallowed the remainder of Stoddard's composition.

Six times the cannon spoke. That was not enough for a proper salute, it was said later, but six cannon were all that the fort possessed, and few would have believed there were that many. As the last roar shook the air and spread its smoke, a Spanish color guard appeared at the base of the flagpole and began to loosen the ropes. The flag of Spain, which had stood out so proudly in the early morning, came down safely and limply. Reverent hands caught it before it touched the ground, freed it, folded it, and carried it away.

Now it was time for the American flag to be raised. From watching Camp Du Bois, everyone present knew what to expect —the gay red and white stripes, the blue field with white stars— but look! That did not describe the flag now going up on the ropes. It had three broad stripes of red, white and black. Cries of rapture, wonder, and unbelief broke out all over the Square, led by those who recognized the royal banner of King Louis—Fourteenth,

Fifteenth, Sixteenth—what did the number matter? It was the Tricolor of France. But what did that signify, many asked? Were they to be French citizens, after all?

"No! No!" came the answer from near the house. "Be quiet now, so that we may hear."

The gallery was by then almost empty. The Teniente and Captain Stoddard, with their aides, had gone into the house. Only Mr. Gratiot remained, and he was explaining about the flag. Certain French exiles, knowing that the territory had been given back to France in the first place and held briefly until Bonaparte had sold it to America, had asked as a great favor for the French flag to fly over St. Louis, if only for a little while, after the flag of Spain came down and before the American flag was raised. Captain Stoddard had graciously consented, limiting the permission, however, as to time. The flag now at the top of the pole could remain there overnight; but tomorrow morning it must be replaced by the Stars and Stripes. Captain Stoddard and Captain de Lassus were in the house now, signing the official papers transferring the government.

"That was a noble thing for the American captain to do," Gabriel said that evening as Saugrain told the story, not only for the enlightenment of his servingman but because it soothed him to review the events, settling each one in its proper place in his remembrance. "But what about the flags, m'sieu? Will you be one of the honor guard at the pole tonight?"

"No," Saugrain said. "I have already stood longer than my feet or legs endure peacefully. I will sit by the fire an hour or two, look over my medicines for rheumatism—it was cold on the Square this morning—then go to bed, to be ready for tomorrow. Meanwhile Monsieur Michau must uphold the honor of the family at the flagpole."

"Not Monsieur Jean?" Gabriel asked.

"No," Saugrain said. "Like me, Jean has no room in his heart for a divided allegiance. We gave ours a long time ago to the American Republic."

"Yes, m'sieu," Gabriel said, "but . . . m'sieu, the sun is about to set, and you have not struck the hour. If you are weary from the long day, I will strike it for you. This once?"

"I am sure you would and could," Saugrain said, "but there is no need. We have still a half minute by my watch. Wait."

On the minute a cannon roared. Gabriel's hands flew to his ears. Then he dropped them, looking foolish.

"That," Saugrain said happily, "is a sunset gun. In the morning it may speak again or there may be a trumpet call. I forgot to say that the American soldiers are now living in the Spanish barracks."

"But will the people in town understand?" Gabriel asked.

"Not all at once," the doctor said, "but it will come. Some day there may be a new Government House with a clock tower, or a church able to support a steeple."

"Also," Gabriel added, "when more Yanquis come, there will be clocks in all the houses. There are six now, I believe."

"I don't doubt it," Saugrain said. "Madame Saugrain has already spoken for one in our hall."

Gabriel's scarred face shone with sudden radiance.

"M'sieu Docteur," he said, "if you are here and Madame and the young ladies and the small son, then I, too, must be content. I thank you for making all things clear to me. With your leave, I will now go and calm Hortense before the stupid animal kicks down the wall of our stable."

PART V

Dr. Anthony ⚜ Saugrain

One ∽

Afterward it grieved Saugrain to admit that, with all his admiration for Amos Stoddard, he never came to know the man. Major Amos Stoddard of the Artillerists—for his smooth handling of the transfer of government he drew a promotion—came to St. Louis in February with a small trunk, holding extra articles of clothing, much paper, and money to cover his expenses, attended by a soldier orderly. On the thirtieth of September he departed with the same accouterments and the same orderly, leaving behind him hardly a mark of his presence.

This was due to no fault in Major Stoddard. He had his orders and he obeyed them to the letter. He occupied Government House, but he was not a governor. His command was temporary and purely military. He directed a count—the first American census—of the inhabitants of St. Louis and the settlements to the south and west which looked upon St. Louis as their capital. In the case of a few disputes, he administered justice, making his decisions accord with statutes already on the books. Finally, he was most careful to alter in no way customs and practices as he found them, a fact which confused and frustrated criticism.

According to Saugrain's thinking, only two events of major importance occurred during Stoddard's six months in command, and neither was of his contriving. The first, the greater, was the departure of Captains Lewis and Clark on their voyage of exploration. By the first of May, after weeks of truly frenzied activity, the keelboat and the two pirogues were loaded and launched, and, with Captain Clark commanding, entered the Missouri River. Lewis remained in St. Louis, to complete and dispatch a final report to the President and to settle some personal business. He had compared vouchers with Stoddard, le Duc said, both men having exhausted their personal expense accounts, Stoddard by responding in kind to social courtesies extended to him, and Lewis by adding a few very special scouts to his company. They had satisfied their creditors with personal notes drawn against the United States Treasury.

As soon as his business in St. Louis was completed, Lewis was to take a shorter route overland, meeting Clark and the boats at the village of St. Charles on the right bank of the Missouri. It was this day, as one of small number of friends escorting Lewis to the rendezvous, that Saugrain knew he would never forget— the pale, cool early morning, mist rising from every ditch and pond, the sun veiled in mist as it appeared, the road a mere widening of a hunters' trail, the fresh, strong horses trotting briskly, ruthlessly ignoring bumps and depressions, the gentlemen alternately laughing and groaning. At last, there was the broad, rolling river, and there were the boats, waiting to ferry the visitors across; but there was no sign of Clark and the rest.

"Never fear, Monsieur Capitaine," the boss ferryman said to Lewis. "Captaine Redhead knows. He is on the way even now. We must hurry, to be in Saint Charles before he arrives."

While the carriages were assembling in St. Louis that early morning, a messenger, it seemed, had ridden off on a very fast horse, to carry the word to St. Charles that Captain Lewis was on the way. From St. Charles another messenger had ridden then to Captain Clark's camp, only two or three miles down stream. If the Redhead was ready, as he surely would be, he could come in sight any minute.

So then there were the boats, one for each carriage, riding the roll of the current, the bossmen shouting orders, the rowers pushing the water away with the blades of their oars until, with a sudden thrust, the boat nosed up a bank of sand and gravel to the edge of the Rue Principale.

This was the St. Charles waterfront. The town had been laid out, not on top of a bluff, like that at St. Louis, but on the slope

(156)

of a large hill almost as steep. The streets had been laid out parallel to the river, but recklessly close to the water's edge. In time of flood, Saugrain thought, the main street must disappear altogether—and no great loss, probably. The street was lined from end to end with huts—the infamous St. Charles grogshops. Saugrain had heard of them through Manuel Lisa. Any patron wanting to keep a crew on his boat always arranged his progress up the Missouri so as to avoid stopping at this trading post. It was because of these grogshops that Clark had encamped his flotilla below the town and held it there until word came that insured a quick pickup of the boss captain and no dangerous delay.

Leaving the waterfront then, the town seemed to gain respectability as it climbed the hill, but before Saugrain could more than glimpse a cross on a church, then whitewashed fences and magnificent trees, sounds from the river drew his attention back to the lower level. Down there Captain Lewis was saying goodbye to his friends and well-wishers. Before he could finish, the sounds from downstream had turned to shouts, answered from the shore. Then came a roaring cheer: "They're coming . . . here they are!"

Here they were, indeed, the keelboat leading, closely followed by the two pirogues. Loaded to capacity with men and supplies, all three boats rode low in the water. Oarsmen labored to make headway against the current, but all were in high spirits until the boats came abreast of the landing and the cheering crowd; and still no order had been given to stop or even to slacken speed. Then the shouts from the boats became groans, answered by jeers from the shore. In the midst of the hubbub Lewis, waiting close to the water, seized his opportunity and leaped aboard the flagship. Two minutes later the cabin hid him from view.

It was neither the spectacular arrival of the three boats nor Lewis's leap that Saugrain carried home with him that late afternoon. It was the going away. The mists which had hovered over the low places in the road in the early morning had now gathered in a patch of fog upstream. One by one, the keelboat first, then each pirogue, entered the fog; and suddenly all were gone—like phantoms. A great hush fell over those who watched.

"Maman," Saugrain said to Madame in the garden that evening, "I know how the people of Cadiz felt when they saw Columbus and his fleet disappear on their first voyage across the Atlantic. Our friends are not embarking on a journey across an ocean of which no man knows the limits. They will be on land or within reach of land the whole time, and yet, the peril, the greatest peril—entering the unknown—is the same for both companies. Even Captain Manuel, who has gone as far up the Missouri as any other, thinks he has not seen even one third of it. And the Missouri is no more than half the distance to the Pacific. They do not know, they will not know from day to day what lies ahead, not the nature of the land or the disposition of the inhabitants. As for us, our suffering will also be not knowing. For a week perhaps, we may have some sort of message. Then there will be no more. They will be lost to us until. . . ."

"Vigny," Madame interrupted, "where are they now—tonight—do you know?"

"Not far tonight," Saugrain said. "They had a late start. If they are as much as ten miles away from Saint Charles, that will be doing well."

"And they are sleeping now, Vigny, do you suppose?"

"Yes, of course," he said. "They will camp on shore, cook a little something to eat, find a rock for a pillow . . . why do you ask?"

"Because I know what I shall do in that case. I will make us a tisane now, and we will drink it. If they can sleep, why can't we?"

Two ⌒

Madame's prescription for calm acceptance of events both ordinary and extraordinary was as good as any. Summer was very tranquil. In the midst of it, Governor de Lassus received his marching orders and, with the Spanish garrison, minus two soldiers, departed—for Florida, it was said, leaving in the keeping of Antoine Soulard his small mahogany trunk. Saugrain, seeing it at the Soulard residence, raised his eyebrows in question. Soulard in reply raised his, but gave no other answer. Le Duc was more communicative.

(158)

"Personal correspondence, I think," he said. "The Teniente did not think it advisable, perhaps, to take it with him to a new Spanish command."

The intimation that Don Carlos had a personal life, apart from and perhaps in conflict with his official duties, sent Saugrain off into one of his deeper meditations, but, before he could solve that puzzle, he himself was involved in a situation open to question— at least on his own part. One September day, shortly after noon, a message came to him from the House of Government. A wooden box, very heavy, addressed to him, had arrived that morning with mail from New Orleans. Would the doctor at his convenience call at the House and identify the box and state his wishes for delivery of the same? A wooden box, very heavy . . . his books? The thought flickered like a weak flame in Saugrain's mind, then went out. Not after all this time, not possibly; but then what?

"Please say to Major Stoddard that I will come right away," he ordered the messenger, and hurried off to the stable to rouse his coachman.

The box did contain his books. Battered, stained with the ocean's brine and some mold, he could have sworn it was the same box that he had stowed in a closet in Paris fourteen years before this. If they were his books, where had they been in the time that had passed since he had been told that they were on the way? The original shipping directions were almost obliterated. Still, they were legible: Dr. Antoine Saugrain, Post St. Louis, Territory of Louisiana, America, via New Orleans. Added to this was other, more recent writing. Deliver to St. Louis. Order of James Wilkinson, Governor, Territory of New Orleans. Abruptly he turned to Major Stoddard, and le Duc like a shadow behind him.

"I am convinced," he said, "that these are books belonging to me, which my family put on a ship for New Orleans two years ago. Have they been in New Orleans two years? Why? And why was it necessary for the Governor . . . but I should not ask. I am grateful to him for discovering the books and sending them. Are there charges?" Le Duc shook his head, leaving it to Major Stoddard to answer the query.

"No charges," he said, "since the Governor sent them. Shall I have the box placed in your carriage? Good."

(159)

Le Duc then followed Saugrain outside.

"You are disturbed about the Wilkinson touch, are you not?" he asked.

"I should not be disturbed about anything," Saugrain said. "I had given up the books for lost."

"I imagine that could still have happened," le Duc suggested. "They probably reached New Orleans when everything there was in a state of confusion and were pushed aside until things began to clear. The General. . . ."

"I did not know about his being named Governor," Saugrain said. "I have been so concerned about this post that I didn't think in terms of New Orleans."

General Wilkinson was only a partner in the government, le Duc explained. A Mr. Claiborne had been named to the post first; but, since he had no military experience, and the Territory of New Orleans was surrounded by Spanish provinces, pirates, and uneasy Indians, he had asked for protection; so General Wilkinson, having had some experience in dealing with all these dangers, had been named a co-governor for the safety of New Orleans.

It was the varied experience of General Wilkinson that troubled Saugrain. "I wish I could think of his sending the books as a coincidence," he said. "You will admit he follows me rather closely."

"Once in five years or so?" le Duc said. "If the box of books was in a corner of a warehouse at the harbor, Governor Wilkinson could have seen them as he made a tour of inspection. His curiosity would have been aroused. He probably wrote his order then and there. You know it was a coincidence."

Wishing to believe that le Duc was right, Saugrain was able, before reaching home, to recover most of the jubilance he had felt on learning that the books had come. So he called Michau Père to look at them and plan a way of placing them where they belonged—in the Saugrain library. Michau Père's first movement was to rip off part of the cover to the box—the board with most of the black writing.

"Ah?" he said. "That one? Again?"

With dignity, he hoped, Saugrain explained about the governors. "So," Michau concluded, "we have no governor and New Orleans has two. That is the way it happens in a republic. One never knows what to expect."

Three ∽

Perhaps the safest way to grow accustomed to a new government was to do no expecting. Saugrain, at least, completely absorbed in the second most notable event of the Stoddard period—the safe arrival of his books—let the days glide by, with the result that suddenly one morning he knew the end of September had come, Stoddard was leaving, and he must ask Willy to hurry the horses into town if he was to reach the House of Government in time to say good-bye. With all that haste he arrived on time, to find the House of Government full of other late well-wishers, and the only unhurried person present—Major Stoddard of the Artillerists.

"Is it permitted," Saugrain asked, when his turn came to make his farewells, "to ask where you are going from here, Major?"

"Home," Stoddard said; then, seeming to realize how the syllable had sounded, he added, "to await further orders."

"And where is home?" Saugrain pursued, determined to have his full turn.

"Woodbury, Connecticut." For an instant the firm, thin-lipped mouth relaxed almost to the point of smiling, but not quite; and Saugrain found himself being pushed—gently—towards the door. He did not mind. Connecticut, he was thinking. Woodbury, Connecticut—the first from there I ever knew, and I did not know this one. Will there ever be another from there in his place? Who knows?

The next day, and for almost two months after that, Michau Père's appraisal of the situation in St. Louis and surrounding territory was correct. Except for a brief supervisory visit by General William Henry Harrison, Governor of Indiana Territory, St. Louis and Upper Louisiana had no governor.

"Congress," le Duc said, "is studying how to handle the large plot of ground that the President took off Bonaparte's hands."

However, with or without supervision, life went on, and finally, on the first day of November, word came that Congress, with the President's approval, had solved the problem. Upper Louisiana, beginning at a certain parallel—say at the mouth of the Arkansas River, to use a more familiar term—would henceforth be known as the Territory of St. Louis, taking its name, as did the Territory of New Orleans, from its capital city. It would have, not two governors, but a governor and a territorial secretary, appointed by the President, and a General Court elected from and by the citizenry, with the right to make the laws governing the Territory. The governor and the secretary had not yet been named and might not appear before the coming year; but, in the meantime a military commandant, empowered to act as a deputy governor, had been chosen. He was already on his way west.

He arrived soon afterward—a man of action who was a complete opposite of Major Stoddard. Robust, hearty, as outgiving and outspoken as Stoddard was restrained and reticent, Colonel Hammond proclaimed Virginia as his birthplace, although at the time of his appointment he had resided in Georgia, the southernmost of the original American colonies.

"Mind you," he said frankly to a spontaneous board of inquiry, calling itself a committee of welcome, "I did not want this honor. There I was, living in comfort and ease on a fine plantation, just enough hunting and racing and visiting to keep me from rusting. I had been elected to a seat in the House of Representatives. Mrs. Hammond was figuring on taking a house in Washington for part of each year, when along came the President, urging me to do him and you all a favor by accepting this assignment. Temporarily, he said. Now there is a word not to be trusted—but Thomas Jefferson is a very persuasive man.

"No," he said a minute later, "really it wasn't anything he said that trapped me. It was something behind his words. Samuel, I thought, this is adventure. Have you had any since Yorktown? Are you ready, still in your forties, to retire to slippers and an easy chair? I said no to that, so here I am."

Here he was—six feet and some inches tall, all bone and sinew and spirit. A gentleman born and bred, and tough as rawhide.

"Indians?" he said. "Fought them in Pennsylvania and Virginia when my beard hardly showed."

(162)

When very little older, he had joined in Lord Dunmore's war on the western Virginia frontier, risking his scalp in a bloody battle on the Great Kanawha. Before that Daniel Boone had not been able to get a foothold in Kentucky.

"I hear," he said, "that the old scout has wandered out this way now, hunting and trapping and making salt on a land grant above here on the Missouri. I must look him up one of these days, and pay my respects."

But the part of his past that he relived most fondly belonged to the American Revolution, especially the last year of that war, when he, with Light-Horse Harry Lee and other southern hot-bloods, had officered the cavalry in General Nathanael Greene's army, then engaged in chasing Tarleton through the Carolinas and Georgia, finally driving Cornwallis north into Virginia, to be trapped on the Yorktown Peninsula. It was in the last fighting of the Revolution that he had become a colonel. The plantation he mentioned was a later gift from grateful Georgia.

Saugrain listened to the talk, fascinated to the point of speech-lessness. Connecticut, he thought, and now Virginia. Two regions, two divisions of the same republic, but so different! Two men sharing a common devotion to one country, but hardly speaking the same language.

Hammond did not arrive with a small trunk and an orderly. He marched over a maze of land and water routes like a patriarch of old. His family followed—his wife and children, with a couple of nephews added for good measure. He brought his slaves, his hunting dogs, his horses. Reaching St. Louis and finding there no vacant dwelling large enough to accommodate his kith and kin, to say nothing of servants and animals, he divided the whole lot, parceled them out in a variety of shelters, proceeded at once to purchase a likely quarter square on Main Street, three squares south of Government House, and built a residence suited to his needs.

A full two stories high, of frame construction, meaning over-lapping boards laid horizontally over upright timbers, it was the first purely American-style house in town. The curious weather-boarding, the spacious rooms, the width of the hall running through the house from front to rear, the many glass windows, furnished conversation for all beholders. A boss carpenter, sent

(163)

by General Harrison to superintend the building, had no difficulty in hiring helpers. It was like learning a new trade, they said, to assist with such building, to say nothing of the pay in American money.

"Have you made the acquaintance of the new *Commandant Militaire?*" Michau Père asked.

"Not yet," Saugrain answered thoughtfully. He had at present no actual point of contact. As a doctor, he had not been summoned to the fort by the lieutenant in command. In town, the seasonal attacks of ague were over and winter coughs and colds had not yet begun. As a mineralogist, he was busy, assaying ore samples for a new patron, named Moses Austin, who was interested in lead deposits. As curious as any other about the Military Commandant, eager to know him, Saugrain felt he must wait for the right time, the right approach.

Four ⌁

Opportunity came on a bright day late in November. Madame Saugrain was in her garden, spreading with Gabriel's help a litter of leaves and dried flower stalks over the roots of her more delicate plantings. When she heard a horseman approach and saw him dismount, looking almost as tall as he had appeared while still in the saddle, she knew who he was. She had just time to remove the gloves which Saugrain insisted on her wearing against cuts and scratches and shake out her skirts while Hammond tied his horse to a fence post, then strode through the gate and rang—to his surprise and Madame's dismay—the alarm bell.

"Good morning," she said hastily. "Please excuse the bell. I am Madame Saugrain. You are wishing to see the doctor?"

"Your servant, ma'am," Hammond said. "I am Colonel Hammond. Yes, I would like to speak to the doctor, if he is at home."

"Oh, yes," she said. "If you will please come into the house, I will call him."

She led the way to the front door while Hammond protested: "If he is on the premises, ma'am, can't I look for him myself?"

(164)

"No, please!" she said in consternation, remembering the laboratory as she had seen it a half hour earlier—the doctor in a smock, blowing up a fire with bellows, preparing to melt some rock. "You will be more comfortable in the house." And she walked on.

"If the doctor is busy. . . ." Hammond said, feebly.

"It is of no importance," she said, mounting the steps. The rock in question, she knew, might or might not be important, but there was no doubt about the visitor. "Enter, please." She showed him into the library, promised that the doctor would be present in one minute, surely it would not be much more, and fled to the rear of the house.

On reaching the laboratory, Madame found it an inferno of heat from a roaring fire, the doctor in his most worn smock preparing to hang over the flames an iron pot full of crushed rock, his face smudged, his eyes red-rimmed, his hair on end. She had to raise her voice to an undignified scream to make him aware of her presence. Seeing her finally, he puckered his mouth, studied her for a half minute, then with a sigh set his iron pot down on the hearthstone.

"What is it?" he asked.

"Vigny," she demanded, "where is your coat? While I brush it, will you please remove the smock—and comb your hair? You have a visitor—in the house, thanks be to God, in your library. So, will you please wash carefully—the face as well as the hands?"

"Who?" he asked now, removing the smock and turning to his washbasin.

"The new Governor," Madame said with emphasis.

Excitement still held her—to such an extent that the doctor was at the rear door of the house before she recalled a smudge under one eye which he had missed in washing. She sagged a little at that, then resolutely shook herself and straightened her back. Colonel Hammond was a fine, rich gentleman and the Governor Commandant; but her husband was still the most distinguished gentleman in the community. Having settled that to her satisfaction, she closed the door of the horrible laboratory and hurried over an outside path around the house and back to Gabriel and her garden.

When Saugrain reached the library, Hammond stood before his

(165)

desk, studying the new bookshelves which now filled the corner above it, each shelf crammed with books. Some were small books, the frayed edges of paper bindings showing that they had had much use. Others even more frayed had no covers. On the other hand, there were many volumes, both large and small, handsomely bound in leather, now somewhat marred but still whole and elegant. His books from France! He himself could not enter this room without making obeisance before them, but he was surprised to see the Virginian examining them so raptly.

Since Hammond plainly had not heard him come in, he took a minute to study the man. What a man he was! Smelling of leather and horse, he had brought the vigor of the outdoors into the house. How well he wore his uniform! The dark green, full-skirted coat showed no insignia of rank but was definitely military. So were the buff breeches, tucked into high riding boots. A light riding crop had the air of a sword. There he stood . . . but it was not polite to study a stranger and guest from the rear.

"Good morning, Colonel!" Saugrain said.

The instant of surprise passed quickly. This time it was the tall Virginian who seemed hesitant. Saugrain felt compelled to put him at ease.

"I am honored by your call, Colonel," he said. "You are not, I think, in need of my professional assistance."

"No, thank God!" Hammond said, then retreated. "Pardon me, Doctor. I mean to say my health is good, and nobody in my house is ailing at present, but. . . ."

Mrs. Hammond had sent him. If they were to live in this town where they were strangers, she thought it most unwise not to have an understanding with a physician who would come to their assistance if they or their dependents should become ill or have an accident.

"And I was recommended," Saugrain supplied. "That was my good friend le Duc. Everyone goes to him for information. Would you believe that he is not a native? He came here from France only two years before I moved my family here from Kentucky. Our surveyor general is also a Frenchman. He was once an officer in the French army. Continually new and interesting people arrive. I shall be happy to attend your family—within the limitations of my knowledge."

(166)

"I am not concerned with your limitations," Hammond said. "I was looking over your books when you came in just now. Fact is, I was counting. I had reached two hundred."

"Do not count any more," Saugrain begged. "I believe the number is a little over four hundred. I have tried to count them myself several times since they came, but I am stopped always by something which I feel I must read immediately. I forget then to put down the number at that point, and there goes my count."

"What I should really like to know," Hammond said, "is how many have you read?"

"All of most," Saugrain said. "Part of all, and at least part of the rest."

Some were schoolbooks, he pointed out, taking the smallest and oldest gently from its place. Others he had accumulated as the years went by. They made a sort of record of his education. In a way their adventures had paralleled his own. Originating in France, with only a few importations, they had survived the French Revolution. They had crossed the Atlantic Ocean and arrived finally in New Orleans; there they had been detained a while, until one day one of the two American governors had discovered the box, recognized his name on it, and sent it on to St. Louis.

"So here we are," Saugrain finished, sounding less jubilant than he wished, "the books and I, reunited at last. A strange story, is it not?"

"Very," Hammond said—too quietly. "Do you happen to know which American governor did you this favor?"

There it was—the question. It had to be answered. Concealment would have been absurd.

"Yes," Saugrain said. "General Wilkinson's name was on the box."

Hammond froze. Color left his face. His eyes narrowed. His genial mouth tightened. One saw then the smashing, slashing cavalryman pursuing Tories.

"James Wilkinson," Hammond said, as one might name a venomous reptile. "A friend, Doctor?"

"No!" Saugrain denied on the instant, then quickly sketched the three occasions when the name by accident had been linked to his—the meeting at Gallipolis, the list of potential settlers

(167)

for St. Louis, and now the books. "We are not even acquaintances," he finished. "Is it not strange that he should remember my name?"

"No," Hammond said bluntly. "Thieves and traitors collect and store such information, never knowing when a friend may be needed. As for sending the books, that, like food for the starving, is the sort of gesture he likes to make. Vain, pompous"—glitter was bright in the Colonel's eyes—"and the damnedest scoundrel ever to elude the hangman; but there! I have spoiled your pleasure in recovering the books. I have used too much of your time. I'll take myself off now."

"No—please!" Saugrain said. "You have sounded a warning. You have indicated that you know this man much better than I do. Your reference to a hangman interests me especially. Would you care to explain?"

Hammond's face warmed. "Fair enough," he said. "Glad to oblige. It is not a pretty story, but here it is."

It was a sordid tale, belonging to the American Revolution. James Wilkinson had been one of a group of discontented officers in the Continental Army who had conspired to pull General Washington down from his high command. The plot had been discovered before it came to a head, and failure seemed to have been the punishment dealt most of the plotters. Some, Wilkinson among them, had been allowed to surrender their commissions and quietly leave the army.

After that, Wilkinson had practised law for a number of years; but law and virtuous living seemed finally to pall on him, and he had sought reinstatement in the army. This was after the war was over, and general officers were scarce. So his request had been granted readily. Being a good soldier when he gave his mind to it, he had risen rapidly, finally reaching top command, which was what he had always wanted, but now was not enough.

"A natural-born conspirator," Hammond said. "Slippery as an eel, but some day . . . now really I must go. I know I interrupted some business you had on hand."

"It was nothing," Saugrain insisted. "When I have a few hours and am not needed elsewhere, I amuse myself with scientific experiment. Today I was preparing to examine some mineral deposits from an area near here. Are you interested?"

"I am, indeed," Hammond said. "I am told that there are rich deposits of lead in the territory."

"That is true," Saugrain said. "And other mineral resources wait to be explored. If you will accompany me to my laboratory . . . no, I have a better idea. You must learn the route preferred by my friends. Let me see. You will leave by the front door—to make your farewells to Madame Saugrain. Then, if you will mount your horse and ride halfway around the square, you will find a rear gate in our fence—with no bell. From it a path leads through a small orchard and a kitchen garden to two stone outbuildings behind the house. The lower one is a kitchen. The tall one, as high as the house, but separate, is my retreat. It is built high like that because when that explosion occurs which Madame expects daily to be the result of my experiments, only so much roof will be blown away. Have you the directions? Good! I will see you soon."

Minutes later Hammond was at the front gate, mounting his horse, and Saugrain was hurrying to his workshop. He was now fairly trembling with excitement. This Virginia gentleman—soldier, patriot, statesman—what an addition he would be to the town and territory! A commandant only? Another stopgap? Ah, he must not be allowed to leave. He must stay. He would stay, but only if some prospect for the future tempted him. Could he, Saugrain, find that hope? He would try.

A sharp knock, which could have been made by the head of a riding crop, struck the laboratory door. "Here I am!" Hammond called.

"Enter, please," Saugrain invited. "Enter, my friend."

Five ∽

Early in 1805 Dr. Saugrain decreed for himself a new holiday—March 9. On that day in 1804, all of Louisiana had become, formally and forever, United States territory. The ninth of March, therefore, would be for the rest of his life his New Year's Day; and he would so celebrate it.

The celebration was as unique and personal as the idea. It

began with a decree of isolation, covering even his household. Nobody was to visit his den or disturb him there—except Gabriel. He needed Gabriel for the second act of ceremony, which was a complete and thorough cleansing of the laboratory—to the point of sterilization. Gabriel was delighted, not to say extreme in his enthusiasm, Saugrain thought as the day wore on; but since he had instigated the confusion, he made up his mind to endure it. He had promised, as soon as Gabriel had finished cleaning all the shelves and cabinets affixed to the walls, to arrange his possessions—treasures and trivia—in absolute order. Naturally, nothing would remain just where he put it; but for twenty-four hours, perhaps . . . he had a new thought. This afternoon—no later—he would hold a levee, inviting his family to view the miracle. This would include the Michaus, to be sure. Even Aristide?

More soberly thoughtful now, and still waiting on Gabriel, Saugrain set himself on a chair out of Gabriel's path and gave his attention to this ever-present problem. Aristide, having assisted Saugrain—seldom to the doctor's advantage—during the past two years, had now at thirteen been enrolled—most unwillingly—in what might become a Latin school, conducted by a young priest sent to St. Louis from Vincennes, Indiana. Incipient rebellion on the boy's part had been crushed by a firm father and a hardly less positive brother-in-law.

"Look, Aristide," Saugrain reasoned, "you have now decided that you wish to be a physician. How can you be a physician of repute without some learning? I can show you how to roll pills; but do you understand the elements that go into their composition? I know. It is all somewhere in the books, but you find reading books of science laborious at present. If you had studied longer and more industriously under our good schoolmaster Trudeau—but no matter. There is now this young seminarian . . ."

Aristide, made desperate by this homily, interrupted by offering to study everything else faithfully if he could be excused from lessons in Latin and Greek. Why must he study those?

"Education," Saugrain said, "is a harvesting of knowledge. Latin will not be easy for you. Greek will be even more difficult, but often translation impresses facts about people and events on one's mind . . . but I see I am talking beyond your comprehension. Do your best, Aristide. I am paying for this schooling and your

(170)

papa has sworn to make you study. You will suffer, but you will learn—about medicine and many other mysteries."

At this point in his reflections Saugrain's mouth twitched and his eyes sparkled as he thought of his young brother-in-law sweating over exercises, sometimes far into the night, within easy reach of his father. He might still grow to be a man. For now at least he was not omnipresent in this laboratory. So much for Aristide. It was now time for Saugrain to return to the immediate business at hand.

The cleaning had gone very well. As he dusted bottles, canisters, and boxes and set each in some new and unfamiliar place which he was sure to forget, Gabriel began spreading water over larger surfaces such as windows.

"The mantel next," Saugrain directed, "if you please. Then I will move my instruments from the table and you can wash it."

"M'sieu, I am through with the mantel. I am waiting."

Quickly Saugrain picked up his microscope, then his apothecary scales. Both needed adjustment, but that must wait. He transferred his Leyden jars and other electrical equipment to the mantel, then took time to laugh as he set Franklin's portrait down in a nest of wires.

"M'sieu," Gabriel said with infinite patience, "I am now finished with the table."

"Good!" Saugrain said. "It will make an excellent island."

Soapy water was now spreading over the floor. He reached sanctuary just in time to escape the tide and sat there until Gabriel went off with his pails and brooms and brushes. A table top was as good a place as any for meditation and reflection.

The winter just past had been remarkably pleasant. In December he had received a long letter from his mother in Paris, in response to one he had written to say that his books had come and he treasured them. After giving a good report on the family in France and saying how happy it made her to think of him in his beautiful home with his charming wife and his children, now a son among them, she had ended with a motherly admonition. She understood that he was pleased with the change of governments, but begged him not to fall a victim of the American's great fault—taking too serious a view of everything. Prosperity was good. Money one must have, but when did he have any fun?

Did he laugh? Did he sing? Above all, did he dance? He had always been fond of dancing.

Chère Maman, he thought from the table top, I can truthfully say I have done all you advise. Gay parties, from sleigh rides to balls, American and French citizens alternating as hosts, had made light of gray skies and snowstorms. As for dancing, he did well enough in French quadrilles, the more dignified pace being kinder to his weaker leg than the lively stepping of a Virginia reel. However, before the winter ended, the reel had often borrowed the pattern of a quadrille, keeping still its lively pace. Presently the two forms of dancing would blend into some new design, he supposed. Very gay, Chère Maman, I assure you.

The picture of the town had also begun to change. New demands for stone from the bluffs had sketched more than one short cut from the river to the principal or main street. One of these paths met a cross street which was the north boundary of the Place d'Armes, then went on west, passing the Auguste Chouteau estate, then mounted a second rise, now generally spoken of as "the Hill." La Rue Bonhomme, old timers had named this lane; but, if it became as prominent a street, as many prophesied, that name would be lost. With trade on the Mississippi now open to all comers, a public market building was being planned, to stand at the foot of it.

Saugrain on his table top stretched his legs and chuckled. The Yankee invasion had begun, and not a day too soon. Old structures, such as the houses of whitewashed wooden posts, the fortifications, the wooden church, had begun to crumble. They would be replaced soon by newer, stronger buildings.

Old customs would go the same way. The post office was a sample. His window sill, always slightly absurd, was now utterly inadequate, thanks again to open lanes of travel and the need for communication with all parts of the nation. So now there was a post office in town, with an official postmaster named by the Postmaster General in Washington. Far from objecting to the loss of his window callers, Saugrain was delighted, especially when he learned the postmaster's name—Rufus Easton—and that his birthplace was Connecticut.

That was, however, about all of Connecticut in the Easton story. Before coming to St. Louis, he had practised law in New

(172)

York state, then in Washington. He was present in the Capital when Jefferson's land purchase was the leading subject of debate. Undismayed himself, he had decided immediately to be among the first to enjoy the opportunities offered by the new Territory. He arrived in St. Louis in October of 1804, and his order to establish a post office there had come so soon after that as to make it seem that he might have carried it there in his own pocket.

Within a week of his arrival, he bought the large stone residence of Joseph Roubidou on Main Street and, reserving that as a residence for his family, proceeded to make over a small stone house on another corner of the same square, but also facing on Main Street, into his conception of a post office.

A wooden partition from floor to roof divided the building into two rooms. The one in front, opening on the street, provided a place under roof where a person calling for his mail could wait if it was not ready or if nobody was there to give it to him. The room behind the partition opened on a path which led to the stone house, also to Main Street at that end of the square. There was no way of passing from the front room to the back room. The partition had only a single window in the middle, where mail was handed to the person claiming it after he had paid the postage. No mail was given out at Mr. Easton's post office until the costs were settled.

Also in the partition wall there was a clever arrangement of small boxes, each marked with one letter of the alphabet. This made sorting the mail go faster. Likewise, it enabled Mr. Easton to find a letter quickly when asked for. People who could not sign their names learned at least their own initials and the large gold letters above the delivery window which spelled UNITED STATES MAIL.

Mail was given out promptly and correctly soon after it came in, and it came more frequently now because it traveled by overland routes as well as the rivers; but it was still anything but regular.

For example, it was January of 1805 before the postmaster or anyone else knew the results of the previous year's presidential elections. Mr. Jefferson had been elected to a second term of four years; but there was a new vice president replacing Aaron Burr, who in the summer before the elections had challenged Alexander Hamilton, a Revolutionary hero and a member of George Washington's Cabinet, to a duel which had resulted in Mr. Hamilton's death. Whereupon Mr. Burr, knowing that further political advancement for him was, for the time at least, out of the question, had resigned from his office as Vice President and gone into exile—it was not generally known where.

"So you see, Antoine," Michau Père said, "that is how it goes in a republic. You have opposing parties and elections. Everybody votes. One man goes up, another falls. Confusion reigns instead of a king."

What Saugrain saw most clearly on this March day of 1805 was that the chief obstacle confronting a republic as extended in area as the United States of America had come to be was the difficulty of communication between the Capital and, say, St. Louis. The duel, the death of Hamilton and the flight of the Vice President had happened in July. To Saugrain it was a monstrous affair, so monstrous that the news should have been in the first dispatches from Washington; but they had contained only warnings of new acts of Congress concerning the government of distant territories. It was not until the November elections were reported that one heard. Now, meditating on the year and this scandal, Saugrain recalled that two residents of Saint Louis— Colonel Hammond and Rufus Easton—were still living in the East when the duel occurred, but neither had talked about it in St. Louis. Why not? Was it considered by them and others merely scandalous and of no great importance? Or had the President asked them . . . Nonsense!

At this point further musings by Saugrain were interrupted by a sharp rapping on the laboratory door. He recognized the sound at once.

"Come in, Colonel," he called, and was off the table and standing when Hammond appeared, sniffing the air.

"What in damnation goes on here?" Hammond demanded. "Are you moving?"

"Every article in this room," Saugrain informed him, "has been moved at least twice today. No, I am not moving away, if that is what you mean."

"Exactly what I mean," Hammond snorted. "You had me

scared for a bit. The whole place reeks . . . soap? I had expected to smell deadlier fumes here."

In this short time Saugrain had made a few observations of his own. Hammond's ruddy face was red from something more than wind. He sputtered about the sterile laboratory because in looking around he did not need to face Saugrain directly, a maneuver most unusual for him. He was troubled by something—troubled and angered. In one hand was his riding crop; in the other, a roll of heavy white paper. If he did not lay it down soon, it would be marked permanently by his clenched fist.

"May I offer you some wine?" Saugrain said soothingly, thinking as he spoke that something warmer on his stomach, like a bowl of soup, would be better. "Perhaps I can find a bottle."

"I doubt it," Hammond said. "Thank you, no. I am near enough to apoplexy without stimulant. I'm here on business. Fresh from the council chamber and in need of other cheer. I"—he saw the doctor studying the roll of paper—"oh, I forgot. I brought this . . . it came by mail—my mail, but it's for you."

"Mail has come?" Saugrain asked.

"Sacks," Hammond said. "You probably have some letters, but our good postmaster did not offer them to me for delivery—not without your order. Meantime there is this scroll—open it, man! What has become of your curiosity?"

Stifled by too many questions sprouting all at once, Saugrain could have told him, but without words he laid the roll on the table, the better to hold it flat as he opened it. The first symbol to appear was the American eagle, wings outspread, holding the American motto: *E pluribus unum,* and below, the striped shield. He felt his eyes and his heart dilate. Farther on, the text, elegantly and clearly lettered, swam so that he could not make out a word until his own name, in black capitals, jumped out at him: DR. ANTHONY SAUGRAIN. Still further on were two words which he in his dazed condition could not begin to comprehend.

"Jesu!" he said prayerfully, "what does this mean: 'Surgeon's Mate'?"

Hammond laid back his head and laughed. "I wondered," he said, "how that would strike you. A holdover, my friend, from our British thralldom. Like quoting the price of cotton in pounds sterling. The equivalent, I should say, of post surgeon. You have

(175)

an army commission there, if you will accept the terms. You haven't read a word, have you, except those in tall letters? You should, you know."

The words were stately: "Reposing special trust and confidence in the patriotism and valor of DR. ANTHONY SAUGRAIN, I have nominated him by and with the consent of the Senate, SURGEON'S MATE in the Army of the United States, to take rank. . . ."

"I have you to thank for this, Colonel," Saugrain said.

But Hammond protested. The doctor had friends in Washington, he thought, with much more influence than he had. There was Meriwether Lewis for one, or it could have been Major Stoddard who had recommended him, or the late Spanish Governor. "Have you noticed the date on the commission?" he asked. "You have been on army pay since the nineteenth of January. The paymaster should be making his rounds soon."

"*Pesos fuertes!*" Saugrain said softly.

"I wouldn't count on that," Hammond said. "We have a nice mint going now in Philadelphia, but the Treasury distributes the coin with caution. You will probably receive a Treasury note, but it will be taken, I am sure, at least for taxes."

Taxes—Saugrain thought again of his father-in-law. While still a subject of Spain, Michau Père had bought the little house in which he lived, and the land on which it stood, with no tax attached to the ownership. Why, then, he demanded, did the new government, having confirmed his right to the property, present such a bill? In the first place, knowing no English, he could not read what was written on the paper. In the second place, he would not pay the tax anyhow.

Quietly, knowing the futility of persuasion, Saugrain had pocketed the bill and paid the Michau taxes along with his own. Now he wondered what his good Bon-père would find to say when he saw the President's commission, and later a Treasury note in payment for Dr. Anthony's Saugrain's services.

As Hammond had advised, Saugrain read on:

The rank of surgeon's mate was his as long as he chose to keep it. Only the President or a successor could remove him. At the end there was the President's neat signature: "Th. Jefferson, President," supported by that of the Secretary of War—Henry

(176)

Dearborn. He would frame the commission and hang it—where? Madame, his wife, would want it in the house, where she could show it to their friends, but. . . .

"Now about your quarters at the new fort?" Hammond suggested.

There had been talk of a new fort ever since Major Stoddard's time. Fortifications planned in the early days to encircle the town on the landward side had never been completed. Only a few bastions and here and there a trench indicated the intent. The bastions were now beginning to crumble. The round tower and the barracks, the latter built after the Indian attack of 1780, were still in use, but the spread of the town up and over the Hill was already leaving them behind. New limits must be charted, but who would know where to place them?

For that matter, who could say what was the western border of Louisiana? It was a shadowy line, somewhere far to the west, so far that one could hardly imagine hostility from that direction. To the southwest, somewhere near the Arkansas River, was the Spanish frontier. To the north there was Canada and the power of England. Locating a fort for the new St. Louis would be a problem for the new Governor to solve when he took office. Still, Hammond had said to the doctor, "your quarters," as if they were ready and waiting.

"I can at least give you the location," Hammond said, with a wry mouth.

But the new Governor had not been named. He would take office in July.

"He is here now," Hammond said. "He arrived late yesterday from New Orleans. He brought the mail."

"I hoped it would be you," Saugrain said.

"No chance of that, I'm afraid." Hammond tried to speak lightly, but his tone was rueful. "I left the old army with the rank of lieutenant colonel. My peacetime promotion to a full colonel is about as high as I can hope to rise now. That is no competition for a major general. It is General James Wilkinson, my friend. It was to be expected, I suppose. The future growth of Saint Louis will be based on its military as well as its commercial importance. Wilkinson may have asked for the command or, more likely, the President bestowed it upon him as the high-ranking

(177)

General of the army. In that case it was an order. Wilkinson had no choice but to accept the post. It was that or return to the practice of law. But you are being very quiet, Doctor. Does this lessen your pleasure in your new commission?"

Saugrain glanced over the top line—that about patriotism and valor. No, he said, he was still proud of the President's trust in him. As soon as he learned what his new duties would be, he would arrange to handle them. He was not pleased with the Wilkinson appointment, but with Hammond's help. . . .

"Surely," he said in sudden alarm, "you are keeping your command?"

Hammond confessed that his first thought had been to resign at once, but he would wait now until he was forced out. He had bought land in St. Louis. He had made a few business connections. He liked the town. He liked its prospects. He would have no title or duties of even an interim governor, but Wilkinson might, for a while at least, find him useful as a military commandant.

"To be strictly honest," he said finally, "if I stay, it will not be for a noble reason. It occurs to me that this may be the place where James Wilkinson may finish in that hangman's noose I mentioned a while back. I may even get myself elected to the General Court here and help him along. Don't look so shocked, Doctor. What were we talking about when we got into this tangle? I remember. Your quarters at the new fort. You knew there would be a new fort? There will be, indeed. Wilkinson has chosen the site for it."

"Chosen?" Saugrain said. "Without looking around?"

He had looked, Hammond reported. He had not made the long trip to St. Louis just to deliver the mail. He had been up since early morning, looking over possible spots for a fort. Once he had seen this spot, he had made his decision. He had turned right back to town and his lodgings in the Pierre Chouteau mansion and sent out runners to call as full a meeting as possible of the General Court to hear his plan.

"Strategically," Hammond said, "the choice is fine—on the Missouri River. It had to be on one of the rivers, the Missouri preferably, but. . . ."

There were objections. Two thirds of the men present at the hastily summoned meeting were original settlers or their sons. They tried to vote down Wilkinson's choice. The Spaniards, they said, had put a fort in that place long ago, but the Missouri had driven them away. It was a terrible river when in flood. But the General had overruled their objections. The Spaniards, he said, had run away too soon. In spite of abandonment and flood water, foundations and parts of walls belonging to the original installations still were there. The necessary new buildings could be erected on those beginnings with a great saving of time and labor.

"He talked about water supply," Hammond said, "a spring and a stream—Coldwater Creek. There is no doubt that he will have his way about putting the fort where he wants it. He expected to spend the rest of the morning writing a report to Washington. Meanwhile I have orders to inspect the site in detail. How would you like to ride out there with me? Have you time?"

For time Saugrain had the rest of the day. Just one word made him hesitate.

"Ride?" he questioned.

"Oh, come," Hammond said. "If you would risk a saddle on one of my gentle mares, we'd see more of each other. I brought the wagonette. Well?"

That, too, Saugrain knew, was hazardous, with Hammond probably exercising a team of half-wild colts, but he asked only time to fetch a shawl from the house—to keep his back warm. Leaving the laboratory, he took up the commission, then laid it down. He would have firmly in his mind where he wished it to hang before he showed it to Madame, his lady.

Shortly after that he and Hammond in the wagonette had left the town behind and were rolling and bumping over what Hammond called "a sort of road," leading northwest to the village of St. Ferdinand on the Missouri River. That, however, was not their destination. When Saugrain finally had begun to count jolts instead of figuring distance, Hammond sighted wheel tracks branching off to the right and turned into them.

Progress was now rougher than before, the terrain unevenly up

(179)

and down, but following generally a downward incline. Hammond, keeping a tight rein on his team, suddenly pulled the colts to a halt.

"Hear anything?" he asked.

The rattle of the wagonette and the snorting of the colts had so filled Saugrain's ears that for a minute he heard nothing. Then, not far away, he imagined he heard the sound of swift water.

"What I am looking for," Hammond said. "Let's go."

Minutes later horse and wagon bounced and slid down a really precipitous slope, but landed whole on a wide stretch of rock and gravel, through which just ahead a sparkling stream raced and tumbled.

"Coldwater Creek!" Hammond announced. "We're here! There's a ford. It should be on a line with the road—" and he drove the colts into it and across.

"You can step out here, if you like," Hammond said. "I'll let the colts have a drink, then I'll tie them and we can look around."

Willingly, however awkardly, Saugrain slid over the wheel, then stood still in awe. "But, Colonel," he said, "it is beautiful. I don't wonder. . . ."

"Take your time," Hammond said. "The river is behind you. What is left of the old fort you will see better when I pull this wagon out of the way."

Saugrain could have cried out again at the widening vista. The level bed of coarse gravel was the floor of a deep valley extending—how far, he could not tell—possibly to the location of its fountain spring, which could be miles away. That the valley had been cut in the first place and later eroded and enlarged by swift water, swollen in repeated seasons of flooding, was not part of a first impression, although he was aware of both banks. On what was now the near side, the rise was gradual, seeming to level off as it rose into sloping but distinctly arable, habitable land. On the opposite side, as Saugrain could testify, all of the land was rougher and more precipitous. Most fortunately, the cart tracks had crossed the lower part of a hillside which mounted finally to a height from which he turned away, shuddering. If the river was beyond, as Hammond had indicated, the hill must

(180)

tower above it like . . . a St. Louis bluff. He was glad to return to the valley.

But the picture in that direction had now changed. The wagonette had concealed the ruins of a small building, half stone, half timber, placed against a background of trees. It stood there in warning, like a sentinel, abandoned to time and death and decay.

"Is that all that remains?" he asked in awe. It had been a proud fort. He recalled a proud name—something to do with a prince of the Asturias.

"Almost all," Hammond said grimly in answer to the question. Then, because they had spent most of what remained of the morning in driving to this spot, he divided the inspection. He would poke around among the ruins, while Saugrain looked over the river bank, giving special attention to the amount of level ground at the water's edge suitable for building. The General's plans included establishing a fur factory for the accommodation of Indian and white trappers and hunters nearby—a store with goods and groceries to exchange for the pelts, and the added convenience of a sutler's stand. He meant to bring in half a regiment of infantry this summer.

When he came to the river, Saugrain promptly forgot all requests and instructions. In the first place, the river was rising. Drift was scattered over the surface from shore to shore instead of being drawn into midstream. There were no marks of falling water on the trees. No sandbars showed. The nearness of the water to the top of the bank made him draw back. He had never before stood so close beside such a rolling mass. However, judging by the tree trunks, the water was not rising, and he laughed at his alarm. After all, March was not the season for great floods. Those came in May or June, when the snows melting on the distant mountains added their volume to streams swollen by spring rains. This small rise was due to a few freshets in the tributaries. The river would fall tomorrow.

Recalling then the report he was to give, he walked along the bank a hundred yards each way from the mouth of the creek, crossing when he needed to on a short causeway of stepping stones almost too regular in pattern to have been arranged that way by nature. Suddenly Hammond was calling.

Saugrain's report was brief. The river bank was smooth and

firm underfoot, and amply wide to hold a store or any other small structure; but, with the river so close, he would recommend that any building—cabin or landing dock—located there be raised on stilts, as was the custom generally where floods were frequent and unavoidable. The Missouri, he said solemnly, was a big river.

Very big, Hammond agreed. Had he seen any sign of such a structure having been built beside the river before this?

No, Saugrain said. He had seen only the water rolling past.

As for Hammond's inspection, he thought the small, abandoned building beside the creek might well have been a station for a guard. It was stouter than he had supposed, the foundations solid, only the wooden walls rickety. He thought he could have knocked them over with his cane, but had not done so, of course. Instead, prowling farther, he had spotted what looked like part of the roof of a second dilapidated building, near the edge of the high ground that walled in the valley along the right bank of the creek.

"I thought you might like to examine it with me," he said. "The view from the top ought to take in the whole panorama. I found a sort of path. I think we can make it."

The path was steep, rough, and in places crumbling, but they made it, Saugrain leading, because if he slipped Hammond could catch and hold him, whereas Saugrain could never have stopped Hammond. Both were breathing hard at the end of the climb. They welcomed a dash of March wind in their faces, but a following gust could have knocked either one over if he had not then stood, squarely braced, on two feet.

The hill seemed not nearly so formidable from the top. No higher than his town house, Hammond thought. The summit was a flattened dome. With a little grading, a platform of level ground would emerge.

"Not enough," Hammond grumbled, seeming disappointed. "It would hold a building or two, a small drill ground, but never a grand parade. A lookout. . . ."

Wherever the fort was built, surely a lookout. The Spaniards had thought so. That explained the skeleton building Hammond had spotted from below—a short colonnade of weathered posts —cedar, perhaps—supporting the tattered remains of a roof.

182)

"Shall we look at the valley from up here," Hammond said then, "before we enjoy the view of the river?"

The valley was all that it had promised to be, seen from the creek level, and more. Gently rolling land, it probably began by following the course of the creek, but extended far beyond that to the south and the west, its boundaries incalculable. Hammond turned from studying it, beaming.

"Magnificent farmland," he said. "Just enough timber for a man's needs. Plenty of water. I'd like one of those open glades for my own. With a strong fort at hand, to scare off the Indians. . . ."

Back to the problem of a fort. More soberly, perhaps more hopefully, they studied the hill and its approaches. Rough, rocky, steep in places, could they be tamed? If they could be reduced to some kind of order—say ground rising in a succession of easier stages, made accessible by a new road or roads—the hill, rather than the creek down below, could be made the focal point of . . . a cantonment, perhaps, instead of a fort?

"If Wilkinson means to move soldiers here by the regiment," Hammond pondered, "he needs a cantonment. But think of the labor, man, during the grading and the building of the roads, and afterwards, with soldiers living in the new quarters, every bit of water must be hauled uphill from creek or river."

But St. Louis, Saugrain reminded him, had from the beginning hauled water for its needs uphill from the Mississippi. The river would probably always be the main source of supply. Nobody complained. The town was placed high above the water to be safe from flood or other invasion. In the highest water, during forty years, the Mississippi had never more than lapped at the town's doorstep.

"But that is a town," Hammond argued. "A town grows slowly. Wilkinson wants at least half a regiment in log houses before autumn. He has other plans for next year and the year after that. He thinks it would be absurd to overlook the advantage of a spring that will supply a thousand men a day."

"So he will build here," Saugrain said, "on the lower level, knowing that the high ground would be better? Tell me, what will the valley down below be like if the Missouri should overflow —this summer or next?"

(183)

"Marshland," Hammond said briefly. "Under heavy rain, marshland. Well, how about a look at your river?"

They crossed the flattened dome, stepped to the edge, and drew back—both of them. The immensity of what they had seen was too awesome for ready acceptance. They looked at each other, smiled in feeble apology, and looked again. Immensity was still there, but they could face it now.

In contrast to the broken land, rough or gentle, on the opposite side of the hill, the picture here was darker, the forest growth, all the growth, denser, the land flatter, shaped not by a creek, however boisterous, but by two rivers.

"I was told," Hammond said, making talk, "that both rivers could be seen from here, but I hardly believed it could be so."

It was so—as if a meeting had been arranged. To their left, at some distance, the nearer of the two rivers, the Missouri, came around a great bend and took a southeasterly course which brought it past Coldwater Creek and the hill where they stood. The Mississippi, farther away, must have come down from the north and also turned, to run parallel to the Missouri. It was at first hardly visible, until one's eyes picked up the line and the glint of water. Farther along, the space between the two rivers narrowed, and the picture was clearer. "Marshland there, too," Hammond said, "that island."

It was not an island, Saugrain knew. It was a magnificent example of what his friend Lisa called a "point"—a green oasis of grass and other vegetation, including trees—to be found wherever two rivers met. The actual joining of these two was somewhere to the east, beyond his seeing but not far beyond. The space between them looked very narrow where distance ended the view.

"The Missouri," Saugrain said, looking down at the rolling water, "is truly the wild one, I believe. You called it my river just now, but I have lived here almost five years and this is only my second view of it." Wistfully he thought of the westward-bound voyageurs disappearing into the mist the year before, but Hammond now was not looking at rivers.

"This spot," he said abruptly, "do you know what I think? What a place for a citadel! I mean to say so in my report. What

(184)

I say may never reach Washington, and I may be citizen Hammond if it does, but I will write it so."

But now the morning was gone, and they were a long way from town.

"Stay up here a while longer, if you like," Hammond said to Saugrain. "I'll go down and feed the colts. I'll call when I am ready." Then, as he started down, he added, "Be careful on this devil's slide."

"You be careful," Saugrain called back. "If I fall, there will be less to carry away." But he would be careful, he promised. He would crawl, if necessary.

He was grateful then for a time alone. His impressions, thoughts and emotions were now in a hopeless tangle. A citadel, he thought. A fortress. Soldiers everywhere. Saws and hammers and the shouts of men, the crashing of trees. Quarters—a house for the commandant, a headquarters building, an officers' row and barracks. A citadel, commanded by a general not wholly to be trusted. How could that be? Did not Wilkinson have a commission reposing special confidence in his patriotism and valor? How could a man be unfaithful to such trust? If he should prove to be unworthy, what could another, knowing his perfidy, do against it? Nothing, perhaps, except stand guard.

With that, a blast of cold wind slapped him hard, and he hurried across the hill to that devil's slide which he must descend. As he reached it, a shout from below blew past his ears. "Coming," he called. "Look out!"

Crawling over the edge, he turned about and, with his face—also his coat and waistcoat—against the ground, groped for a foothold, found one, and eased himself downward. Steps were needed, he thought, or a platform here and there where a man could steady himself. Then he fastened his hand around a protruding root, groped for a second foothold with his good leg, found it, and was perhaps a good three feet below the summit. Again he found a handhold and groped for a footing, but this time found nothing.

Hammond called again, asking if anything was wrong. A man was down there looking for him. He had followed them out from town.

"Ask him to wait, please," Saugrain answered, and tried again, with no better success. Down at the creek, Hammond swore, saying something about a rock that he must have loosened in his descent; and another voice said, "Let me go, sir. I am a good climber. I'll get him."

A half minute later, strong hands seized Saugrain under his arms, and a healthy baritone rumbled cheerfully in his ear: "You can let go now—I'm holding you. I'm on good rock. Hurrah for you! Now for the next step. It looks easy."

Another minute and Saugrain stood beside the creek. Hammond was backing the colts to turn their heads toward home, and a young gentleman, comely and only a little red in the face from his rescue effort, was smiling and saying, "I have wanted so much to meet you, Dr. Saugrain. I remember you well from Philadelphia; but that was a long time ago, and you wouldn't remember. My card, sir, if you will allow me."

Six ✍

"But you have seen this young man only once," Michau Père objected. "It was kind of you to bring him here to your office, to hear what he had to say for himself. It was too cold outside, to be sure, for conversation. But. . . ."

The drive back to town had seemed very cold. Saugrain, his feet now practically in the warm ashes of a fire, shivered, remembering. The young man's lips had turned blue—his resistance diminished by hunger, as the doctor learned presently. That such a stalwart young man, well clothed although perhaps not warmly enough, should have admitted such privation! It had taxed his elegant manners to demur against accepting Colonel Hammond's invitation to ride back in the wagonette to the Saugrain laboratory. There, warmed by a good fire, also a little wine and a few biscuits, he had been able to talk more freely.

"You still know nothing about him," Michau continued.

"The essentials," Saugrain said. "His name is John Hamilton Robinson. He comes from Augusta County, Virginia."

"Wait, please," Michau begged. "That name is familiar. Hamilton—was it not a man by that name who was murdered by the late Vice President?"

"That Hamilton died as the result of a duel," Saugrain corrected. Strange how a man who spoke no English could select such a piece of news and remember it! "That is not considered murder."

"No?" Michau said. "That is how men in a republic settle their differences?"

"Occasionally," Saugrain admitted, although he could not see what bearing this had on the respectability of John Hamilton Robinson, who had said without embarrassment when asked that he was a nephew of the late Alexander Hamilton. His mother, Alexander's sister, was proud of the name that had been hers before her marriage and had insisted that both of her sons—Edward Hamilton and John Hamilton—should have it as their middle names.

As for the duel, Alexander Hamilton had attacked the Vice President violently in the public press, and Mr. Burr, charging that the statements were slanderous because untrue, had challenged Mr. Hamilton to a duel. Robinson in telling the story had showed no rancor. He seemed to think, as did Saugrain, that Mr. Burr's consequent political death and exile had been punishment enough for firing the fatal shot.

So, Michau concluded, the unpleasant notoriety connected with the affair and the family name had been the young man's reason for leaving Virginia. No? What, then, had brought him all the way to St. Louis?

"What brings others?" Saugrain demanded. "He hopes to make his fortune."

Did the doctor think it would turn out so? Saugrain, ignoring any insinuation in that two-edged question, said—more placidly than he felt—that it might take time. A change in government did not necessarily revolutionize everything all at once. John Robinson was a gentleman, well educated. He had studied medicine . . .

"Oh-oh!" Michau groaned. Had he not said over and over that, if the Yankees came in any number, there would be doctors

(187)

among them? Here was the first, and Saugrain had embraced him as if he were a kinsman, not a rival.

In a sense he was a kinsman, Saugrain felt, but how could he make this clear to his father-in-law? He could only repeat what he had always said in reply to Michau's fear of a town full of doctors familiar with American medicine. In science or business, it was healthful for a man to feel that he was running a race against others—possibly fleeter of foot. Otherwise one grew indolent, even dull.

"Besides," he concluded, "John Robinson at present is a competitor to nobody. He is a stranger—except that he had my name."

"I know that," Michau said. "He came to the house first in search of you. I was busy with accounts. Sophie and her sister, your wife, received him."

"And they did not offer him food?" Saugrain said. "A stranger and hungry?"

"Naturally not," Michau said. "A stranger without references, just your name on a piece of paper. They told him where you had gone and advised him to inquire about the road at the House of Government. They did not notice that the man was hungry because they were occupied with more interesting facts—that he was young, handsome, with beautiful manners, and spoke French. Considering their confusion, they acted sensibly, I think."

"They sent him away hungry," Saugrain said again, reproachfully. "He arrived in Saint Louis late yesterday—he had walked most of the way from Vincennes! Where or how he rested at night, I can only guess. Today he walked from here to Coldwater Creek."

"He is entirely without means?" Michau suggested hopefully.

No. He had had with him a draft for sixty dollars, drawn on a Charlottesville, Virginia, bank. He could have had it honored at Vincennes—by General Harrison, who knew his family—but for fear that he might waste the money if it were broken into small notes, he kept the draft whole, though it meant that he must walk the whole way and eat poorly. "I figured," he said, "if George Rogers Clark could walk that distance in midwinter with water up to his chin, I could do as well now with the rivers down."

(188)

He had smiled most appealingly, Saugrain recalled, making his confession!

"So, you endorsed his note," Michau said. "You still have not told me how he obtained your name. From General Harrison?"

No, that was another story. Robinson, as a boy, had visited Philadelphia with his parents in that same winter when a shipload of French émigrés, including Saugrain and the Michau family, had made port there on their way to the nonexistent Gallipolis. The story of their betrayal had aroused compassion and even more curiosity throughout Philadelphia. People gathered about the émigrés wherever they appeared, pointing out this one or that, especially the little man in the full-skirted black coat who was said to be a doctor and a protégé, in France as well as Philadelphia, of Benjamin Franklin. The boy, listening with both ears, had memorized the name—Saugrain—and later written it down on paper to keep. Now he declared that his near meeting had been the chief reason for his choosing to study medicine instead of becoming a merchant, as his mother had hoped, since her father had been a successful merchant in the French West Indies.

"A nice story," Michau Père said. "I can see you believe it, and I know two women who will be enchanted to hear it, but was it worth sixty dollars, do you think?"

"Yes," Saugrain said, restive under this questioning. For five years now Michau had complained because St. Louis held no prospect of a good marriage for either of his marriageable daughters. Elinor, now twenty-eight and seeming more frail each year, was no longer to be considered, but Sophie Marie, called Sophie, was superlatively charming—lovely to look at, as sweet and tender as she was beautiful, radiantly healthy, ready for whatever life had to offer. What she most wanted and needed, a lover, was at her door, and a grumpy father raised objections. Well, Saugrain, brother-in-law to charming Sophie, would not allow the opportunity to pass.

"Sixty dollars is not all," he said. "As soon as he settles somewhere and can send back directions for mailing, his mother has promised the same sum every month of the year."

Even that was not all. Some day John Hamilton Robinson

would share with his brother, Edward Hamilton Robinson, the
entire Virginia estate, now ably managed by their mother.

"Are you sure?" Michau Père said.

Seven ⌐

        Afterwards, when Saugrain had occasion to ask himself
if he might not have done better to borrow some of Michau
Père's caution with reference to Dr. Robinson, he could always
quiet doubt by recalling that at the end of the first year he would
have accepted Robinson for the same reasons which had caused
him to welcome the young man in the first place. John Hamilton Robinson was young, handsome, a gentleman in speech and
behavior, educated, ambitious, talented and—with an assured
monthly income of sixty dollars—anything but penniless. Saugrain himself had settled in St. Louis with less of everything
except experience, and that was something everyone accumulated
in time.

Robinson could have set himself up as a physician and won
favor quickly in St. Louis, but he would not consider competing
with his first and best friend in the town. Besides, for a stranger
to establish a good, steady practice would have taken longer, he
thought, than Saugrain said. So having a second skill, inherited
from his merchant grandfather, he hired himself out to another
trader, a dour Scotsman, named McKenzie, who after a month's
trial offered him a partnership in an independent store and fur
exchange which he meant to set up on the Missouri as near to
the projected cantonment on Coldwater Creek as the new Governor's plans would permit.

He would have hired himself out as a slave, he confessed to
Saugrain, if that had been necessary to prove himself worthy of
marrying Sophie Michau. She was so lovely, so sweet, so precious,
so . . . everything! He would love her and her only, and cherish
her all his life long.

In April he asked Michau Père's permission to call on Sophie,
his object being to win her heart and her consent to marriage.
Michau, for all his previous caution, offered only feeble resist-

(190)

ance. Robinson, it seemed, had had the wit to address Sophie's father in French. After that, other recommendations seemed minor. Michau capitulated. Dr. Robinson might call on Sophie, chaperoned by one of her two sisters, but there was to be no talk of marriage for the present.

"After all," he said, "you have lived here less than thirty days."

"Four weeks," Robinson said, but accepted the terms.

In May the betrothal was celebrated, but that did not end the waiting. A year, Michau said, just to be sure. Robinson turned pale and Sophie wept. They had thought of another month, but a year? It seemed eternity.

So then Robinson begged Sophie not to listen to her father, to run away with him at once. They could find a priest or justice of the peace—someone who would marry them. Where would Sophie like to live, he asked, rather than in this cruel town? There was Mexico. He had never been there, but it was said to be a great and beautiful country. Or he could take her home with him to Virginia. His mother would welcome them, he was sure.

Then it was Sophie who found the strength to resist temptation.

"No, John," she said. "Your mother would like to have you back home, but what would she think of me? What would we think of ourselves? No!"

"Who would believe that anyone so sweet could be so hard?" Robinson demanded of Saugrain. "She is tougher than any piece of leather her father ever handled."

Finally it was Sophie who selected the date for the wedding, artfully subtracting several months from the stipulated year. Since they could not be married in June, the perfect month for weddings, how about December 24, the day before Christmas? The wedding would start off the gay holiday season, with its visiting back and forth, and the New Year would find them settled in their own home.

She presented such a captivating picture that nobody seemed inclined to do any further calculating. So it was settled.

"And I warn you," Saugrain said sternly to Michau Père, seeing signs of the latter awakening from his daze, "don't ask for any changes now, or any further delay. I am surprised that they have yielded this much to your notions."

Eight ✍

If the lovers had dreamed that any crisis, large or small, could occur to threaten their happiness during the new interval of waiting, they would not have stepped into summer so cheerfully and hopefully. After all, seven months seemed to them very short compared to a year. How could they, or anyone else, know?

In July, climaxing a celebration of Independence Day with toasts and speeches in Mr. Didier's beautiful apple orchard, James Wilkinson became officially Governor of the Territory. A bluff, jovial man, with a kind word for the least citizen as well as the foremost, he made an excellent first impression. He enjoyed the company; he enjoyed the food and drink, especially the latter. If he took too much of that, he could not really be blamed. Having just arrived, if he drank with one he could not refuse another.

He was not as handsome as Saugrain remembered. His jowls were heavier, and as the afternoon wore on, his face at times turned alarmingly crimson. Of course, the day was warm and his uniform coat was too tight. When the crowd dwindled and he removed it, setting an example to others present, the red faded somewhat. Still, at its worst it had not looked good.

A friendly man, very kind, everyone said, with a charming gracious wife. No one could find a fault in her, so devoted to her big handsome husband! It was too bad the Wilkinsons did not plan to live in town. They had rented a house temporarily, but the general preferred to have his permanent home near the new fort. If the business of government or an important social affair called for his presence in town, he could travel back and forth swiftly and comfortably in his galley.

The galley already had a mooring place at the mouth of Coldwater Creek, and the General had selected and bought a site for his house adjacent to the area allotted by the Land Office for

(192)

the new cantonment. This came out later, when the allotted area proved inadequate for the cantonment, and the General, very fairly, sold the land at no profit to the Territory, asking only space inside the fort boundaries for a residence. It would have to be smaller than his original plan, but it would do.

Meanwhile, the initial preparations for building the fort had been completed—the laying out of company streets, the plotting of quarters, the felling of trees, the cutting and trimming of logs, plowing, widening and smoothing of the approaching road. Saugrain, venturing out that way alone with Willy in the brougham, found the road a boulevard compared to the original cart track used by himself and Hammond in March, and the hubbub in the valley all that he had anticipated. Wilkinson had held to his original plan for building on the lower ground, and nothing so far had suggested an error of judgment. The forest in the valley was somewhat devastated, but there were the logs, piled and waiting; a brick kiln was in the making; and the wrecked guardhouse had been made over into a stout, though small, administration headquarters for a new commandant in charge of construction—Major Russell Bissell of the First Regiment of Infantry.

His command was to be confined to the fort only, Wilkinson had assured Hammond. An officer on the building site was needed, and Hammond had surely enough duties in the rest of the Territory to justify his title of Military Commandant. Hammond had many duties, but he had begun at once to plan his retirement, and this time he would be really through with soldiering. He would stay on in St. Louis, but only as an interested spectator at the show which, he still insisted, would be played out there.

"Pull off to the side of the road, Willy," Saugrain said as they came near to the creek. "They've put a footbridge over the water for my convenience."

Major Bissell, through a window in the small guardhouse, must have seen the carriage come down the road. He could not possibly have heard the wheels. An erect, soldierly figure in a summer workday adaptation of an infantry officer's uniform—dark blue cotton shirt with white buttons, and white duck trousers tucked into stout gaiter boots—he met Saugrain at the far end of the footbridge and showed him to his quarters in the guardhouse at once, closing the door upon the frightful noises.

"A little warm, I know," he apologized, "but better than outside. What do you think?" And when Saugrain said that the house felt very comfortable, shaded as it was by trees, he seemed quite pleased.

"Good!" he said. "You are the doctor, aren't you? I've been expecting to see you here."

He knew why Saugrain had come. He wanted, naturally, to inquire about his quarters at the fort. No, he had not come too early.

"We can use a doctor," Bissell said. "Incidents and accidents, you know, a touch of sun, a mashed finger. Luckily nothing more serious."

"You have been fortunate in more ways than that," Saugrain reminded him. "No high water this summer."

The major had heard about the flood possibility. He agreed that it was fortunate that the rains that year had been scattered. There had been one or two threats, but nothing had come of them. And yet, he found himself in making his rounds pushing any building that could still be moved uphill a foot or two.

Then they took up the question of quarters. How much time, the major inquired, could Saugrain expect to give to the fort, considering his practice in town?

Saugrain had studied this himself. If he were to come out to the fort two—possibly three—mornings of each week, would that take care of the sick or injured?

"Two mornings would be good," Bissell said. "Three would be better."

So they agreed on Saugrain's being on duty at the fort Monday and Friday morning of each week, with an extra visit between those two days if the need arose.

That settled, the major had a suggestion for the location of Saugrain's office—temporary, of course. Since it was the major's habit to make the rounds of the building operations each morning, the doctor was welcome to the use of these small quarters on his chosen days.

That was very generous, Saugrain said. His only idea had been of a tent—with a floor large enough to hold a table, two chairs, a cot, and a small cabinet for supplies.

"Excellent!" Major Bissell applauded. "Where would you like that tent placed?"

A tree crashed at that moment and Saugrain said instantly, "On the opposite side of the creek, please." A hospital tent was what he had in mind.

Really, he had been so impressed with the new road over that way, it occurred to him now that with a little more work on the same slope they might level off an area large enough for such a tent.

"We'll keep it in mind," Bissell said with an odd light in his eyes, "just in case you find this hut too cramped. Shall I be seeing you next Monday?"

On Monday Willy had to pull up the horses farther away from the bridge. Where he had waited for Saugrain on Friday, a squad of soldiers and hired laborers were busy with grubbing hoes, clearing an area at least a hundred yards square beside the road. He hated to see the doctor walk the extra distance, carrying a tolerably heavy instrument case besides his small medicine satchel, but Saugrain told him to stay where he was. A hickory tree beside the road would shade the carriage from the sun. Willy, of course, must stay with the carriage because the horses, if left alone, might take fright at one of the many noises. As for Saugrain, on military duty now, surely he could walk from the hillside to the guard post, however burdened. He would probably sit idle the remainder of the morning.

He was wrong about that. As he deposited the last of his equipment conveniently in Major Bissell's quarters, the first soldier appeared, a rough splinter embedded in the fleshy base of his thumb. That morning, in addition to removing the splinter, Saugrain mixed cough syrup for a bronchial cold, closed and patched three cuts, and treated a sprain, loosening the affected joint—gently, but firmly—and ordering the man to use it carefully but enough to keep it free. The little guardhouse was cramped for space but adequate.

At noon the major walked with him to the carriage, where

(195)

they found Willy and the horses dozing under the tree. The square of ground on the slope had been cleared of unwanted growth and waited only to be dragged smooth.

"We needed a drill ground," Bissell said briefly.

However, on Friday, when the clearing had acquired a packed, hard surface under the marching feet of a squad commanded by a drill sergeant, Bissell informed Saugrain that there would be space at the far edge for a tent such as he had mentioned. He would be in nobody's way there and would have more room for his medical maneuvers, but there would be no way of keeping out the noise.

By the end of the month, without much attention given to disadvantages, Saugrain was settled in the new location, sheltered by a tent of stout canvas firmly stayed above a puncheon floor. Curtains on opposite sides could be rolled up to allow a breeze to blow through, or fastened down to keep out rain. He could hardly believe his good fortune, and he wondered. Did the major have permission for the tent or, for that matter, for the drill ground? Was his authority absolute in General Wilkinson's absence? In truth the General was more often absent than present. Which it was could be ascertained by the absence or presence of his galley at the mouth of the creek.

Naturally Saugrain did not put these questions to Major Bissell. Just as naturally the major did not give out any information, solicited or not. He was not generally a talkative man. He mentioned his commanding officer just once to Saugrain, when the latter, wishing to make clear his appreciation of the hospital tent, had said ruefully, "I shall like less than ever to see winter come, when I must return to four walls and a roof. Will it be your small station still?"

Bissell answered, "Before winter comes, General Wilkinson expects to have everybody in permanent quarters."

The answer was brief, but complete—the facts as Bissell knew them. Saugrain did not pursue the questioning.

He was thoroughly happy in his new military assignment. His duties so far had not been burdensome. Two mornings a week seemed to give him time to handle everything. In the event that an emergency should arise on intervening days, he had arranged for Dr. Robinson to be summoned from the McKenzie store, now in operation on the bank of the Missouri just below the cantonment limits. This had worked out very well. It made Saugrain happy to hand a case over to the younger doctor—and even happier to have John appeal to him for advice.

As for the noise of saws and hammers and shouting men, it seemed to him to diminish in volume between successive visits. Finally a new sound replaced it—the rhythm of boots tramping up to the drill ground below Saugrain's tent, then marching by twos, by fours, wheeling, turning and whatnot. The officer in command was a rough-spoken sergeant, and both he and the men were the first arrivals from the much-heralded First Regiment of United States Infantry, now quartered at Fort Kaskaskia in Illinois, awaiting orders to cross the Mississippi and occupy Wilkinson's new fort—Bellefontaine. Without any ceremony of christening, when clearing and building had hardly begun, the name by which hunters and trappers identified the spring that fed Coldwater Creek had attached itself to the cantonment. Now it had appeared on military orders, insuring its permanence.

Suspecting that the soldiers drilling belonged to the First Regiment, Saugrain's curiosity was sharpened when crisp, clear, decisive orders replaced the rough barking of the sergeant. This time he put the question directly to Major Bissell, who confirmed his guess, then elaborated. The soldiers were a special detail drawn from the First Regiment. Led by a lieutenant named Pike, they had traveled all the way from Kaskaskia—up the Mississippi, then up the Missouri by boat. Lieutenant Pike. . . .

"Tell me about him," Saugrain said. "He sounds more special than the men."

"Right," Bissell said, that odd light in his eyes contradicting his outward gravity. "I will give you the record: 'Zebulon Montgomery Pike. Born on post, Lamberton, New Jersey. 1779. Two years at school outside. Enrolled as cadet in regiment of his father, Captain Zebulon Pike, at age fifteen. Promoted to rank of second lieutenant, age nineteen. Promoted to first lieutenant, transferred to First Infantry. . . .' All army, wouldn't you say, Doctor? Our General is watching him."

The final remark had the effect of increasing Saugrain's interest in the subject. Would the General's favor prove a blessing or the contrary? And this persistent drilling of a special detail

(197)

—was that army routine or did it suggest some possibly dubious design? This being a question that he could hardly put to Major Bissell, Saugrain took it to Colonel Hammond, who answered freely and frankly.

Wilkinson, Hammond said, would not have been himself if he hadn't a number of plans simmering in his head, none of which he had confided to Hammond, who knew only that the General busied himself considerably outside the confines of St. Louis, conferring with the commandants of other western posts—Michilimackinac, commanding the strait connecting Lake Huron and Lake Michigan, and Fort Dearborn at the foot of Lake Michigan. Had Saugrain not missed him?

"I know that his galley is seldom seen at its Bellefontaine anchorage," Saugrain said. "Beyond that I know nothing about the General's movements."

"Hm!" Hammond said. "Well, I have told you what I know about those. He has been hobnobbing with the gentry among western commandants. He is not going to rest contented with his command here unless he can make it as important as theirs. You say this is a small company that is undergoing special drill?"

"I have not counted them," Saugrain said. "I think there are not more than twenty men."

"Hm!" Hammond said again. "He's beginning softly. This looks like nothing bolder than a reconnoitering move on his part. The territory is large and mostly unexplored. A successful reconnaissance would look good on his record. He may have in mind establishing, after Bellefontaine, subsidiary fur factories."

"But for that," Saugrain objected, "he could join with the fur traders already established in Saint Louis."

"No," Hammond said. "Those are merchants. He is Governor and Commander. He is also James Wilkinson. Well, I'm afraid I've done nothing but stir dark suspicions in your thoughts."

"I have still one question." Saugrain said. "If anything extraordinary is in the General's planning, would he give command of the first venture to a young lieutenant?"

"Yes," Hammond said. "The lieutenant, for the sake of advancement, will take orders without question. Now, don't let my sordid suspicions spoil your enjoyment of your military assignment, but do watch the General and any other preparations you may witness. Bring the evidence to me and I will help you sift and sort it."

Saugrain, however, having little opportunity to observe General Wilkinson, found it more to his taste to scrutinize Lieutenant Pike on the mornings when he put the squad through its paces on the slope below the tent. What Saugrain saw he liked—a young man of medium height, broad through the shoulders but otherwise trimly slender. Blue-eyes, fair-skinned, very fair. Pure Anglo-Saxon, he concluded; but on that particular morning, the weather being warm, a clear, ringing command halted the drill for a period of rest. This allowed the men to ground their rifles and remove their headgear. Pike himself took off his hat to cool his head, and Saugrain, watching from his tent, froze to attention.

His surgeon's eye saw a defect, an imperfection which another might not have noticed. A shortening of the muscles and tendons on the right side of the lieutenant's neck tilted his head slightly toward that shoulder. After the first surprise, Saugrain's next impulse was to offer tribute to the soldier father who had foreseen that military discipline—leading to self-control—would be the only sure cure for a consciousness of a fault that might have plagued his son through life.

As it was, Lieutenant Pike showed no awareness of imperfection, whether his head was bare or covered by the absurd officer's hat with its short plume drooping from the brim. Ah, but what the boy must have suffered in his first exposure to the jeers of other boys! Wry Neck would have been only one of many taunts. Saugrain's heart went out to the boy, the youth, and now to the competent young officer.

So it was with pleasure that he welcomed Lieutenant Pike when he appeared at the door of the tent, a few days later, a paper in hand.

"I have here," Pike said, after obtaining a formal invitation to enter, "a list of men I have selected and am to command on an expedition presently. I wish to request that you report on the fitness of each one to undertake the journey."

"A wise precaution," Saugrain said. "May I see the list, please? I may have treated one or more before this—for some minor ailment. If I believe them to be generally in good health, I could mark off those names, if you like. Then, if you will arrange for the others to wait on me here either before or after morning drill . . ."

"They can be excused from drill, sir," Pike offered, and Saugrain laughed. To him it did not matter, but he fancied the men would like very much to be excused. An appointment was made for him to examine the men the following Monday.

"How about you?" Saugrain asked then. "Do you need a statement as to your fitness? The men, to be sure, will be doing the hard labor, but responsibility is sometimes an even greater strain." A trace of color, he thought, touched the lieutenant's cheeks. "I would like to listen to the heartbeat, the breathing. Now, perhaps?"

"Yes, sir."

The result of the brief examination was what Saugrain had anticipated. "Perfect!" he said. "You are in excellent health, Lieutenant. Now is there anything else?"

"No, sir . . . yes, sir." The color appeared again. "A personal matter. Some day, if you have time. . . ."

"But I am here now," Saugrain said. Willy, to be sure, was waiting, but he could doze and brush off flies a while longer. "Tell me," he urged.

"Yes, sir. I am a married man, Doctor. I have a family. . . ."

A family—a wife and two children, a little girl two years old and a boy not quite six months. They were at present safely and comfortably housed at Fort Kaskaskia, but. . . .

"I don't get to see them, sir. I may not see them before I leave."

So he had thought of bringing them across the river, at least as far as St. Louis. He had hoped to have them in permanent quarters at Fort Bellefontaine by this time. General Wilkinson had spoken very certainly about the quarters being ready before he must leave, but now it didn't seem to the lieutenant that they would be ready. What did Doctor Saugrain advise?

"Leave them where they are," Saugrain said unhesitatingly, "or move them to Saint Louis." He was sure that a suitable house could be found. The population of the town was increasing, but he had yet to hear of anyone unable to locate a vacant dwelling when he needed one. It would be his pleasure to assist the Pikes in their search.

(200)

Nine

It was a real pleasure, then, to settle Lieutenant Pike's family in St. Louis. Saugrain, who knew every fence corner in the town, found a small but attractive house with a garden on Church Street; and Madame Saugrain, aided by Sophie Michau, helped Mrs. Pike fit her personal possessions among the pieces of furniture that came with the house—a dish cupboard, a table, a few chairs, a bed and the Saugrain cradle—on loan. Not that Clara Pike needed their help. Moving about the small house, making it livable, she spoke gaily of previous adventures in cramped quarters—especially in the first year of her marriage, when Zeb had been only a second lieutenant, with quartermaster duty. In Indiana Territory, that was.

"Charming, isn't she, Vigny?" Madame Saugrain said.

Very, Saugrain agreed—a grave, quiet young woman for the most part, with a dignity and self-possession more striking than mere beauty, although she was comely enough, with smooth, dark hair and hazel eyes that brightened at the least mention of her husband.

"I think," Madame continued, "that she has not always lived on a soldier's pay. For her own family, she speaks only of 'Papa,' and a plantation near Covington, Kentucky. Papa is rich and he did not want his only child to marry a soldier; but they were very much in love—one has only to see them look at each other —have you seen that, Vigny?"

Yes, Saugrain had seen that meeting of the eyes, holding, as if neither wanted ever to turn away. So now, after only God and Madame Saugrain knew what heartache they had endured before this, these two fine young people were to be separated—to satisfy the vanity of an ambitious governor.

James Wilkinson's design was now known to anyone who had ears. He was, as Hammond had surmised, planning a reconnoitering expedition—a small sortie, he called it—up the Mississippi. He had the men selected, the provisions contracted for and the boat, but he needed a skilled boatman as a pilot. So he had laid his scheme before the General Court, seeking approval and the man he wanted—Jacques Cardinal.

"He made an eloquent plea," Hammond said. How much did the people of St. Louis know about the upper Mississippi? he asked. Not much, the Court thought, but perhaps enough. It was a very good river as far as the Falls of Saint Anthony. Beyond those, what was to be gained? One could not pass them, going or coming, except by a long, rough portage. The explorers —Marquette, the Chevalier de la Salle—coming from the Lakes, had used a small river that emptied into the Mississippi below the Falls.

Well, but, there must be considerable river above the Falls, Wilkinson argued, or there would have been no falls. Was there no desire to know what that country was like?

The answer to that was that, while beyond a doubt there would be water and fur-bearing animals, there most certainly would also be British fur traders and Indians in the pay of the British. In 1780. . . .

"Ah-h-h!" Wilkinson sighed. The British. Did anyone know how far south the British from Canada had advanced? No. Then he thought it was the responsibility of the governors of frontier posts, with a view to locating a northern boundary for United States territory, to discover what the British considered to be the southern boundary of Canada.

A little more of that and he had the Court's approval—and the loan of the Gratiot boatman.

So it was that very early in the morning of the tenth day of August, Saugrain, Willy, and the brougham picked up Clara Pike and two very sleepy children at the door of their house and carried them out to Bellefontaine to see Pike and his company depart. Two hours later, with the baby sleeping soundly on the cot inside Saugrain's tent, he and Clara and the little girl stood before it, their attention fixed on the valley below.

Promptly at eight o'clock a trumpet sounded, and General Wilkinson, plumes, fringed epaulets, and sword sash, stepped out from Bissell's quarters, followed by the major, in full summer uniform, but not resplendent. At the same time, from some recess in the valley beyond, Lieutenant Pike appeared, leading a column of twos, marshaled by two corporals and a sergeant. Abreast of Wilkinson, the column formed in a double line, the sergeant presented the company to Lieutenant Pike, who presented it to Major Bissell, who presented it to Wilkinson, who gave him in exchange a paper, presumably orders, which finally reached Lieutenant Pike. Finally, when everybody had saluted everybody else, came a ringing order: "Forward, by twos, MARCH!" and the column stepped on down the valley, to disappear where the hill concealed the river and the boat. When Saugrain turned then to Clara Pike, he saw tears.

"You would have liked to see the boat leave?" he said.

"No," she said, not bothering to conceal or brush away the tears. "This was much better. I couldn't have been any nearer to Zeb down there. I couldn't have spoken to him. Besides, there was nothing more for us to say after our good-bye yesterday. I had one question, but Zeb would not answer it positively. Perhaps you will. Do you think they will be home before Christmas? It is four months . . ."

While Saugrain hesitated, a younger, bolder voice spoke: "If they don't make it in that time, ma'am, they're likely to be right chilly where they are going. What is it, Doctor? Did I say something wrong?"

It was John Robinson, up from his store on the river bank, handsome as always even in shirt sleeves and work apron. And he had said nothing wrong. His remark had been thoughtless, but he apologized promptly.

"Mrs. Pike, I am really sorry. Everything favors your husband's success on this voyage. He has a good boat, a first-rate pilot, a company of picked men in high spirits. I personally bossed the loading of provisions. Finally there wasn't room for one more sack of anything. If there had been, I might have stowed away."

"Only the lack of room kept you from doing that?" Saugrain questioned.

"Ha!" Robinson said. "You know better. I have a wedding date for December. Do you think for one minute that I would forget that?"

Nevertheless, when the brougham rolled sedately back toward

(203)

town—Willy instructed to spare the horses—Saugrain asked himself drowsily: After all, what do I know about this young man except that he is handsome, personable, and, yes, venturesome?

Ten ✎

On his next day at the fort, knowing that there would probably be no drilling on his hillside, Saugrain had Willy drive him down to the creek level and crossed on foot to poke around among the building operations. The day's work had begun, but the men knew him and were glad to stop a minute, soldier or civilian, and salute or bid him good morning. Major Bissell did not appear.

Saugrain was pleased to find the buildings as far along as they were, but also dismayed to find so many incomplete. Wisdom, he thought, should have demanded a roof as soon as any four walls were standing. He could make out now, to his own satisfaction, Officer's Row—larger cabins—also two sets of contiguous smaller cabins, which would be barracks, and single cabins behind them—for married men in the ranks, he supposed; but almost without exception, there were no roofs. Some cabins had even gaping holes in one wall, where chimneys had still to be raised. However, as he remembered, roofs and chimneys called for special skill, and returning to the creek he was further pleased—and surprised—to find that General Wilkinson's house was still only a site, marked by a stakes in the ground.

Seeing still no sign of Major Bissell at his headquarters, and nobody near his own tent on the upper slope, he walked down the creek to have a look at the river—his first since his tent had been pitched.

It had not rained since—he could not recall when. The creek splashed and chattered as merrily as ever, but the Missouri was quite low. Sandbars showed here and there, making new islands, and across the river, the green point he had first seen with Colonel Hammond stood out even more boldly. Was he mistaken, or did he see a patch of white on the far side? Before he could an-

(204)

swer his own question, a shout from downstream shattered his speculations. Robinson, from the McKenzie store, had seen and recognized him and was now loping over the smooth surface of the high bank to bid him good morning.

Robinson at work so early? Saugrain thought. He must have slept at the store. As a matter of fact, he had slept there. He often did, he said cheerily. It was great—while summer lasted. Of course, once the weather turned cold, he would not find the lodging so pleasant, but then there would be no reason for a night watchman. Now McKenzie liked the idea of someone minding the store overnight—against prowling Indians.

Yes, of course there were Indians, not hostile, just predatory. The warm weather brought them out. In winter—well, in winter the store would suspend business. For the present, before dark he simply rolled the free whiskey barrel indoors, closed and fastened shutters over the window, barred the door, spread blankets over the counter and slept—"snug as a bug in a rug"—the night through. In the morning he put out the light in the lantern which he kept burning overnight as a sign of his presence, took a quick swim in the river, and was ready for breakfast. Twenty-two, Saugrain thought enviously, was a brave, beautiful age. It was almost a pity to think of clipping the young eagle's wings.

As for the patch of white on the Point—it was a tent, Robinson said. Three more companies of the First Regiment were expected that afternoon. Men, no families. Men were needed to speed the work of finishing the quarters up the creek—as many as could dig, hammer or saw. Skilled carpenters and masons were to be brought from town to boss them. All the quarters must be ready for occupancy before the first freeze, General Wilkinson had ordered. In the meantime the regiment would "sleep out" in tents across the river.

Saugrain looked over at the green point, and Hammond's words echoed in his ears: "Marshland, under heavy rain—marshland." He must have said the words aloud.

"Doctor," Robinson said, "do you have floods here in autumn as well as spring?"

Floods, no. He had been thinking of rain. After a dry spell in summer, sometimes the rains were heavy. "Marshland," he thought still, after he had left Robinson and the river and was walking up the creek. "Marshland." Up ahead then he saw Major Bissell tying a saddled horse to a tree near his quarters.

"You'll never guess where I've been," Bissell called in greeting.

Saugrain guessed at once. Bissell had been to the top of the hill. Saugrain had been aware of a few people on the summit Monday, when the boat was leaving.

"There were more than a few," Bissell corrected. "How do you suppose they got there?"

Saugrain knew how. They had climbed. But the major went on without waiting for an answer. Some of the people had spoken to the General afterwards. Was he not intending to use that height, they wanted to know, for a guard post at least—a lookout? The General, not wanting to make the climb in any fashion, had ordered Bissell to reconnoiter, and he had thought of the horse.

"What did you think of the outlook?" Saugrain asked; he tried to suppress any unbecoming eagerness.

"Tremendous," Bissell said heartily. "Someone—a detail, perhaps—should keep watch up there. The Spaniards did, I am sure." Then he added, with that light deep in his eyes of which Saugrain had learned to be wary, "If we should rebuild on their foundations, would you like to engage a part of the building for summer quarters?"

"Knowing that you will make a road up the long slope before you build anything," Saugrain said, "I will occupy the room the year around, if you will provide a good chimney and fireplace— and one thing more: restore the Spaniards' stairway up the short side of the hill."

With that, he stepped into his brougham and directed Willy to carry him to his hospital tent, leaving Major Bissell to his more serious problems down below. Halfway to the tent, he realized that he had said nothing about marshland to Bissell, but he did not go back. Overhead the sky was a cloudless blue, and all around, grass, weeds, even some leaves on the trees, were shrinking and shriveling against another warm day with no moisture. Marshlands could wait.

But not for long. This was a Friday. On Monday he again walked to the mouth of the creek to look at the camp on the Point. Green sod was almost hidden by the spread of canvas. Woodsmoke rose from fires where camp cooks were hanging kettles in preparation for the noon meal. All looked cozy and secure but the sky was stippled with small white clouds. Driving back to town at noon, he thought he felt a difference in the air. It passed over his face softly, with a trace of moisture on its breath, but it was not until they were rolling through town, south-ward over Church Street, that he saw along the western horizon a line—no, a piling—of gray clouds, and he imagined, if he did not hear, faint and far off still, the first rumble of thunder.

It rained all that night, all the next day, and through another night and day. There was no storm, just rain, quiet, steady per-sistent, finally overabundant. On Wednesday evening, when peo-ple began to ask would it ever end, it stopped as suddenly as it had begun. The cloud umbrella tore loose from the western sky, providing a magnificent sunset and a marvelously cool, quiet night.

Thursday morning the sun shone out hot and bright on streets deep in mud, on sinkholes filled to the brim and running over, on a torrent roaring down Market Street to the river. Fortunately the river was low and could take any amount of water from swollen tributaries. What was true of the Mississippi would be equally true of the Missouri. There would be no flood. But. . . .

"The mud will dry quickly, m'sieu," Gabriel promised. "The land was so dry, so thirsty!"

He was right. Friday morning, by avoiding any puddle that might cover a deep hole, Willy was able to convey Saugrain safely to Bellefontaine, where Saugrain was surprised—and relieved—to find his tent erect as he had left it and several shades whiter, soaked, washed by the rain, then bleached by Thursday's sun. Fog still clung to the creek below, and he wondered about the marshland across the river.

His first patient—Private Collins, Company B, First Regiment—appeared as he was rolling up the canvas flap of what he called a "window" as distinguished from the tent's main entrance.

"Enter, if you please," Saugrain said over his shoulder, his hands now full of mosquito netting, then added as the soldier struggled to suppress a cough, "Sit down. I'll see you presently. But sit down, then! I heard you coughing all the way up the hill." It was not a bad cough—so far. The throat was probably sore, a little congestion in the bronchials. "Well, now, let's see," he said. "Take off your coat." Then he saw that the coat was soaking wet.

"Yes, sir," Private Collins said. "I hung it out yesterday and it dried some, but not enough, I reckon."

Not nearly enough. "I hope you did not sleep in those clothes," Saugrain said.

No. Private Collins had been given a dry blanket and permission to sleep on this side of the river Thursday night. He had taken off his clothes and rolled himself in the blanket on some dry floor and had slept fine. He thought when he woke up some of the clothes would be dry, but they weren't, and his cold was worse.

It was Private Collins who, with a little persuading, told Saugrain how things had been on the marshland during the rain and afterwards. The first night had not been bad compared to what followed. Tent canvas still held water. But the second night. . . .

"We like to drowned," Private Collins said. "Water came through the soaked canvas like through a sifter."

Wednesday morning water was everywhere. Their cots were like rafts except they didn't float. They couldn't build a fire. Those who had taken off their boots could not find them. Barefoot or booted, they waded to the shore, found boats and ferried themselves over to the other side. But there the creek was out of its banks and everything else looked drowned, too, so they went back to their cots.

Thursday morning the sun was shining, they crossed again to the flooded mainland, got something to eat, and went to work. There was plenty to do. What the camp on the Point had been like on Thursday night he couldn't say, having slept on this side of the river.

What he needed now was bed and a plaster for his chest, but Saugrain gave him a bottle of medicine for his cough and a letter to his captain, recommending light work in full sunshine and dry clothing, if available. If his cold was not better by the next day, he was to look up Dr. Robinson at the McKenzie store. Dr. Robinson would take care of him.

Private Collins recovered his health, and so did others who had contracted colds. If that had been the worst, the rain might have been forgotten, but there was more to come. Coldwater Creek and the Missouri fell quickly, but the Point lacked their drainage. The water there shrank, forming large stagnant ponds and small

(208)

evil-smelling pools, with no outlets. Pollywogs were fun, but mosquitoes that stung by day as well as in the dark were a nuisance, then a pest. Ten days after the rain ended the first case of chills and fever was reported. On Saugrain's next visit, there were three, and on the following Monday these three and several more waited for his appearance.

He made the sick men lie down on the bed and the floor while he boiled bark chips over his camp stove. A sergeant in charge of the sick watched him with interest and curiosity, then addressed him respectfully: "Beg pardon, sir. Where I come from we use snakeroot for chills and fever. It works pretty good."

Snakeroot—it grew wild, the sergeant said—a tall plant with yellowish flowers on a long stalk. He'd seen some near the fort—before the rain.

"Poison?" Saugrain asked.

"No, sir. It don't smell good, cookin', but it ain't pizen."

Snakeroot, Saugrain thought, setting his bark infusion off the fire to cool. Sometimes these natural remedies did work. If snakeroot should prove to have the properties of a feverfuge, the drain on his supply of quinine bark—also known as Peruvian—would be lessened. He dosed the sick men, gave the sergeant a large bottle of the fever brew to administer morning and evening, and suggested that he ask his captain for leave to borrow another soldier or two and see if he could find and gather some snakeroot. If he found some, could he cook it at the camp? Yes? Good! In that case, he had Saugrain's permission to substitute it for the costly bark tea. Oh! Would he also on his way back to the camp either go himself or send someone to McKenzie's store and ask Dr. Robinson, in Saugrain's name, to report at the doctor's tent when he could spare the time?

Within the hour John Hamilton Robinson stooped to enter the tent, his expression wholly serious and sympathetic. "Are you in trouble, Doctor, over at the camp?" he asked. "Do you want me to stand watch there?"

"I need your help generally, John," Saugrain said, and explained the situation. Knowing that constant treatment and continued dosage against fever and chills was the only known palliative for the illness, he meant to spend part of every day now at Bellefontaine until dry, cool weather, an early frost, or some other phenomenon brought a decrease in the number of fever cases; but his present concern was medicine. His supply of quinine bark at home and at the camp was not inexhaustible, and he felt he must reserve half of it for the usual autumn ague in town. He would like to devote most of tomorrow to a search for an additional supply. If General Wilkinson were only in town . . . but he was not. His galley had not been seen on Coldwater Creek since before the big rain. Saugrain, therefore, would have to look to others for aid: Colonel Hammond, Mr. Manuel, the Chouteau brothers. Someone would help him. Meanwhile. . . .

"I will take over here tomorrow," Robinson said, "and after that I will keep watch at the camp."

Two weeks went by. The weather was ideal—fair skies, clouding over occasionally, but clearing after brief showers. Quinine and snakeroot seemed to be holding the illness at bay. The hammering in the valley regained lost momentum. Saugrain allowed himself a little hope. Everyone had been so helpful, so kind, thanks be to God! But then there came a day. . . .

He was collecting his things, preparing to go back to town and the sweet, safe isolation of his home, when he heard an odd scuffling on the slope below his tent. He looked out in time to see a new-found friend of Robinson—Lieutenant Hodge of the First Regiment—and two soldiers, leading, pulling, dragging Robinson himself up the hill.

"He wanted to come," Hodge said, when the doctor met them. "He begged us to help him. Then he fought us all the way."

"Delirium," Saugrain amended. John had fought, not them, but his own loss of strength and his other wish, which was to be left alone, to drop down where he was and die, perhaps.

Yes, that was how he had done over at the camp, one of the soldiers said. He had just dropped down where he stood.

They had now reached the tent. Saugrain lifted the mosquito netting and held it high to be out of their way as they took Robinson inside. If they would please lay him on the cot, he directed, and then. . . .

"No. Wait!" he said. "Until I open the blanket." Later it might be difficult to get it under and over him, if he needed cover. So! Now, if they would remove the clothing—the boots surely, and unfasten the rest. Why, he asked, had Robinson worn a coat—this warm day?

"Mosquitoes," the other soldier said. They were bad over at the camp. They stabbed a man right through his shirt. In a minute Saugrain saw how terrible they were. Robinson's chest and arms were covered with angry welts.

"Quiet, John," he said, laying his hand on the hot forehead. "Quiet. I am here."

"He's bad sick, ain't he, Doctor?" the soldier asked, and Saugrain looked at him in surprise.

"Dr. Robinson," he said, "is very sick, but don't despair now. There are many things we can do for him. Would you like to hold his head while I give him medicine for the fever? Hold it tightly. He won't want the medicine."

Robinson tried valiantly not to swallow it, but, with two men against him, most of the dose went down his throat. The pathetic struggle precipitated a small argument. Lieutenant Hodge and the others were needed elsewhere, but Saugrain could not convince them that he could manage the care of Robinson alone. Finally it was arranged that one soldier would stay and the others go back. Later in the afternoon Lieutenant Hodge might send relief, possibly come himself to see how things were going.

Also, on their way back to the camp, one was to walk down to the McKenzie store with a message to a young man who was working there while Robinson was engaged in caring for the sick at the camp—a young man named Michau. "Ask him to bring more blankets, please," Saugrain said, "I am not going back to town, you know. I will stay right here." In that case he would need cover, but that was not all. After the dose of medicine, he had tucked his cot blanket snugly about John and had seen him, in spite of the fever, relax under the added warmth. It was the chill that would follow the fever that Saugrain dreaded now.

The next moment, as if his thought had been a summons, Aristide appeared outside the tent, his arms full of blankets—Robinson's blankets, the ones he used when he slept at the store. McKenzie had sent them to the camp by Aristide in case they should be needed there.

Aristide! His employment by Trader McKenzie indicated no

sudden revolution in the boy's character. Simply, in John Hamilton Robinson, Aristide had found a hero, a pattern of manhood he thought he might like to copy. Soon he was following Robinson everywhere, even to the river-front store. When Robinson said cheerfully, "Do you want work, fella?" he had said yes; and McKenzie with equal tolerance had taken him on.

To Saugrain in the present crisis he was a needed messenger. Aristide must ride back to town with Willy. He could tell the family that Saugrain was spending the night at Bellefontaine and why. He could take with him a list of articles Saugrain needed—medicine, clothing, towels, and Madame Saugrain and Michau Père would fill the order. Aristide objected vehemently. He had come to stay with John; but at once, he was seated at Saugrain's table, writing as Saugrain dictated. When he finished, there was Willy with the brougham.

A bad night followed at Bellefontaine. In the morning, Saugrain, wakened by the sound of wheels from the first sleep he had allowed himself, had to rub his eyes to believe what he saw. There was the brougham with the anxious Artistide, surrounded by everything from a jar of soup to paregoric, and on the driver's seat beside Willy was Gabriel.

Beautiful, homely, faithful, dependable Gabriel! Now Saugrain was sure that all would turn out well. For example, without any qualm, he could leave Gabriel in charge at the tent and go down the hill now to answer a call which he was in exactly the proper mood to answer. Major Bissell had sent him a summons. General Wilkinson had returned to St. Louis the day before. He was now at the fort, and he wished to have a report immediately from Dr. Saugrain on health conditions at Bellefontaine.

Afterwards Saugrain could hardly believe that he had said what he had felt he must say and knew that he had said that morning to General James Wilkinson, Governor. He found the General choleric with rage over what he called the ruins of his beautiful cantonment. He had counted on finding it finished, the regiment settled in winter quarters, everything going. What he had found was a shambles—half the quarters still without roofs, some of them water-soaked for that reason, and why? Because the men who were to have completed the work were unable, because of illness, to report for duty. How did the doctor account for that?

Saugrain began his answer smoothly. He said he had never heard of a doctor being held accountable for conditions which he had no authority to change or remedy. If the General by illness meant the prevalence of ague—chills and fever—he knew of no scientific statement ever made on the exact cause of the autumnal malady. It seemed to be most prevalent—and most violent—in lowlands beside a watercourse. Some said it was caused by vapors rising from the water. Or they spoke of mists—morning or evening mists. Exhalations from swamps were said to be deadly. Lately he had wondered about mosquitoes. Certainly they bred where the conditions he mentioned existed. He described the welts on Robinson.

"Do you mean to say," Wilkinson said, "that a mosquito bite could give a big, strong man this ague?"

"I have heard no mention of a mosquito bite," Saugrain replied, still smoothly, although his anger was rising. "The men do say that the mosquitoes are terrible. I believe them and I cannot help thinking that an infestation such as I found on Dr. Robinson, if it did not implant the disease, could still seriously impair a man's resistance."

Wilkinson continued to fume, his color dangerously high.

"So much for guessing at causes," he said at last, although Saugrain could have said more on that topic. "What are you using for a cure?"

"Quinine bark for fever, paregoric if there is dysentery," Saugrain recited, his wrath coming to a boil, "a homely remedy known as snakeroot. These alleviate the misery. Nature does the rest. Some seem to recover, or they would if conditions were favorable."

"You keep speaking about conditions," Wilkinson fumed. "Exactly what do you mean?"

"I mean," Saugrain said, "that unspeakable, foul, soaking wet, stinking bog where the First Regiment is now encamped. If you will move your men out of that swamp to clean, dry ground, where water drains off instead of collecting, I promise improvement within a week. If you leave them there, I promise nothing but more sickness, even death."

"You mean move them over here—to spread the disease?"

"Ah-h!" Saugrain said. "There is no contagion. If there had

(213)

been, I would have isolated the campground long ago. No, I do not mean that they should be brought to houses without roofs. It is only September. We have a month and half of weather in which living in tents is possible. There is ample high, dry ground on the slope where my tent now stands. It is rough ground, but it will be heaven compared to a swamp. Now I must ask leave to withdraw. I must return to my duties. I have in my tent a man who all last night was as near death as I want to see one."

"And now," he said to Hammond that evening, seeking words of comfort to ease an ache which came from a combination of fatigue and horror over the rudeness of his manner that morning, "I suppose I should be glad that my commission bears the President's signature. Otherwise I might have to turn it in."

"I don't agree," Hammond said. "The General was scared, you know. He saw his whole, beautiful cantonment sinking into the mire. You saved it for him, including the lives of his soldiers. Robinson's, too. Don't you worry. You'll be all right."

And his commission, framed, still hung in the library at home.

Eleven ∽

On the twenty-fourth of December of that year, the marriage of Sophie Marie Michau of St. Louis and John Hamilton Robinson, lately of Augusta County, Virginia, was celebrated. It was a gay affair. The bride had decreed that there be no tears. Everyone was to rejoice with her. It was her day of supreme happiness and she did not want it spoiled. In the morning, before the ceremony, before the arrival of the bridegroom, she could scarcely stand still while her sister Elinor, pale but smiling, helped her with her dressing and Madame Saugrain pinned a veil to her dark hair.

"Sophie!" Madame scolded. "Can you not be quiet for one minute? I almost tore the veil just now. To tear a wedding veil is a very bad sign."

Sophie laughed, but tried. The veil was a square of handmade lace, and precious. Her dear mother had worn it at her wedding.

So had Madame Saugrain at hers, although the doctor had no memory of that, a fact which scandalized his wife.

"If you had worn it over your face," he pleaded, "I would remember because I would have hated that. Nevertheless, do stand still, Sophie. There may be others after you who will want to wear the veil."

Sophie, her mind settled on the marriage and thinking he meant the children who would come of it, blushed; but Saugrain's little girls knew he meant them. Rosalie, now eight years old, laughed, but Elise, the younger one, spoke up pertly: "Will you keep it for me, Maman?"

"For Rosalie first, then you," Madame promised.

At that point the arrival of the bridegroom was announced, and Sophie became truly a bird in flight, but with no sense of direction. A short while later, radiant in a new gown of ivory peau de soie—that material also taken from the family chest— she stood beside John Hamilton Robinson, resplendent in new boots, new blue coat and buff trousers—also glowing with health —and repeated with him the marriage vows as read out by Monsieur Auguste Chouteau, who held a lifetime honorary title as Justice of the Peace. It had to be a civil ceremony. Robinson was not a Roman Catholic, and anyhow, the rickety Catholic church was without a priest, as still happened frequently. As might have been foretold, the lovers had refused to wait for one to appear.

They turned then, after Mr. Chouteau had given Sophie a certificate of marriage, to face a house filled to the last corner. Every family from Frenchtown, the name now given to the Catalan Road area, was represented. From Bellefontaine there were captains and two lieutenants. One of the latter was Lieutenant Hodge, Robinson's friend, who stood up with him for the wedding.

Lieutenant Hodge had also brought Clara Pike from Bellefontaine. In the fall, after all traces of the terrible sickness had faded away, roofs, chimneys and floors had been finished in all the quarters, and General Wilkinson had offered Clara possession of the house reserved for Lieutenant Pike on his return. She had accepted the offer. She and Zeb, she said, had agreed that she might move to Bellefontaine if the quarters were finished and he was still away. She was accustomed to life at a military post—the neighborliness, the mutual dependence and trust. Today, for instance, she had left her children with a neighbor who also had children, knowing that they would be safe, happy and well cared for.

Colonel Hammond came with his charming lady. Jean Michau, in spite of floating ice, had crossed the river from his new farm near Kaskaskia. Tall, filled out now to handsome manhood, he kept still the bold eagerness of youth. To the repeated question: "How did you get across? How do you expect to return?" he said with a twinkle in his eye that he would take that up later with the man who had rowed him over. Just before the ceremony, General Wilkinson, sword, epaulets, plumes and spurs, appeared, and with him his sweet wife. Because of the spurs and sword the General found it difficult to move through the rooms in respectful quiet—and more difficult to hold in check the signs of soaring good humor.

"I haven't seen him like this," Hammond said, "since he got his fort back—thanks to you."

He spoke the truth, Saugrain knew. In September, after Wilkinson's shock at finding Bellefontaine all but ruined by weather and disease, Nature had blessed him and the countryside with a magnificent autumn, drying up surplus water and painting Coldwater Valley all red and gold. As the sick recovered, every man put heart and muscle into shoring up sagging, half-finished huts, laying up chimneys, covering each building as it was finished with a roof. By the end of October every soldier, every family was housed. The wood, to be sure, was green; the logs had not been properly stripped of bark; but the huts looked very solid as compared to tents. The General's spirits had soared with gratification.

But that was October. In November some of his triumph evaporated. A new cause for concern had developed. So far, no word had come from his Mississippi explorers. Before this, no word had been expected. Pike could not spare a man to carry a report back to St. Louis unless some trouble had developed, and the chance of his meeting someone who could be trusted to carry the message was slim.

Nevertheless, in November a murmur of questioning began.

When ice appeared in the river in December faces were longer. If all had gone well, why did not the men return?· Where could they be? But now. . . .

"He has had news from the Mississippi," Saugrain said. "Why does he not say?"

"He will," Hammond promised, "in his own way, when it pleases him."

Hammond was right. Wilkinson waited until the feasting that followed the wedding ceremony was at its height, then called for silence and attention.

Jacques Cardinal, he said, had arrived, in St. Louis late the evening before, having traveled most of the way overland—on snowshoes—with a report for Mr. Gratiot, and to spend the rest of the winter with his family. He had left Pike's company safe in winter camp below the Falls of St. Anthony. All the men were well and in good spirits. The day after leaving Bellefontaine, Pike, finding the boat overcrowded, had divided his company into two parties, one to handle the boat while the other marched northward by land. Alternating these duties daily would provide a change of labor for the men and lighten the boat, besides.

The plan had worked well. The shore party usually traveled at such a pace that, by the time the boat arrived each evening, a campsite would have been selected and a cooking fire would be going. The only delays on the march had been caused by Indians —not hostile but hungry, with their hands out for presents.

Nevertheless, before the expedition reached the Falls, there was ice in the river and snow in the air. So Pike had ordered the boat beached and covered and had set the men to building a winter hut and a stockade.

At this point Wilkinson raised his glass, as if to propose a toast, but Hammond stopped him with a question: "Sir, are we to understand that Lieutenant Pike and all his company are spending the winter in that stockade?"

"Well, no," Wilkinson admitted, his glass still raised. The lieutenant's instructions, he explained, included exploration above the Falls. So, the winter having scarcely begun, Pike had again divided his company. Leaving nine men with Corporal Swift and Sergeant Andrews at the camp, he, with the other nine and Corporal Johnson, had pushed on northward on foot.

(217)

Now, as an audible murmur greeted his announcement, Wilkinson's color rose, but he lifted his glass still higher.

"I entertain no fears," he said, "for the safety of Lieutenant Pike or his company. He knew from questioning the Indians that the first British fur factory was only a two days' march above the Falls and that more were beyond. He planned to stop at each one and, if ever further advance seemed inadvisable, to ask for shelter. Now will you drink with me to the health of the whole brave company and their return in the early spring?"

The toast was drunk, but in a solemn hush. No cheers. Whereupon Wilkinson called for Mrs. Wilkinson's wraps, and they took their leave.

"Please!" Clara Pike was now speaking. "Do go on with the dancing or whatever you wish. Don't think of me. I, too, am sure that my husband will bring everyone home safely. He always does. Please?"

Nevertheless, when Lieutenant Hodge came shortly afterward to ask if she would not like to return to the fort, she was glad to go. It grew dark very early these days, didn't it?

Very early, indeed. The hours sped by. At dusk Sophie clung to Saugrain, saying a tremulous farewell. He was responsible for everything, she declared: this day; her John. . . . Then her John came. Throwing a cape of rich fur around her, he carried her off. God only knew how much of his profits at the McKenzie store or how many Virginia drafts had been pledged for that wrap!

"Vigny," Madame said that night when the house was quiet, "why did you shiver when Sophie said good-bye to you?"

"Did I shiver?" Saugrain said. "Perhaps I did. They kept the door open a long time, saying good-bye to everybody. The wind blew in. . . ."

"Vigny, it was not a cold shiver. Are you afraid Sophie will not be happy?"

"Nonsense!" he said. "She and John will be very happy."

"Then, why?"

"All right," he said. "I will tell, you. I do not like that word 'responsible.' I was in no way responsible for John Hamilton Robinson's coming to this town. After he came, nobody could have prevented what happened here today."

"Vigny, do you think you should have tried?"

"No!" he said in what he would have liked to be a roar, although it never came out that way. "Now, will you please go to sleep or at least be quiet so that I can sleep? Winter is here again, and my bones tell me it will be a cold one. If ever I shiver again where you can see me, kindly stick me with a needle. Good night, you silly Maman. Good night."

PART VI

"This New, Immense, ∽ Unbounded World...."

SENATOR SAMUEL WHITE

November 2, 1803

One ∽

"Vigny," Madame Saugrain said, "there is nothing wrong with this child. Why do you look at him so?"

"I want to see what he is like," Saugrain said, "before you cover him with that long christening robe. Hmm! This one, I think, will be tall."

"How do you know?" Madame inquired.

"His legs," Saugrain answered. "They are longer than mine already."

"Vigny!" This time Madame screamed. "Do not stretch them like that! Give him to me—my poor little baby, my beautiful child."

He was neither poor nor was he little, Saugrain informed her, and most certainly he was not beautiful, this second son. Girl babies were sometimes pretty, even when three days old. Boy babies? Almost never. This one was the color of an Indian, long, skinny. . . . "What do you call him?" Saugrain asked.

"Vigny," Madame said, still aggrieved, "must I always choose the name?"

No, but she usually did. The name came to her with her first knowing that a child was on the way, and she put it away with other bits of things where she could find it when she had need of it. This son, she said now, she wanted to be named for his father; and, when Saugrain objected, saying that it was not good for two men in one house to have the same name, she was ready with an answer. They could turn the name about and call the

(223)

son Frederic Antoine instead of Antoine Frederic. And he was christened so—Frederic Antoine Saugrain, to be called Frederic, or more commonly, Fred, Freddie or even Fritz.

This was March, the first month of an early, precocious spring. Before the end of the month all the rivers around St. Louis were running freely. Early in April Jacques Cardinal, with a second bossman in reserve, took Mr. Gratiot up the Mississippi to a town called Galena, in the center of some lead mines owned and operated by the merchant. There, having been troubled very little by ice in the river, Mr. Gratiot suggested that they continue on to the Falls, to see how the soldiers in the stockade had come through the winter. Three weeks later Mr. Gratiot was back in St. Louis with a report that was good, though indefinite as to Pike himself. The men at the stockade, when he had seen them, appeared to have come through the winter very well. They were by then short of groceries, but had had plenty of meat and fish to eat all winter, and plenty of exercise in procuring the same. Ready to turn homeward now, they had put the keelboat into the water, to hasten their departure when Lieutenant Pike returned. They were expecting him daily, although no word had come from him so far.

However, he must have reached the stockade shortly after the Gratiot visit. On the last day of April the keelboat slithered to a berth in the soft mud of the Bellefontaine landing, and he marched his company ashore.

The company was complete. So was the lieutenant's uniform— weather-stained, eroded here and there, but whole. He wore his plumed hat as jauntily as ever. According to Corporal Johnson, who had been with him all the way, he had worn the hat every day, claiming that it shaded his face where the skin was thinnest and most exposed. The corporal thought it was to show anyone they met—Indian or British—who was in command. As if anyone could have failed to pick out the officer on sight!

Corporal Johnson in Saugrain's winter quarters talked freely, to stifle groans he might have uttered as the doctor manipulated a very lame thumb on his right hand. Indians or British, Saugrain thought, but would not question the corporal. That, it appeared, was unnecessary.

"I see you're looking at my trowsies, Doctor," the suffering

(224)

corporal continued. "That's what gives out first on a march—pants." These in his case were baggy ones of striped ticking. "We had no extras with us. We had to make the best of any replacements we could find. You may have noticed that some of the men came back in Indian leggings. Those were the chaps we left at the stockade. Us on the march were luckier. The lieutenant bought what we needed from the British storekeepers." Fur factories, Saugrain thought, but again he did not press any inquiry. He would have more injuries to care for, he was sure, so gave full attention now to fitting a bandage to the hand, cushioning it generally but leaving the fingers and thumb free.

"Thumb all right, Doctor?" the corporal asked as pain bit into him. "I could wear a mitt—to remind me and others to touch it easy like."

"Very good," Saugrain said, "but you should use it along with the other fingers. A bad contusion there and some inflammation, but I find no bone injury. We'll keep it bandaged for a week or so, but use it naturally, except that I do not advise any fist fights."

"No, sir. Thank you, sir!" The corporal seemed dazed. "There's not much for a man to fight about, quartered amongst friends, and no barrel of Scottish whiskey handy." And he went off, to boast to anyone who would listen about the little French doctor at Bellefontaine, who was a fair master of witchcraft. Just by passing his fingers over a busted hand he could tell how a man had come by it.

As for Saugrain, two sessions at the fort, spent in treating contusions, abrasions and lacerations, and examining frost-bitten feet for gangrene, supplied him with a fairly complete picture of the winter's adventure; and, since the men gave their accounts with no prodding from him and he knew that they talked to others just as freely, he had no hesitation about sharing the information with Hammond.

He began with the British fur factories. At the end of the first day's march northward, having fought a northerly wind the whole way, Pike and his small company had stumbled into the compound of the first of these stations. It was a small station, and new, but the lieutenant had secured lodging for the night— and there, according to the men, was where they should have

(225)

stopped for the winter; but they had no idea of what was still to come. In the morning, with the wind calmer and some sunshine, they had gone on—the lieutenant's orders. By noon, however, they were marching head-on into a full-scale blizzard. Forced to accept the first protection they came upon—a grove of fir trees that shut out the wind—they had dropped their packs and spent the night huddled in a heap under the broad, drooping branches.

"I know," Saugrain said, recalling Ohio woods sheathed in ice.

When daylight came and the wind and the snow seemed less, they had crawled out stiffly and eaten cold rations, which had settled like lead in their stomachs but enabled them to start out. All that day they had trudged on manfully, keeping close to the river, and before dark had turned into another circle of trees. There they were able to scratch out enough dead wood to make a fire. They had boiled water for tea which, with a little rum added, had warmed them enough to make it possible for them to swallow a supper of scorched salt pork and chunks of bread. Toward evening the sun had struggled out, so they went to bed with renewed hope.

The next day, however, had doused their hopes. Morning showed only gray skies, and at noon Pike had sent two scouts ahead on snowshoes to see what shelter they could find before dark or more snow came. By midafternoon the scouts were back with news of a second factory, a larger one. Following the scouts' trail, they reached the stockade in the last half hour of daylight.

They knew, Saugrain's informers said, when the gate closed behind them, that they would be guests of the Hudson's Bay Company for the rest of the winter.

It was one of the company's main factories, built around a sizable compound, with a number of cabins in addition to the factor's house and store; and it was well provisioned. The factor, a Scotsman with twenty Canadian winters behind him, offered Pike lodging and food for a price he could pay, on the condition that his men would volunteer as hunters and lend a hand with the traps.

That was most of the story. In the spring the factor had furnished canoes and an Indian guide to help Pike with the rest of his exploring, but by then the men had wanted only one thing—

(226)

to turn back southward toward home. Finally even Pike seemed to realize that he ought to return at least as far as the stockade, to see how those men there had ridden out the winter.

"Did he find the source of the Mississippi?" Hammond asked.

"I am not sure," Saugrain said. "The men who talked to me complained of a tangle of little rivers and lakes and ponds up Canada way, but made no mention of the Mississippi. I am saving that question for Lieutenant Pike himself. I left a request with Major Bissell for him to see me at his earliest free time. He is busy at present, putting on paper his notes on the expedition. It should be a valuable report—for his story of the British factories."

"Very valuable," Hammond agreed. "When you do see your young friend, he will probably have a captain's bar on his shoulder strap. Also, *de facto*, he will command the next sortie."

"Will there be another so soon?" Saugrain asked.

With a wry smile Hammond assured him that there would be another, and quite soon. That was why His Importance the Governor had been in such a sweat at times over the expedition up the Mississippi. Now that Pike had returned with his valuable information about the British installations, Wilkinson was all on fire to get off a major scouting expedition—this time to the West. He had even gone so far as to lay a sketchy plan for that expedition before the General Court. He wished to send a company of men, under Captain Pike, up the Missouri to the Osage River, then across the plains to the Southwest to establish the source of the Arkansas; also, if possible, that of the Red River of the South, which should not be far away.

"But that is Spanish domain," Saugrain said. "If the American scouts should meet a Spanish patrol, Spain's hospitality would be a Mexican jail."

"That," Hammond said, "is your view of the situation. Wilkinson is thinking only of Wilkinson. If young Pike should bring home a report on the extent of Spanish influence on the edges of the Louisiana Purchase, General Wilkinson will head any commission debating that frontier with Spain's representatives. He is discounting the threat of disaster while he adds up the money and power that success would bring to him."

(227)

"And you?" Saugrain asked, recognizing a familiar glitter in Hammond's eyes. "What are you contemplating?"

"Resigning," Hammond replied without hesitation, "from my perfunctory duties as a military commandant, in the hope of getting myself elected to the General Court. I still believe this is where our arch plotter will come to his ruin, and I want to be in at the kill."

"No, Colonel, no!" Saugrain said sharply, thoroughly alarmed. "Now it is you who in your lust for vengeance would discount disaster to Pike and his company. Also to me whom you call friend. My heart is sick—my mind, too—thinking of those young men and my duty to the Republic which is and has been vital to me for so long. When Captain Pike and his company go forth on this hazardous journey, part of me will go with them, and I in my position may not sound a warning. Perhaps I too should turn in my commission."

"Don't think of it," Hammond said. "You are needed where you are. You man an outpost against villainous design."

"I am a poor sentinel," Saugrain said. "I have no sense of intrigue, no pleasure in it. I have only emotions."

"That," Hammond said, "is the essence of patriotism and valor. Put aside your sufferings and stay at your post. So you will serve the nation and the Territory best. Will you please offer my congratulations to Captain Pike when you see him? And don't forget to ask about the source of the Mississippi. That may inspire him to mention the new venture, if he has been told of it. No, you can't give him warning. But do listen to what he has to say. In return, I will hold back my resignation until we meet again."

But Saugrain had then a sudden inspiration. Would Hammond consent to adding a third patriot to their private council? He had thought of Lisa, the Spanish trader.

Captain Manuel, he explained, had been born at New Orleans, where his father was a clerk in the offices of the Governor General when Wilkinson reputedly was amassing wealth by serving two governments.

Hammond was delighted at the thought of Lisa joining the council.

"Cheer up," he said to Saugrain at parting. "The villain hasn't a chance to escape now."

(228)

Two ∽

Nevertheless, it was with a heart still heavy with foreboding that Saugrain welcomed Captain Pike to his cramped quarters on Coldwater Creek, and it was a soberly thoughtful young officer who faced him. Fortunately, the single shoulder strap on the left shoulder of a new uniform, the insignia of a captain, enabled Saugrain to open the interview with congratulations.

Brightening briefly, Pike thanked him. "General Wilkinson is a generous commander," he said.

"I am sure he is," Saugrain agreed, "but I also think the promotion is merited. Your company is probably the first American military detachment to spend a winter as guests of the Hudson's Bay Company. I heard about that, but I still have a question unanswered. Did you find the source of the Mississippi?"

Pike hesitated, uncertain how to answer. "I think so," he said finally. "That is, I'm not allowed to say no, and I don't like to say yes." Then he, too, spoke of lakes, ponds, creeks and rivers. "In the end, sir," he finished, "we selected the most likely creek, marked it on a chart we had been trying to keep, then turned our canoes about and set out for home. Some day a scientist may judge our choice—correct or the reverse—but he will have had more time to study the problem than I felt I could afford."

"Thank you, Captain," Saugrain said. "I understand that your admission is given in confidence. Whatever happens in the future will not affect you or me. You have brought back an exciting, also a forbidding picture of the Canadian borderland and the British installations in that area. Again I congratulate you. But . . . I had another reason for asking you to visit me. So you know what it is?"

Pike's expression was now more than serious. It was apprehensive.

"The family, sir? Clara told me to be sure to thank you for

(229)

your care of them last winter. She said you sat up one night with the boy."

"I did," Saugrain said, "in January. He was a very sick child. Croup and congestion in the bronchials. If a membranous obstruction forms in the air passages, only a practised hand can deal with that. Fortunately no such crisis developed. The fever broke. By morning your boy was breathing naturally. Well, he recovered. If we have a good summer and he can enjoy plenty of sunshine, he will be stronger when winter comes again."

"But he is not stronger now," Pike supplied.

"No," Saugrain acknowledged, "he is not as strong as I should like him to be. Of course, he is only two years old . . . I will tell you the truth. Because a child is born a male, it does not follow that he is stronger than his sisters. It is a matter of biological composition. Your boy has not the same resistance to coughs and colds that your daughter has, and I thought you should know. Not to tell you is not fair to Clara."

"No, sir. Thank you, sir," Pike said; but he was shocked. "Is it possibly the fort?" he asked.

"No," Saugrain said. "The fort has its faults. You probably have heard what they are: built too hastily, green wood, the logs not properly stripped of the bark. So the wood rots. Not enough stone was put under the houses. The walls settle unevenly and leaks develop. But Officers' Row has a choice location. Your quarters are dry. . . ."

"Yes, sir, and Clara won't live anywhere else."

"We know that now, don't we?" Saugrain said. "Your quarters are home to her. I think she feels that if she waits for you there, it will work like a magnet, drawing you home."

"Yes, sir, I know. It was great to see her and the young ones on the shore last week." But then a look of strain pinched his features. "Doctor, some would say I should leave the army, knowing what you have told me, but I can't, sir. It is all I know."

"Leave the army?" Saugrain cried. "Nothing was farther from my mind. To me you are the perfect soldier. We need you. America needs you. The greater the nation becomes, the more defenders we must have. When I spoke of your boy's health, I had no idea of interfering with your military duties. The condition I spoke of is just that—a condition. The boy may outgrow it. Next winter may be as mild as this one was severe. However that is, you may be sure that I will look after your family. So, take your orders and follow them to the letter, as you would in any case. Just remember what I have told you. When the work is done and you are free to do so, turn your boats quickly once more, and hurry home to Bellefontaine."

"Yes, sir, I will." The blue eyes were bright, the ruddy color was back on the captain's face. "Doctor, I am not at liberty to say what plans are being discussed at headquarters, but I can say this: where we go, if we make this second exploration, there is no chance of our being snowed in."

He would have left then, but, with his hand on the door latch, he turned back. In the winter just past, he had been conscious of one lack in their preparation. Since the journey promised to be a short one and white man's settlements were seldom out of reach, he had taken upon himself the duties of quartermaster and doctor. This year if the journey as planned was made, it would be longer, with no known settlements along the route, and he would like to have a medical officer. Did the doctor know of anyone who could or would assume such duties?

Saugrain said firmly that he did not and watched Pike leave, knowing that he had spoken the first untruth. He knew exactly the man Pike needed. John Hamilton Robinson would have taken the place without hesitation if, with any conscience, he could have done so; but at present was securely tied to home and family. Sophie Robinson was again counting weeks and months, this time until October, expecting the birth of her first child and John's.

Three ∾

As it happened, before General Wilkinson could set in motion any plan for a grand sortie into a truly uncharted wilderness, other events obscured his intentions. First of all, in May Captains Lewis and Clark returned from their voyage to the Pacific Ocean.

The first notice of their arrival was a burst of rifle fire from the direction of Bellefontaine. Had Saugrain been in his quarters there on that day—new summer quarters, built upon the ruins of the lookout from which the earliest Spanish governors had kept watch on the Missouri and the Mississippi—he would have seen the flotilla round the bend of the Missouri and move on past the cantonment. As it was, the salute of rifles found him in the St. Louis post office, seeking Mr. Easton's approval of the address he had written and the seals he had affixed to a letter directed to his mother in Paris, tardily announcing the birth of his second son and namesake. At the first volley from the guns, he stiffened and opened his ears. At the second, he unceremoniously abandoned the letter and made for the street door.

On opening it, he heard other doors opening. All along Main Street people rushed outside, to look and listen, finally to run, when someone or a number of someones shouted, "The boats! The boats from the Pacific!" Then Saugrain ran too. Soon he was part of a freshet of people, racing, stumbling, leaping over obstacles, down the rocky slope to the river.

Abreast of the Place d'Armes finally, he was just able to break free and join a comparative trickle of folk moving more slowly down the easier, although by no means smoother, course of Market Street. The slower pace gave him time to locate a lookout perch for himself at the foot of the descent—a boulder safely off the roadway and twenty feet back from the sandy landing strip.

How he mounted the boulder, he could not afterwards say. There must have been, he thought, a tidal surge of the crowd, which lifted him and deposited him on the top. And not a minute too soon. The firing of rifles on the bluffs had now become spasmodic, indicating that the boats were past most of the lookouts. He had just settled himself on his immovable rock pedestal and begun to enjoy a perfect view of the open river when the captains' boat appeared upstream. Or was it the captains' boat? In color a dingy gray, patched all over with odd pieces of timber not much brighter, this craft bore little resemblance to the galley which had vanished into the fog two years before.

Nevertheless, it moved down the Mississippi as proudly as an admiral's flagship making port, keeping close to the shore but not dangerously close, men with iron-shod poles holding it away.

(232)

Shouts of greeting: "Look! Here they come! Here they are!" measured its progress, swelling finally into a roar as the barge was allowed to drift toward land and two men with ropes in hand leaped from it, then stood waiting for the usual volunteer help to come forward. Taking this for a signal, others of the crew leaped ashore, then stood where they were, met by a silence that seemed more tremendous than the cheering.

For those who waited ashore it was a first close look at the bearded, ragged wanderers. For the wanderers it was a moment of unbelief. Here they were among old friends, old scenes, adventure ending where it had begun. It was not possible to wipe out instantly two years of toil, suffering, peril, in places so remote that one wondered if he would or could live to see home again. Now home—a town with houses, and people speaking a language that a man could understand—was unreal.

The moment of bewildered withdrawal passed, as a father found a son, a sister a brother, and a hysterical wife a husband. Children stared at the wild embracing, each hid from the bearded strangers who would have seized them; and then the cheering broke out again—not so wild or in such unison as before, but noisy enough. A log raft with three muscular voyageurs balancing themselves on it bobbed ashore. Next came a loaded pirogue. One of those made at Camp Du Bois? It looked like one of those, but there was no sign of a second. After the one pirogue there was another raft, then a second barge, heavily loaded, towing a number of skin boats, stuffed with furs, no doubt.

Saugrain, feeling his eyes burn from trying to see everything at once, closed them, blinked to clear his vision, then turned his attention back to the leading barge. The captains should be on it, but in the general excitement he had missed seeing them. He saw them clearly now, Clark's copper-red hair identifying him and pointing to the presence of Lewis nearby; but the doctor's attention was again distracted by the presence of an Indian between them.

By his dress and general appearance, he was a chief of some importance. In contrast to the American captains' buckskins, as frayed and faded as those of their men, the Indian's leggings were of hides that had been bleached and softened. Ornamented garters bound them to his legs below the knee, but their main

(233)

support was a heavily beaded belt, which also covered the string that held his breechclout. If he had worn any covering above the belt earlier that morning, he had now discarded it, exposing a painted and bedizened brown torso to the sun and the eyes of every beholder. A necklace of some animal's teeth circled his throat, and below that hung string upon string of beads, among them a simple leather thong holding a bright, burnished medal.

Eagle feathers were fastened in what passed for a scalp lock on the crown of the Indian's head, although most of the hair was parted from the forehead to the back of the neck and braided, the braids fastened at the end with strips of red calico woven into the braid, reaching almost to his knees. Superbly ignoring the people near the landing, the Indian seemed to concentrate his attention on the fringe of buildings showing at the top of the bluff.

Others in the picture included Lewis's great brindle Newfoundland dog, crouched in an inadequate area of shade against the cargo hold, his tongue out and his eyes brooding on his master, and an Indian squaw, minding a small, dark-skinned boy in a hunter's fringed shirt and leggings. There was also a third man, short, with the black hair and dark skin of an Indian but the more solid, thick body of a white man, who squatted behind the Indian chief and so escaped the notice of Saugrain until the chief suddenly put out his arm to point at something he saw at the edge of the bluff and asked a question. Immediately the short dark man, an interpreter possibly, jumped up, listened, then repeated the question to Lewis. But the latter, although he also had been looking toward the town, must have had his thoughts elsewhere. He did not answer or even notice the mestizo interpreter until the mestizo repeated whatever he had said. Then Lewis, with a brief shake of his head, turned to listen and to answer the Indian's query, smiling as he did so.

However, the change from abstraction to attention was not so instantaneous that Saugrain failed to see and register in his mind the drawn, still face of one whose thoughts had drifted away to some memory, some dream, far removed from the scene of tumultuous welcome. What it was Saugrain did not attempt to guess, and he would not until he could talk to Lewis—preferably alone and he hoped soon. It had been his intention to go down to the barge when the crowd thinned and greet the captains, but now, seeing others—a Chouteau or two, Rufus Easton, Judge Lucas and other prominent ones, French and American—bound that way, he left his boulder and went back up the hill in an absorption of his own. Reaching Main Street, he looked up and down its length trying to remember where he had left the carriage, until finally Willy found him and took him home.

However, not home—the prattle of his children, unfinished experiments in his laboratory—nor his sick people in town or at Bellefontaine, nor his mild participation in the celebrations, receptions and general rejoicing could blot out his memory of that still face he had noted on the day of the captains' return. Could he be mistaken? Had he exaggerated a fleeting abstraction? No.

Finally one day, visited by a slight indisposition, so he said —chills, fever, some nausea—Lewis came of his own accord. He and Clark were then working long hours every day, trying to close out the business of their voyage—paying off the men, releasing them to their former employers. He hadn't time to be sick, but he had felt he could better afford time to visit a doctor than to lie around idle, nursing a stomach which seemed unable to adjust itself to civilization.

He had had a similar spell, he said to the doctor's questioning, during the return voyage. He and Clark and the rest were still in camp at the Falls of the Missouri when he began to feel ill. And then a man with rather poor sight had mistaken him in his hunting garb for an elk and had sent a bullet his way. The ball had cut through the flesh of both thighs—a nasty wound, but Clark, with applications of saltpeter and God only knew what other ointments, had warded off lockjaw; and as soon as healing began, everything being ready for the return journey, the boats had been loaded. They set out with Lewis flat on his back, occupying most of the one pirogue, his legs protected by dressings Clark called tents.

The wounds had healed. By the end of a week he could have walked with no great discomfort. Sitting might have been painful, but he tried neither. There he lay taking up space needed for men and supplies, and he didn't care. He refused food . . . briefly Lewis's expression brightened. No, his ailment had not called for Saugrain's favorite remedy—an emetic for cleansing. His stomach was already empty. He was starving and had no will to be otherwise until suddenly starvation seemed to have worked its own cure. All at once he awoke to a realization of his malingering and ... well, he recovered, or so he thought, but now. . . .

"Good!" Saugrain said. "Now we must consider causes." He had treated more than one member of the exploring party for a deranged stomach, produced, he believed, by food poisoning. They had eaten too much bad food. There was, for instance, that stuff called pemmican. The squaws made it, the men said, out of meat chewed by them for lack of other chopping or grinding, then mixed with bear fat and rolled into balls and frozen for winter meat.

Lewis grimaced. If he or any other had been doomed to die because of what they ate, they would have perished in their second winter camp—beside the Pacific Ocean. The Indians there had been the filthiest of all the savages they had encountered. That, together with fog and eternal dampness ... they had carried out several men when the time came to leave that camp, but none had died. They began to regain health and strength as soon as they had clean air to breathe and something besides fish to eat.

"So," Saugrain said, "we must follow another line of reasoning. I am sorry to hear of your disaffection for the Pacific Ocean."

"The ocean," Lewis said quickly, "is beautiful. I would go back gladly any time that I had the opportunity."

"Ah!" Saugrain said. "Then you have that spectacle to cherish in your memory. Can you forget the filthy Indians as you remember it? Do try. And was there elsewhere some scene, some adventure that you would like to keep always?"

"There were a number." Lewis said. "The Great Falls of the Missouri was one—the water of three mountain streams joining and falling over the edge of a rocky precipice into a foaming basin below, then racing and tumbling onward as one great river." But the best of all, he said a moment later, his face assuming the expression that Saugrain had hoped he would see again, had been a bit of exploring he had done on his own—alone, on foot, with only his dog for company.

On the return journey they had crossed the Continental Divide and come safely through the other passes. Above the Falls they had disposed of their canoes and pack horses to friendly Indians, then had portaged everything that they hoped to carry home

(236)

around the Falls and, weary but in good spirits and good health, had gone into camp below. Leaving Captain Clark in charge of opening a cache where they had buried provisions for the return journey and the salvaging of the one pirogue which had escaped destruction, also the timber of the wrecked keelboat, Lewis had packed a little camp bread and some powder and ball and gone off on foot to explore a small river they had noted the year before but had passed by, knowing it had no importance to their search for the source of the Missouri.

"Alone?" Saugrain could not help protesting. "Surely you knew. . . ."

"I was not alone," Lewis said, his eyes beginning to shine. "There was the dog. He was the best of company. Doctor, I can't tell you how beautiful it all was—the magnificent solitude, the mountains still topped with snow, little rivulets running down their sides. The birds. Some I could not name. Others were enough like birds I did know to be related. Animals barking, squealing, running to their dens at sight of the dog . . . I was never afraid," he declared, "except once for a few seconds."

He was roasting a brace of ptarmigan over the supper fire. Suddenly the dog, who had been watching him hungrily, made a low moaning sound deep in his throat, and his ruff bristled. Lewis looked around at once, and there stood an Indian. He was a big Indian, as western Indians often were—and Lewis was unarmed. He had used his hunting knife in dressing the birds, washed it and laid it aside. His gun was with his blanket under a pine tree—not far away, but not within easy reach. Finally he could save himself only by assuming that the Indian was friendly, possibly curious, very possibly hungry. So, with signs, still feeling queer, he had invited the Indian to sit down and share his supper, then sizzling on its green spit over glowing coals. The dog, however, had not approved of such trustfulness. His growls deepened, his hair stood on end all the way down his spine, and at last he stood up, barking savagely, showing all his teeth. Lewis had never seen him in such a state, and the Indian, no doubt, had never seen a dog that size. Looking at Lewis and finding him also aghast, he had thrown up his hands in a gesture of repudiation and fled.

No, Lewis and the dog had not turned back at that point. They had gone on until Lewis's supply of powder ran low, then had followed another stream back to the Missouri. Arrived at the camp, they had been welcomed joyfully by Clark, who had all in readiness for loading the boats and departing.

It was then, when his heart should have been lighter with each passing day, that Lewis had fallen ill—fever, nausea, chills. . . .

"It sounds as though you were unwilling to return to civilization," Saugrain suggested. "After what you had seen and done, everyday things would seem small."

Lewis flushed, as if this were an accusation. "I am thirty-seven years old, Doctor. I hope I am not that irresponsible. I knew before I ever left Virginia that, if I made this great journey and returned alive, I must give a full report of it to the man who had sent me out—the President."

"I know," Saugrain said, very sure of his ground now. "Nobody who knew you would ever think of your being derelict when it came to duty. You reasoned this all out again, as you lay ill in that boat, and so you recovered. With no return of the distress—until now?"

About to answer with a firm denial, Lewis hesitated. Once, perhaps . . .

He and Clark had brought their company home with two men missing. The first, a Sergeant Floyd, had died early in the journey. They had buried him beside the Missouri and gone on. The second, one of their best scouts, as they were coming down the Missouri on the way home, had taken the pay due him in traps, an extra gun with a supply of powder and ball, a blanket, and a few baubles for trading and asked to be set ashore. He meant to make a long hunt on his own. They had left him at the mouth of the River Platte, facing westward. They would probably never hear of him again; and yet. . . .

"I watched him out of sight," Lewis said, "with the queerest feeling."

Not queer at all, Saugrain thought. A man's thinking mind and his nervous system did not always work together. So now, after tracing a pathway through unknown territory, here Lewis was, lost in a wilderness of paper. That was it exactly, Lewis said, and laughed; but then he ran his fingers through his hair and an ugly little furrow showed between his eyes.

To begin with, there were the journals. Four men—Lewis, Clark, a private named Gass and a Sergeant Ordway—had agreed to keep, to the best of their ability, a day-by-day account of the expedition. The idea had been that any one man's probable omissions would be covered by the notes of one or more of the other three. Mr. Jefferson's idea, Lewis thought, was to publish a compendium of the notes as a book.

"How I envy him the first reading of those entries!" Saugrain felt an actual pang of hunger.

Yes, but nobody could read them at present, Lewis said. Many of them had been written on scraps of paper—any paper on which the chronicler could lay his hand. Now the fragments had to be assembled and put in order—a not-impossible task, except that there were never enough hours in a day or days in a week. Because in addition to the journals, a complete accounting of costs had been demanded. The initial appropriation made by Congress had proved too small before preparations for the exploration had been completed. Now more money must be borrowed to meet day-to-day expenses—payment of the men, civilian and military, respectable new uniforms, lodging and board for the two captains, and board and lodging for the Indians—who were on their way to visit their Great White Father in Washington and must wait here until the captains were ready to escort them to the Capital—boats and crews for that journey. . . .

At this point Saugrain closed the discussion of papers by turning to his medicine cabinet. Expenses were expenses, he said back over his shoulder. Somehow somebody always paid them. Whereupon he took out a large bottle of pale amber liquid, uncorked it, and nodded his approval.

"Extract of anise," he said, once more facing his patient. "Excellent for stomach cramps—in a solution of spirits. I borrowed the idea from a rival pharmacist who has just opened a store on Main Street and is selling an elixir most profitably, which, on analysis, is a familiar medicine in diluted whiskey. The potency of any herbal extract is increased by this method."

But when Lewis would have taken the bottle from him, he drew back. He never offered medicine, he said, of his own compounding without adding a side dose of advice. "In that connection," he asked, "how is your dog?"

"Fat, lazy," Lewis said, smiling, "bored, perhaps."

"Good!" Saugrain said. "It is, then, your duty to give him exercise. An hour each day in the open, with a good run, will benefit both of you."

Also, if Lewis had not yet made the acquaintance of Colonel Hammond, Saugrain would introduce him. Hammond had a new country place west of the town, on a bright little river called the Meramec, and a stable of thoroughbred horses, also in need of exercise. So, a run with the dog every day, and once a week at least a half day for a good gallop on a horse. That could be the best medicine of all.

"I like the whole prescription," Lewis said. He took a firm hold of the bottle and went off laughing, leaving his frown behind. A trace of it, alas, settled on Saugrain's forehead until he turned impatiently to other business, some of which always waited for his attention.

Four 〜

Uppermost in his mind on this bright day in May, 1806, was an invitation from Mr. Brown, the Territorial Secretary, to a reception which Mr. Brown was holding three days hence in honor of his brother-in-law, former Vice President of the United States, who was interrupting a journey to New Orleans to pay a visit to St. Louis.

"Vice President and assassin," Michau Père said, referring to the duel in which John Hamilton Robinson's uncle had met his death. But few people in the town, except newcomers who had settled there since the change of government, knew anything about that unfortunate affair, and if they had known, they would most certainly not have attached any blame for it to Mr. Brown, whom everybody liked. A lawyer of high standing and experience, having practised in New York state for years, he was most kind and fair in explaining taxes and land suits. Having a distinguished brother-in-law, it was not only gracious of him to hold a public reception in his honor; it was almost obligatory.

Everyone would attend, if only to say that one had met and conversed with a vice president.

Saugrain also, as curious as any other, knew that he, too, would go, although, because of his close relationship to Hamilton's nephew, he had a few qualms. He even went so far as to exchange a few words with Rufus Easton, the postmaster, on the subject. Mr. Easton must surely have known Mr. Burr in Washington.

"Know him?" Easton said. "He was my best friend there. He opened the way for me to handle many a case. In fact, he is responsible for my coming here, although only the years can say whether that recommendation was a kind one. By all means, you must meet him at the Brown reception. Mrs. Easton and I will be there."

After that, nothing could have kept Saugrain away, and if ladies were to be present, he knew none would be fairer than his.

Madame Saugrain in truth had never been prettier than she was that day, with a bonnet of her own creation perched on her brown hair, her eyes soft with pleasure and bright with challenge. She wore the silver-gray dress she had made for herself for Sophie's wedding, very appropriate, she hoped, for a matron, the mother of four children; but it was not propriety which caused Mr. Burr, a dark, courtly gentleman, to bow low over her hand, murmuring a compliment in French which brought more color to her cheeks.

"But, honorable sir," she said, withdrawing her hand, "I speak English. My husband prefers that I take every opportunity to exercise myself in it."

"Too bad," Burr said. "Seeing you, I thought I was in Paris once more."

That evening Madame expressed regret that she could not have enjoyed more of Mr. Burr's conversation, but the Eastons had arrived just at that moment and a minute later she was whispering to Saugrain in French, asking him please to excuse her. Mrs. Brown had invited her and Mrs. Easton to visit her garden.

This, of course, left Mr. Burr to exercise his politeness in conversing with his fellow men. He did this very well also. He was even clever about it. Presently, by a maneuver of which nobody was aware, all of the men except Burr and Easton were in a group, and those two were alone, talking very earnestly, Burr in a low tone meant only for Easton's hearing.

(241)

Two old friends reviewing past acquaintance, all supposed, until suddenly Easton turned his back on Burr and walked away. He walked right through the house stopping for nothing or nobody, seeing only the door he wished to reach. He forgot to pick up his hat. He forgot that his wife was present. He had to send for both later.

"Vigny," Madame Saugrain said that evening, "what happened? The Browns hardly knew what to make of it, and Mrs. Easton was alarmed. She thought her husband had been ill. Was he ill, Vigny?"

"I don't know," Saugrain said. "Yes, that could have been it."

He knew that was not it. Only he seemed to have seen wrath on Easton's white, set face. Something Burr had said had outraged him. He had to leave before he committed an act of violence. Meanwhile Burr had rejoined the other guests with an amusing anecdote ready—something about a lawsuit in Washington—which soon had all but Saugrain laughing. Then the incident was forgotten—temporarily at least. General Wilkinson had arrived, also in a state of fume but making no mystery of the reason. Why, he demanded, had he not been notified of Burr's impending visit? He had been up the Missouri a little way and had returned to find Brown's invitation on his desk at Bellefontaine. He had ordered his oarsmen to put the galley out on the river again and had hurried them into bringing him around to St. Louis at top speed, and so had arrived, thank God, before the party was over and the guest of honor had departed. Much the fastest way to come, he said, his anger mellowing, as he spoke pridefully of his galley.

By the way, he added then, the boat was now tied up at St. Louis, provisioned and ready to travel, as he liked to keep it. Burr was welcome to use it for the remainder of his journey, if he liked. Wilkinson himself had business in town and at Bellefontaine which would keep him prisoner for a while. Well?

It was Burr's turn to be startled. Plainly he did not wish to terminate his St. Louis sojourn so abruptly. Mr. Brown also demurred, but then some signal must have passed between Wilkinson and Burr. Before evening set in, Burr's belongings and Burr were aboard the galley, and the journey down the river was begun.

(242)

Five ∽

What a finish to a gala day! Every unbridled tongue in St. Louis wagged. The less a man knew the more he found to say. Mr. Brown, embarrassed by what had happened, was resigning as Territorial Secretary. A new man would replace him, naturally, but that, no doubt, was a time away. For the present, General Wilkinson was in another protracted fit of bad temper, angry at everything and everybody within sound of his voice, which carried far, but especially angry at Postmaster Easton.

The day after the reception he sent a written order, signed by himself as Governor, directing that any mail arriving for him at St. Louis should be sacked unopened and unclassified and delivered to the post office at Alton, across the Mississippi in the Territory of Illinois. He would arrange to call for his mail there and he would direct all his correspondents to address him there.

Nobody needed to guess about the truth of that story. General Wilkinson made no secret of the order. "I will not have my mail handled by that man!" he said—openly and defiantly. Saugrain would not have believed what he heard if, from his Bellefontaine summer quarters, he had not seen the special mail boat leave and return, carrying mail sacks both ways. Alton, Illinois, situated on the Mississippi above the mouth of the Missouri, was easily reached by boat from Bellefontaine.

While people were still happily buzzing over this situation and an added report that Postmaster Easton was much occupied in his back room with correspondence of his own, the Wilkinson galley returned to Coldwater Creek—much too soon to have reached New Orleans and covered the return distance upstream. But this time Wilkinson wasted no time on revelations. With more thrust than usual to his jaw—and less noise—he began to put into action plans which he had made much earlier. Captain Pike, with a work detail of soldiers, and building tools and other supplies loaded in two pirogues, set off up the Missouri, his orders being to select a favorable site on the right bank of the

Missouri for a fort and a trading store, then to measure and lay out the groundwork. He was to return within a month with a report on his party's accomplishment.

Twenty-four hours later, leaving Bellefontaine under the colonel commanding the First Regiment, Wilkinson boarded his galley and set off downriver for parts undisclosed; and Saugrain, sated with speculation and gossip, called a meeting of what he called his triumvirate.

There they sat in the cool comfort of the Saugrain laboratory, three devoted friends and patriots—Colonel Hammond, free now of the last vestige of military command, Manuel Lisa, the fiery, shrewd merchant, and Saugrain, doctor, scientist, philosopher— exchanging views, facts, and opinions.

"So," Lisa said, opening the discussion, "our brave Governor will now borrow a trick from the Hudson's Bay Company, and mark and defend our boundaries with fur factories. Well, the boundaries may some day need defending, but not by James Wilkinson, I hope. I'd sooner trust a Hudson's Bay man. What do the Chouteaus think of this invasion of their hunting grounds?"

"Even a Chouteau," Hammond reminded him, "trades under a franchise. And who gives those, if not a governor?"

"Ah!" Lisa said. "You are right, of course. I might find this new factory a convenient base of supplies, if I could only think of the promoter as someone nobler than a sleight-of-hand artist whose success depends on his turning people's attention away from his baser designs."

"Now that is enough," Saugrain remonstrated from his favorite perch on his work table. "Your opinion, gentlemen, of our Governor is now firmly fixed in my mind. What I don't know is what I want to hear. The confusion which has visited our town goes back, I am sure, to Mr. Brown's reception. What did Mr. Burr say to Mr. Easton that afternoon to send Easton away, white with shock and anger?"

"You tell him, Manuel," Hammond said. "You are our lookout on the Ohio."

So Lisa told what he knew—a tale of such perfidy that it made Saugrain's hair stand out from his head more wildly than usual. On an island in the Ohio, owned by a man named Blennerhasset

(244)

—an odd sort of man, not exactly crazy, but surely not sane—a company of men recruited from outcasts, rebels, malcontents and other unworthies, with perhaps some gentlemen with just grievances, was known to be assembling and going through military drill. When this had begun, nobody knew. It might not have become known now except that, as usually happened in such movements, deserters had given the information. They said that certain gentlemen and former army officers were planning once more to separate the states of Kentucky, Tennessee, Alabama, Mississippi and Louisiana from the United States and form a new nation, perhaps adding the northern provinces of Mexico. Burr visited the island regularly, and Wilkinson's galley had been seen there or at a convenient landing nearby more than once.

"So now you have information," Lisa said. "which gives you no comfort."

"No," Saugrain confessed. "If I had ever known you to give a false report, I wouldn't believe this. The truth sickens me."

Burr's visit to St. Louis had had only one purpose—the recruitment of men and officers for an army of treason. He had dared to approach Easton with this proposition. "Thank God for a patriot postmaster."

All that followed was now comprehensible. Arriving at Bellefontaine, Wilkinson had heard that Burr was in St. Louis, being honored by a public reception; and in a panic he had hurried into town with one idea—to remove him from the scene. Before he left, Burr must have told Wilkinson about his conversation with Easton, and the Governor had made a second hasty, ill-considered move. Not knowing what letters might come for him, he had noisily ordered his mail to another post office.

For Saugrain there remained now only an explanation of the too-rapid return of the Wilkinson galley to St. Louis. Lisa was glad to give it: a United States marshal, with soldiers, had stopped the galley near the Chickasaw Bluffs and taken Burr off.

Where was he now? In custody surely, probably awaiting trial on the charge of treason—conspiracy against the United States.

And where was Wilkinson? Would he follow his friend? Not willingly, the two better-informed men of the three thought. He might have been summoned as a witness.

"I only wish I could be present at that trial," Lisa said, "in

(245)

some corner where I could hear without being seen. I'll wager he will squirm free somehow. Colonel?"

"I refuse to take that bet," Hammond said. "He will win free, also Burr, perhaps—for a while. Cheer up, Doctor. Does this upset you so much?"

"Yes," Saugrain said. "It grieves me to believe that men can be so ignoble in a land so beautiful, of such great promise."

Six ∽

The month was now June. Bellefontaine, in spite of raucous sounds, accompanying repairs on rotting huts, had never looked more fair. Men considered themselves fortunate to be quartered in the beautiful valley. When June surrendered to July, they still could find shade and a cool breeze to refresh them.

In town, Captains Lewis and Clark spent much of each warm day behind the stone walls of the Pierre Chouteau residence, sorting their papers. They hoped to get away to Washington, with their reports and their Indian guests, in the early fall. Lewis's health seemed much improved. Saugrain accepted credit for that, since comment from other patients on the size and friendliness of Lewis's dog told him how much of his advice was being followed, namely, a daily walk, and also, when time could be spared, a gallop on a spirited horse. Hammond was so pleased to have his horses exercised by another Virginian that he had offered Lewis board and lodging free if he would move out to the Hammond farm.

Regretfully, Saugrain was sure, Lewis had refused to do this. He was afraid it might seem an affront to his Chouteau host, especially after Pierre Chouteau had offered to relieve the two captains of their promise to return their Indians safely to their own people by escorting them himself up the Missouri, if the captains could have them back in St. Louis early in the coming year.

This offer Captain Manuel considered not an act of grace, but a sly maneuver. Thanks to a large and active family, he said, the

(246)

Chouteaus had monopolized the fur trade from the Osage River south to the Arkansas; now they were bent on securing the riches of the Missouri for themselves as well.

Lisa would not stand by and see that happen. Two years before this, in 1804, he would have been on his way up the Missouri, extending his trade with the Indians in that direction, but the arrival of Lewis and Clark in St. Louis and their departure for the Pacific had stopped him. Seeing his design as very small compared to the grand design of President Jefferson, he—in common with other merchants, including the Chouteaus—had retreated to old trade patterns. He had persuaded himself that upon the return of the captains he would profit from their observations, and so he had released a number of his best men to them, with the understanding that they would return later to his employ. Now the men were back and he had their promises in hand; but facing this new threat, he felt he needed more if he did not want them stolen.

So began a traders' war which, before it ended, plumbed the depths of chicanery, but it had one virtue. It diverted Saugrain's mind from gloomy contemplation of baser crimes.

"Surely," he said, baiting Lisa, "a Chouteau does not need to steal men for his boats."

"No?" Lisa snapped. "Look! I am, as you know, building a new keelboat. I could have it finished, loaded, the men in their places, the ropes ready to be cast off, and a Chouteau or any other could steal the men right from under my nose—and I could not stop them. Why would they not? I would in the same situation."

There was a law, it seemed, that, if a merchant could produce evidence of an unpaid debt against a man in a rival's employ, he could come with a bailiff and remove that man—when it hurt most to do so. Saugrain must understand, Lisa explained, that the men in a trader's employ—hunters, trappers, *coureurs de bois* —while they were good men, each able to handle an oar as well as a gun or turn his hand to any other duty on the trail besides the one for which he had been hired, were away from home for one half to three fourths of a year, perhaps longer. So they looked upon their return home as a holiday. The patron would have paid each one what was still due him, after the sum paid on

(247)

his debts at the beginning of the journey had been subtracted. A good patron always saw to it that a little extra money was given to each one. This money the men proceeded to spend extravagantly and, when it was gone, to borrow more. A merchant, planning to make a trading journey, expected to have debts to cover. But these were often so scattered that it was impossible for the merchant to be sure he had caught them all. And there was the opportunity for a rival merchant to steal a good crew if he could not obtain one honestly.

"But surely," Saugrain said, both amused and horrified, "there is a way. . . ."

"Surely," Lisa agreed, his black eyes snapping. He must have the thumb print or X or the signature of each man on a paper so strong that even a Chouteau could not prove it worthless. He would consult a lawyer. There was a new one in town—another from Connecticut, Saugrain was pleased to note—a Mr. Hempstead, who, like Robinson, but even more impoverished, had walked all the way from Vincennes to St. Louis, with the added weight of lawbooks on his back. He was now becoming known for his shrewd presentation of claims, but was not yet so enriched that he would refuse to draw up, for pay, such a paper as Lisa desired.

Mr. Hempstead, as it turned out, was quite willing to study the law and draw up the desired paper. Not only that. Before delivering the document to Lisa, he asked Judge Easton, who now had a seat on the Territorial General Court besides continuing as postmaster, to read it for possible flaws.

When Judge Easton's approval had been given, Lisa hurried to obtain the signatures he needed, which not only bound the signers to work exclusively for Captain Manuel Lisa the following year, 1807, but also guaranteed Lisa's responsibility, under bond, for any debts incurred by them between the present—June 30, 1806—and the departure of Lisa's boat or boats not later than April 30 of the said year, 1807, for the purpose of trade with the Indians of the Missouri.

"Now," Lisa rejoiced, "I have only to keep out of the way of hired assassins," and he proceeded to order timber for the building of his new boat.

He failed to reckon on other interference. On the fifth day of July General Wilkinson returned to St. Louis with most, if not all, of his customary bluster. He regretted not having been able to take part in the celebration of the Fourth. Other business had detained him. By this time, however, the nature of his detention had become known. Aaron Burr had been tried for treason before a United States court sitting in Richmond, Virginia, and Wilkinson had been one of the witnesses called. He had admitted acquaintance with Burr, but no more than that. Finally the case had been dismissed for lack of conclusive evidence.

Both men were now free, at least temporarily; but neither, Saugrain thought, would ever again be free from the taint of suspicion. Wilkinson's return brought no applause.

Irritated by this, and more by the fact that town and Territory had prospered under a green new secretary and totally inadequate command at Bellefontaine during his absence—the merchants daring even while at war with one another to complete plans for the next year's trading ventures behind his back—he tried to assert his authority by a proclamation posted on the church door, the post office and Government House declaring that henceforth no trader would be allowed to depart with boat or boats from any town on either the Missouri or the Mississippi River without the express permission of the Territorial Governor.

St. Louis, Bellefontaine, the whole Territory buzzed. Even Lisa was shaken. "Can he do this?" he asked his lawyer. "Can he stop me now?"

"I don't think so," Mr. Hempstead said. "But let's be sure."

Once more he reviewed the local laws on trade franchises and, finding no support for the Governor's proclamation, made Lisa's situation a case in point whether anyone whose intentions were neither criminal nor treasonable could be denied the use of a river for the pursuit of his business by a governor's refusal to allow him to leave a home port. He had found no such law on the statute books, and he asked for a ruling by the Court.

Two days later Judge Easton, presiding, rendered an opinion. Hempstead's statement of the law was correct. Rivers, he said in conclusion, like public roads, belonged to the nation, and only the national Government could regulate the use of them.

That very day, while Saugrain tingled with pride at hearing his own sentiments about the great rivers confirmed officially, James Wilkinson received new orders from Washington which removed him from further participation in the petty wrangling of mere merchants. Since the orders affected the whole First Regiment of Infantry as well as himself, he elected to read them aloud at Assembly the following morning; and Saugrain, saying he never willingly missed a review or parade, stood by to listen. The General was to make preparation forthwith to leave Bellefontaine at the earliest possible date, taking with him all but one company of the regiment, and proceed at once to the defense of the city of New Orleans, now imperiled by a threatened uprising of certain Indian tribes north of that city.

The orders to the regiment had the sound of having been worded by Wilkinson rather than the War Department. The company captains were to see to it that all arrangements were completed speedily, including preparations for removing the families on short notice. These orders were to apply to the entire regiment, even the company which would remain on guard at Bellefontaine. He would not designate which company that might be until a commandant, expected daily, appeared. Also, Captain Pike, who had recently returned from the Osage, was making a list of men for special detached duty. Until the guard company and Captain Pike's selection were named, all in the regiment must follow the general orders.

"So he is still bent on exploring the southwest borderland," Hammond said at the council meeting hastily summoned by Saugrain. "The man's insane. This order from Washington is a reprieve. At the very least it provides him with a blameless exit from his post as Governor here. The President would prefer to remove him decently and quietly. I don't question for a minute the report on Indian unrest. Creek, Choctaw, Cherokee, Chickasaw, they are a lot of disgruntled braves, and they keep Claiborne at New Orleans in a constant sweat. He probably asked for military help and Wilkinson was the answer. He will do a good job, too. He is a good, fighting general and knows something about Indians. With a regiment like the First Infantry he will put the fear of God into the Indians, settle their uprising and then . . .

(250)

retire if he has any sense at all. Louisiana would give him land. The army would pension him. He should have cached money somewhere. If he would only forget these storybook plots. . . ."

The meeting of the triumvirate that warm July day took place in a shallow cave to which Lisa had recently obtained title, in the face of the river bluff below his house and store on Main Street. No more than a deep, jagged hole when he bought it, he had now smoothed the rough edges of the entrance and the inside walls and was planning to extend the entrance with outside walls of stone and a roof. When those improvements were made, and stout doors with iron bars and padlocks were added, he would have a storm-proof and burglar-proof warehouse for his furs, which could be unloaded at the water's edge only a few steps away.

Today it was a cool retreat, the view enhanced by the skeleton of a keelboat on blocks just beginning to take shape in the hands of a master builder. A cool retreat, but Saugrain spoke bitterly because of a bitterness in his mouth and throat.

"General Wilkinson," he said, "is abandoning none of his plans. Captain Pike and his company will leave Bellefontaine by boat as soon after the first of August as they can be ready. Wilkinson will not leave until he has seen them off, but Pike already has his orders. He will ascend the Missouri to the mouth of the Osage, where he will leave the boats and two or three men with provisions to make a winter camp and stand guard over the foundations of the new fort. The rest, under Captain Pike, will strike out overland to the Southwest, in search of the Arkansas River. They will follow it upstream to its source, if possible, then move south in search of the Red River of the South. On reaching it, they will turn east and follow this stream to where it meets the Mississippi. General Wilkinson will be waiting there—in a settlement called . . . Naquitosh? That is how it sounds. I believe it would be spelled out differently in writing, but Naquitosh is near enough."

"You say you have seen Pike's orders?" Hammond said out of a silence as hollow as the cave.

"No," Saugrain said. "I read a copy. My brother-in-law gave it to me to study. He will accompany Pike's party—as an independent medical officer. 'Volunteer surgeon' is how the paper reads."

(251)

Seven ᧐

On reaching home in the early afternoon of the day when Wilkinson had read out the regiment's orders, as Willy turned the brougham into the Saugrain drive, Saugrain found Madame waiting on the path to the house. How long had she waited there? Saugrain asked.

"Not long," she said. "Vigny, you are late again. You are always a little late, but this is the worst. Have you eaten since early morning? No? It is well that I kept hot soup for you. No, it is not too hot. We do not have that much fire in summer. It is just hot enough, if you will come right away without stopping for anything else."

"Without seeing those who wait for me in my den?" he chided.

There was only one, Madame said. He had promised to wait. No, she could not give his name. She had forgotten it. She would think of it while Saugrain ate the soup. She had not forgotten the name, Saugrain knew, but she was in such a state of apprehension that he ate the soup to soothe her, then hurried off to the laboratory.

He was not at all surprised to have Robinson open the door for him. He had dreaded to hear what he knew he would hear ever since Pike had asked him to recommend a medical officer. Now, as he and his brother-in-law faced each other, they were slow to find words.

"John!" Saugrain said finally, and stupidly, "is it you?" Then he added even more stupidly, "Have you had your soup?"

They laughed uneasily at that.

"Twice," Robinson said. "Sophie keeps a pot going, you know. I never thought the day would come. . . ." Then he braced himself. "Doctor, have you . . . can you guess why I am here?"

"To guess," Saugrain said—pompously, he feared, "is not to know. Tell me, John."

Robinson tried then to make his intentions sound good, but failed.

(252)

"I have been asked"—he said—"fiddlesticks, no! I volunteered. I am joining Pike's company for the Southwest."

"John," Saugrain said, "you can't mean it."

But he did mean it. Knowing that there would be opposition, he had studied every possible objection and had answers ready.

He did not know all of everything, Saugrain thought, so began his persuasion with information on the true character of the man who had ordered the march. He held back nothing of Wilkinson's record. All the evidence pronounced him, if not a traitor, certainly an unstable, undependable, irrational, unscrupulous man who, to further his own ambitions, would send brave soldiers to their deaths, or, at the very least, to the doors of a Spanish prison.

"I know," John said, when Saugrain stopped for breath. "That is how people talk who do not like the General. They will not believe that his so-called treason is only an imagination visioning heights that can be attained not only by himself, but, more important, by young America."

To Saugrain's mention of Wilkinson's specific instructions to Pike, Robinson said he knew about those. The General's presence in Louisiana made it possible for him to name a rendezvous to which Pike could report weeks earlier than he could possibly reach Bellefontaine.

In this connection Robinson's real reason for wanting to join the expedition appeared. He had drawn a chart of the route to be followed: the march across the plains to the source of the Arkansas—somewhere short of the mountains, he hoped—the source of the two rivers to be studied. "Doctor," he declaimed, "you know your geography, your history. This is the land traveled by the Conquistadores—one hundred, two hundred years ago."

"I know," Saugrain said sadly, "in search of gold. Did they find any?"

No, they had found only death in the wild, empty land.

"But the gold is there," Robinson insisted. "Such legends are never pure fancy. The gold is there, and some day it will be found. Doctor, please! I do not mean to dig for gold—not this time. I do not mean to look for it. I want only to see the land, to draw a map, to mark it for our country's own."

So it seemed that St. Louis was no longer to this young man the place of golden opportunity. No, it was not, Robinson conceded. All that had changed with the return of Lewis and Clark from the Pacific. St. Louis was now only a door that opened on opportunity. He agreed then that he had improved his knowledge of practical medicine by helping Saugrain when his help was needed, also that he had prospered by sharing the profits of McKenzie's store; but all that was too slow. He did not intend to spend his life trading salt pork or whiskey for animal skins.

"All right, all right!" Saugrain said sharply, desperation sharpening his tone. "Then I have only one more thing to say to you." And he spoke of the child whose birth was expected in October.

"Late October," Robinson corrected. "Three—almost four— months away. We'll be back long before then. We will travel lightly and walk fast. There is really nothing I can do here. Even Sophie says so. She wants me to go. I can't help her. Do you attend the births of your children?"

No, Saugrain did not. He arranged in advance for a good midwife to bring the child. Then he went off—nowadays to his workshop—and locked himself in, closing every door and window, and waited until he was called. He did nothing, but he was there.

"John," he said, "this is Sophie's first child. A first birth is almost always difficult. It can be dangerous. Sophie could die."

At that Robinson laughed. "You know right well she won't," he said. "She is just about the healthiest expectant mother that anyone could imagine. She will be all right. Everything will be all right. You'll see."

Saugrain now reported to his friends in the cave that he had used all his arguments on John Robinson—with no success. "The foolish man asked finally whether I had not enjoyed taking a few risks when I was twenty-four. Have I ever told you, my friends, about that?"

"No," Lisa said, his eyes brightening, as did Hammond's, "but we would like to hear."

"In the year 1787," Saugrain said, "in the company of two gentlemen with whom I had very slight acquaintance, I was exploring the Ohio. One day we were surrounded by what we took

(254)

to be hostile Indians. In trying to get away, one man was killed. The other and I, after frightful difficulties, escaped. I lost everything I had, including a piece of my right foot. Dr. Robinson at twenty-four has known no losses. When he is older and has experienced a few, he may be—who knows?—as wise as I am. *Mon Dieu!* Look at the time. It has been so pleasant here that I forgot to watch. I must go now to find Willy. His shade may have disappeared."

With that the meeting was dissolved, Hammond going uphill to Main Street, Lisa walking down the landing strip with Saugrain to find Willy and the brougham.

"Go with God, *amigo*," Lisa said there at parting, "defender of the weak, the helpless, the foolish, the distressed. You have lost this battle with a windmill but tomorrow you will find another."

Eight

On the sixteenth day of August a company of eight privates, two corporals, one sergeant and one volunteer surgeon, commanded by Major Pike—his promotion so recent that he hardly recognized the rank as his own—departed for the Southwest. For a few days Pike had raised Saugrain's hopes by hesitating to accept Robinson's services. He questioned the ability of a civilian, with no military training or discipline, to endure the rigors of a long march. Finally, however, the advantage of having a medical officer had outweighed his objections. Nobody in the company that day looked more fit than Robinson, a tall, strong young man, smartly handsome in white duck trousers and white linen shirt, jubilantly eager to push off.

They left in two stout river boats, carrying, besides Pike's company and their effects, four other soldiers and their belongings and a variety of tools. These were the men who would winter at the new fort upstream.

Saugrain watched the departure from the lookout on Belle Mountain, as the hill overlooking the river had come to be called —often, more briefly, Belle Mont. The whole picture was very gay. Wilkinson's galley, bright with flags and awnings, waited a short distance above the mouth of the creek. It was Wilkinson's intention to lead the flotilla as far as St. Charles as a token of his good will.

As a token . . . Saugrain wished that he might close his eyes and, while he kept them closed, that the whole picture would dissolve as a bad dream sometimes did. He did close them finally, but all that happened was the sound of a trumpet, then a burst of cheering. When he looked at the river, the boats were moving out. Morosely he watched them disappear; then, with a sigh, turned back to his hilltop quarters—and there, before the door, stood Aristide Michau.

Yes, of course, Aristide. How could he have forgotten? The Michaus, including Madame Saugrain and John Robinson, had arranged this. Was it for Saugrain or Aristide? The dear, good doctor, they reasoned, who had come to depend on Robinson's nearness at the McKenzie store, should not now be left without an assistant. Aristide, to be sure, could not offer as much help as Robinson had given; but here he was, ready and willing. He was now approaching fifteen. To his own satisfaction at least, he had now finished school. For a year, in place of other study, he had followed Robinson around wherever he went. He must have learned a few things.

"He has learned much," Robinson said. "He is quick to learn."

"All right, all right!" Saugrain said. "Aristide will be fine."

So why all the fuss? He would take Aristide around the post a couple of times, so that he would know where to go with medicine and bring back a fresh report on someone confined by illness or injury. Also, when Saugrain was away, he could keep a record of names and ailments of those who had called in his absence.

Aristide, the mischievous, prying boy. He was now taller than Saugrain, but otherwise had changed little. The pointed face was the same, the dark eyes bright, watchful, wary. Right now he looked ready to run.

"Hello!" Saugrain said, the more heartily because of a twinge in his conscience. "I didn't expect—you came to see John off?"

He had come out from town with John, Aristide said, in a

(256)

hired carriage, but he had not waited below to see the boats leave. He and John had said their good-byes on the way out. Then, learning that the doctor had gone up on Belle Mont to watch the boats from there, John had suggested that Aristide follow Saugrain and make his presence known. But he had not wanted to look at the river, so had gone into the office to wait.

"Good!" Saugrain said, hoping that no uneasiness quavered on his exclamation. "Did you have any callers?"

There had been two. One had been a Sergeant Grady's wife—from Washerwoman's Row. The sergeant had fallen out of a hay-mow the night before and hadn't been found until that morning. Mrs. Grady did not think he was much hurt—barring a bruise or two—because he had been too drunk to suffer hurt in the fall, but maybe the doctor should look him over a bit.

There was the note on Saugrain's table—the script as even and legible as Michau Père's. How did it happen that people with a little schooling often wrote like that, whereas a true scholar often could not read his own scratches? Well....

The second caller had been a man with a bad toothache. "Laudanum administered," the note said.

"Laudanum?" Saugrain questioned, with an excess of patience.

Yes. Dr. John had showed him how, Aristide said. A drop of laudanum on a small piece of cotton to plug the ache. The man was afraid the tooth might have to be pulled. So was Aristide afraid. "Do you pull teeth, Doctor?" he asked anxiously.

He did when he must, Saugrain admitted, but he did not like the job. His wrists and arms were strong enough, but he lacked weight. He had been tempted several times to call in the post blacksmith, but now one of the new doctors in town had shown him among his instruments an impressive set of forceps. If, when they returned to the fort—day after tomorrow—the laudanum had not cured the soldier's tooth, it might be best to arrange for him to visit that new doctor. Now, however, they would lock the office, step around for a look at Sergeant Grady, whose relaxed unconsciousness had saved his bones, then find Willy and the carriage, and ride back to town. Surely enough had happened to fill this day.

Three days later, all aglitter, from the cabochon that anchored the plume on his hat to his shining new boots, with colors flying from every appropriate staff, General Wilkinson shook hands with the Chouteau brothers, with Dr. Saugrain, with twenty other leading citizens with whom he had enjoyed friendly relations—at least outwardly—and stepped aboard his galley, waiting at the St. Louis water front; then stood at salute until the current carried boat and General out of sight beyond protruding bluffs.

Behind the galley, hired barges, also with flags flying, carrying four companies of the First Regiment of United States Infantry, made a brave parade out of the leave-taking. Applause, fitful at first, then swelling in volume, replied to the General's salute. It was thoughtful of the General, also right and proper, everyone said, that he should have ordered the boats and the soldiers down from Bellefontaine in the early morning, so that the formal farewell should take place at the St. Louis landing.

He was at heart a good kind man, although some did not approve of him . . . so the conversation ran as the cheering died away. Now he was gone. Generally it was thought that he would not return, since it was known that Mrs. Wilkinson waited at the fort with all her things packed until arrangements could be made for herself and the children to travel. But, one might ask, where would they go now? South? Following her husband? Then what was this talk of war in that direction? Finally an older patient put the question to Saugrain. Was there truly a war on the lower Mississippi?

"No war at present, Michel," Saugrain answered firmly. "Just a few troublesome Indians. The Governor at New Orleans has asked for extra protection. General Wilkinson is an experienced Indian fighter."

That was August. A truly golden September followed—bright, warm days and cool nights. Sophie had a letter from Robinson. He had written on the eve of the departure of Pike's company up the Osage River to the point from which they would strike out for the Arkansas. All the men, he said, were in good health and great spirits. The weather was ideal. He closed with affectionate regards to the whole family. If there was more, Sophie kept it to herself.

(258)

At Bellefontaine, the new commandant was still expected. He arrived finally in October—a disciplined army man of about thirty, Saugrain thought. He seemed rather nonplused by a garrison of two companies scattered over the extensive cantonment, neither company appearing to be at full strength; but he settled himself in the Wilkinson house promptly, deciding that it would serve very well both as his residence and general headquarters.

That was before he visited Saugrain on Belle Mont—where Saugrain meant to cling to his official eyrie until a real winter storm forced him to seek shelter in the valley. Besides, his situation on the hill gave him a ready approach to the Bellefontaine Road. On the first day of October Madame Saugrain had warned him that she saw signs of Sophie's accouchement approaching. Whereupon he had arranged for a livery-stable conveyance to take him and Aristide to the cantonment in the early morning, and Willy to call for them at midday, or sooner if the need arose. His hours at the fort, his program for handling the demand for his services, also the immediate situation at his home in St. Louis, were matters he had still to discuss with Thomas Hunt, Lieutenant Colonel Commanding.

So, he was more than pleased one bright morning to have that gentleman knock on his door and enter. However, he soon found himself forced to defer his personal report. The colonel had a few remarks on his own part that wanted expression. He was, first of all, much impressed by the Belle Mont. Granting that the valley was beautiful and pleasant for most of the year, this height was a commanding position. Had there been a reason for not taking advantage of it in the original plan for the cantonment?

Saugrain mentioned the convenience of being at the river level, the water supply, and the fact that the rear slope of Belle Mont had been much rougher than it appeared now, after much dragging and a year of use.

"But those are minor problems," Colonel Hunt said. "At least a few service buildings could have been located here. The powder magazine for one; headquarters. . ."

And at that point a respectful thump on the door announced the arrival of Willy, with the carriage.

(259)

Nine ∽

Late that afternoon Saugrain stood beside Sophie
Robinson's bed, warming a limp white hand between his, watching her breathing, waiting.

"Sophie?" he said finally. "Petite Maman, are you still sleeping?
No? Open your eyes then. Look at me. That's right. Um-m—
very good!"

Then he had to bend over the bed to hear what she was trying
to say: "Doctor, have you seen the baby? Is he—all right? Sister
said I was to ask you. Why?"

"Because I am a good judge in such a case," Saugrain said,
tucking the limp hand now under the coverlet. "The boy is very
much all right, little sister, although I must say at first I was
frightened. With all that black hair, I thought, *Dieu*, what have we
here—a monkey? However, after Maggie Brule had cleaned him
up a little, I looked again. He is a fine, handsome boy. A big boy—
eight and a half pounds. That is too big for a *petite maman*.
So, sleep now and rest, or you will not be strong enough to hold
him."

"I will be stronger tomorrow," she said, smiling a little at
his nonsense. "You will see." But then tears came, and there was
no stopping them.

Helplessly Saugrain kept watch beside the bed, speaking any
words that flitted through his mind: "For John, little sister? He is
away, I know, but no farther away, surely, than he was last week.
He may be nearer. One of these days the door will open and he
will be here."

Later he hoped that Sophie had not been deceived into believing
him. The year passed with no word from the wanderers. Sophie
Robinson, engrossed in the care of her beautiful—and lively—
baby, recovered her health in spite of disappointment, but she
would hear to no christening in John's absence, although the name
had been chosen before John had left. If John did not return,

their son would be a second John Hamilton Robinson. If or when John should return—Sophie said she was sure he would—their son would be named Edward Hamilton, for John's brother.

"Little Hamilton Robinson," Sophie crooned. "My son Hamilton!"

In January of the new year, 1807, the two captains—St. Louis found it hard to change the familiar title—with very little ice in the rivers, set out at last for Washington, taking with them two large packing boxes of papers and trophies, the Indians, the interpreter, and Lewis's dog. It was said that Clark, besides, had new evidence to offer about those soldiers that Aaron Burr was assembling on that island in the Ohio. What? He continued to do that after being arrested once and tried for treason? Yes, because that trial had come to nothing, it must be remembered, for lack of what the lawyers called conclusive evidence. The Government, however, after that must have watched him more closely, because the first of February brought to St. Louis, as it did to every other town in the nation important enough to have a post office, an order for the arrest of Aaron Burr on sight.

For a week it was difficult to push one's way through the St. Louis post office. Every inhabitant, literate or illiterate, wanted to see for himself the President's order describing the traitor, the dark, smooth-spoken gentleman whom almost everyone remembered to have seen on the occasion of his visit to St. Louis the previous summer.

And what of General Wilkinson? Was he also to be arrested? Nothing was said on the notice about him. Nothing was known for a while, although one could be fairly certain now that he would never return to St. Louis. There was this new commandant at Bellefontaine, and presently there was a new official with the double title and duties of Territorial Secretary and Deputy Governor.

He was new only with respect to the office. He had settled in St. Louis almost a full year before his appointment—another lawyer, very sharp, handsome, well recommended, with good connections, but very young. He did not look a day over twenty. His name was Frederick Bates.

Of course, he was older than he seemed. The President's mes-

(261)

sage, presenting him to the General Court as Secretary and Deputy Governor, revealed that before moving to St. Louis, he had served Michigan Territory as Secretary, establishing there a reputation for exceptional talent as a lawyer, cool judgment, and absolute rectitude. It was the common opinion that, if he had those virtues, his seeming youth could hardly matter.

His dealings with the people of the Territory were direct and honest enough. Having at his command the facts about the end of the Burr-Wilkinson scandal, he made two brief statements. Aaron Burr, after the order for his arrest was published, having assembled only one thousand revolutionaries on Blennerhasset Island, had known that his case was hopeless and had fled into exile, perhaps permanent this time. Where he had gone was not included in the report.

As for General Wilkinson, he had now resigned from the army. His present residence also was unknown.

"Resigned" or "retired," Hammond said at the subsequent meeting of the three wise men, were just other ways of saying he had been dismissed. A New Orleans newspaper had given a more complete account.

Wilkinson in February had been in full command at New Orleans. He had quieted the Indians and put the city under martial law, to prevent betrayal from within; but on hearing the order for Burr's arrest, he had panicked, or he had sought to cover his complicity with action. Anyhow, he had ordered his infantry north to the Ohio to make the arrest. This had stripped New Orleans of its defenses. If Burr had still been at Blennerhasset and known of this movement, he could have marched his thousand revolutionaries south and captured New Orleans, possibly the Louisiana coast, without a struggle. At least, New Orleans thought so and had demanded Wilkinson's dismissal. So Wilkinson also was living in retirement—somewhere.

"I know where he is not," Saugrain said gloomily. "He is not in Naquitosh."

"That's right," Hammond said. "There's that situation still to be unraveled. And you have had no word? Have you spoken to the Deputy Governor?"

"No," Saugrain said. "I am afraid—not because he is young. It is that special virtue the President mentioned—his absolute rectitude. That could make trouble if Pike's company is in difficulties, as I am sure it is. Still, I would like to hear what has happened and where."

Ten ∽

Two days later he had a communication from Washington. He shook before he could bring himself to break the seals; and when he did so and saw, on top of other papers, a letter signed by both the Secretary of War and the Secretary of State, he was more shaken than before. The letter, in brief, presented for his study a transcript of one received by the Spanish minister in Washington from the Viceroy of Mexico, which in turn copied a report to the Viceroy from the Lieutenant Governor at a subcapital named Durango.

The Lieutenant Governor at Durango was holding two parties of American soldiers, each with a different leader, which had been captured by Spanish patrols at different places in Spanish New Mexico. The first captain had papers saying he was a surgeon, name John Hamilton Robinson, residence St. Louis, U.S.A. The second captain was Major Pike, Regiment I, Infantry, U.S.A.

The Robinson party had been taken at Tempe, near the Arkansas River, and brought to Santa Fe first. On being informed that a second party like his had been captured on Spanish territory, Dr. Robinson had refused to state the reason for his presence in New Mexico, wishing to wait for Major Pike's arrival, the said Major Pike being in command over all. Dr. Robinson was ill at the time; he and his men had suffered from extremes of heat and cold before being found by the Spanish patrol. For that reason leniency had been shown, allowing everything to rest until Major Pike appeared.

But Major Pike, on his arrival at Santa Fe, while he acknowledged that the soldiers with Dr. Robinson were part of his command, had denied any acquaintance with the doctor. Whereupon, the Teniente at Santa Fe, at a loss to know how to deal with the trespassers, had sent them all to Durango for safe keeping, and the Teniente there now wished orders from Mexico City. The

Viceroy, however, having by then heard of the monstrous Burr conspiracy—having heard that part of its criminal intent had been a plan to invade Mexico—had thought it best to send all the papers to Spain's minister at Washington, who no doubt could obtain some satisfaction from a direct meeting with the American Secretary of State.

And now the State Department, before presenting the American side of the story, knowing that the presence of the men in Spanish America had been due to the unwisdom of General Wilkinson, wished to have information from St. Louis, where the journey into New Mexico had originated—the reason for it, if available, and most certainly a copy of the orders.

To clear his mind and be sure he understood everything, Saugrain sent for Michau Père and read him all the correspondence, translating everything into French.

"Antoine," Michau Père said at the end of it, kneading his hands as he always did when deeply troubled, "what do you make of it?"

"This much at least," Saugrain said. "I believe the officials in Washington and in Mexico would like to settle the matter peaceably, fairly, and quickly; but they need help. That is why they have written."

"But why to you?" Michau asked. "The commandant at the fort can answer the question about orders."

Robinson or Pike—or both—Saugrain thought, might have mentioned him to the governors involved. John could have claimed the relationship. Washington then, wishing all the information obtainable, had written to Saugrain in addition to Colonel Hunt and Deputy Governor Bates.

The man of absolute rectitude—Saugrain—not knowing what he could do, knew that he must act at once.

"Bon-père, excuse me, please. I must go now. You have heard the news. Tell Sophie what you think she should know—that John is alive but temporarily detained in Mexico. The State Department is negotiating for his return."

"Antoine, that is not true," Michau objected.

"It will be true," Saugrain said, "as soon as we can get a letter off to Washington. And that will be right away if you do not delay me. I am going to call on Mr. Bates now."

"Antoine," Michau said, "he sees no one without an appointment. His clerk writes them down, with the hour and the day."

"He has an appointment with me now," Saugrain said, "if I can get away from here." And he was off at a run for the House of Government.

Opening the door to the Deputy Governor's private office was easier then than opening the portals of the young man's mind. Mr. Bates was stiff at first; he was uncomfortable. There were aspects of the situation to which his code of law did not seem to apply. He was mystified and offended by the Secretaries' consultation of a civilian before giving an answer to the Spanish minister.

"It is only because they believe that the answer to the puzzle must come from understanding the characters of the two men most seriously involved," Saugrain said. "You and Colonel Hunt" —he might have excluded the Governor—"can supply the needed information as to Major Pike's orders, the exact reason for the march; but still the whole story would not be known. Of the three of us—Colonel Hunt, you, and myself—I am the only one who can supply the missing paragraphs. If you will hear me, please. . . ."

"I will be glad to hear what you have to offer," Bates said, "since you think it important."

He would hear, gladly or otherwise, Saugrain thought, but before he began, that clerk whom Michau Père had mentioned tiptoed into the room with word that Colonel Hunt had arrived from Fort Bellefontaine and would like permission to join the Governor and Dr. Saugrain. He was ushered in, begged the others to proceed, then took a chair to one side and listened attentively.

Saugrain began with Major Pike, sketching his life from birth at a military post to the present. Reared to believe in discipline, Saugrain said, Pike was an excellent drill master, also an excellent company officer. He had commanded the preceding expedition —up the Mississippi—with great success. Acting as leader, doctor and quartermaster, he had accomplished his mission, had brought back his entire company in good health, and apparently had got on well with the British fur traders whom he had encountered and a number of strange Indians. On this expedition to the Southwest, Saugrain was sure that he had done nothing but carry out

(265)

his orders to the letter, except that he had been instructed to withdraw at once at the first sign of Spanish occupation. Evidently his meeting with the Spanish patrol allowed him no opportunity to retreat.

"Is it possible," Bates asked thoughtfully, "that the late Governor had some hidden reason for ordering this expedition?"

"It is more than possible," Saugrain said, "since now we know so much more about this unfortunate man. However, if that was the case, I also believe that neither of the men under examination knew of it. Major Pike went because he was ordered. Dr. Robinson went because he wanted to visit in person a region about which he had heard and read many glowing tales, and he thought such an opportunity might not come his way again— Now wait," Saugrain begged, when Bates scoffed at this notion. "I have not yet described this one to you."

He did his best, beginning with his first encounter with the handsome young Virginian and continuing to his departure with Pike. Brave, warmhearted, reared in a comfortable home by indulgent parents—at least the mother was indulgent, and Bates was impressed by the Hamilton relationship—well educated, an excellent doctor. Pike had not liked his joining the company as a "volunteer surgeon," but had welcomed the addition of a medical officer. Impulsive. . . .

"Now," Bates said, "we begin to have a reason why he abandoned Pike midway of their journey."

"But," Saugrain said, "we don't know whether he did abandon Pike. We can reason only that some situation arose over which these two divergent characters could not agree, and so they parted. We will not know exactly what happened until we hear each man's story and compare the two."

"And you have an idea of how we could hear those stories, Doctor?"

"Yes," Saugrain said. The idea had just come to him, but it was a good one. In presenting it, he chose Madame Saugrain's gentle approach to audacity. Would it be possible to write to the Secretaries in Washington, suggesting that they could request or advise or recommend that the Viceroy in Mexico—under some sort of parole—return the captive Americans to the United

States, the idea being that, in the friendly, familiar atmosphere of home, the full, true story of each leader would be told?

"My idea," Saugrain finished, "is to have each one tell his story in the presence of the other."

"Bravo!" Colonel Hunt applauded, finding a reason now for speaking. "Bravo! It's a great idea, Doctor."

But Mr. Bates fidgeted. It was highly irregular, he thought. No mention had been made of a trial or penalty.

"If by penalty, you mean punishment, Governor," Saugrain said, more warmly than he had intended, "these men are prisoners —in Mexico. Have you ever been a prisoner—anywhere?"

"Certainly not."

"It is no disgrace, I hope," Saugrain said, "but it is an experience. When I was twenty, I spent a year in a British prison in Jamaica. My fault was crossing the ocean in a French ship. A provincial prison in Mexico could not be worse, but I doubt that it is much better. The floor will be hard and the food bad. Our young men will return with chastened spirits—that, at least."

Finally the clerk was called in and the letter was written, Saugrain dictating the first text, the other two adding correct phrasing and formality.

"But it was a good letter," Saugrain reported to his father-in-law that afternoon, as he rested on the couch in his library, with the fat volume about Don Quixote for a headrest. "It will have a hearing in Washington. Why? Because somebody in the Capital wants to hear another say what he has been thinking or feeling."

Eleven ∽

The end of March brought the prisoners home to St. Louis. A sorrier lot nobody could have wished to see. Subtropic sun and rain and lye soap had faded uniforms until patches stood out like flags. Dysentery, more than scant rations, had wasted their flesh and hollowed their eyes. "Even after we got back to New Orleans," one man reported, "we couldn't hardly keep down what we swallered." To be confined to quarters at Bellefontaine was no punishment for the soldiers. All a man needed was to be home again, warmed and comforted by familiar food and a woman to fuss over him.

John Hamilton Robinson, paroled to Saugrain, alternately held his Sophie in close embrace, whispering unintelligible endearments into her starved ears, or paced the floor with his son in his arms, making wild promises: "I'll never leave home again, never in this world. . . ."

At Bellefontaine, Major Pike had returned to sorrow. The boy, his little son, had made no gains in resistance and had died during an epidemic of membranous croup in February. After Clara Pike's awed greeting, "Zeb, I hardly know you," Saugrain saw them one day standing beside the grave of their son. He did not need to hear what they had to say to each other, if they found any words. He turned away with a constricted, aching heart.

Then came the hearing—in the day room of Colonel Hunt's headquarters house. April sunshine dispelled all memory of the vagaries of March. Through an open window came the merry sounds of spring—the splashing of the creek and a great fussing of birds. Inside, the atmosphere was either chilled or overheated by hostility. The two principals, after all they had been through, had come home not on speaking terms, and nothing had happened since to bridge their differences. When the hearing began, each faced his interrogator squarely, but never once looked at the other. Hostility mounted, especially when they gave their separate reasons for the division of the company. Bates had brought out two clerks to take down the testimony, hoping that in that way not a word should be missed. Repeatedly now one clerk or the other raised his hand for delay.

"It was that mountain," Robinson said first, "that damnable mountain."

"Such a mountain I had never seen before," Pike said. "At first it was just a great, white cloud floating in the sky. Morning and evening there might be a glow of color, but mostly it was white. We were away from the river, with no trail to follow; but here was a marker—due west. . . ."

"For two solid weeks," Robinson reported, "we marched through bush and bramble, scrub growth and desert, trying to

(268)

reach that mountain. We knew soon enough that it was a mountain. Still we went on. When we came to it, it towered above us. . . ."

"Like a sentinel," Pike said. "There was no sign of hut or other marker on it. I felt we must climb it, claim it by planting a flag, as I marked the beginning of the Mississippi on the other march. We rested two nights and a day. Then I ordered the climb. I wanted not only to plant a flag on the summit, but also to examine the view. It seemed our best opportunity to study the land on all sides. It was still October. At the base the mountain was green, with flowers blooming. Flowers bloomed at the edge of the snowcap."

"It was bitter cold," Robinson said. "We wore summer uniforms. Every man had a blanket, a gun, powder and ball, and a hunting knife. Some of us had traded for extra moccasins back on the Osage River. That was all. Nights were the worst. At the base, where we had some cover, we could roll up in our blankets and sleep after a fashion. Above that, before we came to the snow, there were rocks—bare rocks, as hard as flint. Still, we could huddle on the lee side of a boulder and make out to stay alive. There were misshapen trees—terribly tough wood. We hacked and broke off enough for fires—to scorch the meat we killed—hares mostly, a few birds. We ate the meat without salt, washing it down with melted snow water, and rested—in heaps, for body warmth. At dawn we pushed on, too dazed to rebel. . . ."

"The climb," Pike said, "was often arduous, but never impossible. There was always a way around the steepest slopes. We stopped short of the summit. The view was magnificent. Allowing for the deceptive distances of the plains, I knew we could see for miles. Off to our right the sun shone on a whole range of mountains, snow-covered, marking the western horizon. I knew if we followed the line of those mountains, we must reach the river we sought. There would be plentiful wood and water and game at the foot of the mountains."

"We had with us a sort of guide," Robinson said. "We didn't pick him up. He joined us—several days after we left the Osage. A Plains Indian, he spoke almost no English, more Spanish; but he could read footprints, man or animal, where we saw only dust. And he never seemed lost. He knew the country."

(269)

He had refused to climb Pike's mountain, but when the men came down and spoke of the mountain range beyond it, he named it at once: Sangre de Cristo, Blood of Christ, and crossed himself as he said the words.

As for Robinson's abandoning the march:

"I was stunned," Pike said. "From the day we left Bellefontaine, he was more than faithful in his care of the men. At any hour, day or night, he would respond to a call, giving aid to any ailment—sickness, a wound, an insect bite. On the mountain, although he objected to climbing it, he carried a pack of instruments and medicines, and used both. Then, when the worst was over, to take off without a by-your-leave. . . ."

"I was not sure that the worst was over," Robinson said. "I refused to climb one more mountain."

When Pike had mentioned marching along the Sangre de Cristo range, the Indian had said, "No!"—one of his few English words—and pointed . . . well, if the mountain range went southwest, his direction was south. With stumbling words and wild motions he had indicated that they should go that way. They would reach the river in—he showed four fingers—four days. When Pike still refused to change his plan, the Indian seemed very dejected, and that night he disappeared.

Robinson had been the first to learn that the guide was gone. All that day he had been too busy dispensing medicine and liniment, bandaging wounds and open sores, to think of the Indian. When darkness came, he disposed himself for rest in a position that insured his being awakened by light striking across his eyes. The makeshift alarm worked; he was awake at the first hint of dawn. Not finding the Indian guide in his usual place was a shock, but he had no time to waste in pondering that. He fastened on his back pack, rolled his blanket and hung it over the pack and his shoulders, took up his gun, and was ready. Remembering how the Indian had faced, pointing southward with his arm outstretched, he faced that way, fixed his eye on an outcropping of rock, and hurried off.

He had no idea that he was being followed. Never in his life had he felt so alone as he felt that day. It was like walking through empty space, but he went on, keeping to a sort of line from one objective to another. He allowed himself a brief rest

(270)

at noon in the shade of scrubby trees around a pool of water, so brackish that he did no more than sample it. Instead, he sipped a little water from his canteen, then got to his feet again.

Toward evening, when he came to a trickle of water over a rocky bed, stumbling weary, he dropped his burdens and sat down to stretch his legs; then, for fear that they might stiffen and he couldn't use them again, he forced himself to rise and, with gun and canteen in hand, walked slowly up the course of the stream, hoping to find enough water to taste. Sure enough, the trickle slowly increased, spreading out finally into pools among the rocks. At one of these he risked a mouthful, found the water sweet and clear, and buried his dusty face in it after he had drunk enough to satisfy his thirst. Feeling refreshed, he hurried back to where he had dropped his blanket and pack.

He was assembling loose rock to form a basin in which he meant to build a small fire—to toast some dried meat he had brought from camp and heat water for tea—when he heard the rustle of movement. Snatching his gun, he turned, and there, to his horror, at the edge of the arroyo, stood four men from Pike's command. In a huddle the evening before they had concluded that Doc was making ready to turn back home. His attentions to all during the day had been too painstaking. Moved by a terrible longing of their own, they had decided to follow him. That night they had slept a little apart from the other men, with the one who had the sharpest ears nearest to Robinson. The appointed guard had heard him rise and next morning, had watched him leave, then had awakened the others. They knew he would send them back even if he had to go with them. So, all day they had followed just close enough to keep him in sight without his seeing them.

Yes, Robinson had known that they should be returned to their unit, but here they were. He scolded, he urged, he persuaded, he reasoned, he pleaded, but they would not heed his warning. He reminded them that by the military code they were deserters, and they knew the punishment for that. They were in for it now, they argued. Major Pike would not forgive their going off without leave. He would drag them over the other mountains and shoot them afterwards. There was nothing Robinson could do but accept their company.

(271)

At the end of the third day, as the Indian guide had foretold, they came to a regular river. It might or might not be the Arkansas, but after four days of arid marching, it looked impressive. Moreover, it flowed from west to east. They decided to rest where they were that night and in the morning begin to trace the river to its mouth, wherever that might be. They would have water, probably game and some fish. A little farther on they might even manage to make a raft to carry them downstream.

At Bellefontaine, the small board of inquiry stirred restlessly. As he might have foreseen, Saugrain's heart ached for all the men involved.

"Did you not think," Colonel Hunt asked, "of the possibility of hostile Indians?"

"We were desperate," Robinson said. "We thought only of our needs."

Their plans made, they had stripped, washed the dust from their bodies and from such of their clothes as they thought would dry quickly, eaten supper from their dwindling rations, rolled themselves in their blankets and slept. They knew nothing until the following morning, when they wakened to find themselves surrounded by a Spanish military patrol.

"The officer commanding," Robinson said, "knew no English. One word—Americano—got over to him. He decided we were spies and marched us off to Santa Fe."

The lieutenant there had proved to be more literate. Either he understood Robinson's simplified explanation of how he had come to be taken while wandering about Spanish territory, or he made a good show of comprehension. Unfortunately, by this time an Indian runner had brought word of the capture of another lot of Americanos in the Sangre de Cristo mountains, their comandante a man named Pike. When the Teniente asked Robinson if he knew this Captain Pike, Robinson, grasping at any straw, unblushingly told the truth. Yes, he knew Major Pike and he felt sure that the major, when he arrived, would set everything straight.

"Another error on my part," Robinson said now, ending on a note of bitterness. "Gentlemen, I have told the truth as I remember it."

The rest was Pike's story. Asked why at Santa Fe he had denied knowing Robinson, he answered with characteristic terseness, biting off each word before choosing another, and yet, it seemed to the tormented Saugrain that Pike was not without feeling. Rather, he suffered with an unaccustomed emotion to which he would not yield.

"I was angry," he said. "I felt disgraced. In all my army life I had never witnessed or dealt with desertion. I thought, I still think, his conduct was outrageous—to leave without warning, and no word of explanation after he had gone. He took half my company."

Reminded that Robinson had said under oath that he had not taken the men and had not thought of anyone following him, Pike continued, "I still maintain that they would not have deserted if he had not shown them the way."

As for their meeting at Santa Fe: "I could not look at him. I could not forgive what he had done. I hated him."

The atmosphere in the room grew heavier by the minute. Saugrain's heart was now a lump of lead. Asked if he thought that by staying together his company might have avoided capture, Pike said it was possible. At least their number would have equaled the number of the Spanish patrol. Such a company would have looked more like exploring and less like spying. But would not the same have been true if he had taken the Indian's advice and led the whole company southward to look for the river?

"That," Pike said, "looked to me like turning back. I did not consider our duty accomplished."

At this point anyone would have said that blame for the sorry ending of the venture rested more heavily on Robinson than on Major Pike.

"Well, my dream is over," Robinson said to Saugrain at the end of the day. "I might as well pack our belongings and take Sophie and the boy back to Virginia."

"A dream," Saugrain said gently, "does not die so quickly, John. Please do not say anything to Sophie of your intent. Wait."

Before the end of the hearing a slight turn had come in Robinson's favor. It hinged upon a question put by Colonel Hunt. Would Major Pike please repeat what he had said about Robinson's service before he had abandoned the company?

(273)

"Excellent," Pike repeated. "Never derelict in the performance of duty. Willing to answer a call by day or night." And when Colonel Hunt commented, "Then you must have missed him the more for that reason," the reply was crisp but unhesitating: "Yes, sir."

With that the hearing was over. Robinson and Pike were dismissed, the one to return to his home in town, the other to his quarters. The judges remained—to review the evidence and write their recommendations to Washington.

All had been deeply impressed, shaken, by the testimony of the two men—their hardships, their sufferings, their parting in anger at the base of the beautiful, damnable mountain: Pike's Mountain. Above all, they had come to know the awesome extent of Jefferson's purchase, the barren empty wastes waiting to be claimed and used. Now the judges must examine their feelings, their thoughts, and make a recommendation.

Here, they agreed, were two fine, brave men, whose valuable service should not be discarded lightly or hastily. They were guilty chiefly of errors in judgment, under extremely difficult circumstances. Even Robinson's irregular conduct had been innocent of evil purpose or intent.

"Gentlemen," the Deputy Governor said at this point, "what we are suggesting amounts to pardon for every offense, major or minor, a reward instead of a penalty."

"You don't agree then," Colonel Hunt said quickly, "to a recommendation for leniency, really an acquittal?"

"I do indeed agree," Bates said just as quickly, "but not because of circumstance. Rather, because of their value as men and officers. What Major Pike may consider a failure in the way of accomplishment may prove to be the reverse. His and Robinson's observations may supply much-needed information some day— when, for instance, it becomes necessary to fix a boundary between American and Spanish claims. In that connection it is regrettable that the notes, with some drawings which Dr. Saugrain says Robinson made, were confiscated. You still think there is no hope of recovering any of that, Doctor?"

"None," Saugrain said. "The men have been returned, but no papers. If there is still a king of Spain, these will be sent with the Viceroy's report to the Royal Council in Madrid, which will give them honorable burial in the royal archives. Some day, hundreds of years from now, scholars may be allowed to look at them, or copy a few lines from the written text, but now all we can hope is that the two men may keep their remembrance of what they saw and experienced long enough to set it down in some form on paper. That is a thing they can do while they wait for a reply to our recommendations."

"Gentlemen," the Deputy Governor asked solemnly, "are you ready to make those recommendations?"

The gentlemen were ready. The report began with a summary of the hazardous situation in which the company found itself at the time of the leaders' seeming misdemeanors—their physical exhaustion, their isolation, their remoteness from human habitation. In view of those things and their record of perfect service up to that point, it pleaded for leniency of judgment. It recommended the restoration of personal freedom to all the men involved, also that Major Pike should continue to hold the rank of Major and the men of the company should keep their company ratings.

It was a good report, but Saugrain suppressed a sigh as he signed it. If only the President and the Secretaries of War and State could have heard the brave young men tell the story! God grant them understanding and a degree of imagination!

Twelve ↶

The weeks of waiting for a final word from Washington were not easy to endure. At Bellefontaine Colonel Hunt relaxed "confinement to quarters" to cover the post. The men in the ranks drilled with their companies and shared the daily tasks as ordered. Major Pike displayed his experience as a quartermaster to assist in the ordering and storing and issue of supplies. One Sunday, when Colonel Hunt was indisposed, Pike commanded a general parade. John Hamilton Robinson, on the other hand, was by turns humbly grateful or jubilant to be sacking dried beans and peas and weighing out salt pork at the McKenzie store on the Missouri, filling a big order for Manuel Lisa, whose boat was now complete and ready to be loaded for his trading voyage.

As for Saugrain, he suffered these days from an affliction heretofore rare in his experience—a period of indecision, of self-doubt. In the simple act of administering a dose of ipecac, he would ask himself, Am I doing the right thing? Could I do better? More largely, he wondered whether his advice had been good in the matter of John Robinson, Zebulon Pike and the rest. Colonel Hunt said he had done wonderfully well. Mr. Bates was most respectful when they met. Still, he wondered.

He knew this was simply a manifestation of nerve strain, but, except when he was furiously busy at some exacting task, he could not shake the mood. As the weeks went by and each day meant that waiting to know must be relieved that much sooner, his suffering grew worse instead of better.

Finally on a Monday morning in mid-April, he reported for duty at Bellefontaine, determined to slay the monstrous thing that was disturbing his peace of mind. He would on that day make a vital decision and act upon it—just to prove that he could. With the decision vaguely framed in his head, he visited several bedfast patients, then turned over the rest of his general round to Aristide and marched off to his quarters on Belle Mont. There he closed the outer door firmly, insuring at least a warning in advance of any call, opened a window to let in the good spring air, turned from that to the wall that held his commission as SURGEON'S MATE, lifted it off its nail, and laid it face up on his table, meaning to study it.

Knowing every syllable engraved on it, he nevertheless read every word from "Reposing special trust" to "Th. Jefferson, President," then, with undiminished resolution, sat back, closed his eyes and composed mentally a letter of resignation:

Mr. President, I have now for three years filled the post of surgeon's mate at this Fort Bellefontaine. I have enjoyed every hour spent here, faithfully answering every call made upon me, applying such skill as I possess to the curing of the sick and mending the wounded. I have served you and this much of your army with devotion and absorption, laying aside other duties and calls. I am not tired. I am in good health. I shall miss being here, knowing the men who come and go—and their families; but

I feel that now is the time for me to withdraw, to turn over my duties to a younger man. I can then with an easier conscience devote myself to certain professional matters which I have lately neglected.

If he could have stopped there, he had a fair letter composed; but it was not in his nature to stop without saying all that he was thinking. For instance: I am not an old man, Mr. President. Forty-four is not old, but old age draws nearer. I am by nature meddlesome. I make trouble for myself and others by meddling. I cannot resist an opening. I make a show of wisdom, knowing that I have no great store. Sir, I do not wish to occupy a position of trust when I am not more than a meddlesome old man. . . .

In sudden horror at this admission, he gasped and drew back from the table. What had he been thinking of, to address a president so, one whom he had never seen, to drown him with silly words? He had never been given to hysterics. Why now?

He knew why. He was offering to resign and he wanted to stay. Here he was, tearing himself into two parts again.

At that point came interruption, without a knock or call. The door was thrust open and there stood Aristide, perspiring, breathless.

"Doctor!" he panted. "Come quick. No, don't come. Let me say it. A thing has happened. I have read in your books and I have heard you say that a first sign of smallpox is a putrid smell —corruption. I . . . Doctor, Mrs. Grady, Sergeant Grady's wife . . . their son is visiting them. He has a fever and a breaking-out—an eruption. . . ."

"Aristide!" Saugrain, on his feet now, pushed the commission back on the table. "You did not go into that house, I hope!"

"No!" Aristide said, still fighting for breath. "When Mrs. Grady opened the door, I started to run, but she cried out at me to stop. She wanted to know why I was there instead of you. She needed a doctor. She wrung her hands and began to cry. Her son was dying, she said. So I told her I would fetch you. She said I had better do that or she would come after you. I said, 'No, please, Mrs. Grady. Please go inside. I will bring him.' But you can't go into that house, either, can you?"

"I must go," Saugrain said, and wondered at the quiet of his voice. "I must go at least where Mrs. Grady can talk to me as she did to you. If she will stay at her door, I will be safe enough. Did she go back into the house? Did you see her go?"

"Yes, sir. When I said I would go for you, she said, 'Well, go then. Why are you standing there?' Then she went into the house, still wringing her hands."

"Good!" Saugrain said. "Before I see Mrs. Grady, we have a few things to do here. First, go quickly to headquarters. Ask for Colonel Hunt. If he is not there, another officer will be—perhaps Major Pike. I saw him going that way this morning. Whoever is there, say I sent you and I request a guard, to be stationed at twenty paces before the Grady door to keep anyone from entering or leaving the Grady house. If you are asked why, say it is a small-pox case. You understand?"

"Yes, sir."

"Good! When the guard is ordered, you will go with him to the Grady place and wait until he takes his stand. If Mrs. Grady appears, tell her I am coming as soon as I have medicine ready. Then, leaving the guard in command, go down to the river front and find John. Bring him here. If I am not here, come again to the Grady door. *Dieu*, Mrs. Grady will have not one doctor—she will have three. Go!"

The door closed. Aristide was on his way. Alone, Saugrain allowed himself a short pause, not for thought but rather for arranging his thoughts. He must have everything in order in his mind before taking further action. The commission, still on the table, was now an unwelcome interruption. He hurried to place it back on its nail.

Now, then. First, John Hamilton Robinson. He must arrange to sleep at the fort. He could spread his bed in this office—on the floor, if the table was too short. He would not find the floor hard now. What else would he need besides blankets and a pillow? Clothing, a change of linen surely. John could ride back to town now with Willy, to get what he needed—and see Sophie. Sophie must not object to this absence. It would be only for a week or two this time, God grant.

Next, Mrs. Grady might need help with her son, a man grown, possibly delirious. Who? Gabriel? Assuredly Gabriel. Immune to the disease, still strong. Time a drag for him now that he had lost his good Hortense. John could gather him up, too, when he went to town. At the fort he could have a tent within the proscribed line, before the Grady house. Medicine, food, could be set down at the line. He could pick up the medicine, empty the food into a bowl or kettle from the house, then leave the clean, empty containers at the line to be gathered up. He could keep a low fire going, a kettle with water at the boil above it. Yes—Gabriel. He would know what to do and he would do it.

What else? To keep the disease from spreading, Sergeant Grady must be located, confined somewhere under observation. It was possible that when the son had arrived, probably not feeling well, the sergeant had already quartered himself elsewhere. Still, Sergeant Grady must be confined and watched for a week at least.

Now for the promised medicine. He set out his jar of quinine bark, poked his fire into a blaze, and hung a kettle above it. The infusion temporarily would end his duties for the day at Bellefontaine. Town was another chapter. Willy, having carried Robinson home and then returned him to the fort, would be expecting to take Saugrain away. But not directly home. Not at first. Before that he must set the doctor down at the river front to do what he had neglected to do or put off during the full years that had passed since his coming to St. Louis.

On the waterfront, he would find a boat and the boat's master. At any price he would commandeer boat and man and send the man off with an imperative order for smallpox vaccine, to the nearest likely source. Authority? Governor Bates would give it to him. He must see the Governor in any case, to request a quarantine examination of boats and people arriving at St. Louis. He must. . . .

The door burst open again. This time Robinson filled the space. Never had he looked so young, so strong, so dependable!

"John!" Saugrain grasped both his wrists. "We are in trouble, John. Aristide told you? Then listen, please!"

PART VII

Number 300
෨ South Church Street

One 〜

It was past noon of that April day when Saugrain felt free to drive away from Bellefontaine, his responsibilities temporarily entrusted to others. First of all, he had reported the situation to Colonel Hunt, who was properly horrified. "Are you sure?" the colonel asked.

"As sure as I can be," Saugrain said, "without seeing the patient. You understand, if I examine him personally, I, too, must live under quarantine. I could not then visit anyone else here or in town. I hope I can obtain information from Mrs. Grady which will complete my diagnosis without my going into the house."

"You are right," Colonel Hunt said. "You should not remove yourself from your duty to others. But . . . what precautions am I to take?"

Saugrain had thought that out. He recommended ordering a General Assembly, at which the news could be given out and further orders issued. Washerwoman's Row should be evacuated and families settled in other vacant buildings. Sergeant Grady must be apprehended and held for observation. He could have been exposed to the infection. He should be quartered in a cabin and not allowed to leave it for another fortnight. Any relaxing of the regulations might spread the fever through the fort, the countryside and the towns roundabout.

"If you wish," he offered, "I will speak to the men when assembled. I will try to make it clear that the safest thing for all will be for everybody to remain here at Bellefontaine, where any fever can be reported and the proper attention given to it at once." He himself would report for duty daily until the danger of an epidemic passed.

"Thank you, Doctor," Colonel Hunt said. "I will do everything you say. I will double the guards at all posts—and yes, I think it would help to quiet some of the fear if you would add a few reassuring words."

After that, while the colonel prepared his orders, Saugrain visited the Grady cabin. The interview with Mrs. Grady, called to the door and stopped there by the guard, was not easy. As Aristide had described it, she wept and wrung her hands.

"You will not step inside to see my boy," she wailed, "even when he is dying."

"No, Mrs. Grady," Saugrain explained firmly when he could make her listen, and explained why.

"Oh, Gawd!" she said. "Is it as bad as that, and I'm to have no help?"

She was to have the best of help, he assured her. He would be at the fort every day now, to hear how the sick man was coming along and to prepare his medicine. Best of all, Dr. Robinson, whom she knew, was going to live at the fort in Saugrain's quarters, to be on hand night or day. He was in town making his preparations. When he returned to Bellefontaine he would bring a strong, kind man who had had the smallpox and so could pitch a tent beside her house and help her care for her son. She might need help in giving him his medicine, and he must take it, if he was to live. A large spoonful now, another in the afternoon and again in the evening. With the third dose the fever should be less. He might even sleep. Then he asked about the eruption.

"Oh, Gawd!" she said again. "All over his chest, his arms. . . ."

"Ah!" Saugrain said, suppressing a shudder. "Are they like this, Mrs. Grady? Each one a swelling with a pit at the top, filled with matter? Pus, we call it."

"How did you know?" she said in awe. "Horrible, and the smell. . . ."

"Mmm," Saugrain said. "At their worst. They will be bad for two or three days, Mrs. Grady. Then, with God's help and a reduction of the fever, they should dry off and heal."

(284)

He set the medicine bottle on the ground and walked away with the guard while Mrs. Grady came to pick it up. She turned back to the house with it in her hands. At the door, in spite of new ravings from within, she turned. "Between doses," she said, "I'd best hide the bottle. If Sergeant Grady sees it, like as not he will drink all of it before he knows his mistake . . . and where is that good-for-nothing while all this is going on?"

When Saugrain told her of the plan to apprehend the sergeant, she actually laughed. "Arrest him, is it?" she demanded. "It would serve him right, the drunken ape. But I warn, you. It will take three men his size to do the trick, and a strong jail to hold him." Then, resurrecting a sob, the poor woman disappeared into the infested house, and Saugrain hurried off to headquarters to quell any panic that might visit the Assembly.

However, as Hunt had predicted, his presence drew respectful attention. He was able to convince all that the only thing they could do now was to obey orders without question and through isolation keep the single case of smallpox the only one. Repeating that he intended to be at the cantonment every day while the danger lingered, he added an order. Everyone who had any trace of sickness was to report to him promptly for examination.

Then he went to his quarters to rest, to reread his commission, and to wait for the return of Robinson with Gabriel. When the brougham arrived, it held not only Gabriel but everything else, even to an outdoor cooking kettle. The picture that Saugrain carried away later included the unloading and more—the spectacle of Zebulon Pike and Robinson discussing the disposition of guards on an enlarged isolation area, as if they had never been anything but friends.

After that, the greening countryside on the way to town and the town itself, drowsing through the early afternoon, were a startling contrast. More startling was the river, with not a boat moving on it, and a landing strip almost deserted. Two keelboats at some distance from each other were beached on the sand. One, near Lisa's cave, was Lisa's new boat, with Lisa himself hovering lovingly around it. The other, farther downstream, a little below Market Street, was an older craft, with the owner also present. Hovering in his case included a frequent kick at the timbers of the hull, suggesting fear of rot.

(285)

Hoping for some information about the stranger, Saugrain left the carriage on Main Street and made his way directly down Lisa's path to the new keelboat. Willy, meanwhile, was to drive around by the old wagon road to his usual spot of shade and rest himself and the horses there.

Two ✍

"*Madre de Dios!*" Lisa said when he heard about the smallpox. "Am I to be stopped by that now?"

Saugrain thought that unlikely. He hoped that there would be quarantine regulations about boats, but right now the first to be examined would be those arriving, not leaving. Meanwhile, if Lisa would tell him about this other boat and its master....

"Who is he?" he asked. "Where is he going? Can I trust him with an important errand?"

Lisa was only too glad to talk about the stranger. He was young, yes, but very able. He had reached St. Louis the afternoon before, with a most interesting cargo from New Orleans Territory—hemp, cotton cloth, sugar, molasses, rum, handmade jewelry, perfume, and dried figs. Lisa had bought half the load out of hand. So now the young master, with some choice pelts aboard his boat, was ready to start for home. Ribald noises from the tavern at the foot of Market Street were his crew, fortifying themselves before taking up poles and oars again.

Yes, but who was he and where was his home?

His name, Lisa said, was unpronounceable and he had not bothered to remember it, but mention had been made of Kentucky. Without waiting to hear more, Saugrain abandoned his friend and hurried off to interview the stranger.

A first scrutiny told him at once that Lisa's description had been accurate. The young man reminded him of Jean Michau at nineteen—principally, perhaps, because he wore rolled-up cotton breeches and moccasins. However, it was with much more maturity than Jean had displayed at nineteen that he listened to the doctor's problem. He thought over his answer before he

(286)

gave it. Yes, he said firmly, he was sure he could deliver the doctor's urgent plea for vaccine to the post surgeon at Louisville, either the one that the doctor remembered or whoever might have replaced him. The errand would not take him out of his way. He was leaving this afternoon for Kentucky. The voyage up the Ohio would be delayed at Louisville by the Falls. While the crew handled the portage, he would hurry to the fort. Would the doctor care to write out what he wanted?

On a page torn from a notebook, with a pencil, both objects always in his pocket, Saugrain, leaning against the cargo box on the boat, wrote out his plea to whom it might concern: fresh vaccine in such quantity as was available and could be sealed in a tight container, wrapped safely, and entrusted to the master of the first boat on its way to St. Louis or to the postal carrier at Vincennes, whichever one was likely to arrive soonest at the town, now threatened by the possibility of an epidemic. Reading over what he had written, he thought that more words could not make his plea more urgent, but he should, perhaps, name the messenger and write out his own promise to pay all costs of completing the transaction. Having set this down, he read aloud all that he had written, just in case some of it might later prove undecipherable.

"You will notice a couple of omissions," he said, handing the paper to the young man. "I do not know what the costs will be, and I do not know your name."

The young man studied the paper thoughtfully, soberly, until he came to the end. There something excited him, bringing out again his resemblance to young Jean Michau.

"Dr. Saugrain," he said. "I've heard that name many a time. I—excuse me. My name is von Phul. Henry von Phul. I live in Lexington. You were gone before we moved there; but you are well remembered—you have many friends still."

Briefly Saugrain suffered a touch of vertigo. Could this young man have been sent in answer to his need for help?

No, it was chance that had brought him. In Lexington, he explained, he worked for a Mr. Hart, an established trader. He, Henry von Phul, was only a senior apprentice in the establish-

(287)

ment. This was the first time he had been sent out in command of a boat loaded with merchandise—Kentucky tobacco, grain both dry and distilled, and manufactured goods from Pittsburgh and Philadelphia—his destination New Orleans. If he should be successful in disposing of his goods there, he was to reload with whatever the port city offered in exchange and return to Kentucky. Instead of that, on his return up the Mississippi, he had made two side trips—the first up the Red River, where he had sold his entire boatload to planters at a profit which enabled him to drop back to New Orleans for more merchandise. Feeling now very bold and capable, he had brought this load on to St. Louis, a city of which he had heard much talk during his sojourn on the lower river.

In St. Louis, it had been his good fortune to meet Manuel Lisa, a name also familiar to him, and Lisa had all but emptied his boat again. However, with some excellent peltries in the vacant cargo space, also some fine white flour and cornmeal from a new gristmill and a sample of local wine, he was now ready to set out for home. He was not sure how Mr. Hart would receive the report of his wanderings, although every step had worked out to a good profit; and certainly Mr. Hart would have wanted him to accept an errand for Dr. Saugrain.

But now he had another inspiration. How would it be if he himself, after locating a source for the wanted vaccine, should bring it to St. Louis instead of trusting another to deliver it? He would like to return, he believed. He had seen nothing of the town on this brief stop. How much time could the doctor give him to go home and return?

To this near rhapsody Saugrain had listened with approval but only half of his complete attention. The other half had been devoted to Henry von Phul himself. Von Phul—interesting name, German—Saxon German, he thought, considering the fair skin, the clear blue eyes. Far-seeing eyes, one could be sure, their vision strengthened, not dimmed by use. A fine young man, a healthy specimen . . . suddenly he realized that Henry von Phul had put a question to him which he had not answered. What was it? Enthusiasm, or possibly impatience, had deepened the color on the smooth cheeks and brought out a light sweat.

"I don't believe," Henry said, "that it would take any longer for me to go and return than it would take to locate another carrier. Would a month be too long?"

"A month?" Saugrain said, still dazed. "What is a month compared to seven years?"

With that, Henry was off to the tavern to collect his crew, and Saugrain was on his way to Willy and the brougham. At home, however, he delayed his report to Madame Saugrain—and his soup —while he got out his spyglass and scanned the river. He found the boat all right, bobbing along at a good rate downstream, but he put down the glass with a sigh. Hopefully, he had put a chip afloat out there. That was all—a chip.

Three ✍

On his arrival at Bellefontaine the following morning, Saugrain, after a night's rest, was able to receive with proper gratitude a cheerful report from Washerwomen's Row. Young Grady's fever had lessened. Delirium had passed.

"Good!" Saugrain said, receiving the report from Robinson in his quarters on Belle Mont. "Day after tomorrow we will know whether he will live or die."

Meanwhile Sergeant Grady had appeared and was now a prisoner in a cabin at the far end of the Row. Enraged by not being allowed to enter this own hut or to communicate privately with his wife, he had given everybody a rough time until he was incarcerated. He was quieter now, since Colonel Hunt had prescribed a measure of rum as a sedative, to be administered with each meal. This Saugrain approved thoroughly. The sergeant must remain where he was, under guard, for another week at least, in spite of his protesting that he had never been near his son since his arrival at the cantonment. After a week, if he showed no signs of illness, he might be given his freedom, but only on the condition of obeying strictly the quarantine orders.

After that, Saugrain would have liked to send Robinson home to his family for a proper rest and relief, but while they were discussing the safety of that, a summons to headquarters came

(289)

for Saugrain. Mail had arrived, and Colonel Hunt would like to see the doctor whenever he was free.

"You are free now," Robinson said. "I will wait right here. Go, but be careful. Don't stumble. You don't suppose. . . ."

Yes, of course, Saugrain supposed. The summons could have only one cause. The long-awaited word from Washington had come.

There were three letters, finally, expressing the gratitude of the President, the State Department, and the War Department to Colonel Hunt, Governor Bates and Dr. Saugrain for their able handling of a delicate situation. They also expressed appreciation for Major Pike's and Dr. Robinson's complete and honest report on their actions under trying circumstances and the information they had gathered applying to territory hitherto unexplored by the United States, in particular, Major Pike's mountain. Therefore, with the approval of the President and Congress, General Dearborn was enclosing in the Colonel's letter two commissions which had been recommended by General Wilkinson before his retirement and had waited only on the men's return and Congressional approval.

One informed Major Pike and anyone else concerned of his promotion to the rank of lieutenant colonel. The other offered Robinson the rank and rating of assistant surgeon in the United States Army, if he would take it.

"Do you think he will accept?" Colonel Hunt asked.

"I believe he will. I hope so," Saugrain said. "Have I your permission to tell him the news?"

Minutes later he was laying a bar of lye soap on Robinson's supply of clean clothing and ushering him out of his quarters. He was to take the shortest path to the river, scrub himself all over thoroughly, put on the clean clothing, and be off to the town with Willy, to share the glad tidings with Sophie. In the evening, to spare Willy and the Saugrain horses the extra trip to the fort, he was to come out in a hired rig, which would take Saugrain back to town for his rest.

"Yes, sir, Boss Doctor!" Robinson said, saluted, and ran.

On the following day, young Grady's fever left him. Three days later he was able to crawl out of bed and do a few things for himself—to spare his mother. It was too late. Before he had all his strength back, when people were beginning to think that the scare might be over and asked when one might expect the quarantine to be lifted, Mrs. Grady collapsed, and the quarantine had to be extended. Worn out by anxiety and the care of her son, she hadn't a chance to recover. She died as if burned to ash inside and out. Her son prepared her shrunken body for burial while Gabriel made a coffin. Sergeant Grady, gone berserk against this second blow, was not allowed to see his dead wife. They buried her quickly in a secluded corner. Saugrain stood by while Colonel Hunt read the burial service. No one else threatened to come near.

Turning away afterwards, Saugrain thought forlornly of the chip he had set afloat on the Mississippi—Henry von Phul, with the order for vaccine. How long ago had that been? Three weeks as he counted.

The next morning Henry von Phul was at the door of the laboratory, in his hands a small, carefully wrapped parcel. When it was opened, most of the contents were more wrappings. Finally there were four small glass bottles, sealed and labeled, "Vaccine—Smallpox. Goforth, Cincinnati, Ohio. May 1, 1807."

When Henry had reached Louisville on his way home, Saugrain's friend was no longer there. Other officers, however, had been most helpful. They had recommended this chemist at Cincinnati, Dr. Goforth by name. He had understood at once Dr. Saugrain's problem: how to carry vaccine a distance and keep it fresh for use. He himself had been working on that, and he was happy to send Dr. Saugrain a sample of his latest solution, asking in return nothing but the Saugrain's report on his success, or lack of it, in using the vaccine.

After this fruitful meeting, Henry had to hurry on to Lexington to report to his family—a widowed mother, a sister and a sixteen-year-old brother—and to his employer, Mr. Hart. A joyful reunion had followed, and then not so joyful. In his solitary travels, Henry had had time to do some thinking and observing. Deeply impressed by the brisk trading at several places on the Mississippi, he had concluded that he would like to set up a business for himself at some promising port—St. Louis, preferably.

Henry's family had been most understanding. Mr. Hart had been troublesome. Pleased with the profit on Henry's first trading voyage, he had for that very reason been unwilling to release him from the few months remaining of his apprentice agreement. However, against all blandishments, even the offer of a partnership, Henry von Phul had held out stubbornly for his freedom. Finally Mr. Hart had let him go—and on very generous terms.

"Naturally," Saugrain said. "In that he is like our mother country, England. He hopes you will not be too successful in your independence, and so will return to him and Lexington."

Still unexplained, however, was the speed with which Henry had twice covered a distance it had taken Saugrain and the Michaus two months to cover once.

"I bought a horse," Henry said.

But, of course! At Lexington! "A race horse?" Saugrain asked.

No, Henry had not wanted a racer, but at a racing stable he had found a bargain in a young horse which had disappointed the breeder but still had good blood lines and very good, strong legs, promising endurance. So mounted, he had crossed the Ohio by ferry, ridden overland to Cincinnati, then through Indiana Territory, and finally, by way of another ferry—a new one, wasn't it?—over the Mississippi to St. Louis. On the journey he had rested only to give the horse respite.

"My head swims to hear of it," Saugrain declared. "So now I am indebted to you, the horse, and a fellow scientist. Let us take another look at what Dr. Goforth has sent."

For this examination he picked up one of the bottles—or what he had thought were bottles—and discovered it to be, instead, a simple tube like many he had blown, closed at one end and open at the other. The tube had been corked, then sealed by a coating of wax over both cork and the original opening. Inside were three miniature, narrow, knifelike blades, white—ivory or bone, Saugrain thought. Somewhere he had seen something like them . . . there was a tool in his wife's sewing basket that she called a bodkin, the right shape but much larger and heavier than the Goforth blades . . . but now he saw Madame again, wailing over the loss of a tooth from an ivory comb she sometimes wore in her hair. That was more like it. He wondered, but he could study that later. More important now was the fact that one end of each Goforth blade had been dipped in some substance now turning brown. If it was vaccine, he could have thought it worthless, had not a closer examination of packing under the tubes brought out a paper on which the Cincinnati chemist had printed a message: "DO NOT MOISTEN VACCINE IF DRY. HOLD APPLICATOR UNDER CUTICLE UNTIL VACCINE DISSOLVES."

Distaste added to doubt settled heavily on Saugrain's diaphragm, and he turned back to Henry von Phul.

"Tell me," he said, "has the good Dr. Goforth tried the vaccine in this form on a person?"

"Yes, sir," Henry said—ruefully. "On me, and if a sore arm is any sign, it is good stuff."

Two days before this he had been really sick and had regretted leaving Cincinnati. Then, suddenly, the day after that—yesterday —the pain was gone.

"Mmm!" Saugrain said. "May I see, please? Beautiful!" he added when Henry had bared a muscular left arm with a ripe pustule rising from the healthy flesh of the upper half. "Healing begun. Inflammation receding. Good scab. Care must be taken not to knock it off before the sore closes. Bandage? No. Better healing without. Some protection indicated, however. Linen handkerchief knotted above wound, not too tightly, held in place by the shirt sleeve? Very good. Have some linen pieces somewhere, must think where."

All this was given in running comment as cheerful as the whistling of a bird with a new nest. Appropriately, he did whistle when he found a drawer full of linen pieces. Choosing one, he folded it deftly and knotted it above the sore.

"You will have a nice scar," he prophesied, "but no smallpox, I think."

Henry, buttoning his shirt, was concerned only about the vaccine. Was it all right? Had he for all his haste come too late for it to be of use?

It was very much all right, Saugrain declared. "You have probably arrived at just the right time. I should have no trouble in finding twelve volunteers to submit to vaccination—at once— today!"

"Twelve," Henry said, "seems a very small number."

It was a small number, Saugrain agreed. It would hardly make an impression on the cantonment or the town, but it was a beginning. He must use the vaccine where it would do the most good. He would have liked to begin with his friend Lisa, but the Spaniard was now well on his way up the Missouri, dealing with strange and very savage Indians. Some day Lisa might like to carry the vaccine to his savages, although not soon at the present rate of supply.

Well, enough about that. He would find others for this first dozen treatments. In the meantime Henry von Phul had done Saugrain and St. Louis a great service and deserved a look at the town and a few people. They could begin by visiting another good friend, Colonel Hammond—but later. A glance at his watch told Saugrain that the morning was gone. They must have a bite to eat before they set out, a bowl of Madame Saugrain's good soup . . . but of course they would do this. Madame would know by now of Henry's presence. She was expecting them.

Wearing a fresh cap of lace with new lilac ribbons, with her two young daughters in neat pinafores behind her, Madame Saugrain certainly was expecting company.

"I began to wonder," she said as she welcomed Saugrain and his young man caller, "but no matter. The soup is always ready. Please take chairs and eat with good appetite."

The kitchen was bright, with the green of trees tempering the sunlight that streamed in through the windows, and fragrant with vapor rising from the soup, mingled with clean wood smoke and some faint feminine potpourri hiding possibly in an apron pocket. A gay half hour followed. Madame ladled the soup into bowls, and the girls set it on the table, with crusty bread and cheese and wine within easy reach. Rosalie, now ten years old, shy, sweet, and lovely, stole a glance at the handsome young man when she thought no one was looking. Elise, eight and already a conscience-less flirt, was a little bolder; but neither said more than "yes, Maman; no, Papa." It was not their place, they knew, to enter the conversation when *chère* Maman had so many questions and the young man was so polite in answering, although twice a question had to be put to him a second time because he had not heard it as first spoken.

Bemused, Saugrain thought, when the silver watch said it was time to leave for their call on the Hammonds. Bemused, he thought again, when he and Henry von Phul were in the brougham and Henry sat staring at nothing visible, bereft of most of his faculties. Abruptly, Saugrain decided to allow the Hammonds to show the young man the town while he went on to Bellefontaine, where he meant to show the Cincinnati vaccine to his two assistants, Aristide and Robinson, then to use the first three doses on them and—with Robinson's help—himself.

Four

"Such a nice young man, Mr. von Phul," Madame Saugrain said that evening, when the hour had come for her and the doctor to count the blessings of the day.

"Mmm!" Saugrain said.

"I wish," Madame continued, following her own thoughts in the subsequent silence, "that he might settle here. Is there any chance of that, do you think?"

"I think," Saugrain said with sharp emphasis, "that is his firm intention."

"Vigny, why? Was he so charmed with the town?"

"I don't know what he thought of the town."

"But I thought . . . oh, I see. You had to go to the fort and Colonel Hammond showed him."

"That was not necessary," Saugrain said. "Mr. von Phul had already seen all that he needed to convince him that this is where he wants to live."

There was silence in the fragrant garden.

"Vigny," Madame said then, "how you speak! I thought you liked him. In presenting him you said how grateful you were for his bringing that vaccine, which you wanted so much."

"I know," Saugrain sighed, "but I didn't know then that he would prove to be a horse trader and a robber of bird's nests."

"Vigny, who traded horses? What horses?"

"His horse," Saugrain said. "A good horse, which had brought him all the way from Lexington. He traded his horse to Colonel Hammond for one of the colonel's best fillies. The colonel told me."

"Filly?" Madame said thoughtfully. "What is that, Vigny?"

"Filly?" Saugrain repeated. "That is our word *fille*. A filly is a horse *jeune fille*. Do you understand?"

"Yes, Vigny." With that, Madame put her head against him and began to shake. Was she laughing or crying? He could only wait for her to reveal which.

When she could speak, it was to say, "Vigny, which of our *jeunes filles* do you think attracts Monsieur von Phul the more?"

"Herr von Phul," Saugrain corrected. "It is a German name." As if that mattered.

"My dear," Madame said then—soothingly—"if it is our Rosalie, she is only ten. It will be seven more years before she is seventeen and we must choose a husband for her. You know?"

He knew what she meant. Seventeen had been her age when she had married a penniless doctor. Nevertheless. . . .

"What have we to do with choosing?" he demanded.

Madame shook some more. Now plainly she was laughing.

"Vigny, my adored one," she said. "You sound just like Papa. This charming young man—who brought you the vaccine you have wanted!"

"A small package," Saugrain permitted himself to say now. "Twelve doses in all. I was at my wits' end to know how best to use them. Also I am not altogether happy about Dr. Goforth's invention of a way to give out the vaccine. It takes time to prepare, and in the end it . . . well, I don't like the looks of it."

So it was the vaccine that troubled him, Madame thought. But, with something in his hand that he did not like, she said, surely he could invent something better. Not right away, perhaps, but soon.

Madame was right, he knew. If he did not like what fortune had put in his hand, he must study and discover something better. He would try. He surely would try. Meanwhile, he had used Dr. Goforth's gift of vaccine rather fairly, he thought. At Bellefontaine, besides himself and Aristide and Robinson, he had vaccinated Colonel Hunt and the first two of a line of soldiers who had responded to a call for volunteers. Returning to town then, he had offered the dubious privilege of vaccination to Colonel Hammond, Lawyer Hempstead, and Deputy Governor Bates. The last three doses were awarded to his friend le Duc and his neighbors—Messieurs Soulard and du Breuille. Not one had rejected his offer, although several had hesitated. Now, with his own arm beginning to make itself felt, he wondered how his friends were feeling. He would hear tomorrow.

Tomorrow, however, was a distance away. Resolutely he turned away from anxiety, allowing the charm of his immediate surroundings to steal over him.

"*Chérie*," he said, "what smells so sweet this evening?"

"At last, you notice!" Madame sighed. "It is our locust tree. This is its first good blossoming."

"The one you planted?" he asked, remembering a small brown wizard man tramping through the village with a bundle of switches under his arm. Scions of trees, he claimed, from President Jefferson's home in Virginia. He sold them for—well, that did not matter. The widow Chouteau had sent him to call on Madame Saugrain. Naturally Madame Saugrain's tree had grown— better than any other. The fragrance of its blooms—bitter and sweet—drowned every lesser distillation. A sign? Yes. Of faith, no doubt, but also of devotion and patience.

Five

Patience? Wisely, Saugrain did not count the hours he spent, sitting before the twelve Goforth applicators, arranged in a row on his work table. He knew now that they were ivory, and hence precious. He must return them and the tubes to Dr. Goforth at his first opportunity.

The applicators, however, he knew almost at once, would present no real difficulty. Madame had said—reluctantly—that he could have her treasured comb if he could not find the teeth he needed elsewhere. He had then gone to Manuel Lisa's store and stated his need to the clerk in charge during Lisa's absence.

"Broken combs?" the clerk said. "Sure. We get some in every shipment of goods. Too many—ivory, shell, bone—what would you like?"

Saugrain's choice was ivory, because it was easy to clean and could be shaped to a point without danger of breaking, but he went off home with a sack filled with varied pieces of combs—material for dozens of applicators, he thought. With the Goforth packing of vaccine for transportation, dozens were needed. That realization brought him back to what he was convinced was the real necessity—devising a less clumsy container, which could be filled and sealed at or near the source of supply. That might be the solution.

The image of a tube occurred to him—a narrow tube, just wide enough to hold a single dose of vaccine and permit the insertion of the applicator. Permanently sealed at one end, it could be sealed with wax at the other after the contents had been added, to be opened only once at the moment of vaccination. That would insure only brief exposure to the air. It was such exposure, he felt, that had produced the ugly dry lumps at the ends of the Goforth applicators.

His thoughts at that point took a great leap forward. If he could produce such a tube in reasonable quantity, it might not be necessary to insert the applicators before the time of vaccination. In that case, if he could have someone beside him to cleanse the applicators after use, he would not need so many applicators. A handful in reserve . . . Rosalie, who had quick, deft hands, entered the picture, but not too clearly.

The laboratory saw little of Rosalie these days. A Miss Maitland had opened an English school in town, and both Saugrain girls were enrolled there. They were to become familiar with American customs and American speech. Beyond question, it was a good school. The girls learned the new ways quickly. The only trouble was that they seemed to grow as fast as they learned. It had been a long time since Rosalie had drawn pictures on a slate or laughed over strings of dancing paper dolls while he fussed and fumed over his experiments, none more baffling than the present problem. Choosing an assistant was now rather premature. If the time should come when he had real need of extra hands, there was Aristide. Of course! He should have thought of Aristide in the first place. With a deep sigh, Saugrain scratched out a few notes on a slip of paper, made a neat pile of the Goforth applicators and closed his shop for the day.

The following afternoon he was back at the same table, staring into space, thinking. A tube—he could blow a glass tube that fine, even finer. He had done it often, making thermometers; but nobody knew better than he how fragile those fine tubes were. At the least mishap they shattered. Bits of glass got into everything. A glass tube was impossible. He must find or make some other material. What, for instance? Completely frustrated, he crumpled the paper with his notes, threw it into the fire, and went out to seek peace by pacing his favorite path, well marked now by other frustrations, along the top of the river bluff.

Six ∽

The year 1807 was generally rather frustrating—a standstill sort of year. The growth of the town seemed halted. The fear of a smallpox epidemic, although it came to nothing finally, and that business of examining every boat that tied up at the water front did not invite new people or trade.

A greater threat to commerce was national. For some time England, fighting the imperial ambitions of Napoleon by land and sea, had harassed American shipping by halting and boarding vessels on the high seas and taking from them men she claimed were of English birth, impressing them as sailors on her warships. By 1807 the practice had become so general and so bold that President Jefferson, not wanting to go to war with England, had signed into law an act of Congress closing every American port, forbidding ships either to enter or leave it. This became infamous as the Embargo Act. Word of it, reaching St. Louis, produced prophecy of ruin even in that inland city. Leading merchants had now no foreign market for their furs. Why would anyone settle in a city doomed to ruin?

A few did settle there, however. By the end of the year St. Louis could count enough taxable, voting citizens to qualify for incorporation as a town, a first step toward recognition as a third-class city. This would not only erase the appellation of "village," but it would give the town a stronger local government under five trustees elected from the citizenry.

Enthusiastically the taxable voting citizens voted, only to be told afterward that they should have presented a petition for incorporation to the Court of Common Pleas before electing the trustees. All would have to be done over again next year.

How could anyone not be glad to see the last of 1807? The New Year could not possibly be worse. Just possibly it might be better.

It began well enough. The first eastern mail brought word of the repeal of the ruinous Embargo Act and a new ordinance permitting coastwise trade and commerce with a few islands and some South American ports. This was not exactly freedom of the seas, but it allowed the more venturesome shipmasters to clear home ports. In St. Louis the leading merchants, ruthless competitors before this, seeing that, united, they would have a better chance of survival than each man could have alone, banded together to form the Missouri Fur Company, its one purpose being to find an outlet for their furs.

In April Manuel Lisa came home from a rigorous but prosperous voyage, during which he had established a fort in the land of the Mahas, then continued northward to set up a stockade in the land of the Dacotahs, after successfully standing off such British agents as the New Northwest Company. He was invited to join the alliance. He listened to the proposition with a lift of his Mephisto eyebrows, then cannily stored his handsome furs in his new cave house on the edge of the Mississippi before he threw in his lot with his former rivals. That done, he set out for the Ohio to consult with his trusted partner, Colonel Vigo, and learn from him more facts about the condition of affairs. Also, since he was going that way, he would happy to see what could be done about an order for more vaccine, which had been placed the year before with Dr. Goforth of Cincinnati.

"Vigny," Madame Saugrain said, knowing about the meeting of Lisa and the doctor but nothing of what they had agreed upon, "that nice young man from Lexington does not return to St. Louis this year? I hope nothing was said to him last year which offended him."

Nothing, Saugrain assured her, that could offend had been said to Herr von Phul. He was not one to take offense, unless it concerned some pursuit which he had in mind at the time. If he was determined to settle in St. Louis, nothing would stop him. If, on the other hand, he had changed his mind about that, nothing would induce him to come.

"Vigny," Madame said, "you are never so nice as when you pretend to be mean. I, too, will wait anxiously for Captain Manuel's return from the Ohio. Perhaps I may be permitted to have a few words with him, to ask if possibly he has any news about Mr. von Phul."

She had his permission to question Lisa, Saugrain said, and he was sure that Lisa would tell her whatever he knew. Meantime there was more waiting.

In that interim Meriwether Lewis returned from Washington as Governor of the St. Louis Territory. "The quiet one?" people asked in surprise. They had thought, if either of the two captains were chosen for governor, that it would be the handsome, dashing redhead, Major Clark. So quickly had people forgotten that Lewis had been the senior in command on their memorable voyage.

And yet, Saugrain himself had felt some dismay on learning of the appointment. Surely the President needed men of such ability and integrity in other and livelier positions. With the possibility of war threatening the nation, he needed commanding officers of known ability and experience; but in this case, at least, the President wished to honor his former secretary by appointing him governor of the territory he had explored.

So that was how it was. William Clark was named Superintendent of Indian Affairs, Lewis was named Governor. He would give to this new responsibility all his heart, Saugrain assured everyone. Ah, that was what he feared. Wanting to think of him riding a spirited horse, he saw him riding a stool, poring over papers.

Saugrain's second pang of dismay came when Lewis arrived. He had made the journey from Washington alone. He had left his dog in Pittsburgh, returning him to his former owner, an active hunter. He would have no time now for a dog, he said; he would be much too busy.

He took his oath of office with quiet dignity, then cheerfully faced his duties. Clark had remained in Virginia to marry his sweetheart, Julia Hancock. It might be a month or more before he came on, and Lewis wanted everything going smoothly before Clark arrived.

For an official residence he leased a house on Main Street. What he liked best, he said in showing it to Saugrain, was the gallery around three sides of the house, and especially a little room closing the gallery at one end. He thought of furnishing it with a desk and a couple of chairs, making it into an office. The house, then, would be for receiving company, and the office would be a personal retreat.

(301)

The room looked out on ground which had formerly been an orchard and garden. Having been reared on a farm, Lewis thought of growing vegetables there. The tools were probably still in a shanty at the far corner of the garden—it was not a shanty, exactly, but rather, a small, old house of "posts in the ground"— melancholy enough in its present state.

However, any dismay Saugrain felt after inspecting this property was obscured by other concerns. When Lisa returned from the Ohio in May, much of his cargo of merchandise was marked plainly for Indian trade, which indicated that, market or no market, he would launch another voyage up the Missouri the following year. He also brought a substantial package of vaccine from Dr. Goforth, and with it a report on the whereabouts of Henry von Phul. The young man had visited Cincinnati in the preceding summer on his way home to Lexington and had left an order with Dr. Goforth for as much vaccine as he could spare, with instructions to deliver the parcel to the first reliable boat master bound for St. Louis. At the time he had thought it probable that he would not return to St. Louis in 1808, meaning to visit the Eastern markets in the hope of gathering some interesting merchandise for the opening of his exchange in St. Louis the following year. As Saugrain read the letter, Henry von Phul was no doubt shopping in Philadelphia or Boston or New York.

Meanwhile here was Saugrain with twenty-four doses of new vaccine to distribute and, more troublesome, a note of warning from the Cincinnati scientist. He wished to advise the eminent Dr. Saugrain that this was the last vaccine in the present form that he would give out. He was now working on a new invention, hoping to discover something more practical.

Seven ∽

By turns amused, defiant, depressed at the thought of Dr. Goforth coming out ahead of him with a discovery which he wanted to make, Saugrain went doggedly on, bestowing the boon of vaccination on likely and unlikely subjects until finally he had but one dose left. He offered it to a newcomer, Joseph Charless, who was seriously considering the publication of a news paper in St. Louis. He already had one to his credit in Louisville, Kentucky, and why he had thought of moving the enterprise to St. Louis he had so far not said.

Charless—the spelling in two syllables was correct, because that was the way it had been handed down to him by his Irish ancestors, although he pronounced it "Charles." Other Irish features were his intensely blue eyes, a mop of black hair, and a very long, narrow face, especially long in the lower jaw.

"It is not wise, perhaps," Saugrain said, "to offer you my last dose of vaccine. A sore arm will not make you more friendly toward our town."

"No?" Mr. Charless said. "Now I regard it as enterprise that you have offered inoculation against smallpox here. But . . . must you peddle the stuff this way? Would not a notice in the newspaper be better?"

"Yes," Saugrain answered, "if there were a newspaper, and also, if I had a more plentiful supply of vaccine." He explained then the problem that he faced.

"Very interesting," Mr. Charless said gravely. "Good luck attend you."

With that, offering still no explanation of his movements, he left town as suddenly as he had come. However, he had done a bit of business there before leaving. Almost immediately—that is, within a month of his departure—a printer, Jacob Hinkle by name, a short stocky man with permanently blackened fingernails and a generally smudged appearance, moved a crude printing press, two cases of lead type and a keg of ink into a room which Mr. Charless had rented on Main Street, in the same square that held the post office. There he oiled and inked his press and produced a notice, which he pasted inside the one window looking out on the street:

HOME OF THE MISSOURI GAZETTE
Cards and Handbills
Printed at Reasonable Rates

On the twenty-first of July, the first issue of the paper appeared, printed on sheets of foolscap seven and three quarters inches wide by twelve and one half inches long. The name spread proudly across the top of the sheet above two columns of identical news, one in English, the other in French. The text was not easy to read in either language, a word being lost here and there in the spread of a blot. The news, however, was not all-important, the source being what it had always been. A notice at the bottom of page 1 promised that the *Gazette* would appear each Thursday if the mail, due at Cahokia across the river on Tuesday, arrived on schedule.

Nevertheless, whatever its shortcomings, the first appearance of the newspaper created a sensation. Realizing the limitations of his sheet, Mr. Charless had noticed only the very important local events and given a line, no more, to each. He announced, for example, the arrival of Major Clark and his bride, but left it to local gossip to supply the details, namely that the bridal party, having reached Louisville safely, could go no farther until Governor Lewis sent two barges to carry their personal belongings, including a pianoforte, on to St. Louis. He spoke respectfully of the death of Colonel Hunt at Bellefontaine, but did not describe the military funeral with plumes on the hearse and rifle salutes; and Dr. Saugrain had to say finally why the colonel had died so suddenly: he had a weak heart, and one night it stopped beating. The paper noted that a new Catholic bishop was promised but said nothing of the new brick church that the bishop was going to build.

Most of the space for news was filled with an account of the triumphant journey of a steamboat up the Hudson River. The boat had been invented and built by a man named Robert Fulton.

"New York to Albany, Bon-père," Saugrain boasted, the homely little sheet in hand, "in two days of eight hours each—that is almost ten miles in one hour."

"The Hudson," Michau Père suggested, "is not so difficult to navigate as the Mississippi?"

"Even so," Saugrain said, "it has a current. Let us say five miles an hour. It is two thousand miles from New Orleans. How many days would that come to?"

"Fifty," Michau said—on the dot. "That is less than two months."

"It was not news really," Joseph Charless said, when Saugrain congratulated him on the piece about Fulton. "I keep such stories on file for the weeks when the mail does not come on time." Still, Saugrain knew that without a newspaper St. Louis might have waited a long time before hearing about Robert Fulton.

Eight ↶

On a bleak day in February of the new year, 1809— so cold that it was necessary to have hot fires going under every chimney to keep the house from freezing into a two-story igloo —Saugrain sat in his library, an open volume on medicine on his lap, from which he had so far gleaned not one interesting bit of information. Sharing the room and the bright fire with him was his daughter Rosalie, struggling over what was to be, when finished, an English composition. Any man in the world, Saugrain thought, would have found a study of the profile of the girl at the desk more absorbing and more informative than an out-of-date scholarly treatise.

His child, his Rosalie, was twelve years old now. Her body was changing, he knew; but what had that to do with the new lift of her chin as she threw her head back, looking at nothing in partic- ular, searching for a word, a thought, perhaps, listening, he would have said, her lips parted, waiting? Then, when whatever she sought still eluded her, up went both her hands into the dark cloud of her hair, ruffling it in exasperation. She sighed. She thought again . . . ah, now she had what she was looking for! In a flash she changed back to her more familiar self. She smoothed her hair. Her face became quiet, tranquil, beautiful. She dipped her pen into the inkwell and wrote, the pen making a whisper of sound on the paper. Oh, oh! Again she was stopped.

"Papa, may I interrupt your study? I have a question. How do you spell scientist? It seems to have too many letters!"

"Ah!" he said. "You are writing about me again?"

A smile dimpled her cheek. "Do you object?" she asked. "All the girls in my class are writing about their fathers. Miss Maitland approves. We should be able, she says, to express ourselves clearly, being so familiar with the subject. Papa, the word, please. S-C-I-E-N—that much is from science, but then —T-I-S-T? It doesn't look right, but it is? I am glad, because the next sentence has it again. 'A scientist is one who wants to know all about everything, even a lump of dirt. Of what it is made. . . .' Papa, you look so strange. What have I said that's wrong?"

"Nothing, *ma petite*, nothing. It is that pen you hold. May I see it, please?"

If he looked strange, it was because of a tremor building up inside him. With the pen in his hand, he really shook.

"Mmm!" he muttered. "Just what I need. Tubular, the right size, semitransparent. A little accumulation inside now, but that can be removed. . . ."

"Papa," Rosalie protested, "what are you doing? Don't break it, please!"

"I can't break it," Saugrain said. "It is too tough. I can't bend it. To break it one must use pincers, strong ones, and sharp."

"Papa," Rosalie pleaded, "if you are making an experiment— please, I have other pens. This is my favorite. You gave it to me on my birthday. In the shop you have a jar full of quill pens. Grandpère uses them for his accounts."

"Mmm!" Saugrain said, still admiring the pen. "I have others, you say? Good! They will not be so white, or so clear, or I would have seen in them what I see in this one. But there! I give you back your pen now. Treasure it. I will tell you why one day. What kind of bird gave us that feather, do you think? A swan? A goose? Well, go on with your writing, while I examine the pens in my shop. When you have finished that composition, you can see if you wish how I take them apart. What was it you said about scientists—that they must see how everything is made? You can now add to your lump of dirt, birds' feathers."

In his laboratory, excitement persisted. Perfect, he thought again, holding in his hand an inferior quill pen. Not so white, not so clear as Rosalie's, it still was tubular and tough. Pincers were still needed, with a strong bite and a sharp cutting edge. Setting the jaws of his best pincers close to the sharpened point of the pen, he squeezed with all the might he could put into his hand and wrist—and the quill snapped.

With a great sigh of satisfaction, he sat back on his stool to study his handiwork. The edge of his cut was rough, but he knew he could smooth it. Now he must consider how long he wanted a tube to be. Not too long, but long enough to be held firmly in one's hand, also long enough to take an applicator. He laid one along the quill. *Dieu!* If he were careful, he could have two tubes instead of one! So he made a chalk mark three inches below his cut, then marked another length below that, and picked up his pincers.

A minute later two tubes lay in the palm of his hand. All the edges were rough and the tubes tapered some, but the applicator entered the narrower one with space to spare. He would seal the narrower end of each tube permanently, leaving the wider one open to receive the vaccine. With that in mind, his next move was to clear a bit of fluff out of each tube, then pour water through them. He could see the water running through, and when he closed the narrow end of one with a fingertip, he could measure the amount of water in it. If he should be so fortunate as to seal fluid vaccine in his tubes. . . .

But there experiment for that day ended. Strength went out of his hands, his arms. General lassitude followed. How absurd! He had not worked that hard. No, but consider how long before this he had toiled and fretted, trying to perfect a tube as simple as the stem of a feather from a bird's wing.

What remained? From some source still a mystery he must obtain a number of quills. When he had them, he must make them all into tubes. Then he must find or compound a wax to seal them. Common sealing wax might do for the permanent seal. The other must be something more pliable—soft, but firm. It must close the wider opening of a tube, but it must yield when the time came to remove it. Finally he must find a nearby source of the cowpox vaccine, so that it would be fresh when he filled and sealed the tubes. He would take that up with Jean Michau, farmer, across the river at Kaskaskia. Jean knew every cow in that territory.

So now, having the whole operation in neat order in his mind, he turned back to the first step—obtaining quills. He could take one or two more pens, unnoticed, from the jar in the laboratory. More than that would draw question from Michau Père. He could buy . . . no, he would not be so extravagant as to buy quill pens

(307)

only to destroy them. What, then? Feathers? With every man of his acquaintance a hunter—for sport, for profit, or from necessity—feathers should be available, once he had decided on the right bird.

Two days passed. On the morning of the third, as he was preparing to leave for Bellefontaine, Madame delayed him.

"Vigny," she said in her gentle, firm way, "the turkey wing we use for dusting the fireplace in your library is missing. Can you think where it has gone?"

He did not need to think. "I borrowed it," he said. "I wanted a few feathers."

"But you have a wing in your laboratory."

So he did; but, he explained, it was not as good a wing as the one in the library. It had been used more roughly. Must she have a turkey wing for sweeping the library hearth? Would not a broom do as well or better?

"No," Madame said. "A broom raises more dust. A turkey wing sweeps more gently, gathering the dust with the soft ends of the feathers and holding it until one can shake it outside. Vigny, this was our best wing. Mrs. Hammond gave it to me and showed me how to use it. It is an American invention . . . have you destroyed it?"

"No, indeed," he swore. "I wanted only a few quills from the under side."

They were, naturally, the strongest quills. Taking them left the wing rather incomplete and the feathers nearest to those he had withdrawn somewhat loosened, but the wing was still good enough for a hearth, although not good enough for Madame Saugrain. He knew that, now that the harm had been done. He remembered well tears shed years before this when he had borrowed a little mercury, which he needed for a thermometer, from the back of her French mirror. Dolefully, he explained now his need for feathers—and what did his charming wife say in reply?

"Vigny, you should have told me. Turkey feathers are black, homely. For white quills you need goose wings."

But the turkey feathers had been available and good enough for experiment. As for white quills, must he now go through the town, seeking someone about to slay a white goose, and ask for the wings?

(308)

No, indeed. Madame knew a better thing. Many of their friends down the road, especially those who farmed, raised geese —the du Breuilles, the Soulards, the Sarpys—and there was her brother Jean. Did he not have geese on his farm? Had Vigny inquired of Jean? Why not?

Well, for one thing, the river was now full of ice. It should begin to break up presently; but when it did, weeks would pass before navigation was possible. Also, if the ice went out with a rush, Jean might have flood water to handle on the Illinois side. Really, he was reserving Jean for the last step in his operations —the vaccine itself. In the meantime the turkey quills had done all right for a beginning.

Finally there came the truly halcyon day when all the preliminary preparations had been completed. Thanks to Madame Saugrain's discreet solicitations, he had a box filled with small tubes from the wing feathers of white geese and, in reserve, a smaller supply of perfectly efficacious dark turkey quills. He had with Jean's help located a herd of cows infected with the pox near Ste. Genevieve, which he could reach quickly by boat, or more surely by land. The road south was now a much traveled highway, well beaten by use and kept smooth by frequent dragging. He had ready a large lump of white wax, which he had compounded on a beeswax base. Thanks to the help of Gabriel, who had become most skillful at loosening feathers, cleaning the quills and cutting them the proper length, Saugrain could now begin plugging the tubes in preparation for filling them. In fact, he had plugged all the darker ones with sealing wax and was making ready to plug the better ones when he suffered an interruption. Perhaps "suffered" was too violent a term, although some pain attended the fact.

Henry von Phul returned to St. Louis.

Nine ∽

It was a fine April day, the most beautiful of the season so far, so beautiful that Saugrain was visited by a great restlessness, an unwillingness to shut himself up in his laboratory or any other enclosure. His mood, no doubt, was the result of too-intense labor over his experiment. It . . . well, whatever the cause, he wanted to unbar the door, fling it open, and rush outside. And then? To walk along the rim of the bluffs, dangerously near the edge, to view the spread of the river in flood, to feel its great, eternal pulse, to listen to the sound of rushing water, to walk until he had breathed out all the staleness of confinement and breathed in the freshness of another spring. To walk until his legs were weary. Only his legs, understand, not the rest of him.

He was so enchanted finally by this prospect that a knock on the door of his laboratory was an interruption, threatening invasion. He did not recognize the knock. It was not sharply imperative, like Colonel Hammond's, or respectfully restrained, like that of Governor Lewis. Lisa would have rattled the door and entered. This knock was not demanding, but. . . .

"Enter, please," he said, curious as well as puzzled.

At once the latch was lifted, the door swung open, and in stepped Herr von Phul. There was an awkward moment. *Dieu!* One would have thought they had never met before. Surely Henry had not been away that long. Laughing at himself, Saugrain went forward with both hands extended. He had to touch this elegant, well-groomed, fashionable young man to be sure of him.

"Henry!" he said, laying hold of von Phul by his arms, because his hands were inaccessible. One held a bulky parcel, the other a carefully tied roll, suggesting a newspaper, a calendar, a map— "Henry, I hardly know you."

"It's the clothes," Henry said, also laughing. Mischievously? Triumphantly? Expectantly? What did it matter? "I didn't pole the boat on this trip."

Surely he had not poled a boat or ridden and slept with a horse. The cut of the brown cutaway coat, the fawn-colored trousers, the white shirt with narrow ruffles down the front, the collar and cravat were the wrappings of a gentleman of consequence.

"Henry, tell me," Saugrain demanded.

"I will," Henry said. "That is why I am here. But first let me put down these things. This is for you, Doctor."

And he handed Saugrain the parcel. Saugrain weighed it in his hands. It had little weight beyond that of the wrappings. Appre-

(310)

hensively he read some of the writing on the upper surface, and apprehension became a certainty. "The Jenner Laboratories, Philadelphia," the superscription read. Jenner—the laboratories had used the name of the celebrated Dr. Edward Jenner, credited with the discovery of smallpox vaccine.

"Henry, you made that long journey just for me?" Saugrain said, wanting only to conceal his dismay. The box was still in his hands.

"I had other business in Philadelphia," Henry said, and now he, too, seemed uneasy.

"You know Philadelphia?" This was more temporizing on Saugrain's part.

"I was born there," Henry said. "We lived there until my father died. After that was when we moved to Lexington."

Oh, to be sure—the widowed mother! Saugrain put the parcel on the table.

"Now tell me everything," he said.

"It is a long story," Henry warned. "Wouldn't you like to open the package first? You don't want the vaccine? You don't need it now?"

"I want it. I need it—all I can have," Saugrain said, but his eyes looked at the parcel and away. "Henry, I have to confess something about a mystery package like this."

As a child, he had been given a toy. Jack-in-the-box was the English name. It was supposed to be amusing, very clever. A clown's head was concealed in the box. The lid was held down by a brass hook. At the release of the hook, the lid flew up and out sprang Jack. He was only a papier-mâché clown, with a peaked hat and a ruff for a collar, but to a young child he had seemed a monster.

"I was that kind of child," Saugrain said. "But enough of nonsense. I will find a knife. No, not yours. Can you imagine a surgeon being without a blade of some sort ready to his hand? Ah! Here we are. Now then!"

Resolutely he cut the first strip of twine, but it was Henry who impatiently loosed the other knots, stripped off the wrappings and laid them aside, Saugrain repressing a shudder as he watched.

Now the box on the table waited for his examination. He had only to lift the lid . . . he did so, releasing not a spring but the front of the box, which fell toward him, disclosing three trays of transparent short white quills, sealed with wax.

"Clever, don't you think?" Henry said.

"Wonderful," Saugrain agreed. "You cannot know how wonderful until I show you." With that out came his box of quills and the two kinds of wax. "You see?" he said.

Henry saw. Saugrain truly had no need for the vaccine he had brought.

"Oh, but I do need it. I want it." Perversely, Saugrain was determined now to cheer the crestfallen young man. "Look at those beautiful Philadelphia tubes, all filled and sealed. Then look at mine, still empty. We have only recently found a suitable source for the vaccine we want. Now, with your gift in hand, we can proceed more surely, with better heart. And that is not all. Think what it means—that I, working here alone, have obtained the same results as those Philadelphia men of science, none of them so isolated as I have been. Your generous gift is an endorsement of my efforts. My resources now seem to me to be unlimited."

At present, however, he wanted to talk about Henry von Phul.

"You have returned to Saint Louis this time meaning to stay?" he asked.

Yes. A new boat, loaded to capacity with choice merchandise, was now beached on the river front, waiting under the protection of a trusted crew for the owner to rent a room in town large enough to accommodate the store and himself, since for a while he meant to live with his business.

His business—the boldness, the confidence, the sureness with which the young man had come this far at once excited and appalled Saugrain. He must have pledged all his own and his family's working capital on this venture. Paying no attention to prophets of gloom, who forecast a ruinous war with the mightiest nation on earth—discounting Bonaparte's fantastic empire—he had gone to the busiest port on the Atlantic to purchase his goods; but why he had gone there was no longer a question in Saugrain's mind. Henry had lived in Philadelphia until he was sixteen. He had gone to school there. He had acquaintances still in the port city, people who remembered the von Phuls. Also he was sure that he would obtain there merchandise of quality, and along with it some excellent mercantile counsel.

Since he was sure, he had found what he was looking for. There had been considerable gloom, grumbling, even despair among ship owners and merchants whose prosperity depended on open sea lanes; but in Philadelphia and elsewhere up and down the coast, he had found bold men ready to risk war with England and a growing belief in the ability of the United States to come off victorious.

Where, the bold ones demanded, were better ships built than in the yards of America, from Maine to the Carolinas? What nation had such areas of forest? Where were there men more skilled in shaping hulls and rigging masts and sails? For arms there were iron foundries, dating, some of them, back to the Revolution. Powder mills were also plentiful. So let the ships now rusting and rotting in the harbors be scraped and mended and rigged to sail the sea once more, armed to defend their right to be there. Sailors? Skippers? Was there to be only one John Paul Jones in American history?

This was bold talk, overbold perhaps, but it was strong talk. Saugrain felt its strength as Henry von Phul continued his report. As for business, the eastern states, he said, forced to live upon their own resources, were now trading briskly among themselves. Manufactories of all kinds were multiplying. He had in his boatload of merchandise lengths of excellent gingham, calico, workaday cotton and woolens. No silks or velvets, naturally, except for two pieces of brocade, brought around Cape Horn from China. Generally, such luxuries must wait on that hoped-for settlement of differences at sea.

Henry's inventory went on and on. Besides woven cloth, it included shoes, hosiery, ribbons, laces, buttons, thread, glassware, queen's ware—everything, it seemed, except baubles meant for trading with Indians. He had been deeply impressed on his brief earlier visit by the sound good taste and evident prosperity of the people whom he had had the privilege to meet. So now he was opening a store, stocked with merchandise which he hoped would attract such purchasers.

Meanwhile, as he talked, Saugrain had been doing a sum. Sixteen years old when he had moved with his family to Lexington in 1800—almost coinciding with Saugrain's departure for St. Louis— Henry von Phul was now twenty-five. He had been twenty-three when Saugrain saw him for the first time, kicking his boat with a

(313)

boy's disgust, wearing youth's careless clothing; now, two years later, he was in every aspect a man. Mature was too staid a term; determined was better. Very sure of himself and his plans and purposes. That he would know success was a forecast not to be challenged, but how had he known this so surely that he had dared to cut loose from a pleasant life in Kentucky and put every dollar he could scrape up into this trading venture? Had he never been in the least afraid, Saugrain asked?

Yes, Henry admitted. In the beginning, when almost everyone said he was crazy, he had trembled some, but then it had seemed to him that what he feared were things that might or might not happen—phantoms of unreality, compared to his certain knowledge of what he wanted to accomplish. Surely every achievement of consequence must be accompanied by the risk of failure. Knowing this, he had brushed the phantoms away and gone on with his plans. From that day opposition never mattered.

Finally, his strongest motives for wanting to join the merchants of St. Louis had been two. First of all, he liked the people. But he had known only a handful of those—Manuel Lisa, the Hammonds, and the Saugrains. Including Rosalie? Rosalie most of all, possibly. There had been some attraction at their first meeting, enough to disturb her father. But she had been a child, hardly ten years old at the time. She was only twelve now. Saugrain had almost forgotten the incident. So, no doubt had Henry von Phul. A young man of his extraordinary judgment would hardly permit the memory of a child, however lovely, to shape his plans for a prosperous future. People, he had said; and now he was talking about the second attraction that St. Louis held for him— the river. Not the Missouri, which he had never seen, but the Mississippi; and not the Mississippi as it looked now—with a keelboat or two, a few pirogues and one inadequate ferry —but the Mississippi as it might look a few years from now. In the East he had seen Robert Fulton's boat, the *Clermont*. Granted that the Hudson was not a mountain river, also that the *Clermont* had barely covered the distance to Albany and return and had needed extensive repairs afterward, the first successful upstream journey by steam had been accomplished. Fulton was now making over his boat. Others were working on other boats. The day would come. . . .

(314)

Surely it would come, Saugrain agreed; and who was he not to understand that Henry would like to be present when the great day arrived? The mellow resonance of a bell cut through the doctor's slightly wistful musings. He counted the strokes. Eleven o'clock? How was that possible? What had become of ten?

"A town clock?" Henry asked.

"A bell ringer," Saugrain corrected. "It is an old bell which the new Catholic bishop has had mounted temporarily on a wooden frame. We have been promised a new church with a regular belfry—but you are not a Roman Catholic, I think."

"No," Henry said. "Something Protestant, if anything."

In Philadelphia he had gone to a Quaker school, but he was not a Quaker. It would have been quite all right if he had been, Saugrain assured him. St. Louis did not stress the importance of creeds as much as the missionaries who visited thought was proper.

"But here we are talking," he said now, "and both of us with business to attend to, although mine is more easily deferred than yours. My assistant surgeon lives at the cantonment Bellefontaine now, and my hours are less strictly kept. I mention the fort because Willy will have the carriage ready. It will help us look for that room you need. Where shall we begin? The newspaper office? We have a newspaper now, printed once a week—usually."

"I must take a subscription," Henry said, smiling, "but before we leave, may I have the pleasure of paying my respects to Mrs. Saugrain? I have a small remembrance here for her—and the young ladies."

The remembrance was that whatever-it-was on the table beside the gift of vaccine. Stripped of its wrappings, it proved to be a ladies' fashion magazine, illustrated in color—the latest empire modes.

"Madame will be delighted," Saugrain said. "All the women in town will want to borrow the magazine."

Again Henry made respectful mention of the young ladies.

"They also will study it," Saugrain promised, "page for page. Their lessons may suffer, but not their needlework. I am sorry to say that they are not at home right now. There is a new school for young ladies. I myself see them only in the early morning or evening and on Sundays. You must share our *déjeuner* next

(315)

Sunday. Madame will insist upon it. In the meantime there is soup—daily fare in Frenchtown, which is what our Yankee citizens call this end of Saint Louis."

Henry von Phul snatched at the straw offered. He would be most grateful for the soup, he said. He was hungry.

"Such a fine young man!" Madame Saugrain said approvingly that evening. "I like him even better than I did the first time I saw him. So do you, Vigny, I think."

"Mmm!" Saugrain muttered.

"So brave, so sensible . . . the whole family seems to be like that," Madame continued.

Over the soup Henry had filled out his story. He had an older brother, William, married, living in Ohio. At the time of the elder von Phul's death, William, although he and his wife had begun a family of their own, had taken the two youngest orphans into their home, leaving Henry with the widowed mother, a sister, Maria, and one younger brother, Graf, to care for. It was William who had moved the family to Lexington because he liked the town and was sure Henry could find work there to his liking.

Henry admired his older brother greatly. William, marrying, had not abandoned his family, so Henry now felt the same obligation. He meant to watch over the von Phuls even after he had settled in St. Louis.

Madame now ended her praises of Henry with more adjectives: brave, devoted, et cetera. Saugrain listened patiently. Since noon he had learned something about Henry that he was sure Madame did not know. Mr. Charless, the newspaper publisher, had obtained the information.

"Henry will be successful here," Madame was saying, "all his family having been merchants."

"Not all," Saugrain said smugly. "His father was not a merchant. He was a master brewer. When he settled in America he brought that accomplishment with him from his birthplace—Westphalia, Germany."

"Brewer?" Madame said. "You mean beer?"

Well, what else was there to brew except beer—or ale, as the English called it?

"And we have no brewers here?" Madame asked.

Not so far, Saugrain told her. A group of young men, among

them Edward Hempstead, the brilliant young Connecticut lawyer, had tried. Mixing ignorance with a slight knowledge of
process and ingredients, they had stirred up vats of mash, added
yeast and clear spring water, and allowed the mash to ferment;
then, when the time was right—they hoped—they had drawn off
the liquid into kegs, which they loaded in pirogues and pushed
into caves at the edge of the Chouteaus' millpond to cool. The
resulting brew had a good amber color. It foamed invitingly
in mug or glass; but the taste was never right. Now, however, with
the son of a master brewer added to their councils, they thought
success was assured on their next try.

In vain Henry had protested that he was as ignorant as any of
the other amateurs. If his father had possessed a secret formula,
the company for which he worked in Philadelphia had kept it.

"Never mind," Mr. Charless had said to that. "If the beer is
not a success, you will be. The young men will welcome you for
the relationship, and some day on a purchasing trip to Philadelphia, you can inquire about the formula."

Ten ✍

Afterwards, when war came—a war that few wanted
and nobody, especially in the western territories, believed could
really happen—prophets abounded who swore that they had seen
it coming. Saugrain laughed at them. The three years preceding
it had seemed very like any other three years, with the usual
mixture of good and bad. In spite of, perhaps because of, conditions on the eastern seaboard, St. Louis grew—slowly, imper-
ceptibly, but surely. So did the reputation of Antoine Frederic
Saugrain as an explorer in the field of medicine.

The *Missouri Gazette* of May 26, 1809, carried a brief notice
of his vaccine. The wording had been a matter for serious discussion between the doctor and the editor. The first sentence, for
instance, was pure Charless fanfare: "Dr. Saugrain gives notice
of the first vaccine matter brought to St. Louis." The second and
final statement was Saugrain's: "Indigent persons vaccinated
gratis."

(317)

"I call that overly generous," Charless objected. "A doctor lives by his fees."

"A doctor lives to serve people," Saugrain retorted. "As many as possible. Long ago in my mind I promised the people of Saint Louis that, if I succeeded in bringing vaccine here in quantity, never again should there be an *Année de la Picotée*."

"But the poor," Charless contended, "may not relish being called indigent."

"Who is to know whether they pay or not," Saugrain said, "except me? I do not allow my father-in-law to set down their names in a book. Please print this as I have said it."

The result was a busy fortnight for the doctor. Beginning on Friday morning after the appearance of the notice, a steady parade of curious, fearful, uncertain applicants presented themselves at the laboratory. Gabriel guarded the door, allowing no one, high or low, regular patient or stranger, to enter until the person preceding him had left. He tuned his manner to harmonize with that of the applicant. To rude pushers he said loudly and firmly, "Wait! Get back in line." To the more cheerfully obedient, he said, "If it please you, will you wait? The doctor does not wish to see more than one at a time. It does not take long. Thank you."

This was gratifying response to the first notice, but not overwhelming. While the flow of applicants continued, Saugrain excused himself from duty, thus finding a little time each day to cut and seal at one end with hard wax a reserve supply of tubes. These were delivered to the farm near Ste. Genevieve, where his assistants in the field, Jean and Aristide Michau, filled all the tubes he sent with fresh vaccine, then capped them with the removable white wax.

At the end of a fortnight, Saugrain, finding himself not at all wearied but, rather, refreshed by these activities, appeared at the printing office with a notice even more beneficent than the first one. After the usual argument, it said:

Dr. Anthony Saugrain, having been politely favored by a friend with the genuine Vaccine infection, has communicated that estimable preventive of Small Pox to a number of the inhabitants of St. Louis and its vicinity, and wishes to announce that he has acquired a fresh supply, enough to treat as many more if they will apply within the next two weeks. Persons in indigent circumstances, paupers and Indians, will be attended gratis.

"Indians?" Charless questioned. "Now, why. . . ."

"You sound like my father-in-law," Saugrain said, laughing. "He is now keeping a separate account of my benevolences—to frighten me."

"Good for him!" Charless said in approval. "After all, you do have a family to consider."

"My estimable father-in-law," Saugrain replied, "sees to that also. For myself I like that word 'benevolences.' I have received so many in my time that I am consumed with a desire to have some to my credit. Many Indians visit our town these days. There are always tepees on the Chouteau grounds, and now Major Clark has his new Council House ready to receive them."

The missionary aspect of new benevolence in that direction went much farther. The Chouteaus now, through the multiplying branches of their family, had complete sway over the tribes between the Missouri and the Arkansas Rivers. They were petitioning the War Department for a garrison at the new fort at the mouth of the Osage. Manuel Lisa matched them with a fort among the Mahas across the Missouri from Council Bluffs. He had also a second fort among the Sioux and other tribes trading at his station at the great western bend of the Missouri. He was planning to establish a third on the Yellowstone River on his next voyage. Lisa, having had a good "take" on his own vaccination, was carrying with him on this voyage, besides seeds of pumpkin and beans, a package of the magic quills.

This, Saugrain pointed out to Charless, was spreading the use of his vaccine far beyond his fondest expectations. So the invitation to Indians in and around St. Louis must stand. Then he mollified the publisher with a promise that his next notice in the *Gazette* would threaten lawsuits against debtors who could pay and did not.

This gratified Charless, but offered only temporary appeasement to Michau Père. In the same June issue of the paper which carried the notice of vaccine, a new doctor, the seventh since the territory had been handed over to the Americans, announced that he had established himself in the stone house, the former home of Joseph Roubidou, where he would practise medicine.

"This one, I believe," Michau said grimly, "is related to Major Clark. His wife is the Major's niece."

Even this information caused Saugrain no trepidation. He had still more patients than his father-in-law could cover with collection, and he was as busy as any man could be with his work, both profitable and unprofitable. Once more he was thinking—wistfully—of turning in his army commission, now that John Robinson had established his family, including a second son, at Bellefontaine. However, again he held his hand from acting on impulse. With the completion of Fort Osage, it seemed to him that he saw that certain gleam in Robinson's eyes which he must always associate with the search for adventure and, possibly, treasure. If a garrison were ordered to Fort Osage, an army surgeon, no doubt, would be needed there, and Robinson would surely take the place if the opportunity were offered. Ah, well, one could only wait and see.

Eleven ∽

The year 1809, begun so bravely, ended in calamity—a great and wasteful loss, not to any one person, not to St. Louis, but to the nation. Early in September Meriwether Lewis, having assembled his papers, chiefly statements of debit and credit, sacked them neatly, together with some evidence that the national Treasury still owed him recompense for expenditures pertaining not only to his office as Governor but going back to the great western voyage, and set out for Washington to have the claims examined and adjusted. He had to do this, he confided to Saugrain, because certain men of prominence in the Territory had accused him of misconduct in office—of yielding to influence—not theirs, naturally—even of misappropriating Government money and credit. The house he had leased on returning to St. Louis was cited as evidence of personal extravagance, although it was generally known that he had occupied this house only a short while before he turned it over to Major Clark and his bride. After that he had lived for a while in the room he had furnished at the end of the gallery. This, however, had not been far enough away

(320)

from the gay life in the big house; and in order not to disturb or be disturbed by that, he had retired to the little house at the far end of the garden.

Now this reserved, gifted, amiable gentleman, assailed by more calumny than had ever accrued to the duplicity of James Wilkinson, had felt compelled to take his books and papers to Washington. If, protected by his friend and patron, the late President Jefferson, he could not clear his record, how could he clear it?

He himself chose the route he would travel, the danger of brigands on land or pirates at sea—including the river—being almost equal.

Deciding for his health's sake to go by water, he left St. Louis in August on a boat captained by a man with a perfect record in eluding pirates. His plan was to obtain passage at New Orleans on a coastwise merchantman bound for some port on the Atlantic. All aboard, including Lewis, were in fine spirits. If they should be attacked, he said, he could handle a gun better than most, and so could his trusted servant.

"No, I am not afraid," he said to Saugrain's anxious question. "At least not for myself or my money. I will say this. I will guard my papers with my life."

The next word, the only word anyone had from him after that, was in a letter to Clark and a verbal report made by the master of the boat. All had gone well on the journey, both reports said; but at Chickasaw Bluffs, halfway to New Orleans, Lewis had changed his mind about continuing on the long way around by New Orleans and the sea; and he and a Mr. Holt, also a passenger on the river boat, had engaged horses for themselves and Lewis's servant and had ridden off, meaning to follow the Natchez Trace to Nashville and so, on safe well-traveled roads, to reach Washington sooner.

The boat master said he did not blame them for leaving the river. At the Bluffs, tales of river pirates below had been fearsome. He himself had been glad to be paid off and to hurry back to St. Louis.

The next word to reach St. Louis was an item in a newspaper which Clark had read and clipped during a visit to his family in Kentucky in October. Meriwether Lewis was dead. By his own hand, the newspaper said, at Grinder's Stand on the Natchez Trace. "Slit his throat," Clark said bluntly, quoting the paper.

(321)

"I don't believe it," Saugrain said. "It is not easy to cut one's own throat. He had pistols. If he had been bent on suicide, that would have been his way."

Later, when men from Nashville, New Orleans, and Washington came to investigate the circumstances, pistol wounds were found on the body, any one of which could have caused death. Missing were Lewis's watch, his wallet, his papers, and the servant. Mr. Holt was present. He had stopped before the party had reached the tavern, to look for an extra horse which had gone astray. Lewis and the servant had ridden on without him to engage rooms for the night. Lewis was dead when Holt arrived.

Then the missing servant returned and told his story. He and Lewis had reached the tavern in the early evening, and the Governor had taken separate cabins for himself and Mr. Holt. He and the servant had eaten supper when it was ready. Then the Governor had gone to his cabin with a light, and the servant had gone to a stable nearby to care for the horses. While there he had heard pistol shots and had hurried back to Lewis's cabin. Mrs. Grinder was there, having also heard the shots, she said; and there was the Governor, all over blood and near to fainting. All he could say was something about its being hard to die. Then he was gone, and the servant was running for his life. Into the woods—anywhere, to get away. None of the missing articles was on the servant's person when he returned to the cabin. Missing also were most of his wits.

"And so, *chère* Maman," Saugrain said to Madame in the quiet of their home, "most unworthily a fine, true gentleman has died, and, of those who knew him best, I am the only one to say he did not take his own life. Still, I must say it. He was too brave a man to kill himself."

"Vigny," Madame pleaded tearfully, "you are sick with all this grieving and argument. Others have died or gone away and you have not felt so much sorrow. A terrible thing has happened, but you can do nothing about it now."

"I know," Saugrain said, and drank gratefully of the tisane she offered. "Death is the natural end of living. It is those who live afterward who suffer the pain of loss. I felt such loss when I heard that Dr. Franklin was gone, but he was an old man when he died, wearied by much living. Meriwether Lewis is the first brave young man to go of those whose lives I have been permitted to share. So let me weep for him, *chérie*. Sorrow is all I have left just now. That, too, will pass; but I cannot, I do not wish to part with the ache of it just yet."

Meanwhile the Territory was again without a governor. Another would come in the natural course of events. But when? There was now a new commandant at Bellefontaine, replacing Colonel Hunt. The new officer was Colonel Daniel Bissell, not related to Major Russell Bissell. Another brisk, able soldier who promised well, he had already sent a report to Washington, including plans for a great rebuilding of the cantonment during the coming year. He advocated the use of brick and stone. So now Colonel Bissell at Bellefontaine and Secretary Bates in St. Louis—who had once been Deputy Governor as well—supported by five trustees, governed the Territory.

"They do very well," Michau Père said, when this had gone on for a month and nobody's manner of living seemed disarranged. "Perhaps we do not need a governor."

But of course they would have a governor, Saugrain said, though perhaps not until spring. After all, this was the end of the year, not the beginning. As he spoke, he looked out the window and saw a shower of snow riding the rain and the wind.

In St. Louis, the snow shower was merely a warning that winter was on the way. At Fort Osage, up the Missouri, where the Robinson family—Dr. John, Sophie, and two little boys, with a third child on the way—were now settled in stout, weathertight winter quarters, it was a full-scale, howling blizzard.

Winter at Fort Osage, Sophie wrote, promised to be half again as long and just as dreadful as the one she remembered from the year when the Michaus and the Saugrains were new to St. Louis and the Saugrains had to live in their barn because their house was not ready.

It was Sophie who had insisted on the whole family moving to the new fort when John was ordered there. Now she gave promise of being almost as capable as her sister, Madame Saugrain. From the day of the family's arrival in the new quarters she sent a letter home by every boat that carried a mail sack. Life at Fort Osage, she admitted, was very different from that at Bellefontaine. The fort was more primitive—a stout stockade with a barred

(323)

gate and a sentry on watch day and night. Quarters for soldiers and officers were small cabins, opening on a bare parade. There were two other officers' wives at the fort, each with a small daughter. The wives, who were very friendly, helped her acquaint herself with the customs of the post. In addition, a married sergeant had quartered his family on the far side of the parade. His wife was Irish, young, and glad to add to her husband's pay by doing laundry work for the officers. She was said to be also a good midwife. This, Sophie thought, the dear doctor might like to know. All the children, including the sergeant's two—a boy and a girl—played together, paying no attention to rank.

Another letter was a merry report on John's growing skill as a hunter, and the deliciousness of prairie chicken for table poultry. John had also shared in a buffalo hunt, being determined to cover all their bunks with buffalo hides. However, after the first hunt, resulting in one hide, he had decided to buy the others. Sophie feared after that he might smother them all in their beds some cold night. The snows were said to be deep on the prairies, and the winds bitter cold; but, if the Indians survived in their shaky huts, surely people in snug cabins could do as well—if they did not set fire to the cabins. She was very well so far, and so were John and the boys, but she was happiest when a supply boat arrived with mail from St. Louis. Her dear ones must write often while the river remained open. Groceries, too, had to come from down the river, but meat was plentiful. Indians brought in game in addition to what the hunters killed. The quartermaster salted and dried half of it for a supply later. When spring came John had promised her a cleared space outside the stockade for a garden where she could plant the seeds she had taken from home, and a henhouse where she could raise chickens—to scratch out the seeds she planted in the garden.

One could laugh at the bright humor of the letters—and then turn thoughtful. Little Sophie, way off there, surrounded by wild animals and Indians, awaiting the birth of another baby. Drifted snow might be a blessing as a barrier.

Then winter struck St. Louis. It came suddenly, with a wind that rose in the late afternoon, then howled all night. In the morning everything outside was frozen stiff, and snow was falling. After that, one snow followed another with only short respite

(324)

between, allowing one to stir abroad briefly, to enjoy the sun, to inspect traps, to attend church or a town meeting. Styles in dress ceased to matter; they were the same for everybody—a hooded blanket coat over shawls and a variety of other woolens.

The two great rivers froze over. Roads crossed them as far upstream or down as there were settlements. People joked about them. It was easier to cross a river that way than by ferry. Certainly it was cheaper. Sometimes a crossing was too simple. Hungry Indians came to the towns, begging for food. Some had furs or quarters of deer to trade. Many simply begged or stole. If they obtained rum, they were dangerous. Finally a strict ordinance made it a felony to give or sell rum to Indians. If they stole it, naturally the offense was on their part.

Saugrain visited the sick in the town when the sun shone and the snow was right for snowshoes. He left supplies of medicine at the fort, but appeared there only when the roads were packed hard enough to bear the weight of a cart horse and a sledge, which was a wagon bed with oak runners.

With all the hardships, however, life asserted itself. In one interval Colonel Bissell gave a ball at Bellefontaine. Fiddles also screeched or sang in the humblest houses in the town. A dancing master opened a school, promising instruction in the latest figures. Many a day and night, his house was dark, but when the weather relented, it could not accommodate his pupils.

Finally, good health, good humor, courage brought almost all through to spring. Another year began, when its arrival had seemed doubtful in prospect. Days marched in order, it seemed, in spite of prankish Nature. Spring brought a new governor, another army man, a stranger to most, General Howard.

Spring brought also new disaster. In March warm, southerly winds spread a false spring over the central plains from the Appalachians to the Rockies. It could not last, many said. It did not last for long—just long enough to melt the snow on the slopes of the mountains and the ice in creeks and branches; and the water rushed down to swell the little rivers. Presently the ice in the greater rivers began to heave and break away. Then it went out with a rush and a roar, and the water rose. Cold weather came back then, to add to the misery of those caught by the flood. The waters in the lesser rivers and creeks could not recede because the flooded big rivers pushed the surplus back instead of receiving it. The St. Louis landing strip was lost to view almost immediately, and the water rose almost to the level of Main Street, but not quite. Looking eastward across the river, there was no far shore.

"Poor Jean!" the Michaus said. "What has happened to him, do you suppose?"

"Nothing," Saugrain said with confidence. "He has hill land for his animals, if he drove them to the new pastures in time; and, as for his fields, he can now demonstrate the truth of his belief that land is richest where it is flooded frequently."

The most complete loss, the most utter destruction, befell Fort Bellefontaine. Every building on the lower level, from Wilkinson's Headquarters House to the blacksmith's shop, was lifted off its foundations and demolished. The men who had tried to tell General Wilkinson that this could happen to his beautiful valley, including the ghost of the first Spanish Governor, could have said with justice, "Didn't we warn you?" Except that the destruction was too awful for triumph. General Howard, on viewing the scene after the waters went down, said merely to Colonel Bissell, "Well, you can rebuild now without the extra labor of wrecking." And he turned his attention from then on to the general welfare of the Territory.

Which may have been what Colonel Bissell wanted. He built a new cantonment, all on high ground, leading from a headquarters building on the summit of Belmont, as he—and other mapmakers after him—wrote it. Once more, in spite of new brick from the colonel's kiln, the bite of the axe and the whine of saws filled the air with discord. Except in days of smothering heat, Saugrain kept window and door of his quarters tightly closed. Even so, he said to Willy each day at noon, "Let us get away from here quickly. My ears ache."

Still, it was interesting to see new skeletons of buildings rise on the upper slopes of the hill. Presently tents bloomed on the lower slopes—temporary quarters for new soldiers coming in. Immediately after the flood, while the remainder of the old First Regiment still camped on any high ground they could find, those companies were withdrawn and replaced by men of two new regiments of infantry. These were chiefly raw recruits. Between

(326)

assignments of labor on the building, they drilled on the new parade under company lieutenants with more knowledge but not much more experience than their own. None of them, Saugrain thought, matched a lieutenant he remembered—a smart, crisp drill master with a plumed hat disguising the tilt of his head toward one shoulder.

Colonel Pike had been moved back to Ohio after the smallpox scare. All the new troops were strangers. Once more Saugrain thought of turning in his commission. Sometimes the wish was based on nothing more than the fact of new uniforms. The coats were all to be single-breasted, which gave them smart lines but less warmth in cold weather. Madame packed his old winter coat away carefully, in case of need, and waited for him to be sure. At other times his impulse came from loneliness. Finally he spoke to Colonel Bissell of resigning.

"Now?" the Colonel said with what looked like real dismay.

"But," Saugrain said, "is it not possible that a new surgeon will come with the new regiments?"

"I have had no such information," Bissell said. "Until I do— and after that—I'd be obliged if you would stay on. Your knowledge and experience give a man in my position something solid to tie to."

What could Saugrain do then but order a new uniform coat?

Meanwhile, at Fort Osage, at the end of winter, Sophie Robinson's third son had been born, and Anthony Saugrain Robinson had begun the adventure of living. Sophie had come bravely through the birth. "I think," she wrote, "I am almost good enough to be named an honorary squaw. Indians don't even go to bed with their babies. If we stay on here. . . ."

In St. Louis Manuel Lisa had returned from a most successful voyage. He came down the Missouri leading a flotilla of bullboats and rafts, laden with magnificent furs, riding the falling waters of May. His eyes glowed with triumph. He had raced up the Missouri the year before against a fleet of boats carrying—besides the necessary hunters and oarsmen and scouts—merchants, geographers, botanists, even a writer named Irving. They had been westward bound to visit ultimately a settlement on the Pacific Coast named for the Mackinac trader from New York, John Jacob Astor.

Manuel had kept ahead of them all the way up the river as far as the Dacotahs, where he had lost them after arranging, at their request, to supply them with horses to carry them by land the rest of the way. He had learned later that some had turned back, but others, including the writer named Irving, had gone on. Had Saugrain seen any of those who had returned? When Saugrain admitted that he had seen one or two and heard of others, but had not talked with them, Lisa's eyes snapped.

"What I wanted to do," he said, "was to meet the Indians on the route I had marked out and do business with them before others got to them."

That he had succeeded his peltries showed. Finally he had established a new fort on the Yellowstone, with a stockade and a small, stouthearted garrison to guard it. That had made it possible for him to make trading treaties with all the Indians of that area. He named some of the tribes: Dacotah, Crow, Shoshone, and many bands of Sioux—Ogalalla, Unkpapa and the like, their names impossible to recall. If any Sioux Indians should come to St. Louis, he had promised them, he said, to show them the den of the medicine man who could by scratching a man's arm keep off disease.

Then, laughing wickedly, he was off to discuss Indian treaties with his newfound friend, Major Clark, as Superintendent of Indian Affairs.

As Lisa returned, Henry von Phul, delayed until then by rumors of floods on the Ohio, departed on a purchasing journey to the East. Lost as he was in a fever of impatience—his store, he said, was practically empty of merchandise—he took time to ask the Saugrain ladies what they would like him to bring them from Philadelphia or New York. Madame Saugrain demurred politely, but the girls spoke up at once: "A new fashion magazine, please, Mr. von Phul." Elise added a request for some pretty silk pieces. At eleven, she was somewhat weary of flowered dimity.

Henry laughed, but Madame was horrified. She scolded the naughty one, saying that she hoped Mr. von Phul would overlook her boldness. She was, of course, much too young to think of silk dresses. Elise pouted prettily, not over the rebuke but over being told that she was too young. Rosalie said nothing, even more eloquently, her mouth wistful, her eyes soft with dreaming.

(328)

Twelve ∽

It was at this period in his life that Saugrain found himself reverting to at least one custom of the villagers he had known in old Pain Court—their way of remembering a year not by a number, but by its most important event. For example, 1810 was to him the year of the great flood, which destroyed the first Bellefontaine cantonment and led to the fine new brick buildings on high ground. It was also the year when two new regiments moved into the new buildings, after they had helped to finish them.

It was the year of the new single-breasted uniforms and odd, helmet-shaped hats—with no plumes.

It was in 1810 that Lisa, having raced the Astorians up the Missouri had sent them on westward while he attended to the business of establishing friendships with the Indians of the Great Plains.

It was in 1811 that Lisa returned triumphant and richer than ever and held conferences with General Clark. General because now, besides being Superintendent of Indian Affairs, he was commander of all the Territory militia. It was no longer the Territory of St. Louis or Upper Louisiana, but the Territory of Missouri. From 1811 onward it was so written on the records: Missouri, Territory of the Second Grade, with a representative in Congress.

So it was also in 1811 that Saugrain had the proud privilege of casting one of the votes which selected young Mr. Edward Hempstead to that office. Whereupon, in response to this vote of confidence, Mr. Hempstead brought the rest of his family from Groton, Connecticut, to St. Louis, thereby adding, to the census count of 1,400 inhabitants, two parents, three brothers, one brother-in-law and a wife, and two sisters, one a widow with one male child.

That they would all match the young Congressman in wit, fortitude and endurance was demonstrated by the record of their journey. They had traveled from Groton to Pittsburgh by stage, then down the Ohio and up the Mississippi by barge, buying their provisions and cooking them en route. Young Edward's famous walk from Vincennes with his law books on his back seemed a pleasant stroll by comparison. Elijah Beebe, the brother-in-law, on arriving in St. Louis opened a hat manufactory and store on Main Street, and Mr. Edward settled the others on a farm on the Bellefontaine Road overlooking the Mississippi and left them to work out their own futures.

This they did most ably. Stephen Hempstead, the father, was a devoutly religious man, an elder in his church—Presbyterian. His first public act, after seeing to it that his house was supplied with food and fuel and a strong servant to fetch and carry, was to assemble there all in the community who were members of his church, or inclined that way, for Sunday worship. The first meeting included only Hempsteads and Beebes. At the second two more families appeared. There would be more, the gratified elder thought; and he wrote to the national presbytery a plea for an ordained minister, and to a Bible society an order for Testaments.

A first result of these devotions was an awakening of other religious groups—Episcopalians, Methodists, Baptists—and the new Catholic bishop ordered immediate delivery of stone and brick for the church he had promised.

In the midst of these major events, really going back a few years, a third daughter had appeared in the Saugrain home. She came so quietly that the doctor, immersed in smallpox vaccine, elections and the like, forgot to examine her critically at birth and, in fact, was hardly aware of her until one day she laid a small hand on his knee and said, "Papa?" in a tone so reminiscent of her mother that his heart jumped.

"When did this one come?" he asked, exaggerating his surprise.

"A year ago last November," Madame said. "You knew."

Mademoiselle Henriette Saugrain was a full three years old when James Madison, fourth President of the United States, yielded to an outraged Congress and declared the still young nation to be in a state of war against Great Britain.

(330)

PART VIII

The State
~ of War

One ∽

The President's declaration, when it became known in St. Louis, produced first of all a sort of benumbed silence, from which many quickly took refuge in unbelief. How could a war which had begun at sea affect their town or territory? The only war St. Louis had ever known was the great American Revolution; and only the very old remembered that, there had been the threat of an Indian attack in 1780 which had come to nothing because of the presence of General Clark's older brother and some new fortifications, of which now only the old tower on the Hill remained. Only one man had been killed—the Cardinal brothers' father. War?

Saugrain knew nothing of war except what he had heard or read. Now approaching fifty, he had been less than twenty when the treaty negotiations had begun in Paris. The understanding of war, he concluded, by any person from a commanding general to the lowliest soldier in the ranks, from a president to a plain citizen, was limited to what that one person experienced in a small area immediately surrounding him at any given point of time.

The War of 1812, as it came to be called, was to Dr. Saugrain in St. Louis, first of all, handbills distributed by a town crier—since illiteracy still abounded—summoning all male citizens above the age of twenty-one to assemble in that same barnlike structure in which all voting had taken place since the Louisiana Purchase, to hear the President's declaration read and opinions on it expressed by leading citizens.

The meeting was very well attended. So many came that chairs or benches were out of the question except on a speaker's platform at one end of the room. Standing was made uncomfortable by the density of the crowd. A person who began to feel faint because of the close atmosphere must cling to two or more neighbors to keep his footing. Consequently the meeting was shorter than had been planned. Governor Howard read the declaration with suitable dignity, but not loudly enough to be heard at the far end of the room. Shouts were raised, asking for a second reading by a stronger voice, William Clark's name being heard oftenest. So he read the document. Then Judge Easton explained the reasons which had led to the declaration of war. Murmurs and groans greeted his explanations. Finally shouts of anger and sympathy for the President were molded into resolutions supporting the national Government and declaring the readiness of St. Louis and, if was to be hoped Missouri citizenry, to serve in any way needed to insure a victorious outcome.

Finally, when all who had tried to speak were hoarse, and evening darkened into night, and no supper had been eaten, the meeting hall emptied and everybody went home, stepping high but stumbling frequently, since nobody's thoughts were on the ground before his feet and it was rough, as always.

Morning of the following day showed clear skies and full sunshine on land and water—as peaceful a picture as could be imagined; and duties waited. Man and animal had to be fed. Cows had to be milked and driven out to pasture. Wood must be brought to each house, to keep fires going within and also under outdoor kettles. Water must be carried. There was everything to do. War? Thanks be to God, it was still far away. Until it drew nearer, which one hoped it would not do, man or woman could only go on living and working.

Dr. Saugrain, more sensitive to hidden possibilities, kept his thoughts to himself as he breakfasted in his cheerful kitchen, chatting pleasantly with his young sons and his two older daughters, but he sent them off to school in two groups in the family brougham. As a rule, the girls as well as the boys walked, in company with schoolmates their own age from down the road, escorted by a servant, also on foot. Today they and their school-mates would ride.

Madame Saugrain, with grave eyes and no smiles, stood by, watching the preparations but saying nothing, until a half-dozen chattering laughing girls, had packed themselves in the now-aging brougham and disappeared. Then it was: "Vigny, you think it is not safe for them to walk?"

The thought had just come to him, Saugrain said, wishing to erase anxiety from her usually bright face. The carriage was ready and so was Willy. On this day he could spare the time for Willy to drive two loads of children to town. Another day this might not be the case. They could walk—all of them—as usual.

Really, the kitchen, the childern, had aroused a protective urge in him that was stronger than he would have supposed it could be. Sending the young people off in the old brougham hardly expressed it. Saying that he had a few things to see to at home before he left for Bellefontaine, he kissed his wife, patted her reassuringly, and bade her kiss the little ones for him, then turned to his laboratory.

There, however, he did not turn his hand to any of several experiments waiting for him. Instead, he stood inside the closed door, viewing the general clutter as if he had never seen it before, or rather as if, by looking at each piece of it, he could hold it fast and keep it from slipping away. War: if the ones who had asked for it could not make good their boasts, would it sweep westward like a fire beyond control? Would it. . . .

A knock of warning preceded the entrance of Gabriel with wood to build up the fire on the hearth.

"M'sieu Docteur," Gabriel protested, "you are early today. It is cold in here. I thought perhaps after the meeting you might sleep late. . . ." he waited expectantly.

"Would you like to hear about the meeting?" Saugrain asked while Gabriel stooped to blow a spark into a flame and add a little wood. "Very well, I will tell you."

Talking something over with Gabriel was as good a way as he knew to restore mental equilibrium—common sense, Gabriel called it.

It had been cold in the meeting hall, too, Saugrain began, then reviewed the proceedings.

(335)

"Was that all of it?" Gabriel asked at the end. "Speeches? But, m'sieu, war is fighting. When will that begin? Where?"

"Things have not advanced that far as yet," Saugrain said. "There are always preliminaries."

The President's declaration of war might not have reached London at this time, he thought. It must cross the ocean, probably in the hands of a courier, who would deliver the paper to the American minister, who would hand it to the King or the King's prime minister. Then the British must hold meetings, to plan what ships and soldiers could be spared to fight against England's former colonies.

"But," Gabriel said, "the English always have men for their armies. If they don't find them in England, they hire them from other countries. And here there are the Indians. Indians are always on the side of the English because the English give them the most presents—red calico, which they prize, and sharp scalping knives. I think we have to fear the Indians first of all. I remember . . . ."

There were others who remembered, Saugrain reminded Gabriel, among them William Clark. He not only remembered tales told by and about his older brother, but he himself, along with his friend Captain Lewis, had fought in the Indian wars in Ohio which followed the Revolution, the English being unwilling to release their hold on that rich land.

So, war became presently a grand muster of militia from all five counties of the Missouri Territory, and a drilling of volunteers, who were brave enough but needed practice at marching in formation and obeying military commands. There was also target practice, not only for those who had been hunters before they became soldiers, but also for lawyers, merchants and clerks. At the first pop of a gun in St. Louis, mothers shooed their children indoors like young partridges.

War was also good news and bad. All the first outside news was bad. In August an army of British regulars and Canadian volunteers, supported by Indians, attacked the stronghold of Detroit and captured it—the first recovery of territory surrendered to the United States in 1783. The worst feature of that news was that the loss was due, not to lack of brave men defending the fort, but the cowardice of General Hull, of the American commander. He, it was said, surrendered to fear before he tried resistance.

This was disaster in more ways than one. Detroit must be retaken. But how? Who would rally the dejected, defeated troops on that now wide-open frontier? Who would stop the British advance through Michigan into Ohio? In those dark days many a one spoke wistfully of Meriwether Lewis. He had won his spurs fighting Indians in the old Northwest Territory. He was a born soldier and leader. Now they said it—too late. There was nobody, it seemed, who could fill the place that he could have filled with honor. Several, including even the discredited James Wilkinson, tried, but failed on the first testing.

William Clark's name was prominent then in the choosing of a commander; but St. Louis was a strong and vital bastion on another frontier. If its defenses failed, the new Northwest, the whole Louisiana Purchase, would be lost. Clark was a fighter, his name was potent; and he had never been more needed than he was needed now at St. Louis. When General Howard was re-moved as Governor of Missouri Territory to take military duty elsewhere, Washington added the office of Governor to Clark's title of Indian Agent, and he had accepted the extra burden with cheerful gusto. After that he could not leave Missouri to go to the defense of Ohio. Still, many inhabitants of western America, including Doctor Saugrain, trembled for their safety until word came that President Madison had called General William Henry Harrison to take command of the Army of the West.

Some asked, would he take the command? That had been a near thing—that battle on the Wabash. Harrison had won it, but he could have lost it. He had crushed a flaming Indian uprising —eight hundred desperate whites against swarming Indians, led by Tecumseh and his brother, the Prophet, aided and abetted from Canada. Would he want to go through that bloody business again? Leave his peaceful, comfortable Indiana home?

But there was no peace possible on the Western frontier, with Canada massing troops along the chain of Great Lakes, and Tecumseh and the Prophet singing war songs again. The next word was that Harrison was mustering his old army and adding not only paleface warriors, but also some Indians who thought it

(337)

best to keep the treaties they had signed after Tippecanoe. Harrison was on his way to retake Detroit.

Two ∽

Meanwhile, before the hopeful report came from the Ohio, Missouri Territory was faced with the threat of savage massacre.

"One wonders why, m'sieu," Gabriel said one day, it having become a habit with him to discuss the more puzzling aspects of war with Saugrain as he tried daily to put the laboratory into some kind of order. "We have always had Indians, but since that one time long ago, they have almost never been dangerous."

That was true, Saugrain agreed. Occasionally a wandering brave, having bought or begged too much rum from a sutler, had created panic in the town with upraised tomahawk and screaming gibberish, but such an Indian in one way or another was quickly subdued. His tribe might even make apology later for his behavior, showing no rancor even though the offender had been killed during a fracas.

But these were new Indians who threatened—chiefly Sac and Fox warriors from up the Mississippi. They did not attack strongholds like Bellefontaine or even Fort Osage. They struck at isolated farms, pre-empted by migrants from the eastern states—land-hungry men, who could not resist the rich prairies in the western reaches of the Territory. They took as much land as they could have and settled their families in large double log cabins, meaning to replace those later with elegant manor houses.

The Indians began hostilities by visiting such a place by stealth at night, driving off horses and other livestock, butchering the animals they took for meat boldly on the owner's land. Then they grew bolder.

One night they shot and killed a man as he sat, reading from a book with a light beside him—a foolish thing to do. Gabriel said, to show the Indians where he was. This man was shot through an open window. At another house, a band of Indians murdered an entire family except one woman, the wife of the owner. Somehow, crazed with terror, she managed to escape in the dark and, with a baby in her arms, made her way to the house of the nearest neighbor. This had happened, Gabriel understood, near the place where the Boones went every year to make salt.

"Gabriel," Saugrain said, "how do you gather such stories?"

"I hear," Gabriel said. "I am not as young as I was when you first saw me. I am not strong in my legs any more, but I hear very well."

He was strong enough, Saugrain thought. He would probably live to bury his friend and patron. What a thought! Saugrain brushed it aside and sharpened his ears to take in other information that Gabriel had gathered.

"It is the English," Gabriel said. "They give guns to the Indians, besides scalping knives. The English have the Indians dancing the war dance once more, telling them that the Yankees will steal all their wild land if they are not driven away."

There must have been truth in what Gabriel had heard. Soon after the murders began, a military order was published in every village and town, closing Missouri to further settlement until peace came. No grants of land would be made, no claims would be honored and no protection would be given to any who tried to settle outside the established towns.

Following this order, the garrison at Fort Osage was sharply reduced. All married soldiers and officers were moved out, and only a small guard patrol remained—to quiet the Osage Indians and serve the needs of traders and hunters still active on the Missouri.

Five Robinsons then filled every corner of the Michau house in St Louis, but not for long. As soon as Dr. Robinson's presence in St. Louis was known, Governor Ninian Edwards of Illinois, who was collecting a volunteer army on that side of the river, invited him to be his aide de camp. Not knowing exactly what the duties of an aide might be, but presuming that in his case medicine would have a part, Robinson accepted the Governor's offer, and was ordered at once to Fort Kaskaskia.

He had no objections to that, because he had agreeable army acquaintance there, but settling his family there was another matter. The overcrowded fort had no accommodations for them, and

(339)

he had to be content with housing them in the little town of Ste. Genevieve on the Missouri side of the river.

"They could have remained here," Michau Père complained. "Why not?"

"St. Louis," Saugrain said, "is too far from Kaskaskia. To reach Ste. Genevieve, John has only to untie a boat any time he has leave, and he will be there in half an hour. Ste. Genevieve is a nice town—French people. French customs. Anyhow, three boys are too many for your house."

"They could be four this time next year," Michau suggested.

"It is possible," Saugrain conceded. "That is how things go."

That was how things went in St. Louis, Missouri Territory. Days, weeks, seasons passed. Life went on much as usual. Hunters and trappers went out after furs and meat, and the furs went to the eastern markets or to New Orleans in the spring. Lisa went farther and farther up the Missouri, circumventing British traders and adding new Indians to his alliances. The Chouteaus extended their trade to the southwest. Henry von Phul, seeing his merchandise again disappearing, made a quick, venturesome sortie eastward after new supplies.

Imagine Saugrain's surprise, then, when one morning shortly after the completion of that journey, that successful, enterprising young robber of birds' nests called at the laboratory dressed in a fringed hunting shirt, buckskin leggings and moccasins. A broad, mischievous smile and a gleam in Henry's eyes recalled the youth in cotton breeches and gingham shirt whom Saugrain, in need of a messenger, had accosted on the river landing—was it five, almost six years ago? Yes, this year was 1813.

"What is this, Henry?" Saugrain asked. "Have you turned Indian trader, after all?"

No. He was now an Indian hunter. He had put his business in order, with a tried and trusted clerk in charge, and had joined a band of young men calling themselves Boone's Rangers. Their special service was to patrol the Territory and protect outlying settlements against continued depredations by the bolder Indians.

The name alone was expected to frighten off some of these. Nathan Boone, who commanded the Rangers, was the youngest son of the celebrated wilderness scout, Daniel Boone. Daniel had settled in the Territory on a grant of land given him by de

Lassus when the latter was named Lieutenant Governor of Upper Louisiana. Since Daniel preferred unoccupied land—preferably remote from the nearest habitation—the grant, bounded on the north by the Missouri River and on the east by the Femme Osage Creek was generous, allowing space for his family, his sons' families, his wife's kin, named Bryan, and a son-in-law with more kin, named Callaway. As time went on, they had multiplied and prospered—and Indians gave them no trouble.

Nevertheless, Boone's Rangers might be confronted with Indians who were strangers. There was that danger, and Saugrain felt he must warn Henry.

"If it should happen that you must fight Indians," he said, "do be careful, Henry. Do not be too brave or needlessly reckless. You have much to lose."

"Only my life at present," Henry said gravely. Then, after another minute, he went on. "I cannot contemplate marriage now, sir, but when the war is over, I hope to marry . . . it is Rosalie, Doctor. Ever since I first saw her, I have not been able to think of any other. I want to marry Rosalie. I want this more than anything."

"Does she know?" Saugrain said feebly. So this was the reason for a member of Boone's Rangers calling on him, disguised in buckskins!

"I think she may have guessed," Henry said, "although I assure you, I have never mentioned marriage to her. I wouldn't—without your permission."

Then he waited—in vain. Saugrain could not speak.

"Have you any objections, sir?" Henry asked, shaking some himself.

"Yes," Saugrain said. "I have one objection. I am her father. It is not easy for a father to give away his heart's treasure."

"Yes, sir . . . but. . . ."

"I know, I know . . . at the same time I cannot stand in the way of my child's happiness, if this is what she also wants more than anything else. We must leave the decision to her, I think."

Having made this statement of surrender, he blinked—once, no more—but in that instant Henry von Phul, ranger's buckskins and all, disappeared.

"That robber," Saugrain said to Madame that evening, "must

(341)

have been born under a rare union of the planets. He will be rich—he already is rich for a young man, but he will be richer. He will give Rosalie a fine house, silk dresses—he will take good care of her, I think. . . ."

"Vigny, of course he will. You should see the two of them together. They are so happy, so much in love. . . ."

"Mmm," Saugrain murmured. "You know where that leads, don't you? Rosalie will be having the babies instead of Sophie and"—he squeezed her arm—"you."

"Vigny, you knew?"

But of course he knew. Her face bloomed as it had when she was carrying her first; and this, her sixth, would be her last, she said.

"Vigny, I mean it. It is not fitting that a grandmother should continue having babies."

Three ⌁

War, then, besides all the other things which it was and was not, was the miracle of young love—rapturous meetings, doleful partings, and fear, which crept in where fear had seldom been before, tearing apart the tissue of dreams. Rosalie Saugrain spent more time now helping her father in his laboratory, offering a pair of hands where extra hands were needed, asking in return only the solace of his pretense at wisdom.

"Dear Papa," she said one day, "how long do you think it will last—the war, I mean?"

Saugrain, whose wisdom to his own mind was seldom adequate, had trouble in answering the wistful tone of this query.

"How long?" he said finally. "It is hard to measure time in advance. But I can tell you this. A year when one is sixteen is much longer than a year seems to one who is fifty. The end will be hard then to remember."

War also saw the flowering and the harvesting of another kind of love. In towns like St. Louis, or smaller, or larger, people leaned on one another for support. Those who were stricken by grief or simple hunger, receiving help, were hardly more grateful than

(342)

those who were able to give—and were grateful for the privilege of sharing their better fortune.

Most memorable to Saugrain was the day when Mr. Stephen Hempstead Senior, accompanied by his older daughter, Mrs. Keeny, called on a matter of business.

"I am delighted to see you," Saugrain said. "I have been looking forward to the pleasure of making your acquaintance."

He meant it. Elder Hempstead, soldier and patriarch, was the first battle-scarred veteran of the American Revolution whom Saugrain had seen at close quarters. He might never see another to match him; and the Widow Keeny, with her fresh apple-blossom complexion and her bright blue eyes and her voice and her laugh, when she spoke or laughed, with the timbre of bells, was—well, she was equally the daughter of New England.

Saugrain at once invited them to go with him to the house, to meet Madame Saugrain. They would be more comfortable there, he thought, but they said, "Another time, please." They really had business to attend to.

"Daughter Keeny," the Elder said without more preamble, "in Groton, Connecticut, where we lived before coming out here, did nursing for a living. She was considered the best...."

Daughter Keeny laughed merrily. The sound lingered in the laboratory afterward, Saugrain thought. She was not that good at nursing really, she said. More truly, she had no rivals. Most women she knew preferred to weave or piece coverlets, but she liked to take care of people. Beyond simple homely remedies, she did not pretend any knowledge of medicine.

She could, however, see that a sick person took the medicine which the doctor had ordered. She could make up a bed fresh, smooth, and comfortable. She talked to sick folk, read to them, sang to them, if that was what they wanted—nursery rhymes for the little folk, hymns or ballads for the older ones, although they were not particular. They like the sound of singing. Sometimes, with the very ill, she sat in a rocking chair within view of the bed all night long, a piece of knitting or a book in her lap. It comforted the sick to waken and find her there. It was very little she did really, but it filled hours which otherwise would have been wasted, at first when her husband was away at sea and more lately since he had died.

"Son Edward advised us to call on you," the Elder said. "He thought you might know someone in need of daughter's care."

Need? Saugrain could have named a dozen cases where Daughter Keeny's presence would have been a godsend, but today he thought particularly of Polly Charles, Manuel Lisa's poor, demented wife. Briefly he told the Hempsteads the story—the years of captivity among the Indians, the Spaniard's impulsive ransom of Polly and the child she had carried away with her. He told how Lisa had married the poor woman and adopted the child, then had brought both to St. Louis and given them a comfortable home, with a servant to care for them, and—well out of his whole acquaintance Saugrain could not name a more devoted husband.

Under these circumstances Polly's daughter had forgotten anything she might have remembered out of the past, but it was not until a son had been born to Polly and Lisa that Polly showed any sign of returning sanity. Unfortunately, it was only a sign, not recovery. Recently, in two different winters, the daughter, twelve, and then the son, eight, had died—of lung fever; and Polly's hold on reason had broken, giving way to old hallucinations. Lisa, who had adored his son, had been most patient and understanding. A second son had been born; but Polly either clutched the child to her, to keep specter Indians from murdering him, or rejected him altogether, saying he was none of hers.

To this narration the Hempsteads, father and daughter, listened in awestruck silence. Now Mary Keeny spoke.

"Doctor, do you think that I could help?"

"I think," Saugrain said, "that you might succeed where everyone else has failed. A woman near her own age, sympathetic, compassionate, who speaks her own language . . . Mrs. Keeny, would you consent to visit Polly Charles with me this morning?"

Soon after that, having deposited the elder at his son's office, with the promise that he would be picked up later and carried home, Saugrain, with Mary Keeny at his elbow, knocked on the door of the living quarters of Lisa's home on North Main Street, called out his name and, as the Negro servant opened the door, stepped inside, with Mary Keeny, as instructed, following him closely. The servant, who had opened the door with a smile of welcome for the doctor, saw Mary with him and closed it apprehensively. Her mistress was watching from the far side of the room, and one never knew. . . .

As it happened, Polly saw only the doctor.

"Good morning, Doctor," she said in her vague way, "I was not looking to see you today. I have plenty of medicine. I slept all right last night and am feeling very well. . . ." Then she became aware of the stranger and a shadow settled on her pale face. Saugrain saw the shadow but ignored it.

"I have brought you a visitor, Polly," he said quickly and drew Mary forward to present her. "Mrs. Keeny is new to Saint Louis. I think you two might be friends."

"A visitor for me?" Polly said, studying Mary. Something about the stranger—the widow's bonnet, the shawl, the bright face— must have been familiar. The shadow lifted, and out of the past good manners asserted themselves.

"I am pleased to see you, ma'am," she said. "Would you care to lay aside your bonnet and sit a while?"

When Saugrain returned later in the morning to call for Mrs. Keeny, the two women had just finished a pot of tea and were chatting like sisters after a long separation. Polly had brushed her hair and dressed it neatly, and the two-year-old boy, also scrubbed and neatly dressed, played contentedly with a string of empty wooden spools on the floor beside his mother's chair.

This was the beginning of Polly Lisa's second and almost complete return to sanity, if not to perfect health. Everyone marveled, including Dr. Saugrain, but nobody's wonder equaled that of Manuel Lisa, when that composite saint and sinner returned to find his house in order and his family at peace.

"Never," he confessed to Saugrain, "at least not since I was a boy in my mother's house in New Orleans, have I known a home like this. *Mi amigo*, what do I owe you? And Mrs. Keeny?"

"To me you owe nothing," Saugrain said. "Buy your lady a new dress or save the money to send your boy to school when he is old enough. But you should by all means pay Mrs. Keeny. I will give you an account of the hours she has spent with Polly. She also has a boy to raise."

The ministrations, then, of Mary Keeny to the sick, the suffering, the sorrowing, the dying, in St. Louis became a legend—a gift of grace, perhaps, to offset the grimmer aspects of war.

(345)

Nevertheless, the grimmer aspects were there, and not to be ignored. Early in the war, Joseph Charless, editor of the *Missouri Gazette*, anticipating a delivery of mail even more erratic than in times of peace, had subscribed to various papers printed elsewhere—Cincinnati, Louisville, Philadelphia, Washington and so on. When he had read an issue and taken from it for his files any item he thought he might need, he would place the paper on a shelf in the printing office, making it accessible to any subscriber who might like to stop by and browse through the general news. Saugrain was one of the first to take advantage of this opportunity. Every time he passed the office, if he thought he could spare a half hour, he would go in, settle himself in a chair with the top paper off the stack in hand, and devour every item even to the casualty lists released by the War Department. One day, as his eyes traveled down this sad column, a name seemed to spring out at him: "Zebulon M. Pike," and then two lines of identification: "Colonel, 16th United States Infantry. Killed while leading an assault at York, Upper Canada."

"No." Rejection was a sigh, rather than a spoken word. "Ah, no!" He stood up, to put the paper away, and, as he turned, the printer stared at him, his forehead wrinkled with question: "Bad news, Doctor?" he said. "You have had a loss?"

The ink-spattered features swam in space as Saugrain steadied himself to answer. "Yes," he said, "yes." Then, finding no other words applicable to his loss, he made his way unsteadily out to the street.

Four ∽

War then became the death or survival of heroes. Names never heard before appeared in the news: Commodore Perry, fighting a victorious naval engagement on Lake Erie; another sailor, David Lawrence, crying out, "Don't give up the ship," and in the next breath falling, mortally wounded; on land a new general with a homespun name—Andrew Jackson—subduing another Indian uprising south of the Ohio.

At the same time there was another Indian alarm in the West, centered about a town on the upper Mississippi—Prairie du Chien in Wisconsin, remembered by the old ones in St. Louis as the place where the British had gathered Indians for their unsuccessful attack on St. Louis in 1780.

"Prairie du Chien?" Madame Saugrain questioned. "What does that mean—a dog's prairie?"

Absently, his mind on other matters, Saugrain explained about burrowing gophers. At this place, he thought, they must occur in large numbers.

The year was now 1814, and nobody knew how the war would end. In April General Clark, commanding two hundred picked militia men, and Colonel Kennerly, commanding sixty regulars from Bellefontaine, accompanied by five barges loaded with arms, ammunition, dry rations, and tools, set out for the north woods. Boone's Rangers, including Henry von Phul, remained on scout duty in Missouri. John Robinson, army surgeon, was commandeered for medical service by Clark and marched with the others to Prairie du Chien.

In St. Louis two anxious families wondered about Sophie. Would she come home now? To their most urgent pleas she steadfastly said no. It was best, she thought, for the Robinsons to remain where John had settled them. They were quite a family now, including little Harriet, born right after they moved to Ste. Genevieve. She was—all the children were—charming. Sophie wished her family could see them. Some day, when the war was over . . . but it was best not to think of that now, although John wrote cheerfully from Prairie du Chien. He did not seem to expect hostilities in that quarter. It seemed to her that almost any day he might open the door of their little house and come walking in—for a visit, or to stay.

In some ways 1814 was the worst year of the war. In August the British abandoned the Canadian border as a base for invading the United States and attacked at other points. Men-of-war entered Chesapeake Bay and bombarded Baltimore. Miraculously the defenses held, but there were no such defenses before Washington. Admiral Cockburn of the British Navy led a landing force all the way to the Capital, meeting no real opposition. When he reached Washington, he found a city all but empty. Congress and

(347)

half the population had fled at the first rumor of attack. Madly then, he set fire to the city, beginning with the President's House.

It was a long time before those who witnessed the holocaust could judge how nearly the Capital had come to being destroyed that ghastly day and night. The President's House appeared to be a blackened ruin. Every state building had been burned to some extent, together with surrounding houses.

In that early, shuddering appraisal, however, the most astounding fact was that the British had disappeared. When had they gone? How? Where to?

Had Admiral Cockburn, awed by the extent of the conflagration, thinking how many miles away were the boats which had set him and his men ashore, been seized by a panic of his own and ordered a retreat? They were gone, leaving useless ruin behind them—useless except that a nation, angry before, now was roused to fury.

In September it was generally known that the British fleet had sailed out of Chesapeake Bay, taking a southerly course. In October it was harbored at Pensacola, Florida, for repairs, being readied for battle. Then word came that Mobile had been taken. New Orleans would be next.

Oh, God, not New Orleans! A British army in force, with ships to carry men and guns, was assembling among the offshore islands. If New Orleans fell, what then?

Before that question could be answered, America spoke. New Orleans must not fall. An army must be gathered for its defense. To collect that army, to organize the defense, Andrew Jackson was called from his home in Tennessee. He answered the call, growling about the impossibility of erecting defenses on the low, marshy ground of the Mississippi delta. He could not do it if he had a year. He didn't have a year. He had only a month, perhaps not that much; but he came. Where was he to recruit an army, he demanded? Where could he find regulars to train volunteers? But he issued the call. He wanted strong men to build breastworks. He wanted men who could load, aim, and fire a rifle gun, marksmen who could bring down a squirrel hiding in a tree, or a raccoon located only by its blazing eyes.

He got his army. Before a proper summons could be published, men left their homes—north, south, east and west, drawn by the

General's name, driven by fierce determination. They traveled by foot, horse, boat—whatever offered. They were every kind of man—one a young medical officer absent without leave from a guard post in Wisconsin. . . .

On a day in December Jean Michau, farmer of Kaskaskia, Illinois, braved a river filled with floating ice to tell Saugrain what Robinson had done. Saugrain embraced him warmly, as always, then held him off to take a second look. "Jean," he said "should you be here? I mean. . . ."

"I know," Jean said. "The ice; but I had to come."

He had crossed the river the day before, had spent the night at Sophie's house in Ste. Genevieve.

"Sophie?" Saugrain asked. "Is something wrong there? She has seemed so content. She writes cheerfully. . . ."

Then Jean told him. Robinson was on his way to New Orleans.

"Ah!" Saugrain said. "I knew he wanted to go." When the first mention had been made of a possible attack on New Orleans, he had written to General Clark to ask for leave to go. As Clark knew, there was no danger of any fighting at Prairie du Chien. There would be bloody fighting at New Orleans. Doctors would be needed. "I think he wrote to Washington also," Saugrain said. "Jean, you saw him. Had his leave come?"

Jean did not know. He rather thought it had not come. Robinson had not mentioned such a thing when he stopped at the Michau farm—two days before this. It was midafternoon then and he was in a great hurry to get across the river—to tell Sophie and the children good-bye and be on his way before dark.

It was not the dark that Robinson feared, Saugrain knew. He had run off without leave. He wanted to reach New Orleans before the battle and he did not mean to be stopped. If his promise to Sophie, to Saugrain, would not stop him, he could not be held.

"Jean," Saugrain asked, "How will he travel? How did he reach Kaskaskia?"

He had walked, Jean said, most of the way. Occasionally a farmer gave him a lift. The latest farmer on passing his home had put up the cart and walked on with Robinson. So Robinson would not travel alone. Besides that, Robinson had left Prairie du Chien with only a knapsack on his back, carrying his stock of medicines and a few personables. Now, however, the two men could carry more. So Jean's wife had packed some food for them, and added a worn sheet and a few other rags that would do for bandages. Robinson had been most grateful.

"And what else?" Saugrain asked. "Did he have any money?"

"He had his last army pay," Jean said, "but he wanted to leave that with Sophie."

"So you gave him money," Saugrain sighed. "How much, Jean?"

A little, Jean confessed finally, but the little finally came out as sixty dollars, which Sophie was to repay out of the Virginia drafts.

"It was because of Sophie I gave it," Jean said. "And for the wounded. I have done so little."

He had done a great deal. Farms like his fed armies. Every quartermaster for miles around knew the Michau herds and fields. Now Jean had arranged with a neighbor that, in case the fighting at New Orleans went badly, one would replace a fallen soldier while the other managed both farms. They would draw lots for the first choice. After that they would serve in turn.

Such was the anxiety of at least one family among the many that waited for news from New Orleans. John Robinson reached the battlefield in time. He found a ragged army assembled there, he wrote in a hurried letter to Sophie, men trained and untrained, gentlemen and clodhoppers, dressed in broadcloth, buckskin, and cotton jeans. Jackson took them all without question. If they could not shoot, they could dig. Every man soon knew his post behind the entrenchments and the breastwork of clay, straw or baled cotton. The British would find them ready.

Five ↩

The grand assault came on the fifteenth day of January. Again and again General Pakenham ordered his redcoats to charge, but he could not break through Jackson's lines. Evening found him in full retreat to his fleet offshore. January in New Orleans,

(350)

however, became February before a report reached Missouri and St. Louis; but that in no way dimmed the celebration. Twenty-four hours of rejoicing were decreed, with at night a lighted candle in a front window of every house up and down and across the territory. In Ste. Genevieve Sophie Robinson lighted hers that night and every night after that for a month, until at last another letter from her husband allowed her to snuff the candle and turn her face homeward.

Jean Michau again brought the word—and the letter—to Saugrain. Robinson, finding himself after the battle very near the Mexican border, had crossed over. A war of rebellion, he wrote, was spreading through the Spanish provinces, which he thought all of America should support, anticipating the time when the United States would want to extend its territory in that direction. There he was convinced, lay a source of wealth greater and more immediate than any other. So, much as he hated to prolong a separation as painful to him as it was to his darling Sophie, he had accepted a generous offer for his services from the commander of the Revolutionary Army. Sophie and her devoted family must wait with good hope for his return. He would return, he was sure —although he would not say when—with sacks of money to pay off all his debts.

"Well, Jean," Saugrain said to his young brother-in-law, "he is right in one way, at least. We will take care of Sophie and the four little ones. Your father and sister Elinor will make room for them in their little house. Yes, I think it best for her to return here; but what you—what all of us—must remember is that we must not say anything to Sophie which will sound like criticism of her husband. She will hear that from others. She carries the truth in her own mind. It is part of her grief that sacks of gold mean more to him than she does. At least, it looks that way, you see, although it is not strictly true. Sacks of gold did not take him to New Orleans. She will hear presently about his heroic help during the fighting. So will we. It was the nearness of Mexico, as John says, that revived his madness. I had such hope for him after his first experience there, when he came back to live at Bellefontaine, then Fort Osage. Now here it is again, but Sophie loves him. So do we all."

(351)

"But it is not fair," Jean Michau said, his eyes stormy, his face clouded. "You have no sacks of gold. Neither have I. You will take care of John's family, and I will help, but it is not right."

"It is right, and you know it," Saugrain chided. "You gave him sixty dollars to help him run away, and you hold the note he signed, which you will probably never collect. Jean, caring for Sophie will not be so bad if the drafts from Virginia continue to come."

"How do you know they will continue?" Jean demanded.

"His mother sends them," Saugrain said. "She knows her son as Sophie knows him. Both want only one thing—to bring John home, and they will have him back some day. You will see. Their love will bring him."

Six ✍

So now, as far as battles were concerned, the war was over. Once more a treaty of peace with Great Britain was drafted in Europe—at a meeting of Peace Commissioners, this time in the city of Ghent, East Flanders. However, certain local problems, notably that of the shadowy western frontier of the American Republic, had still to be solved. Indian alliances and trade agreements dictated the terms of peace in that quarter. Knowing that, Governor Edwards of Illinois and General Clark of Missouri called on the tribes of the North and the West to send their chiefs to a great council to be held in St. Louis in June. To that council Manuel Lisa alone brought forty-three chiefs, representing tribes of the upper Missouri from Minnesota westward to the Yellowstone.

Here was local news that Editor Charless printed with a flourish, but the inhabitants of the city barred their doors. Indians, singly or by twos and threes, had visited St. Louis since its beginning, but never so many at one time, and never such Indians. These were tall, strong, haughty savages, with bears' teeth strung around their necks. Serpents' rattles, sewed to their leggings, clacked as they walked or stepped to the rhythm of a ritual dance. One breathed more easily when no place in town provided space for their meeting and camp ground had to be found elsewhere. The site finally chosen was the strip of land between the Missouri and the Mississippi opposite Fort Bellefontaine, where in Wilkinson's time flood water and malaria had nearly destroyed the old First Regiment. There was no flood water now. The Grand Powwow would be held near a trading post on the Mississippi shore known as Portage des Sioux.

The story was that once upon a time, when Indians fought one another instead of the white man, a wandering band of Sioux after raiding a Sac village in Missouri had been forced to run for their lives, pursued by vengeful Sac warriors. They reached the Missouri, where they had hidden their canoes, with just time enough to allow them to jump into the boats and paddle across to the opposite shore. Then, carrying their canoes overland to the Mississippi they launched the canoes once more and so escaped up that river to their homes in Minnesota.

Portage des Sioux would be remembered forever now as the place of the Grand Powwow; but no one, Indian or paleface, would remember it more vividly than Antoine Saugrain. On a day when everyone was busy with final preparations for the pow-wow, especially the women—squaws having been brought along to set up tepees and perform other duties too menial for warriors—Manuel Lisa brought one of his chieftains to Saugrain's quarters on Belmont. In fifteen years of familiarity, Saugrain had achieved a measure of tolerance for Indians, at least if he faced them in the company of someone like Lisa; but only he knew how thin that tolerance was. The scalping incident before his house and several occasions when drunken braves had terrorized the town with yells and upraised tomahawks had planted, then cultivated that area until fear was always his first reaction on meeting a warrior, even a peaceful one. His vaccinations, given free, had been inspired, not by concern for the Indians, but by his knowledge that their villages were breeding grounds for epidemics.

This Indian, however, was no Kickapoo crazed by rum, nor was he a guileless aborigine, curious to see the paleface medicine man make lightning jump across a table. Judged by his ornaments, he was a chief of consequence, and a giant besides. His dark features were either contorted by a scowl or permanently furrowed by deep scars. And there was no mistaking the meaning of the mono-syllabic gutturals that expressed his contempt for the little doctor. There continued throughout Lisa's hurried statement the situation which had led to this visit.

Chief Running Horse had brought his daughter with him to the council—his only child, his only hope for male progeny. She was now of an age to marry and produce the grandsons he wanted; and it was the thought of finding a suitable mate for her that had brought him to this gathering of chiefs. Now death threatened to extinguish hope.

During the evening of the day before, while the young men in camp were indulging in sports—running, archery and the like —an arrow had gone wild and struck the girl in the chest as she stood in the doorway of her father's lodge, watching the fun. It had pierced the tender flesh between her breast and her arm and gone clear through the shoulder until it was stopped by the broad shoulder blade. There it seemed to have embedded itself. It might have been better, Lisa thought, if it had gone on through the bone. Then the shaft could have been broken and the arrow withdrawn in two pieces. As it was. . . .

No, Saugrain said, that would not have helped. The bone would have been shattered. Well, but, Lisa argued, as it was, none of those who had tried had been able to move the arrow. The girl was in great pain, and the anguished father had turned to Lisa, demanding that he seek help from his medicine man.

"Amigo," Saugrain said sadly, "you would do this to me? The girl will die if the arrow is not removed. It is just as certain that she may die if it is taken. There are other doctors in the town." He mentioned the one with the case of beautiful instruments. He mentioned Dr. Farrar, husband of General Clark's niece. Had Lisa consulted Clark? Clark must give permission. . . .

It was Clark, Lisa informed him, who had said, like the Indian, "Find Dr. Saugrain. He can take the arrow if anyone can."

As a last resort, Saugrain spoke of the chief's derisive growling. On seeing Lisa's wizard, Chief Running Horse did not think much of him. No, Lisa said. The growls meant only that Running Horse was afraid that Saugrain would not come to the girl's aid. So was Lisa afraid of this, and General Clark, too, perhaps. Everything—Lisa's influence with the tribes, the success of the great council—seemed to hang on Saugrain's consent or refusal.

But in the end none of these things brought his answer. He looked once more at the Chief's rugged face and saw there beads of sweat—a father's agony over his wounded child. Suppose the girl had been Rosalie, and he the father! One by one, in quick review, his children passed through his thoughts, even the latest, Eugenie, a fairy princess not quite two, flitting about the house like a moth from her mother's garden.

"Say to your friend," he bade Lisa, "that I will remove the arrow. But make it clear to him: it will be a bloody operation and I do not promise that his daughter will live after it."

Soon—very soon—he stood beside a hammock, hung between two trees, where the girl had spent a night of torment. Her eyes were glazed by fever. Her skin was hot and dry. He laid his hand on her forehead and spoke to her gently: "Daughter?" She tried to smile, but could not; and he laid a folded napkin over her eyes.

An army tent was ready and waiting, every curtain rolled up, mosquito netting over the opening. The sergeant in command knew Saugrain's ways. The table was boards laid upon wooden trestles and secured with knotted rawhide. One of Madame Saugrain's discarded sheets covered the boards. Of these Saugrain kept a supply at both his offices. On a stand nearby Aristide had laid knives and a probe on a clean towel. A washbasin was there, with pails of fresh water on the ground. At the fort, Saugrain, seeing Aristide looking pale, would have excused him, but the young man had rallied. He would be all right now.

The army sergeant stood at the foot of the table. He was to hold the girl's ankles. The father waited to hold her hands, although he had said she would not move if the doctor commanded her to be motionless.

"She must not move," Saugrain said to Lisa. "Tell him so."

Seeing everyone and everything in place, Saugrain shed his uniform coat, washed his hands, clipped on the long white surgeon's coat, nodded to his helpers, and took up the scalpel and probe. As he did so a kind of coolness settled on him. His eyes, his brain cleared. His hand steadied. The feathered shaft of the arrow gave him his angle for approach. Quickly, but calmly, he made a

(355)

first incision. The girl's lips quivered, but she made no sound. Perhaps she fainted. He did not pause to investigate. Working now with probe and scalpel, using the probe for eyes, in less than a minute he touched the rough edge of the flint arrowhead. Now he must be careful not to sever the strip of deerhide that bound it to the shaft. Again he let the probe guide the scalpel as he worked around the piece of flint, loosening it wherever it held fast. At last it moved, but not enough. A little more probing and lifting, and it was free. Cautiously he ventured a pull on the shaft, then more, and more. Suddenly, feeling no resistance, he made the final decisive motion and the arrow emerged—whole. As it did so, the Indian girl, who must, after all, have been conscious throughout the ordeal—the time could have been measured in minutes —breathed a long, shuddering sigh, and died.

Aristide, who had been busy sponging away the blood, spoke first: "Doctor, there is no more bleeding."

"Yes," Saugrain answered, in French, "I know. There is no pulse."

Laying the bloody arrow on the table, he motioned to the Chief and the army sergeant, indicating that they could release their hold, and said to Lisa, "Tell her father her spirit fled as she was freed from the arrow."

But then it was the father he had to face, not his good friend Captain Manuel. Rage superseding grief, the savage giant towered above him. His eyes blazed. His hand was on a knife at his belt. So, Saugrain thought, this is how it will end, after all.

For a long minute the two of them stood so, each staring into the other's eyes; but just as Saugrain realized that his legs were giving way, if not his eyes, the Indian shivered, and his hand left the knife. Seeing that, very quietly Saugrain turned aside.

The Indian girl still lay on the table. Aristide had wiped away the blood and removed the towel from her eyes, but he had not thought to close them. Gently Saugrain did so, then fumbled in his pocket, found two copper coins, and laid one on each eye. He would have left the table then if movement behind him had not warned him that Running Horse had been aware of his every motion.

What? Would there be more rage now? Vengeance still? No. The father had wanted only to see. What he saw led first to another convulsive shiver, then a howl of anguish. Still howling, the Indian snatched up the bloody arrow and fled.

"Bravo, Doctor *amigo*," Lisa applauded. "If you had wavered only once . . . but let him go now. He will find a place where he can howl as long and as loud as his spirit demands. So, with the help of our sergeant and Dr. Michau, shall we gather what belongs to you and leave? The girl? Women are already on the way. They will wrap her for burial. Day after tomorrow they will begin the journey home."

Seven ◡

War in the West ended then in the light of council fires at Portage des Sioux. Indian and paleface chieftains moved in shadowy silhouette through the flickering light of the flames. Long harangues were delivered. The pipe of peace was smoked. Pledges were made. Gifts were exchanged. Saugrain, watching from a safe distance, was glad that he had been persuaded to attend. He would have been sorry not to have viewed this tableau. And surely his sons. Alphonse and Frederic, who were only twelve and nine years old at present but would live to see the Territory reach its maturity as they reached theirs, should have this night to remember.

Still, he was glad, while the fires continued to blaze, to be in the brougham with the boys and on his way home. There, contrary to his orders, Madame Saugrain waited to welcome them, to hear the boys' excited report.

"It is time for bed, my sons," Saugrain said finally. "Tomorrow we will go over it all again. Now I wish only a few moments with your *chére maman* before sleep. It is so sweet and peaceful here in the garden, and I am tired—very, very tired."

"You are tired, Vigny," Madame said, when they were alone. "It has been a long day for you."

"I slept away three hours of it this afternoon," he protested "You must take them off when you make a count."

"I know," Madame said. "I was glad you could sleep. You had callers. Did you know? The Governor. . . ."

"General Clark?" On the instant Saugrain was awake, alert. "And you sent him away?"

"No, Vigny. He was the one who said you must not be disturbed. He told me about the Indian girl, Vigny. It was a cruel thing they asked you to do—to take that arrow."

"Not altogether cruel," Saugrain said. "I did not want to do it until I saw the girl. She had suffered to the limits of her endurance. I did not know the power of an arrow. I still do not know what damage it did to the scapula. I like to think now that the pain ceased while she still lived. She sighed such a sigh, and died so peacefully. *Chérie*, I learned about Indians today. Manuel tried to tell me, but being told is not the same as experience. They are brave. They must be brave. Their way of life makes it necessary. They are warriors, quick to anger and savage in their anger, but they are also men, with man's joys and sorrows. I think I shall never be afraid of one. I must remember to tell Manuel that. He did not call this afternoon, I think."

No, Lisa had not called, but Colonel Hammond had, and he, too, had refused to have the doctor disturbed, but he had left a message. "Tell him," Madame quoted, "that he is a braver man than I ever was."

"Ah, bravery!" Saugrain said, "I had no choice. That is what bravery comes to in a tight corner. Did he tell you that he is thinking of leaving Saint Louis now and returning to Virginia?"

"He spoke of Carolina, I think," Madame said. "Mrs. Hammond is homesick."

"Is she truly?" Saugrain mocked. "She will say the same of him. A strange man, this Virginia gentleman soldier. As long as there was something to fight for or against, he was happy here. Now, with peace . . . really, he is having twinges of rheumatism, and the growing hustle and bustle of this place does not encourage life in an armchair, with one's feet on a pillow. So—he is going home. Yes, to the Carolinas. Mrs. Hammond has a patrimony there, I believe. The colonel has none now. He sold everything he had in the East to move west. Now, by selling all he has here, he will just about clear his debts."

"But I thought he was a rich man," Madame sighed.

"No," Saugrain said. "No more than I."

(358)

"Vigny, you have no debts, I hope."

"None that burden me," Saugrain said, "but I leave all that to your papa. No burdensome debts, but also no sacks of gold. Not that I came here in search of gold. I had been led to believe that here American history would some day be made. I wanted to see that happen, to play a small part . . . well, my wish has been granted. That is all my wealth."

"Not all," Madame said. "I still have the *peso fuerte* you gave me when we first came. It is our amulet. . . ."

"What? You never spent it? But the coin itself is worth more than you think. You may have done well to hoard it. *Chérie*, at last I am cleaning out my desk and my cabinets at Bellefontaine, and am coming home to stay."

"Vigny, they will miss you."

"They know where to find me if they need me. So, now we can hang the President's commission in our house, where people can see it. We can knock down the fence."

"Vigny no! Never . . . the fence!"

"But I thought you hated it."

"Vigny, I never did. It is ugly, but it is one reason for the sweet peace of our home. It keeps out what you call the hustle and bustle."

"But not robbers," Saugrain teased. "Henry von Phul. . . ."

"Vigny, Rosalie is now eighteen. . . ."

"All right, all right! Henry will carry her off soon enough. Don't be so pleased about it. I concede that it will be a good marriage. Sacks of gold there, no doubt. And presently Elise will go the same way."

"Elise," Madame, said, "can wait a year or two. She is happy right now with six or seven young men in pursuit. She will take her time about choosing a husband."

"She will do the choosing?" Saugrain asked.

"But, of course. It is always that way."

"Even you?"

"Even I. Vigny, if I had waited for you to come after me, where would I be now?"

He had not thought that day could end in laughter, as it did.

"Not here, I am sure," he said in the midst of merriment. "I can see now—you were always the bold one. Well, what do you think of your choice now, Madame?"

"I think no woman has the right to be as happy as I have been every day since our marriage."

"Then," he said, taking her hand and pretending—only pretending—to raise her to her feet, "if you are content, *chérie*, so am I. Shall we go in now?"

End